Praise for *Mrs. Rochester's Ghost*

"What's more delicious than a novel with so many twists and turns that you don't know who's telling the truth until it's over—and even then you're not so sure? Lindsay Marcott's *Mrs. Rochester's Ghost* is just that book. A contemporary Gothic novel haunted by the ghosts of du Maurier and Henry James that is impossible to put down. Go for it."

—B. A. Shapiro, *New York Times* bestselling author of *The Collector's Apprentice*

"Gothic and elegant, *Mrs. Rochester's Ghost* captivated me from the first page and kept me reading all night. Lindsay Marcott has created a seductive Big Sur landscape; peopled it with brilliant, complicated characters; and set in motion a thriller both terrifying and emotionally satisfying. I loved it."

—Luanne Rice, *New York Times* bestselling author of *Last Day*

"Smart, thrilling, and completely unexpected, Lindsay Marcott delivers the goods in the brilliant *Mrs. Rochester's Ghost*. Highly recommended for readers who like incandescent prose and deep deceptions."

—Gregg Olsen, #1 *Wall Street Journal* bestselling author of *If You Tell*

"This imaginative take on Charlotte Brontë's Gothic novel has several satisfying nods to the source material, but veers away just enough to create a refreshing new experience. Marcott's Jane is a formidable protagonist . . . Fans of *Jane Eyre* who enjoyed Rachel Hawkins's *The Wife Upstairs* will appreciate this equally enjoyable retelling from Marcott."

—*Library Journal* (starred review)

SHADOW
SISTER

ALSO BY LINDSAY MARCOTT

Mrs. Rochester's Ghost

The Producer's Daughter

SHADOW
SISTER

A NOVEL

LINDSAY
MARCOTT

THOMAS & MERCER

Text copyright © 2022 by Lindsay Marcott
All rights reserved.

Published by Thomas & Mercer, Seattle

www.apub.com

Amazon, the Amazon logo, and Thomas & Mercer are trademarks of Amazon.com, Inc., or its affiliates.

ISBN-13: 9781662500046 (hardcover)
ISBN-10: 1662500041 (hardcover)

ISBN-13: 9781662500053 (paperback)
ISBN-10: 166250005X (paperback)

Cover design by Lucy Kim

Printed in the United States of America

First edition

To Virginia Dorothy Maracotta
Greatly missed

"Is something the matter, dear," she said,
"That you sit at your work so silently?"
"No, mother, no—'twas a knot in my thread.
There goes the kettle—I'll make the tea."
—Edna St. Vincent Millay, "Departure"

She nourishes the poison in her veins
and is consumed by a secret fire.
—Virgil

PROLOGUE

It happens in the millisecond between two thoughts.

First thought: the earth beneath my flip-flops is solid. In the next, there is no earth. No vaporous white moon in the sky, no ragged clouds. No sky at all. Or black, pounding sea below.

The bluffs, with their straggling long manes of ice plant, have disappeared.

There's nothing at all except me in free fall. Weightless; without boundaries. No up or down. It's like dancing in outer space. I feel such joy. I'm finally free.

But now pictures flood into my mind. Images of things I'll never get to do. I'll never see Paris or Tibet. Or eat a papaya or lick a pistachio ice cream cone. I'll never have a baby. Or even own a dog of my own.

I'll never fall madly in love with somebody who loves me back.

I no longer feel joy; I feel rage. It's so horribly unfair. And in the final split seconds of my falling, I'm consumed by one thought.

I don't want to die.

It's too late, I know, but please, please, I want to have more life. I want more things, more experiences. I want some fun. I want to be loved.

Most of all, I want revenge.

CHAPTER ONE

AVA

I grew up in a haunted house. And for a while, it was a lot of fun. And then, horribly, it wasn't.

The house even looked haunted. Crumbling blackened stone, with two gloomy flanking wings and pointed dormer windows, shrouded by half-dead pines. It would have looked at home on a bleak Yorkshire moor, the ancestral estate of some grief-maddened lord, but it happened to be nestled on the last and mostly uninhabitable stretch of private land on the Monterey Peninsula, some 120 miles south of the Golden Gate Bridge. It had been built in 1927 by an ancestor of mine—an eccentric San Francisco bootlegger with a romantic streak. He stashed his illegal cash in niches hidden behind sliding panels and threw lavish gin-washed parties for mobsters and movie stars and flappers until one of the mobsters murdered one of the flappers—slit her throat from ear to ear—in a small wing behind the kitchen called the servants' quarters.

The house was occupied fitfully afterward by various members of my maternal family: it had sat isolated and abandoned for over a decade when my mother went to look at it. A white elephant that nobody would buy. You could access it only by a quarter-mile drive that jounced and bounced you with ruts and potholes, while thick cypress forest pushed in on both sides and flagellated your car's doors and windows. Inside the house, mice ruled, water dripped, and the stairs and passageways shivered with mysterious drafts.

But for Mom, it was love at first sight. She loved the broken dumbwaiter in the kitchen. The claw-foot bathtubs. The ballroom with echoing coffered ceilings and the gargoyles on the library fireplace, copied from a painting of hell by Hieronymus Bosch.

She had just come into her Blackworth family trust money. She wrote a check for the back taxes on the spot, and the property was hers.

"Are you out of your goddamned mind, Christina?" That was Dad's reaction. He'd been a tennis player, ranked as high as number eighteen on the pro tennis circuit, until some vague scandal at Forest Hills—a seventeen-year-old on the Italian women's team—coupled with an injury to an ankle put an end to his career. Now he chased deals instead of balls. A gas well (demolished by a hurricane). A rejuvenating face cream (caused hives). No way he was going to live in the middle of freaking nowhere.

But then a pal tipped him off: real estate on the Central Coast was about to skyrocket. And so when I was six and my brother, Jamie, seven, we left our flat in San Francisco and moved to the bootlegger's eccentric old house. Blackworth Mansion, Dad dubbed it, even though our own last name was Holland. "Bought and paid for by Blackworth ill-gotten gains." The name stuck.

We knew right off there was a ghost.

You'd wake up late at night to a clatter of kitten heels on the back stairs. Or a window would suddenly whoosh open in a room when there wasn't even a sigh of breeze.

Or maybe you'd be brushing your teeth, and there'd be a jitterbug of steps right behind you even though the mirror showed nothing there, and the hairs on the back of your neck would stand up straight.

And we knew it had to be the ghost of the society girl who'd had her throat slit in the servants' quarters.

There'd been a fire in that wing some years before we moved in, and the damage was never repaired; and so Mom named the ghost Cinderella. "Because she lies in ashes now," she said in her own kind of ashy, murmuring voice. "In cinders and ashes, just like Cinderella."

Jamie and I bragged about our ghost to our friends. We competed with each other to have the most encounters with her.

It was all so much fun.

And then Mom actually saw her.

It was early March. we'd been living at the mansion for seven years by then. Jamie and I were in the front hall, waiting for Dad to drive us to our school, Sanderson Day Academy, in Pacific Grove. We were nervous. Dad's tempers, always tricky, had been scary lately: all his latest sure-thing deals had fizzled; he was drinking nonstop. The morning mist hadn't cleared yet, and both his temper and his driving would depend on just how much booze he'd put away the night before.

Mom, always a late riser, came floating down the central staircase, cradling O'Keeffe, our longhaired white cat. She wore drifting clothes that blended with the fog—a pale-gray linen shirt and long skirt. Two or three vintage rings—Blackworth family heirlooms—sparkled on the fingers of each of her hands.

"Guess what, my sweet loves?" she murmured. "I saw her last night. She appeared to me."

"Cinderella?" I said eagerly. "Where, Mom?"

"In my studio. I was working till the wee hours. I was trying to get a shade of blue exactly right." Mom was a painter. Still life paintings that looked like Dutch old masters, except with creepier subject matter. She made many of her own colors in a mortar and pestle, like an alchemist. "I kept mixing and grinding, but I just couldn't get what I wanted. Then suddenly I saw her. She was in the corner between the two windows."

"Was she nude?" Jamie said. He was going on fifteen; he'd become snide about Cinderella's existence. "She's ectoplasm, so why would she need clothes?"

Mom looked at him with fond amusement. Both beauties, the same tawny eyes and chestnut hair. And Dad had wolfish good looks—I'd heard a cleaning lady describe him that way. Mom said my looks—my nearly black hair and too-big, too-wide-set eyes—were intriguing. "When people look at you, Ava, they will always want to keep on looking." Though from my experience so far, that hadn't been the case.

"She was too hazy for me to tell what she wore," Mom said to Jamie. "But oh, she was lovely. Small. Dark. Her eyes were so sad."

"Who killed her, Mama?" I said. "Did she say?"

"She said nothing at all. She winked at me. And then she just dissolved into the air."

I felt a tick of envy. Only Mom could get a ghost to wink at her.

Dad's footsteps approached, and we all shut up. Sometimes even just a mention of Cinderella could make him go apeshit. "Superstitious crap," he'd sneer with such venom that spittle flew out of his mouth.

He appeared now, grasping a mug that said ADULTING IS HARD. We all knew what was in it—coffee, black, with a generous pick-me-up of Johnnie Walker Black Label. "You guys ready?" The hand holding the mug was trembling.

Mom said, "I'll take them, Kevin."

Jamie and I exchanged glances. Mom rarely left the property. Her car, a twelve-year-old Jeep, still looked almost brand new.

Dad just said "Let's move" to Jamie and me and headed out the door.

"I'll go find my keys," Mom told us. She went back upstairs and returned with her purse. And then, ignoring Dad at the wheel of his Mustang convertible, she drove us—barefoot, bedheaded—the thirty-five minutes to our school.

❧

"We should try to see Cinderella too," I said to Jamie. "It's not fair Mom gets to see her and we don't."

It was several days later. We were down at the wild rock-strewn beach below our house. Some of his friends were horsing around in the freezing, turbulent surf. Jamie had just waded out to untangle a snorkel strap.

He shot me a look. "You don't think she really did, do you? It's Mom. She talks to butterflies."

I shrugged. I was nearly thirteen and didn't really believe in Cinderella anymore, either. Except at the same time I didn't not believe in her. There were moments I could swear I felt her presence. "We should at least *try*."

A slender blond boy climbed out of the surf, shaking off water like a frisky dog. I felt a drawing sensation in the pit of my stomach. Thomas Rainier. His family was enormously rich. They jetted among three or four homes; he'd been kicked out of two boarding schools back east—for simply not giving a shit, Jamie said—and was now barely attending the same academy in Pacific Grove that we did. He had a kind of aloof manner. Not superior aloof, I thought. More like a loneliness, even in the middle of a crowd. And I was secretly, hopelessly in love with him.

"'Sup, Ava?" he said.

I flushed deeply.

"She wants to conjure up our ghost," Jamie said. "You know, the girl who was murdered in our back room?"

Thomas turned his eyes to me. Blue eyes that looked deceptively sleepy until you noticed the sharp light in them. "You got a spell you plan to use?"

"I thought maybe . . . well, if I went to her room late at night and just let her know I want to see her, she might appear."

"So how are you going to get in?" Jamie said. He explained to Thomas, "The door to that hallway is locked. Only Mom's got the key, and she won't give it out."

"Break a window," Thomas said. His wet body was shivering a little. It made me shiver too.

"If my dad found out, he'd lose his shit," Jamie said. "And believe me, he'd find out. But you know what? I could jimmy those old locks pretty easily. They're all rusted out."

"Then do it," Thomas said. "Tonight."

"In the wee small hours." Jamie imitated Mom's whispery tones. He was a terrific mimic. "What do you say, Ave? One a.m.? You in?"

I felt a sudden sense of dread. Like the feeling I'd had just before our goat, Dora, was killed by a coyote. My best friend, Grace Zhao, once told me she'd heard Mom was a witch who knew when people were going to die. I'd never heard Mom predict any such doom, but maybe if she could, she'd passed the power on to me. And I was having a premonition that something bad was going to happen.

But Jamie's eyes were fixed somewhat sardonically on me. So were Thomas's.

"I'm totally in," I said.

I didn't get undressed. I kept myself awake reading one of Mom's old Judy Blumes and also spinning romantic fantasies about Thomas Rainier that always ended with him declaring his never-ending love.

At the dot of one, I got up. Tied on Skechers. Crept out into the hallway. Jamie's door was still shut. I scratched softly.

He sidled out wearing jeans and one of Dad's old cashmere sweaters, a large screwdriver in one hand and the flashlight from his sleep-away camp in the other. He glanced at the end of the hall—Mom and Dad's bedroom suite. Placed a finger to his lips.

With exaggerated stealth, we went down the back stairs to the kitchen.

O'Keeffe slunk out from a shadow. "Don't let her out," Jamie said. He cracked open the back door and edged outside. Keeping O'Keeffe back with the heel of my sneaker, I followed him out.

There was no fog. The sky was speckled with stars, and a yellow half moon bobbed directly overhead. I could hear the ocean pounding below. My heart was pounding, too, as we proceeded around the side of the house.

Jamie suddenly stopped. "Mom's still up."

I glanced up. She stood silhouetted in the window of her corner studio, gazing out at the blackness. "What's she looking at?"

"No idea. But she can't see us down here. Let's go."

We continued around to the north side, where the servants' quarters were. A juniper hedge was planted in front of the windows. It had long grown wild: its trunks were gnarled and twisted. As we edged behind it, sharp branches clawed our hair and clothes.

Jamie stopped at the first window. "It's this one." He inserted the screwdriver blade between the rotted-out sill and decaying frame, then glanced at his sleeve. "Shit. I got a rip in Dad's sweater. He's gonna kill me."

"It's already got a moth hole," I pointed out.

"Like he'll care." He jammed the blade farther in and gave it a hard wrench. The sash lock popped loose. "Told you. Easy." He pushed up the window frame. It rose a third of the way, then stuck.

"I can get through." I wriggled facedown over the sill and dropped inside.

"Coming in." Jamie squeezed through and came down hard next to me. He switched on his flashlight. "Whoa."

I turned. Gasped. The walls oozed with black mold. Slabs of gray ash covered the ceiling. Stilettos of petrified dust twisted down from it. There was a tiny dresser draped in dust and cobwebs. Two cast-iron bed frames pushed together. "It's like we're inside a tomb," I said.

"Yeah, a tomb for beds." He trained the light on the bed frames, and their shadows flickered on the walls. "That's their skeletons."

I shuddered. "Don't talk like that."

We both jumped as the window slammed shut behind us. Ash like gray snow rained down from the ceiling.

"Holy shit!" Jamie said. "We're lucky it didn't fall on one of us."

I slapped greasy ash from my hair. "So, what do we do now?"

"Just wait, I guess."

He lowered himself to the cruddy floor, resting his back against a bed frame. I sat down next to him. The smell of mold and old ash made me gag. I wished I could still hear the surf but couldn't.

Minutes dragged by. Jamie jiggled his foot. I folded and unfolded my legs. Our breathing sounded very loud.

I gave a start. "I think I felt something. Like maybe she pulled my hair."

He beamed the flashlight on me. "I don't see anything. Let's just concentrate on her, okay? Send out some brain emanations." He giggled. He was nervous too.

I squeezed my eyes shut and tried to concentrate on Cinderella the way Mom described her. Small, dark haired. Sad eyes.

And then my eyes shot open. It felt suddenly like all the air was rushing out of the room.

Jamie leaped wildly to his feet. "We've got to get out of here!"

"What?" I said.

"She kissed me. On the lips."

He moved fast to the window and hoisted it with all his strength. "Come on, Ava."

He ducked under the sash and jumped out; and I reached the window just in time to see him stumble and fall into the sharp claws of the juniper.

After that, it was no longer fun to be haunted.

It was more like a curse. Like Cinderella had cursed our whole family for whatever reasons of her own.

First, there were Jamie's twenty-six stitches, including in his eyes, and then surgery, which still left him mostly blind in his left eye. And the reconstructive surgeries that didn't erase all the scars on his face.

Mom and Dad had always argued, but now they began to fight for real. Murderous, name-calling fights from behind their bedroom door.

And then Dad was packing his bags. And Mom was shrieking at him, and Dad was stomping down the stairs with two unzipped duffels, and Mom yelled, "Have fun being homeless for the rest of your pathetic shit loser life!" and Dad bellowed back, "Better than staying with you, you fucking mental space cadet!" and he left the house for good, slamming the door behind him.

And in less than a year, Mom was dead.

CHAPTER TWO

My memories of Blackworth Mansion become sketchier after Mom's death. Just flickers until the day after we buried her ashes in a leafy old cemetery in Oakland.

That day I see vividly. Dad was in the sunporch, slumped on the glider, rocking to and fro. The ice in his glass of Black Label clinked. Great-Aunt Wilhelmina was there, too, on the green wicker chair with the high fanback. At seventy-two, still beautiful, with thick deep-red hair (dyed by then) and the Blackworth tawny eyes. She lived in Sausalito, near where all the houseboats docked, and she kept a loom in her attic on which she wove tapestries patterned with fantastical beasts.

How long had Dad and Aunt Willie been here? I couldn't remember.

The pills I was taking were making my mind thick as mud. *Take these, Ava. You'll feel better.*

Who gave me the pills? I couldn't remember that either.

Jamie was pacing. Back and forth relentlessly.

I was hidden in the hallway near the sunporch door, clutching O'Keeffe.

Everything was surreal. Living people were like ghosts. Ghosts didn't exist.

Mom was dead.

"It's possible . . . ," I heard Dad say. "That she poisoned herself."

I leaned forward and peeked in.

"What are you talking about?" Jamie stopped pacing. He looked ready to punch Dad.

"I mean accidentally. From making her paints. Grinding things up, plants and bark and what have you. Some plants have cyanide in them. Fruit pits. Apricots. Cherries. I think peaches too. She could have ingested small amounts over time."

"Ingested." Aunt Willie gave a disgusted snort. "For God's sake, Kevin, are you saying she ate her paints?"

"Not on purpose. But she'd get paint on her hands and fingers. Her hair. I once saw her dip her brush in her tea instead of the cleaning water."

Jamie said, "This is so fucked up. I've got to get out of here."

He came bursting out into the hall where I was huddled.

"Where are you going?" I said.

"Away from this house. Thomas is driving over to pick me up."

"He's not sixteen yet. He can't drive."

"He does anyway." Jamie stomped furiously on through the house. I heard the front door slam.

I wished he had taken me with him.

Inside the sunporch, Aunt Willie said to Dad, "You didn't have to be so damned quick to pull the plug, Kevin."

"For Christ's sake, Willie. She'd been brain dead for over a week."

Brain dead.

Mom had started going from being floaty to a klutz. Dropping things. Stumbling over her own bare feet. Sometimes jerking out an arm or a leg for no reason at all. But she'd been getting better. She'd gone back to being Mom, all floating and whispery and wonderful.

And then suddenly she got worse.

She was in the hospital, in a coma. Jamie and I were in the front hall, waiting for Aunt Willie to take us there to visit, and then Aunt

Willie came down the hall. She was walking so very slow. *Your mama is gone, my darlings. She slipped peacefully away.*

And I had imagined her spirit just sort of rising to embrace the air.

No one had said anything about Dad pulling the plug.

Dad now mumbled something I couldn't hear. Aunt Willie said, "Well then, there should have been an autopsy."

"There was no point. Brenner confirmed the diagnosis. It was Creutzfeldt-Jakob."

Dr. Brenner was a nerve specialist in San Francisco. Mom had started seeing him when she became so klutzy.

I squeezed O'Keeffe so tight she gave a hiss. She had a streak of green paint on her haunches.

Mom got paint over everything.

We weren't going to live with Dad. Mom had cut him out of her will. She left all her money in a trust for Jamie and me, and Blackworth Mansion as well.

Dad had exploded in a rage. He said no way were we going to live with him. He couldn't afford us. The way he said it, it meant he didn't want to. We were going to go live with Aunt Willie in Sausalito.

"We were working things out," I heard him say now. "Getting back together."

"That's bullcrap." Aunt Willie let her head drop into her hands. Her shoulders were shaking. She was sobbing without making any noise.

Poison. The word clawed up through the sludge in my brain.

Mom had been poisoned.

Somehow, I knew that was true.

A door slammed shut upstairs for no reason at all.

Cinderella. The hairs on my arms stood up straight.

DIDI

It's Wednesday, so Didi has gotten home before Mimi, even after making a pit stop at the Quiki Mart for a family-size (ha!) package of Double Stuf OREOs. She's already wolfed down most of them and hidden what's left under her mattress. *Like bank robbers' loot,* she thinks sarcastically. *Or a priceless string of pearls.*

Poor old Mimi. Mondays, Wednesdays, and Fridays, she works at the Hollands' place, way in the wilds of the hills below Carmel, about an hour's drive from Monterey. Any minute, she'll drag herself back. Exhausted to her bones. Slumped in the doorway like a question mark.

It's a bitch of a job, cleaning lady. But Didi gives her credit; Mimi's a star in her own way. At the top of the daily house cleaner game. She can pick and choose her clients, and she only picks the best. And to Mimi, the Hollands are the best of the best.

They're sort of famous, the Hollands, all over the Monterey Peninsula. Didi sometimes hears kids at school talk about them. They're supposed to be awesomely great looking but weird at the same time—like, they think their house is haunted by some kind of evil ghost. Mimi's mentioned the ghost, too, but mostly she rhapsodizes about the mom, Christina Holland. "Magical" is how Mimi describes her. "She makes everything around her sparkle."

Except, if you ask Didi, it's poor old Mimi, lugging around her scrub mop and Comet cleanser and Mr. Clean, who's the one making it all sparkle.

But what Mimi loves most about Christina Holland is that she's originally a Blackworth—one of those old money families who used to lord it over San Francisco society until the tech billionaires took over. Mimi's a snob, when you get right down to it. She actually dresses up to go scrub Christina Blackworth Holland's toilets. She puts on these swingy V-neck tops and tight designer jeans instead of her usual cleaning lady ensemble—baggy cargo pants with that stained old blue shirt untucked. She even screws in all three of her zircon studs.

But here's the really absurd thing. Even though Mimi worships Christina, she steals from her. Or actually pilfers (a word Didi loves). Little stuff. Like a bent old butter knife with a fancy *B* monogram (*B* for Blackworth family, of course). Or last week a crumpled and unfinished charcoal drawing Mimi must have fished out of the trash. She never uses any of this stuff, she just keeps it in a JCPenney bag in the back of her closet.

Didi gives a deep sigh. Mimi can sometimes act batshit crazy. But she's the only mom Didi's got, and she tries, really she does. She's had such a lousy life, she deserves to have anything she wants.

She definitely deserves a better daughter than Didi. Chunky and ugly, with frizzy dishwater hair and in a permanent crappy mood.

Tough luck, Mimi, she thinks sourly. Better luck in the next life.

She sticks a CD into her player. Red Hot Chili Peppers. They sort of suck, but she listens to them because Sarah Davis raved about them on MySpace.

Something acid bubbles up in Didi's throat. Sarah Davis. Her new best friend. At least she was until today.

Didi's never had a best friend before. Or any friends at all since grade school. She's mostly been shunned or just ignored. Sophomore year, she'd tried to go Goth, all death makeup and bleached platinum hair and black clothes, but the Goth crowd ignored her too.

Weird-ass Goth nerds rejected her. How pathetic is that?

Then at the beginning of this semester, Sarah Davis transferred into her school. A babe—all creamy complexion and perfect nose and golden brown hair brushing her delicate shoulders. The hot crowd quickly took her up. But amazingly, she chose a seat next to Didi in AP English and actually began talking to her! And continued to through the semester, and then walked with her to their next classes, and they talked and giggled together, just like best friends. They haven't hung out after school yet because Sarah's got lacrosse and on weekends she's busy with her family, but during the summer, Didi is sure they will.

Except today . . .

A burp of acid. She swallows.

Today, in English, while Mr. Di Rizzo was enthusing about Beowulf's great virtue, Didi whispered to Sarah, "So, like, Beowulf's a virgin, right?" Lame joke, yeah, okay, but Sarah didn't even roll her eyes. And afterward, when they were leaving the classroom, Sarah walked in dead silence for a minute. Then said, "Listen, don't put anything in my knapsack, okay?"

Didi had turned bright red: she could feel the blaze burn right up to the roots of her hair. "I didn't . . . I mean, I thought you'd like getting surprises."

"I don't, okay? Nobody would. It's creepy. Why would you even think it wasn't?" She'd softened a little and added, "Look, that was kind of harsh. But seriously, Didi, you've got to respect other people's boundaries."

Didi had gone all sullen and, like, "I'll respect yours, don't worry." And then she'd walked stiffly ahead.

She slams the eject button on the sucky Chili Peppers, and the disc shoots onto the floor. Didi kicks it under the bed. She's probably blown it with Sarah.

Then she thinks, *Oh crap. I'm gonna eat the rest of those OREOs.*

She's got no freaking willpower at all.

Maybe she should just kill herself.

Or kill somebody else. Anybody, really. She could.

There's really no reason she couldn't.

She's already done it once before.

CHAPTER THREE

SARAH

Psyc 204 Abnormal Human Sexual Behavior
An intensive approach to human sexual behaviors that deviate from traditional cultural standards. This class will integrate concepts of psychology, sociology, and neuroscience.
Instructor: James Blackworth Holland
Freemartin Hall Rm 111
Mon., Thurs. 2:30 p.m.–3:20 p.m.

I'm late, drat it. The lecture's already started.

Like an idiot, I hadn't checked the exact location of Freemartin Hall, and so I parked in Structure 3, which was at the opposite end of the campus—a fifteen-minute schlep, in addition to getting turned around in all those modern science buildings at Steinman Plaza.

I hate being late for anything. It's a not-so-subtle sign of contempt. *My time is so much more valuable than yours.* Or else it's sheer ego. Make a grand entrance, get every neck to swivel as you come twirling in the door.

I don't want to seem superior. And I definitely don't want to attract attention. I just want to blend in. I hope I do. I'm thirty-five, over a decade older than most of these students, but I'm fairly sure I look younger than I am. I'm wearing my hair student-style—long and loose. And I've got on the unofficial regulation student outfit: jeans, down vest, UGGs. Granted, my vest is Chanel. And my jeans, Brunello Cucinelli—light wash, midrise, over a thousand bucks at Neiman's. But I doubt any of these kids will recognize that.

The UGGs, at least, are just UGGs.

The lecture hall is packed. Abnormal Human Sex—it promises some pretty juicy stuff. S&M with leather hoods and safe words. Fetishes involving frogs or your great-grandma's panties. I've got to admit I'm looking forward to it myself.

I spot an empty seat a few rows down in the middle. I edge past knees and a few dirty looks. The boy who's manspreading in the seat beside it grudgingly knocks his knees together without even a glance at me. I sit down. Fish out a notebook and Montblanc from my tote.

James Blackworth Holland, PhD in psychology. The name had leaped to my attention in the catalog. When I was in high school in Monterey for that one semester, it was impossible not to know about the weirdly glamorous Hollands. I'd had a real curiosity about them back then. So I immediately registered for the class.

Dr. Holland is turned to a white screen, clicking through PowerPoint images. Even from the back, he gives off the attitude of a man who knows he's hot. Slim build. Thick shock of chestnut hair. He wears his tweedy sports jacket with a slouchy insouciance. A jacket that, by the way, is in a league, price-wise, with my Chanel and Cucinelli.

Dr. Holland obviously has money.

He stops on a diagram of a section of the brain. It looks like a spiral with bulgy parts to it. The bulges are all labeled, and there's a larger label above the diagram: LIMBIC SYSTEM.

He turns to us. "The limbic system, sometimes referred to as the reptile brain. It's evolved from our most primitive ancestors."

His face is boyish, fine boned, with just a touch of rakishness. Horn-rimmed glasses. Sexy-nerdy.

"Briefly, it's in charge of our most basic and automatic behaviors. You might think of these as the four *F*s. Feeding. Fight or flight. And that other well-known f-word . . ." He pauses provocatively. "Fornication."

A ripple of laughter from those who'd been expecting the more basic term.

He clicks an enlarged view of one of the bulges. "The amygdala. From the Greek word for almond, because . . . well, you've figured it out, it looks like an almond. The amygdala has complex functions, but the most important is in processing emotion. And, arguably, the most important of our emotions, at least from an evolutionary point of view, is fear. Anybody want to guess why?"

For a moment, no one is bold enough to speak. I consider raising my hand. But then a girl down front says, "To run away from danger?"

"Exactly!" Dr. Holland says. "Beginning with our earliest ancestors, fear has been critical for survival. Fight or flight. For example, if you're an early *Homo sapiens* and you happen to spot a saber-toothed cat, it's good for you to receive an instantaneous signal to back away and not try to go up and scratch it behind its ears."

Robust laughter. Dr. Holland's got us charmed now.

"The amygdala is also associated with aggression. Fight as opposed to flight. And where this will get very interesting for us is its role in male sexual behavior. Interesting fact: in men who are castrated, the amygdala shrinks more than thirty percent."

The boy next to me squirms and squeezes his thighs together.

"We're going to see that when these two behaviors, aggressive and sexual, become confused, it plays a strong role in psychopathic sexual violence."

Now he's talking. The stuff of Hannibal Lecter and *Criminal Minds*. The entire room rustles in expectation.

I do too.

Dr. Holland is punctual: he wraps the class at exactly 3:20. Like all charismatic teachers, he's already got groupies. There's a stampede toward the front of the lecture hall, both boys and girls.

I stash my pen and notebook and head back out onto the campus. Bradford is a private university nestled in an area of Orange County just a stone's throw from Disneyland. It's modeled on the Ivy League— all quadrangles and buildings with pediments and noble colonnades. Though this being Southern California, there are a lot of palm trees and not so much ivy.

I've got time to kill before my next class, so I wander across the sunken plaza to the outdoor sculpture collection. I go directly to a monumental abstract sculpture mounted on a black base. The Henry Moore. The prize piece of this collection.

My eyes fix immediately on the bronze plaque on the base:

Two Forms
Henry Moore (1898–1986)
Gift of Sarah and Gideon T. Ellingham

I flash back five years. My thirtieth birthday. Gideon bringing me here. He's using a cane, not his wheelchair, and being helped by our driver, Manuel. As we approach the sculpture collection, Gideon stops. Gestures to Manuel, who takes a sleep mask from his pocket and hands it to me.

"Put it on, Sarah," Gideon instructs me. "Cover your eyes."

Since our marriage, blindfolds have not been unknown to me. But never before in public.

I know better than to ask why. I pull it over my eyes, feeling a little surge of panic at being blinded. But I don't let it show. Miguel takes my elbow and guides me, leaving Gideon to stumble on his own.

After a short distance, we stop. "You can take the mask off now, Sarah," Gideon says. I push it off my eyes.

"Happy birthday, my dear!"

It's an ugly metal sculpture. Like two huge dinosaur pelvis bones made of bronze tilting against each other. Gideon is chuckling with delight.

I didn't get it then. But I get it now. A multimillion-dollar sculpture with my name on it for posterity.

I squat down and run my fingers over the engraving, or at least the only words that count. *Gift of Sarah . . . Ellingham.*

A gust of Santa Ana wind blows up from the desert, and it cuts right through my Chanel down. I straighten up, hugging myself. I pull up a campus map on my phone. The Student Union café is close by, and I walk quickly to it.

A large, clamorous place. From the hot-beverage dispenser, I fill a cup with rich, frothy chocolate. I pay the cashier, slot a twenty-dollar bill into the tip jar (it will make his day, I'm sure—most students leave nothing), then turn to search for a table.

I catch my breath.

Dr. James Blackworth Holland is sitting alone, just one table away. Reading on his phone, holding it a little closer than someone normally would.

I can see his face distinctly now. The left eye, something odd about it. A slice of the eyebrow missing. And faint scars, darts and arrows on his cheeks and jaw, accounting for that rakish look. They stop him from being too pretty.

I hesitate, then approach him. "Excuse me, Dr. Holland?"

He glances up with a quizzical look enhanced by that missing chink of eyebrow.

I duck my head a little shyly. I'm not used to talking to good-looking men anymore. "I just want to say I'm taking your class, and I, um . . . I really enjoyed your lecture. It was very informative." Informative. I feel like biting hard on my tongue.

"Thanks," he says perfunctorily. But then he registers the fact that I'm not a kid, I'm actually close to his own age. And that I'm pretty. Maybe even very pretty. "And you are . . . ?"

"Sarah Ellingham."

"Like Ellingham Hall in the Business School?"

"Yes." I give a modest little twist of my lips. "My husband, Gideon, endowed it. He was a trustee here."

Dr. Holland's brows raise. Or more accurately, his right eyebrow raises to match his perpetually lifted left one. "Are you auditing?"

"No, I'm enrolled. Gideon died two years ago. I dropped out of college sophomore year, so I thought now would be a good time to finish my degree."

"I'm very sorry about your husband. But great that you're finishing your degree." He indicates the opposite chair. "Would you like to join me?" When I hesitate, he adds, "Please."

"Thank you." I sit down and set my cocoa on the table.

"Are you majoring in psych?" he asks.

"Yes, but I don't intend to go into the field. I mean, I'm not going to be a therapist or anything. I have a more personal interest." I hesitate, and then I say, "You see, there was a girl I went to high school with who tried to kill me. I guess I'd like to figure out her motivation."

"Seriously? She tried to kill you?"

"Yes. She was one of those outcast kids that others make fun of. A real oddball named Didi. I was new at the school. I felt sorry for her and tried to be friendly. She went overboard; she began stalking me, at school and on social media, and hiding presents in my knapsack. I had to pull back. And then at a beach party, she pushed me off a bluff."

His attention is riveted now.

"I survived, obviously. There was a ledge beneath the cliff covered in vines, so I really wasn't hurt much. But it scared me nearly to death. I remember thinking that if I did survive, I'd somehow get even."

"Did you have her arrested?"

"No. It would have been complicated. My family was moving again. My parents were both air force, and they were transferred to a base in Texas." I pause to take a sip of cocoa, hoping not to leave a mustache. "But I suppose I've never totally gotten over it. Somewhere in my mind, I'm always afraid she'll pop up at me again."

He says carefully, "Have you ever talked to anyone about this?"

"You mean a therapist? No." I give a little smile. "Maybe that's the real reason I'm a psych major. So I can begin to do therapy on myself." I add quickly, "I don't know why I'm telling you this. I hope you don't think I'm trying to sneak in a free session with you."

He smiles. "I'm not that kind of psychologist. I teach and do research."

"Experimenting with rats?"

"Better known as grad students." His smile turns flirtatious. I feel a little thrill.

"So what made you go into psychology?" I ask. "If it's okay for me to ask you?"

"It's okay." He hesitates. "I guess it was also trauma in my youth. My parents separated when I was fourteen, and my mother died a year later."

"Oh God, that's really hard," I say softly. "What did she die of?"

His eyes dart very briefly away. "Natural causes," he says.

He's a terrible liar. I find that endearing. "Why abnormal psych? I mean, it's a fascinating subject, so I guess there doesn't have to be a reason . . ."

He gives a little laugh. "My family was not what you'd call normal. Not in the realm of deviancy, just out of the ordinary. So perhaps I think of more ordinary people as a little dull." There's a teasing expression in his eyes, and I can't tell whether he's joking or not.

He glances at his phone. I wonder suddenly if he's finding me a little dull, despite what I've told him. This has been so fortuitous, but I don't want to presume on it. I stand up. "You're busy."

"No, I was just checking the time of a departmental meeting. I've still got half an hour."

"But I do have to go, I'm afraid. I've got a seminar on the other side of campus. I don't want to be late."

He looks disappointed. "Whose seminar?"

"It's not psych. English. Contemporary American Women Writers. I almost majored in English. I took AP English in high school, and it was really inspirational." I extend my hand. "It's been very nice to talk to you, Dr. Holland."

"Oh, hey. It's James." He takes my hand warmly. "I'll see you in my next class, I hope?"

"Absolutely," I say. "I'll be the one in a middle row scribbling notes like mad."

I turn and head to a bin to dump my nearly full cup of cocoa. Not the most elegant of exits. I can tell he's still watching me.

Didi. Why did I say that name to him? I haven't spoken it out loud in a very long time.

Like always, I look around to see if she's anywhere in sight. Not because I'm frightened of her. Because of something I did not blurt out to Dr. James Holland.

I still very much want revenge.

CHAPTER FOUR

AVA

Choose a beanbag, Ava. Dr. Patti offers me a basket full of beanbags shaped like animals. A toad. A white rat. A lobster.

I grab one at random. An octopus. It's purple.

Okay, very good. That octopus is your fear, Ava. See those tentacles? They're your feelings of guilt. Your fear has got you all wrapped up in them. But they belong to the octopus, not to you.

I look at the purple octopus. It's kind of sweet.

Throw it away, Ava. Throw it hard against that wall. Scream and howl and slam it hard against the wall.

I can't hurt any creature. Not even spiders. Dad once accidentally drove over a black snake. Mom wept tears over it, and so did I.

I'm unable to throw the purple octopus at the wall.

Dr. Patti with her basket of animal beanbags. Why had she popped so suddenly into my mind?

My life was basically fine. It was true that, four months before, my brief marriage to a brilliant and temperamental engineer named Noah had ended, but it was an amicable divorce.

Almost ridiculously amicable.

We'd met in Boston, where I'd been living since college. Noah had wandered into the hole-in-the-wall photography gallery on Davison Street that I was managing: he worked for SpaceX south of LA and was killing time before leaving for the airport. Our attraction was instantaneous. For the next five months we conducted a thrilling long-distance relationship. Texting each other until all hours of the night. Racing to catch planes. Some awkward phone sex.

And I had felt, for the first time since Mom's death, something other than sort of just okay. A spark of being intensely alive.

We married in Aunt Willie's flower-strewn garden, and I moved into Noah's modern house in Manhattan Beach. I began doing my own photography, staging photos that told a complete story. I dressed models—not fashion models, real people—in out-of-style clothes I dug up at Goodwill or the Salvation Army. I posed them in eerie locations doing things that looked ordinary but weren't, in some nightmarish way, and I lit their faces with a beyond-the-grave pale glow. "A horror flick in one frame," Noah called them, and he wasn't far wrong.

He had pretended to like my work. "It's unusual. It makes you look twice."

What he meant was he hated it. The ambiguity disturbed him. He was a tech genius, he got heady on algorithms and codes, and his work was equally baffling to me.

We had almost nothing in common. We'd mistaken the spice of long distance for real and abiding love. I began to draw into a shell. Noah became excessively polite. We slept curled on opposite sides of the bed. Ate our meals in murderous silence.

Divorce was the sensible thing, we finally agreed. It was the only thing we'd agreed on for months.

After signing the final papers, we celebrated at a bistro in Brentwood. Toasted each other with Veuve Clicquot. Ordered cake for dessert, devil's food with dark truffle shavings. We waved our signed legalese like winning lottery-ball tickets. Outside the restaurant, we chastely kissed goodbye. "We'll always care for each other," I said, and Noah replied, "You bet we will." And then we left in our separate cars, knowing the chances were good we'd never see each other again.

I'd rented a charming bungalow in Santa Monica with a pink silk tree in front. Since then, I'd sold a number of prints through a downtown gallery, and the owner had been talking about a solo show.

I was poised for the start of a gratifying new life.

So why Dr. Patti?

She had been the best of the string of therapists I'd had after Mom died. I'd sunk into a seemingly depthless black well. Aunt Willie, scared senseless, had me observed in a psychiatric institution called the Pavilion, where I was kept under an intense suicide watch. After that, there were psychologists, and a grief counselor, and once a healer in a royal blue caftan who waved stinky candles around my face and feet, and psychiatrists who scribbled prescriptions: Lexapro, and when that didn't work, Prozac, and for a disastrous time, lithium.

By the time I left for college, I had pulled out of it. Strands of black dread like octopus tentacles sometimes tickled at the corners of my mind, but I was good at brushing them away.

Until now.

I was sleeping less and less. Waking up feeling there was something urgent I needed to do. Something I'd left undone. And when I squeezed my eyelids shut in a desperate attempt to get back to sleep, images played out behind them—of my family, back in that haunted house we called Blackworth Mansion. Jamie, his astonishing beauty, his face still free of scars. Dad, vigorous and handsome but losing his shit over the smallest provocation.

And Mom. Her voice sometimes murmuring in my ear: *Ava, sweet love. Why won't you help me?*

Jamie called. We hadn't seen each other since Aunt Willie died several months after my wedding (of a massive stroke at the age of eighty-seven doing what she loved best—weaving fantasies into fabric at her loom).

"We need to talk about the house," he said.

"I was just about to call you," I told him. "It must be sibling ESP."

He gave a snort. He was a scientist: he had little use for things like ESP. "I want to put the property up for sale," he said. "It's worth a fortune now. I've been talking to a lawyer. It's possible to break the trust."

I felt a twinge of alarm. "It's not possible until I turn thirty-three. That's nearly another four years."

"Look," he said. "The house is rotting away up there. Neither of us has set foot in it since we left it. The upkeep is enormous. The lawyer says we can claim it's an unreasonable drain on our principal."

"Since when do you care about money?" I said. "We've already got more than we need."

"I've had some expenses. I could use some extra, and I'm sure you could too. It's not like we inherited a major fortune."

This didn't sound like Jamie at all. "I don't want to sell it," I said. "In fact, I'm going back to live there for a while."

"You can't be serious," he said.

"I'm perfectly serious. I'm going to move in as soon as it can be put in shape."

He paused. "I think we should talk about this in person."

I drove to the university a few days later. His office was in one of the oldest buildings on the campus, a mock-Renaissance structure with a tall campanile. His door on the second floor was partially open. I started to go in, then realized he wasn't alone. He was standing in front of his desk, deep in conversation with a young woman.

I rapped, and he looked up with a start. "Oh, hey, Ava. I lost track of the time. Come in."

The young woman turned to me. Not so very young—about my age. She was strikingly lovely: a tumble of golden brown hair framing dark eyes, a perfect nose, good bones. But there was an almost hesitant quality about her beauty, as if it had only recently been given to her as a present and she wasn't quite used to owning it yet.

"Ava, this is Sarah Ellingham," Jamie said. "She's taking one of my classes. Sarah, my sister, Ava Holland."

A student? I extended my hand. "Nice to meet you."

She grasped it warmly. "I'm very happy to meet you, too, Ava. Your brother is an outstanding teacher."

"Which class are you taking?"

"My abnormal psych," Jamie said. "Sarah is one of my best students."

"Don't believe him. I have to study like a demon, and I'm definitely not one of the best."

"She lived in Monterey for a while," Jamie said.

"Really?" I glanced at her. "Maybe we knew people in common."

"James and I already compared notes. We don't. I only lived there the second half of my senior year. But I knew about your family. You were local celebrities."

"We were that weird," Jamie said.

"You were that interesting," Sarah said with a pleasing smile. "We found out we both played lacrosse, though. When I transferred into Monterey Regional, they let me be a substitute attacker."

"Jamie was an attacker too," I said.

"I know." She plucked a lock of her hair and started to twist it but tucked it behind her ear instead, and as she did, I noticed a small ring on her middle finger—a sapphire encircled by pearls in a vintage setting.

"I love your ring," I said. "It's Victorian, isn't it?"

"Yes. I love vintage. I bought it in a tiny shop in London some years ago. The owner said it had belonged to a niece of Queen Victoria's."

"Our mother had one very similar to it. An old family ring. Do you remember, Jamie?"

"She had dozens of rings. But I'm fairly sure none of our family were royalty."

"You never know. You should do one of those Ancestry things." Sarah's tone was teasing. "But listen, I know you two want to catch up, so I'll let you be."

"Don't forget this." Jamie handed her a thick book. *Diagnostic and Statistical Manual of Mental Disorders.*

Sarah shot me a playful glance. "My bedtime reading tonight. I'll fall asleep and dream about schizophrenia."

"I hope not," I said with a smile. But there were worse things to dream about. That much I knew.

Jamie walked her to the door. Said something low to her, and she murmured something in reply. He turned back and sat down at his desk, and I took the chair facing him.

"She's very pretty," I said.

"Yes, and very smart too. She's a widow. Her husband died a couple of years ago, a wealthy guy who left her well taken care of. To her credit, she's finishing her degree, not just going to the gym."

A wealthy, smart, and beautiful young widow. She could have seemed intimidating, but she didn't. I said, "Is there something going on between you?"

He gave an evasive smile. "We're seeing each other, but we're keeping it quiet. As long as she's my student, it could seem unethical." He put on a pair of glasses. His trademark horn-rims. "Okay, let's talk plain," he said. "Give me any rational reason you'd want to live in that godforsaken house."

"You know the gallery, 66 Church, that sold some of my work? I've been talking to the owner about a solo show. I have an idea for a new series of photos she's excited about. I'm going to photograph my past. *Our* past. Growing up in a haunted house." My voice rose with excitement. "I'm going to stage all the shots in Blackworth Mansion, like making it one big set."

"Jesus, Ava. You should never go back in that house again. It could trigger very traumatic memories. And you definitely can't live there by yourself."

"Sure, I can. It's my home."

"You think of that place as home? God."

"I do. And besides, I want to trigger memories. I've been thinking a lot about all of us back then. Especially Mom. The way she died."

He looked at me warily. "What about it?"

"I think there might have been something I could have done to prevent it. Something that I knew and didn't do anything about."

He gave a sigh. "Her death was in no way your fault, Ava. It was a rapidly progressing neurological disorder. Possibly Creutzfeldt-Jakob. I know you've never really accepted that."

"Have you?" I said. "I mean, honestly?"

"It's the only thing that makes sense. All her tests indicated it."

"She didn't even do most of the tests. And you know there were things that didn't fit the diagnosis. I think . . ." I hesitated. "I think somebody killed her."

"Do you have anybody in mind?"

I hesitated. "What about Dad?"

"He's a mean drunk and can't keep his prick in his pants. But he's not a murderer. Jeez, Ava. You're suggesting that our father killed our mother. It's crazy to even think that."

"Is that your professional opinion, Dr. Holland?" I said.

"No, just my personal one. You want my professional opinion? You've never let go of your adolescent guilt for being unable to control things that were completely out of your control."

Let it go, Ava. Dr. Patti's purple octopus blinked through my mind.

"I've lost so many of my memories of that time," I said. "I think making these photographs could help me get some of them back. And then who knows? Maybe I'll agree with you that it was a nerve disease."

He made a disgruntled face. "You're talking about dissociative amnesia. Memory loss due to trauma. It can happen, but only temporarily. You would have regained your lost memories by now unless it was head trauma or you were on drugs."

"Maybe I was on drugs," I said.

"You weren't. You hadn't been put on any meds yet."

"I think I was. I remember somebody giving me something. Telling me it would make me feel better."

"Who gave you something?" he said sharply.

"I don't remember. A woman, I think. There were so many people there that day. They all came running after I found Mom in her studio."

"Ava." Jamie's tone now became shrink-like, gentle. "Nobody was there except you. It was the end of the day. Everybody working for us had gone home. I was still at practice, cross-country, remember? Some parent drove me home. An ambulance had just gotten there, but otherwise it was just you."

I stared at him in confusion. I remembered people . . . footsteps. Running. "Who called the ambulance?"

"You did. You still had the phone clutched in your hand. That green cordless one from the Monster Room. You were out of your head, I could hardly get a word out of you."

"Are you sure Dad wasn't there?"

"I'm sure."

Images dashed and flickered. They seemed like real memories. They had to be. He was wrong.

His tone became shrink-like again. "Ave, listen. You're coming off a divorce. You're thinking emotionally, not rationally. Are you still taking your meds?"

"Faithfully," I said. "I'm not out of my head, Jamie. And I'm not going to agree to sell Blackworth Mansion. Not now, maybe not ever. You can sue me if you want to try to break the trust, but it's not going to work."

"You're not going to find Mom there, you know," he said. "She's gone, Ava. You're not going to conjure her back up."

"I'm really not delusional, Jamie. So stop psychoanalyzing me."

He screwed his mouth in frustration, an expression that was so *Jamie* I couldn't help laughing. "Come on, let's go to lunch and talk about completely different things. I haven't seen you in ages. I'll take you somewhere nice."

"Okay," he relented. "But let's just go to the faculty lounge. I've got midterms to grade."

The lunch was strained, even though we said nothing more about Blackworth Mansion or Mom. I hoped he'd tell me more about Sarah, but he didn't bring her up, and I didn't press him.

But I thought about her as I was driving the monotonous, soulless stretch of freeway back to Santa Monica. The rich, beautiful widow with that pleasing, slightly shy manner about her.

Could she be the reason behind Jamie's sudden interest in money and lawyers? The thought jolted me.

And then I thought of something else.

The ring she was wearing. Vintage sapphire and pearls. Suddenly, it seemed to me that it wasn't just very similar to Mom's.

It seemed like it was the exact same one.

But that was just crazy. I shoved the thought out of my mind.

CHAPTER FIVE

SARAH

Ava Holland should have looked freakish. Those eyes, so big and too far apart, and her black hair cut boy short. She should have looked like some nocturnal creature. A lemur or something. But she was stunning.

And that way she had of looking like she'd just tossed on any old things—that khaki shirt could have used an iron, and her white sneakers had seen a lot of jogging. But somehow the result was also stunning, for all its carelessness.

James is the same way, with his frayed collars and scuffed John Lobb loafers. An old money thing, I suppose.

And like James, Ava tries to button up her emotions. And just like with James, they tattle on her anyway.

Or at least they do to someone who notices.

I was nervous about meeting her. He's told me about her breakdown after her mom's death. The meds. The suicide watch. I hope she's not going any kind of crazy again. Not when things are going so well between James and me.

He also told me she plans to go live at their family's home. Lenore Wyatt, my attorney and life manager, says California has strong squatters' rights. Ava could end up with total claim to the property if James doesn't stop her. I haven't said that to him, though. It's not my place to say it.

Or at least not yet.

I wonder now, as I leave his building, whether they are discussing me. How much he's telling her about us. It's all happened so fast between us I can hardly believe it.

Running into him in the cafeteria was a lightning strike of luck. And it could have ended with just that one brief encounter. But I made sure it didn't. For the next class, I came prepared with a question. I raised my hand before he launched into the lecture, and when he acknowledged me (with a pleased smile), I stood up. "In the last class, Dr. Holland, you mentioned the role of abnormal male aggression in sexual behavior. I was wondering if we'll be looking at similar behavior in women."

Several of the female students began popping up in whack-a-mole fashion, and they took up the question as sort of a feminist challenge to James. Like, "We demand recognition that women can be just as pervy as men," though not in those words, naturally.

James handled it beautifully. "I understand your issues, ladies, but don't worry. The female frontal cortex is going to get equal scrutiny in this class."

I'd shot a sly glance of amusement at him, and he had locked eyes with me, echoing my amusement. Afterward, I received a message on the student portal. "I've been mulling over your question. I'd love to discuss further. Coffee?"

Absolutely, coffee.

Followed some days later by a breakfast "discussion of your last paper." Which led to a very nonacademic dinner date. And a second dinner in a romantic restaurant, with a nightcap at his house in Laguna Beach. Followed directly into his bed with very normal, not in the least abnormal, sexual behavior.

I had intended now to go to the library to work on revising my midterm paper, but suddenly I'm not in the mood. I retrieve my car from the parking structure and drive instead to Costa Mesa. The South Coast Plaza mall.

In the mall, I head to Saks. The women's designer department. I seek out an older saleswoman, a tiny sixtysomething with bags under her eyes. Debra, she says her name is. I tell her I'm looking for a simple but elegant daytime dress. Something in a pale color. But not white.

Definitely not white.

I try on quite a few dresses. Finally, I select a belted georgette dress in a pale-green print. Loro Piana. Nineteen hundred dollars. Inexpensive compared to the clothes I bought when married to Gideon, but it's for what will just be a casual event, really.

I hand Debra my Platinum Card, and she efficiently rings the dress up. She adjusts it on its hanger, padding the shoulders with tissue paper, and fits it almost reverently into a plastic dress bag.

She'll never get to wear a dress like this, I think. As I slip my credit card back into my wallet, I have an idea.

"Debra," I say. "I'd like you to have this."

She looks at what I'm offering with some suspicion. Wondering, *What's the catch?* I assure her there's no catch. Just something extra for her.

"But don't mention it to anybody," I tell her. "You might put your job in jeopardy."

"I won't," she assures me.

I head to the handbag department. Browse the Chloés. The Bottega Venetas. Maybe I should buy one as a gift for Ava.

No, I'm pretty sure she'd think that was gauche.

I'll have to find a better way to prevent her from becoming any kind of an obstacle.

DIDI

Mimi can't be at Didi's graduation today because she's got to work. Though not for the sainted Christina Holland this time.

For a filthy rich family named Rainier. They own three other homes and are practically never even here but for some reason decided to blow in for the weekend—Didi's graduation weekend—and Mimi couldn't say no because then they might never call her back.

Didi understands. Mimi does it all for her. So she can eventually elevate herself and not have to break her back for rich people the way poor old Mimi does.

Didi isn't even sure why she's come to the stupid graduation herself. There's a swirly cold fog, and all the seniors are flapping up to the podium in their black robes, looking like alien seals in some soupy alien sea. They're going in alphabetical order, so Didi's turn is right in the middle.

The invisible middle.

She would've been first if she had been valedictorian. She could have been. But she had slacked off in chem and world history, getting eighty-three and eighty-five respectively instead of high nineties, like she could've easily. Because no way was she going to stand up there and give a lame speech that was all "We've been through some amazing times together, guys," and "Don't be afraid to chase your dreams."

Because what about when your dreams chase you? When they come at you like the most scary, terror-making movie you've ever seen—worse than *Saw II* or *The Hills Have Eyes*—and all the exits are blocked.

What then, you guys?

'Cause that was the speech she would've made. And they'd have rushed up and stuffed a gag in her mouth and dragged her right off to the nearest nuthouse. So Zoe Gotsch was valedictorian and up there going "follow your bliss" and blah, blah, blah, barf.

Now finally everyone's collected their stupid diplomas, and they're running around hugging each other and signing each other's yearbooks and shrieking about a party tonight at Shoehorn Beach, and who's gonna bring the brewskis? Nobody is shrieking at Didi, of course, and she hasn't collected one signature.

"Hey, girl!" Didi whirls. It's Sarah! Her face is flushed with excitement, and she's got a yearbook tucked under her arm, and she's grinning at Didi. Didi feels her heart swell: they're friends again. "Give me that thing." Sarah grabs Didi's yearbook and flips it open and writes something sort of long. "I wrote on your picture because I don't have one. I transferred in too late." She makes a mock pouting face. "You going to this party tonight? Sounds like it's gonna be wild!"

Another girl barges up and grabs Sarah's shoulders from behind, and Sarah turns, and this girl has her sign *her* book, and some other kids are waiting their turn with Sarah. Didi's got to catch a bus. She takes off her robe and cap and sticks them in the provided receptacle and leaves.

But she wonders: Are she and Sarah best friends again, or what?

She goes straight home without stopping at the Quiki Mart. Mimi's taking her for a celebration at Chipotle, and Didi's been tasting guac and carnitas and that great tomatillo salsa they make there all day long in anticipation.

But then Mimi staggers in and immediately collapses on the ratty couch. "My knee is on fire. Be a love, hon, and get me an ice pack."

Didi goes to the freezer. The ice pack is almost frozen over, and she has to chip it out with a knife. "What happened?" she asks, bringing it to Mimi.

"The Rainier boy shoved me on his way out the door, and I fell." She winces as she presses the ice pack down. "The blond one. He was in a hurry to leave, and I accidentally stepped in his way."

"They've got two blond sons." Didi had helped Mimi clean at the Rainiers' a couple of times. "Which one, the dumb one or the smart one?"

"I can't keep them straight, hon. But hey, how was the graduation? I'm sorry as heck I missed it."

"A thrill a minute," Didi says. "So I guess no Chipotle then?"

"Oh, hon, not tonight. You can pick up some subs from Manny's. You like those, don't you?" She adds in a musical voice, "I got you a present. It's in my bag."

Didi digs into Mimi's vinyl knockoff Prada. There's something wrapped up in paper towels. A squat jar with a silver cap. Le Parc Antiaging Facial Crème.

"It's a high-end product," Mimi says, still in that chirpy voice.

She's pilfered it from Mrs. Rainier. And when Didi unscrews the cap, she sees the product inside has gone a rotten shade of tan. Mrs. Rainier had probably tossed it.

Maybe she should just bash Mimi's head in with it. Put her out of her misery.

She's immediately ashamed of the thought. It's not Mimi's fault she's a klepto. She can't help it. "Thanks, Mimi," she says. "I'll start using it right away."

She goes to her room and sticks the jar in a drawer. Flops on her bed. Opens her yearbook to her photo to see what Sarah Davis had written.

Didi's proud of her photo. For the shoot, you were supposed to come as you really were, like deep down, and not just the way you normally look. What a farce! All the popular kids were hair-flippy gorgeous like they always were, and the arty crowd looked all arty. And the jocks wore the team sweatshirts of the moron colleges they'd been accepted to, just like always. But a few kids did take it seriously. Suze Wallenstone came in drag, per her intention of transitioning to tranny male at eighteen. And that kid Winston Peet came in clown makeup, but he was special needs, so they allowed it.

Didi had taken the instructions very seriously. Didn't wash her hair for a week so it dribbled dirty into her face. Canceled out her lips and eyelashes with mud-colored foundation and wore these beige glasses that used to belong to Gram and a no-color beige top—Wal-Mart, extra large. It made her look exactly like who she really is.

Invisible.

So invisible that Sarah scrawled right across it:

Girl, you are smart and beautiful and perfect just the way you are! Don't ever let anybody make you change!!!

Didi reads it a couple of times. The first time with a flush of pleasure. The second time, not so much. Beautiful? Perfect?

Bull bull bull!!! Shit shit shit!!!

She grabs a Magic Marker and cancels out the message. Which also cancels out her photo. But she doesn't scribble out the quote next to it—one word in Classical Greek. Τιμωρία. Ms. Varnado, the geography teacher who was supposed to monitor the quotes to make sure nobody slipped in anything racist or claimed it was Walt Whitman when it was actually Snoop Dogg, wanted to know what it meant. "Valor," Didi told her. "Courage in the face of battle." Ms. Varnado said, "Very inspirational," in this fakey voice, like she thought Didi was going to need a shitload of valor to make it through her sad future life.

It doesn't mean valor, though.

It means something else entirely.

She decides, suddenly, she will go to that party on Shoehorn Beach tonight.

CHAPTER SIX

AVA

I had to be on the wrong road. I'd made the turn off Highway 1 by instinct. As if my hands on the wheel of my newish Volvo SUV had been directed by some invisible guide risen from the past.

The access road I was on, below and parallel to the highway, should have been rough and crumbling, but I was sailing on a smooth surface. And there were driveways leading off the road down to the shoreline: I could glimpse homes under construction—elaborate spectacles of modern architecture—through the trees. I heard the gangster rat-a-tat of nail guns. The whine of electrical saws. The beep, beep of a large vehicle backing up.

Impossible. The land that bordered Blackworth Mansion was too rugged and steep to ever build on. I'd definitely taken the wrong turn.

But then, abruptly, the smooth pavement ended, and my car was jostling over ruts and depressions. And there it was, almost invisible— the driveway to our property. I steered onto it, dense cedar and pine pushing in from all sides as if trying to reclaim what was rightfully theirs.

And then my heart began pumping hard as the familiar view came into sight. The old stone house set among mournful pines. The broad grass lawns. And far beyond and below, the misty blue expanse of the Pacific Ocean.

I came to the low wall surrounding the sculpture garden. Not really a garden. A large octagon-shaped area filled with gravel. There were six dry fountains and a few partial plaster statues listing on their bases. Other statues had long ago toppled, and the fragments were thickly scattered over the gravel. Mom used to come here and hunt for plaster body parts for her still life paintings: the crook of an elbow or a jagged section of a naked breast.

The driveway looped around the wall and continued on past a long line of cypresses to the circular front drive, sparse gravel crunching under my tires. An old, lovingly restored Dodge truck sat parked in the drive. The caretaker, Michael Fiore. I was early for our appointment, but he'd gotten here earlier. I pulled up behind his truck and stepped out of my car.

The ocean. I'd forgotten how aware of it you always were here. The sting of salt in the air, now intensified by the late-afternoon mist. The crash and tumult of the surf below. I gazed out at it a moment, breathing deeply, until the wind changed, carrying now the smell of the forest and the discordant sounds of construction from the next bluff.

I turned away from the ocean and walked toward the house. Crumbling, blackened. The windows boarded with splintered wood. The red front door, faded to the color of dry blood, drooping slightly off its hinges.

I climbed the stairs, so cracked now and full of weeds, to the front porch. The door latch rattled in my hand. I pressed it firmly, opened the sagging door.

I took my first tentative step into the foyer.

A reek of mildew and must. A frosting of dust on every surface, and dust motes waltzing somnambulantly in the air. The furniture hunched beneath dingy drop cloths like misshapen ghosts. The rugs rolled up in old blankets were like bodies awaiting burial.

I shouted, "Michael? Are you in here?"

My voice sounded as dead as everything else in the house.

The light was very dim: only a few feeble bulbs burned in cobwebbed sconces. I moved through the front hall: the sagging chandelier, the umbrella stand shaped like an elephant's foot, the stopped grandfather clock pointing to 12:35. The marble staircase, grand and sweeping, now covered in dust and grime, the banister looped with webs. I stood at the base and gazed up to the second floor.

A large shape flittered in the shadows.

"Michael?" I called tentatively.

No, it wasn't Michael. There was no one—nothing—there.

I heard footsteps overhead. I hesitated, then climbed the stairs.

The footsteps remained above me. Heavy, measured.

He's on the roof.

I let out a puff of relief. Then glanced down the hallway to the right. That mauve floral wallpaper, so faded now. Faded cream-painted doors: my old bedroom; Jamie's.

Home.

I turned down the opposite hallway—the north wing—and I continued to the last door on the ocean side. It was shut. I paused and suddenly felt a dread so strong that my legs began to give way. I clung to the doorknob a moment.

Then, resolutely, I turned the knob and stepped inside the room.

Mom's painting studio.

My legs wobbled again, and I sank into a chair. Her swivel chair that had squeaked when she turned this way and that. It was rusted now. No longer swiveled nor squeaked.

There was very little light—only what seeped through cracks in the boarded windows. But I still felt her presence here. Her long wooden table, splattered and splotched with paint flung from her brushes. The gauzy curtains she'd tacked up to filter the sea light, fluttering a little in one of those mysterious drafts that wafted through the house.

But her clutter was missing. The jumble of brushes and palettes. Her mortar and pestle for mixing her paints. The heaps of bizarre objects for her still lifes—desiccated jellyfish and shards of ancient Coca-Cola bottles and decapitated rag dolls. All of it gone.

A memory stabbed at me. One that had often groped at the borders of my mind. But now it suddenly flooded in as vividly as if it were happening right now.

I've come bursting in here, wanting something from Mom. What? Permission for an overnight with a friend or to settle some argument with Jamie . . . it doesn't matter. Because I see Mom in the corner—that corner, right over there between the big windows—and she's doing some kind of horrible dance. An ugly, jerking kind of dance. Making grinning faces like a jack-o'-lantern. Her rigid lips spitting out nonsense words I can't understand.

Except I can. There's one word that she says not once but over and over.

Poison.

"Knock, knock."

I gave a start. Michael Fiore was standing in the gloom of the doorway. "Whoa, didn't mean to scare you, Ava. I thought you heard me coming up the stairs."

"No, I heard you on the roof, but I was just . . ." I lost the words. Tears began trickling down my cheeks. I swiped them with the back of my hand.

"Sad memories, huh?"

"Yeah," I said. "Very sad. How are you, Michael?"

"Real good." He'd been our handyman back then, and he'd been left in charge of keeping a basic eye on the property. He looked very much the same: wiry frame, weathered-to-reptilian face, scraggly gray-blond hair pulled into a rat's tail. His aloha shirt was open to the navel. "You're looking good, too, Ava. And how's your brother?"

"He's got a doctorate in psychology now. Teaching at Bradford University."

"Sweet. How about your dad?"

My face hardened. "No idea."

Michael nodded without evident surprise. "I was checking for loose shakes up on the roof. We've had heavy rains this winter, a lot of debris flooded down off the hill and came right up to the house. Dirt, rocks, gravel. Some mud seeped inside. I just got the last of it cleared out." He nodded again. "This place must look kind of run down to you. My job was always just to keep it standing, you know."

"I know, Michael," I said. "It is a shock to see it like this. But it still feels like my home."

"I hear you. The places we come from run real deep in us. We don't never get them out of our systems." He scratched his bare stomach meditatively.

"I can't believe all that development up the road. We used to be so private here. That bluff was so steep and rocky we thought it was impossible to build on."

"For the right price, you can build on thin air." He made a sour face. "Those places are gonna sell for fourteen million and up. Worth the expense of developing."

"I suppose we could get a lot for our property."

"I believe so, Ava," he said. "You and James thinking of selling?"

"No," I said firmly. "Definitely not."

"Smart. It's gonna keep appreciating. So do you want me to take you around the house? You can point out anything you want particularly done."

"No, I think I'll just walk around by myself for a while. Soak it all in."

"Good enough. I'll be on the roof if you need me. If not there, in my truck."

He disappeared. I remained in the studio a little longer. I let my mind wander back to Mom, my finding her here that evening, doing that hideous dance.

She had collapsed on the floor, her body in convulsions. One arm jerking up to me as if begging for my help. I'd stood frozen, unable to move. For how long?

Seconds? Hours?

Until finally I ran out, screaming, and people came running upstairs.

Except that wasn't true.

There weren't a lot of people here. Nobody but me.

And if I was wrong about that, maybe I was wrong about everything. Even the word *poison*. Maybe Mom didn't say that at all. Maybe it was something I hallucinated later.

Why couldn't I remember?

I got up and looked around the room again and then turned to the bank of narrow drawers on the far wall, where Mom had stored her finished canvases. The drawers were empty except for a sketchbook in the lowest one. I took it out.

I began to open the sketchbook, then hesitated. Mom had always been sketching. Capturing us unaware in awkward moments, yawning or stuffing blueberries into our mouths.

But she never showed her sketches to anybody. These books were her private journals, she said. Nobody allowed to see.

I placed it back in the cabinet and shut the drawer.

I went out of the studio and began walking through the house, glancing into one familiar room, then another. My old bedroom with the jumping-horses wallpaper. Jamie's, his wallpaper with rocket ships. I went down the back staircase to the kitchen, with its haphazard improvements.

Phantom sounds reverberated in my mind. The whir of daiquiris in a blender. O'Keeffe yowling. Bare feet padding down a hallway.

I wandered down the corridor to the sunporch. Hurricane boards over the plate glass. The lush potted plants were gone, but the old wicker furniture remained.

Memories came in a rush. Dad on the wicker swing the day after we'd buried Mom, glass in hand. Jamie pacing, clenching and unclenching his fist.

Aunt Willie in the fan chair. *You were damned quick to pull the plug, Kevin.*

Ice in Dad's glass clinking. *We were getting back together.*

He'd been coming back to the house more frequently in those last months before Mom died. Acting like a doting father. Courting Mom. He'd thought he was succeeding.

But he wasn't. She hadn't forgiven him. She'd cut him out of her will.

He had motive to kill her.

I shuddered. How could I ever prove it?

The house was getting too dim to see much more. I headed back to the front hall and started to go outside, but I suddenly turned back to the stairs.

There was a small closet built into the wall beneath them. I crouched down and swiped away cobwebs, then opened the closet door and crawled inside. I tapped a spot on the back of the closet, and a panel slid open. One of those secret niches where my ancestor had hidden his bootleg gin. Jamie and I used to leave secret notes for each other here.

I reached into the niche. Groped and felt something. Not a note. A small bottle. I grabbed it, tapped the panel closed, and wriggled back out.

A prescription bottle of pills. I peered at the yellowed label. Nembutal.

A heavy sedative.

A faint voice drifted into my mind: *It will make you feel better.* It vanished before I could grasp it.

I stuffed the bottle into my purse and went outside.

CHAPTER SEVEN

Michael was leaning against his truck, squinting at his phone. A heavy mist was rising from the recently drenched foliage: he looked painted in pastel.

"Could I ask you a question?" I said. "The day my mother was taken to the hospital . . . were you here?"

He furrowed his brow. "You know, I was here that morning, Ava, but not when it all went down. I'd gone back into town. The drywall place, and then Value Strong, that old hardware store, to pick up some hinges. That's gone now, Value Strong. Got bought out by Ace some time back. The big chains swallow up everything, the SOBs."

"But that morning . . . ," I persisted. "Do you remember if my father was here too?"

"I'd have to give that a think, Ava. After all the shit I've smoked and put up my nose, it's hard to come up with my own name."

"It would be good if you could remember. And anybody else who was here that day."

"Well, you see, the same problem. A lot of years jumbled up in my head."

And yet he'd remembered the drywall place and the hinges from the hardware store. "It was the last day I ever saw my mother conscious,"

I said. "After that, she was in a coma, and none of us could ever talk to her again. So I'd like to remember as much of that day as possible."

"I hear you. Don't know if I can help you, though." He jammed his phone into the pocket of his sun-bleached jeans. "So are you done here? I'll start locking up."

"Done for now. How long do you think it would take to get it ready for me to live in? Just the main rooms."

"If you don't mind work still going on, you could move in maybe two, three weeks from now. We'll get the dust and bugs gone by then. Some painting. Get it wired for 5G. You gonna be here by yourself?"

"Any reason I shouldn't be?"

"Not really. But one thing you should know. A couple times I've been down here and saw somebody had gotten into the house. It beats me how. It's all boarded up good, and the locks are okay."

"Maybe raccoons?" I said.

"Nah. Some stuff got moved around. Another thing. A month ago, I came here and a vehicle was parked in front. I told the driver he was trespassing. He said he'd been here years ago. Like that gave him permission." Michael gave a snort.

"Who was he, did he say?"

"I already knew. Real estate developer, name of Thomas Rainier. It's his company that's putting up all that new shit over there."

The name shot a thrill through me. Ridiculous, after all these years. "He used to be a friend of my brother's," I said. "What did he want?"

"Didn't ask. But my guess is he wants to get his hooks on this property. Knock down this house, put up eight new ones, each bigger than a Home Depot."

"So you think he was the one who broke in?"

Michael sniggered. "Not him personally. He might have hired somebody. To scope things out, get an advantage if he comes at you with an offer. My advice is get a real mean dog. He won't come around again."

"I'll keep it in mind," I said. "Send me an estimate, and we can get started."

"Will do, Ava. And if you want, I can get Fran here working for you."

His daughter, Franny. I remembered her, a little kid who'd follow you around asking disconcerting questions—*Ava, do you have your period yet? Is Jamie always going to have those marks on his face?*—until you finally had to tell her to go away. "That would be great," I said. "How's she doing?"

"Gave us some trouble for a while. She ran off with a dude when she was sixteen. The feds picked him up in Utah on a burglary charge, and they brought her back here pregnant. She's straightened out now."

"How old is her child?"

"He didn't make it. Crib death. SIDS, they call it now."

I widened my eyes in horror. "I'm so sorry."

"It happens," he said. "So. Who's gonna pay for the work? The trust?"

"No," I said. "It will be on me."

I began driving back up the long rough driveway, the mist thickening by the minute. It was easier once I turned onto the access road. As I passed the new construction, barely visible now through the fog, I thought of the name Thomas Rainier. That slender blond boy who'd seemed so glamorously aloof to me at thirteen. My hopeless, all-consuming crush on him.

And now he was a real estate developer. Ruthlessly cutting down old-growth forest to put up McMansions. As if his family wasn't rich enough.

I flashed to the last time I'd seen him. Mom had been sick, but then she'd gotten better; it was all going to be okay. Jamie had his friends over again. I was on a step outside, pulling off my riding boots, and Thomas suddenly sat down close beside me. He wore nothing but swimming trunks and, like always, four or five bracelets stacked on his wrist. Leather. Twine. Silver.

"You know that cleaning lady of yours?" he said. "She used to work for us. My mother said she stole things, and fired her."

I was tongue-tied. My body was quivering.

"My mother's a fucking bitch," he said. He got up and went down to the beach.

I'd continued to sit there, one boot on, one boot off. My entire body on fire.

I suddenly became aware of a dazzle of headlights in my rearview mirror. High-mounted headlights very close behind me, the vehicle itself obscured by the yellow-tinged fog. I had the strange sensation that the lights were floating of their own accord, that they would pass straight through my car and appear on the road ahead of me.

I merged onto Highway 1; the lights merged right behind me and kept the same close distance behind. I swung off at the first exit, and so did the invisible vehicle. A feeling of alarm trembled through me.

At the stop sign at the end of the exit road, I turned sharply left. The headlights swung right and vanished.

Just some driver from the construction site in a fever to get home.

I checked into the Hyatt in the nearby Carmel Highlands. I had timed my visit to coincide with an event that evening. A gender-reveal party for my best friend from childhood, Grace Zhao, now Grace Zhao-Greenwald. We'd kept in touch, even during the blackest of my years after Mom. Grace had supported me in my divorce; I had cried with her over her two miscarriages. She was now a third-year associate at a Monterey trial law firm, married to a hand surgeon named Darsh, and five and a half months pregnant again.

I texted her. I'm here. Just checked into hotel. See ya soon!

She replied: Come early so we can gab first.

I sat down on the bed. I took out the prescription bottle that had been hidden under the stairs.

Nembutal, 100 mg.

A heavy barbiturate. In the right amounts it could kill you. And this vial was almost empty. Was I the one who had taken the rest?

The drug was prescribed for a Beverly something. I couldn't make out the last name.

I flashed on a memory: Jamie and I leaving here to go live with Aunt Willie. Grief-filled confusion. O'Keeffe in her carrier mewling piteously. Aunt Willie checking our bags, making sure we just packed essentials. *We'll be back for the rest.* And I had hidden something in the secret compartment. Something I hadn't wanted her to see.

We never did come back.

Who was this Beverly on the drug label? I texted Jamie: Just came from house. I found a bottle of Nembutal in our secret place.

He answered. Mom took sedatives. Had friends get them. I sometimes hid them from her. Never told you.

I stared at this with shock. Mom took drugs! I pictured her, so floating and dreamy, but that wasn't drugs, that was just Mom, part of what made her so special and different and wonderful.

I texted: Think it was me who put it there. Somebody gave them to me. Prescribed to a Beverly somebody. Familiar?

Nope. Still planning to move in?

In 3 weeks.

You know what I think. And am still pursuing option to sell.

Fine, I wrote.

He's with Sarah, I thought. The beautiful widow. She was the one behind his sudden desire to sell our property.

But why? She was rich, according to Jamie. She had not seemed greedy and acquisitive. Maybe even the opposite.

I couldn't think about this now. I had to get ready for Grace's party. I stuck my phone in my bag and opened my overnight case. I'd tossed in some mail I'd pulled out of my box just before leaving Santa Monica, and I glanced briefly through it. Mostly junk. Bills. A copy of *Aperture* magazine. And, strangely, a greeting card.

I peered at it a moment, then ripped the envelope open. A condolence card. *With Sympathy* written in white looping letters against a background of pastel doves and daisies and a droopy little angel gazing heavenward.

For me? I checked the envelope. It was my name scrawled in black ink. My address.

I opened the card. A vapid verse and below it a signature written in block letters with a charcoal pencil:

CINDERELLA

DIDI

Didi waits until Mimi has fallen asleep, about ten minutes into *Jimmy Kimmel*, dead exhausted after toiling for the Rainiers. Then she fishes the keys to Mimi's Fiesta from her purse and tiptoes out the door. She drives to Shoehorn Beach. It's one of those hidden little coves that are kept secret from tourists.

The parking lot is jammed, so she parks illegally, the Fiesta sticking out halfway onto the walking path. The cops won't be cruising this dinky park tonight. Too much major partying going on all over the city. She gets out, pauses at the top of the concrete stairs.

The party below looks like one of the circles of hell in Dante's *Inferno*. Tiki torches jammed into the sand flicker like flaming tongues, licking the misty air. They cast huge writhing shadows on the bluffs— like souls in hell, Didi thinks.

She heads down the stairs to the beach. Music is blaring. Coldplay. How original. The cranked-up bass competes with the boom of the surging breakers.

She starts to move through the crowd. Lit-up phone screens cut through the dark like laser swords. Every girl is shrieking at the top of her lungs, every guy is bellowing, and gangs of dogs make a doggy racket as they race in and around legs.

She spots Sarah Davis. Low-rise jeans and a cropped-off tee: she looks superhot. Didi debates with herself, then starts to head to her, but Sarah is in a tight little circle: she's holding a beer bottle even though she told Didi she doesn't like to drink, and she's laughing as hysterically as everyone else. So Didi just walks past.

She's all dressed up. She's pulled her hair into one high ponytail spouting from the side of her head. Squashed her legs and butt into skinny jeans she thought she could never get into again. Flip-flops, like every other girl. And she's wearing bling! Gold-toned dream catchers and about a dozen tinsel-bright bangles on one arm.

Nobody gives her a second glance.

She might as well be back at school. Invisible.

She hits a beer cooler and grabs a Sierra Nevada. Mimi was brought up a Mormon, and even though she hasn't set foot in a Mormon church in thirty years, she still won't allow alcoholic beverages in the apartment. Didi turned eighteen a month ago. Old enough to enlist in the army and get her head blown off. Or be sentenced to death by lethal injection.

But have a sip of beer? Nooooo.

She twists off the top and chugs the Sierra Nevada straight down. Flings the empty bottle into the sand.

Then picks it up and drops it into the Hefty that's lining a large container. Good citizenship. Mimi's taught her that.

She starts for a second beer, but a guy, Cody McCreery—he was her lab partner, Microbes and Us was the class—dives for the cooler, stomping on her toes in the process. "Shit!" she howls, but Cody is scooping an armful of bottles and bellowing to some a-hole, "Five gonna be enough?"

"Screw you," Didi mutters, but he's already charging back to his Neanderthal pals. She could have stripped naked and bent over and waggled her butt right in front of him, and he probably just would've set his beer on it.

She takes another Sierra. Chugs half, nurses the rest.

A wave slaps the naked legs of a girl, who shrieks like she's getting her throat cut. A couple of dogs crash into the receding wave and come yelping out like they were being attacked by a great white.

Everybody at this freaking party seems to be everybody else's closest friend. Pretty soon they'll all start pairing up and melt away into secluded nooks in the bluffs and bang each other's brains out. But there's dancing now, and that Didi can get into. She begins to move to the music. She waggles her head, making her ponytail thrash and bobble.

She notices that Sarah is not so surrounded anymore. So is she Didi's friend or not? Didi boogies her way toward her.

"Hey, girl!" she shouts. "Come on out here and dance with me!"

Sarah lifts her head, and a look of horror comes over her face—a look like *I'd rather die than be seen dancing with a freak like you.* The hottie guy standing next to her says something in her ear, and she laughs, and Didi knows it was about her.

She boogies more strenuously, like she's totally caught up in the bacchanalian beat, popping her fingers, shaking her butt and boobs, and moves off like it's the music that's carrying her away.

She gets to a place where the party thins out and stops her bogus dancing. She grabs a third beer from a cooler. A Blue Moon White this time. The real moon is just an occasional shimmer through patches of fog blowing in from the water. She heads to the tide line. Lets the cold surf drench her flip-flops.

"Bullshit," she screams at the water. "It's all freaking bullshit!"

Somebody laughs. She whips her head.

A blond dude. He's standing by himself in the foam, smoking a cigarette.

She recognizes him. One of the rich Rainier sons. The smart one. Thomas is his name.

He looks kind of lonely. Maybe a kindred spirit? She wades up to him.

"What's your preppy ass doing at a plebe party like this?" she asks in a surly tone.

The surf and the music's beats are so loud she thinks he didn't hear. But then he says, "Just passing through. Same as always."

"So where are you going next?" she says.

"Fuck if I know."

She laughs. Offers him the can. "Blue Moon?"

He gives a slight smile. "No. But thanks."

Of course. Just because he's at a plebe party doesn't mean he wants a plebeian beer. Except it's not, it's a premium beer. Defiantly, she pulls the tab and takes a long gulp.

"I know you, don't I?" he says. "You've been to our house a couple of times, right?"

She shrugs. "I don't think so."

"Yeah, you were. Your mom is one of our maids."

Her face turns fiery red. "My mother is a professional house cleaner. It's specialized work, and she's an expert, not a frigging maid."

She turns and starts back up the beach, flip-flops scuffing up sand. The word *maid* burns in her ears, and so do her own stupid words. Specialized work. Like Mimi utilizes the latest in high-tech equipment instead of mops and rags and brooms.

There's a hatred boiling in her that transcends every other feeling. She hates Thomas Rainier and Sarah Davis. Mimi too. And everybody at this fucking party.

She plods back up the concrete stairs to the parking lot. *Shit!* Her car is hemmed in by another—a brand-new Toyota RAV4. Some snot-nosed rich kid's graduation present. Maybe the Rainier son's, though he's too young to be a graduate. A present just for being alive.

She considers ramming the Fiesta hard into the side of the RAV4. But that would also ram the hell out of Mimi's already dinged-up car. She imagines Mimi examining the new dents. Breaking into tears.

Instead she turns and begins down the wood-slatted path along the top of the bluff. The path winds around, and now she can no longer see the party below, though she can still hear the thudding beat of the music. She steps over the low guardrail onto the projecting point of the bluff.

And then a miracle happens.

A full moon breaks through a thin patch of fog. A bright, beautiful white disk throwing a shimmering ribbon onto the ocean. It illuminates a girl now standing at the far edge of the bluff, gazing out at the water.

It's Sarah Davis.

She's by herself. None of those other hottie shitheads are with her.

Didi suddenly knows what she's going to do. It won't take much.

No more than a thought, really. Just the merest quick summoning of willpower to do it.

She tosses the Blue Moon can onto the ground. She summons the will.

She starts moving silently forward.

CHAPTER EIGHT

AVA

It seemed like a vicious joke. My instinct was to rip the sympathy card up and flush the pieces away.

Instead, I looked at it again, examining it as if through the long lens of a camera. Noted the too-pat composition of the drawing. Its sugary quality. Cheap, off a pharmacy rack. Selected with ironic intent.

The stamp was a generic "Forever" stamp, a waving flag. The postmark was Monterey.

From Grace? Maybe as a silly joke?

No. Impossible to imagine.

She might have told people I was coming back. Former classmates from Sanderson Day Academy. Maybe one of them playing a joke?

It felt more like a taunt. *I'm watching you. Coming for you.*

Dad.

He'd somehow found out I was coming back to the house. The property he'd been cut out of.

He was enraged. Had followed me down to the house and tailed me up the hill afterward. But I hadn't seen or talked to him for about three years. How could he have known?

I stuffed the card into the bottom of my case and began to dress for the party.

The Greenwalds' house was newly built, up a steep series of roads on a cliff above Monterey. A beautiful structure of glass and stone that in the heavy mist seemed to hover amid the pine and cedar around it.

Grace flung open the door as soon as I pressed the bell. She was fourth-generation Chinese American, with a heart-shaped face, a long and silky black bob, and the same infectious energy she'd had as a child. "Oh my God, you're here!" she exclaimed.

We hugged exuberantly, crushing the large bouquet of purple irises I was cradling.

"We're ruining the flowers." I laughed.

"And they're so gorgeous!" She gathered the bouquet with one hand, then tugged her stretchy mint-blue dress tighter with the other, showing off her sizable bump. "Look, Ave, it's real! And this time my ob-gyn thinks I'm safe!"

"Oh God, I sure hope so." I amended that. "I'm sure you are."

She beckoned me inside—open plan, high ceilinged, as airy and sophisticated as the exterior.

"This is breathtaking," I said.

She grinned. "Be sure to tell that to Darsh. He's become disgustingly house proud. Come on, he's in the kitchen, getting in the caterers' way."

We headed to a large kitchen, all slanting skylights and dazzling stainless steel. Darsh Greenwald loomed over a center island, peeling grapefruit twists, while several young people in plum-colored jackets busied around him. "Ava, welcome!" He stooped even to kiss my cheek. He was a foot taller than his wife, with a shock of prematurely silver hair. His hands, as befitting a hand surgeon, were exquisite. "I've mixed some Belvedere martinis. Can I tempt you?"

"Yeah, you may," I said.

He poured a glass, fixed a grapefruit twist on the rim. "What do you think of our new digs?"

"She said they were breathtaking." Grace pulled a vase from an upper shelf and began arranging the flowers.

"We gave our architect free rein, and he was brilliant," Darsh said.

"Except for a few issues . . ." There was a snap in Grace's voice.

"Minor," Darsh said. "They're getting resolved."

For a moment, tension crackled in the air. Then Grace grabbed my arm. "Let's find a cubbyhole before the crowd arrives."

We went to an alcove off the living room and sat on a low modern couch. "Is everything okay with you and Darsh?" I said.

"Yeah, don't worry. Except that the house went way over budget, and in the end, our hotshot architect had to cut some corners. I think Darsh was just too dazzled by him." She waved a dismissive hand. "I want to talk about you. You're really doing it? Moving back to that scary old house?"

"Do you think it's scary?" I said.

"Hell, yes. I always did. Your ghost scared the pants off me. What was her name? Cleopatra? Those sleepovers you had, five or six of us on futons, I could never sleep a wink."

"Her name was Cinderella. I always thought you just pretended to be scared. That all of you did."

"Maybe the other girls. But not me, I was genuinely until I was about ten. And don't hate me, Ava, but I was scared of your mom too."

I gazed at her, stunned. "Mom? I thought you loved her. You used to say she was more like my sister than a mom."

"I did love her. But I also thought she was an actual witch. Making potions up in her studio. One time I watched her grinding up some gravelly looking stuff. She said it was dried bugs. It totally freaked me."

I grinned. "Cochineal bugs. She ordered them from an old lady in El Salvador to make a scarlet paint."

"That's what I mean." Grace laughed. "My mom cooks some weird things. Duck feet and this dish called stinky tofu. But not weird as that."

"You're right." I laughed too. "How come you never told me?"

"I didn't want you to think I was a scaredy-cat little nerd. And I knew how much you and Jamie adored her. And really, sweetie, I did too. I was heartbroken when she died." Other voices sounded from the living room. "Oh crap, people are here already. I thought we'd have more time to catch up. But we will when you're back for good." She grabbed my hand. "Come on, let me start showing you off."

The party filled up fast. I met a lot of people in quick succession. Good-looking, friendly people. Lawyers, medical workers, teachers. Grace's parents—her bubbly mom, Coral; her taciturn, kindly father, Steven—greeted me fondly.

But I felt adrift in this sea of faces, and even Grace and Darsh, always circulating back to me, seemed at a distance. Outside the walls of glass, the evening had darkened to match my state of mind. My thoughts dwelled on my own house, the memories it had evoked, and the disturbing sympathy card.

I fueled myself with martinis. Accepted a third drink, or was it a fourth? When I couldn't remember, I requested a glass of water and retreated back to the alcove where I'd been with Grace. I sat down on an ottoman, nodding at a woman on the adjoining couch.

A nun was my first thought. Mid-sixties. Severely cropped gray hair, plain white shirt, navy slacks. Deep-set eyes that telegraphed detachment.

"Are you Christina Holland's daughter?" she said.

"Yes, I'm Ava Holland," I said. "How did you know?"

"Grace told me about you. You're the only one who looks like you don't actually fit in here. And you bite your nails, just like she did."

I glanced at my fingernails. Bitten ragged. Mom's always were too.

The woman stuck out a businesslike hand. "Margaret Zhao. Grace's godmother. I'm married to her uncle." She shook my hand firmly but briefly.

"How did you know my mother?" I asked.

"I was a cop, until I was stupid enough to get shot. I used to advise the board of a women's shelter up in Salinas. Your mother was on the board. She showed up only once to a meeting, but she was memorable."

"She was on a lot of boards, but she almost never went to board meetings. She rarely left our property."

"Agoraphobic?"

"Not really. I mean, she would leave from time to time. But mostly people came to her. She had lots of friends, old and young and rich and poor, and they were forever visiting at our house."

Margaret Zhao gazed at me with that expression of nunlike detachment. I suddenly noticed the folded cane beside her. Wondered how she got shot.

"I met Christina a second time," she said abruptly. "A couple of years later, right before I made detective. I was on patrol with my partner, and we got a call. Domestic violence."

I looked at her warily. "My parents?"

"Yeah. When we showed up, they said everything was fine. Their stories lined up—a loud argument, and a maid jumped to the wrong conclusion. We saw no signs of physical abuse. The maid wasn't very clear about what she'd heard or witnessed. So that was that. It wasn't long after that I heard Christina died. Creutzfeldt-Jakob, correct?"

I flinched. "It was never definitely diagnosed. She fell into a coma and died before she'd done most of the tests. There's an MRI now that can diagnose it with ninety percent accuracy, but not back then."

"No autopsy?"

"My father refused it."

"Somebody must have signed the death warrant."

"The neurologist she'd been seeing before she was taken to the hospital. He's long retired."

"She was young for Creutzfeldt-Jakob."

"Only forty-three," I agreed eagerly. "It usually comes on at about sixty or seventy."

The deep-set eyes fixed on me. "You have another theory?"

I hesitated. "There are other possibilities. Maybe some kind of toxin."

"Was she around a lot of pesticides? Or chemical waste?"

"Not that I know of."

"Her doctors might have run tox screens. Have you looked at the hospital records?"

"She had a DNR, so the hospital wasn't allowed to do anything. And she didn't do many of the neurologist's tests before that. But a lot of poisons don't even show up on tox screens."

"Some don't," she acknowledged.

"It could have been accidental," I said. "She was an artist. She made a lot of her own paints. It could be she used something toxic."

"You believe that?"

"No," I said emphatically. "I think it wasn't accidental. I think she was deliberately poisoned, and I'm determined to find out for sure."

"What makes you think you can after all this time?"

Because it's buried in my memory, I wanted to tell her. It got sunk into blackness, and I'm going to dig it out. But Margaret Zhao would probably scoff at this. Crime labs. Footwork. That seemed more up her alley. "I don't know if I can," I said. "But I'm going to try."

The music piping in the background stopped. Darsh's deep voice sounded from the terrace, summoning everyone out there.

"I think we're about to find out if it's a girl or boy," I said.

"You go. I lost a lung, and these days, once down, I don't budge for a while. And it's cold and damp out there."

I stood up. "Can I get you something first?"

She shook her head curtly. "I've got a daughter around here somewhere who'll be back to wait on me." She reached for her bag at her feet. Took a card from a wallet. "I consult now for police departments. Grace said you were moving back, so get in touch with me when you do. I'd like to hear more about this."

"I will. Thanks."

I headed out to the terrace. Fairy lights strung through the railings glowed softly in the mist. Darsh and Grace stood at one end, Grace's parents with them, as well as Darsh's mother, a stately woman from Calcutta with the same thick silver hair as her son. The caterers were passing out confetti guns—long tubes with twist bottoms—to the kids old enough to use them. Grace and Darsh's moms gave a countdown: "Three, two, one . . ."

A series of loud pops, then pink confetti and streamers and a shower of glitter burst into the air above us. Cries of "It's a girl!" People surged to congratulate Grace and Darsh.

A tiny boy came toddling past me in pursuit of a streamer. A beautiful child: straight black hair, brown skin, bright-blue eyes. Grabbing the streamer, he fell hard on his bottom and let out a wail.

I dashed over to him and crouched down. "Hey, hey." I made a funny face. He stopped wailing. I made another, funnier, face. He gaped at me. Stuck the streamer in his mouth.

"No, not for eating." Laughing, I pried it out of his mouth. I closed it in my fist. "See, all gone." He stared at my hand in astonishment. Then slapped it and shrieked with glee.

A man came bounding up and scooped him into his arms. "There you are!"

I looked up. Ash-blond hair. Blue eyes beneath sleepy-looking lids. I tumbled back to being thirteen years old: my face flushed; my heart beat fast. I got to my feet and said, "Hello, Thomas."

He smiled. "Ava?"

"Yeah, it's me. It's been a long time."

"Yeah, it has. Hey, thanks for rescuing this bruiser. I looked away for one second, and he was gone."

"Your son's a very handsome boy," I said.

"He's gorgeous, but he's not mine. He belongs to my brother."

For some ridiculous reason, I was glad to hear that.

Then a thought sneaked into my mind. This was not a coincidence. He knew I'd be here. He'd come purposely to see me.

The toddler squirmed impatiently in his arms. "What's your name?" I asked him. Suddenly shy, he buried his face in his uncle's shoulder.

"His name is Anson. And he's too big to be acting like a baby, aren't you, Anson?"

Anson squirmed harder, demanding to be put down. Thomas set him on his feet, pulled an electronic toy from his pocket, and turned it on, all flashy bleeps and colors. The child grabbed at a silver bracelet his uncle was wearing, one of five—silver, leather, braid—stacked on his wrist, but the flashing colors on the toy proved irresistible, and he took it and plumped down on the floor with it.

"That should keep him busy for about three minutes," Thomas said.

I grinned. "You still wear all the bracelets," I said.

"I still do, yeah. So what are you doing here? Visiting?"

I said, "I'm moving back next month. To our old house, in fact." But I was sure he already knew that.

"Blackworth Mansion? Do you still call it that?"

"Yes," I said. "To both counts. I'm having it put into shape just enough for me to live there."

"Alone?" he said.

"Yes." It was a question I was getting tired of answering.

"That big old house. You'll be lonely."

"I don't think so," I said. "I'll have neighbors in those homes you're building down the road."

"They won't be occupied for a while. Not till the end of winter, and that's if I'm lucky."

"You must have had to clear a lot of old forestland for the development."

"We did some clearing. We kept as much of the old growth as possible."

"But not all of it."

"That would have been impossible. But we're replanting more than we took out."

He spoke so evenly, as if destroying ancient forestland was something perfectly ordinary and fine—which of course it was, in his business. "There were trees that were over six hundred years old," I said.

"And there still are a lot of them, many even older. It was one of my chief concerns when I designed the project."

"You designed it? You're not just a developer?"

"Not just," he said with a wry smile. "I designed this house. Didn't you know that?"

So he was the hotshot architect who had dazzled Darsh. And, according to Grace, had cut corners. "No, I didn't. It's quite beautiful."

"Thanks. Would you like to see one of the new ones? I'm at the site frequently, and I'd be glad to give you a tour."

"And do you ever drop by my family's house when you're there?"

A tighter smile. "I suppose Michael Fiore told you he chased me away."

"So you know Michael?" I said with surprise.

"Sure. My construction managers hire him from time to time. He does first-rate cabinetry."

So Michael, who loathed developers and had bad-mouthed Thomas, didn't mind taking Thomas's money.

"Are you looking to acquire my property?" I asked him bluntly.

"Is it for sale?"

"No. And never will be."

"Then there'd be no use in my trying to buy it, would there?"

Anson suddenly let out a piercing shriek and tossed the flashing device away. Thomas picked it up, stuffed it back into his pocket, then swung the little boy onto his shoulders. Anson grabbed a fistful of his uncle's hair and tugged hard. "Ow!" Thomas said.

I couldn't help a laugh. "Anson, you mustn't pull your uncle's hair."

"Hair!" Anson repeated with unbounded joy. He tugged harder.

Thomas pulled the boy's hand off, then bounced him lightly on his shoulders. "I'd better get him home. It's way past his bedtime. My sister-in-law is going to kill me."

I looked up at the little boy. A few stars of confetti fell from his hair onto his round cheeks. "Bye-bye, Anson," I said. "It was really nice to meet you."

He smiled—a smile of such radiant sweetness that my heart shattered.

"It was good to see you again, Ava," Thomas said. "Good night." He started to turn.

"I'll be in touch," I said impulsively.

He turned back, with a questioning look.

"About looking at the site."

He held my eyes a moment. "Good," he said.

I watched him leave, balancing the gorgeous child on his shoulders. And I suddenly felt an almost unbearable yearning. Though for what, I wasn't sure.

I just knew it had nothing to do with being thirteen.

CHAPTER NINE

Where am I?

I was in a tangle of confusing images. Some of them dreams. But some not.

I was in bed in Mom and Dad's suite. I knew that's where I was because of the wallpaper, lavender with a jazzy 1920s pattern. I seemed to hear voices nearby. Jamie: *Where did I leave my boogie board?* Mom's ashy whisper: *She dissolved into thin air.* Dad bellowing: *You fucking mental space cadet.* But the light from the facing window was wrong: at eight a.m., it should have been brilliant in my eyes, but this was a pearly northern light. And the bed was the queen with the white headboard I'd slept in with Noah, which had gone to me in the divorce.

Past and present all tangled up.

A cat crouched on the bed. A cat as black as Mom's cat, O'Keeffe, had been white.

Was he real?

He was real. I'd adopted him right before leaving Santa Monica. Named him Stieglitz. Georgia O'Keeffe's mentor and lover.

I wasn't in my parents' room. I was in the identical suite in the north wing of Blackworth Mansion.

I'd driven up yesterday evening, three weeks after I'd come the first time, my car loaded with suitcases and boxes. I'd hit a late-for-April storm. Torrents of rain slammed down in cyclical bouts. Blinding me for seconds at a time as I navigated the treacherous coast highway with its curves and narrow bridges and sheer drops to the sea. My nerves were frazzled by the time I turned onto the parallel access road. The new construction, halted by the rain, lurked invisible behind drenched vegetation. Our long rutted driveway was muddied and puddled, a challenge even for my Volvo. The house was dark and deserted. The ocean subdued, the surf muffled.

I got soaked retrieving the key from under a rock beside the circular front drive. Even wetter as I hauled Stieglitz and suitcases inside. There'd been changes made. The boards were off the windows. The drop sheets lifted from the furniture. Ladders and buckets strewn everywhere, and a pervasive smell of fresh paint and cleaning chemicals.

A cold wind howled down a corridor. I followed it to the kitchen. The top of the dutch door in the adjoining mudroom had blown open, flooding the floor with water and sodden leaves. I bolted it shut, wearily mopped up the mess with a drop cloth. I let Stieglitz out of his carrier, rubbed down his wet fur. Unpacked his litter box and carton of Fancy Feast and opened a can for him.

It was so damned cold. Where was the thermostat? A sudden moment of panic. Did we even have one?

I jumped as the dutch door banged open.

"Ava?" A young woman swaggered in. Small square face, unruly reddish-blonde hair. Her slicker swamped her small figure. "I was meaning to be here when you came to make sure you got in okay, but I got held up by a rockslide on the Cabrillo."

"Franny! Thank God you're here. Is there any heat in this house?"

"Sure. The thermostat's in the hall right off the Monster Room. I'll show you."

The Monster Room: what we used to call the library because of the gargoyles carved on the fireplace. Funny she'd remembered that.

I trailed her to the old-fashioned thermostat mounted on the wall. It was instantly familiar. "It never went on very high," I said.

"That's for sure. I'm gonna blow out all the radiators for you, as soon as I get around to it. But you might want to put on a thicker sweater."

I went to the luggage I'd dumped in the foyer and pulled out a heavy wool jacket.

A horn blared out front. The movers, bringing what furniture I hadn't given away or sent to storage. Three guys, very surly: their truck had gotten bogged down on the muddy driveway, two of them had to push. It took three hours for me to direct them where to cram my things into the already overstuffed rooms, even with Franny pitching in. I tipped them extravagantly.

Franny shrugged on her rain slicker. "What time you want me here in the morning?"

The house suddenly seemed immense. The surroundings so dark. "Would you be willing to stay the night, Franny?" I said. "I mean, just for tonight?"

"Well, you see, Ava, I've got a boyfriend. Are you afraid to stay here alone?"

Was I? "No, it's okay. I'll be fine."

I bolted the dutch door, top and bottom, behind her. It was still cold. I went into the narrow butler's pantry and opened the liquor cabinet. The bottles were dusty, but alcohol kept forever, didn't it? I picked one at random. Johnnie Walker Black Label. Dad's favorite. Good for warming the blood.

I poured a stiff measure and took a sip.

That memory of a voice: *Take this, Ava. It will make you feel better.* The Nembutal. And something to wash it down with.

Black Label scotch. I felt a cold shudder.

Heavy sedatives and scotch. Whoever had given them to me could have killed me. Maybe wanted to.

I tossed back the rest of the scotch, then tramped through the house, turning on those few lights with working bulbs in them. And then I went upstairs and got ready for bed.

The water in the taps was frigid. I grabbed a pile of blankets from the airing closet and huddled beneath three of them. I flipped on the bedside lamp that had arrived with the movers.

Noah's beloved Tizio lamp—it should have gone to him in the divorce.

I'd offer it back to him. He'd probably like that. I pulled out my phone to text him.

No. I'd heard on the grapevine he was seeing somebody new. A programmer at Cisco. Brilliant and very pretty.

I put the phone down.

An icy cold current snaked into the room. There were creaks and groans everywhere. The rustling of old drapes. Leaky water giggling down pipes.

And then a rapid tapping of little feet in the hallway coming toward my door, and it made the hairs on my neck prickle.

Stieglitz jumped onto the bed. I gave a laugh of relief.

He curled at my feet. A fresh band of rain pounded the roof and splattered the window. It was cozy now. My eyelids floated closed.

Someone coughed.

Outside. Low, almost inaudible, but not far away.

My eyes flew open. I lay very still, listening hard.

There's someone out there.

Dad, I thought. His rage at being cut out of Mom's will. He'd contested it. Claimed she was sick, not of sound mind. He'd lost the case. But over the years, he'd called Jamie and me, drunk, hurling abuse. "You ungrateful snots. I kept that freak show of a house together, and you cheated me out of what was mine. You owe me, you all fucking owe me."

I'd stopped taking his calls. Changed my number. It was three years since I'd last heard from him. But now he was out there. Watching the house. Waiting.

Ridiculous.

The rain pattered. The distant surf shuddered and thrashed. There'd been no cough. Just rain. Ocean.

But I had kept very still, listening, until I eventually drifted to sleep.

And now I had woken up in that tangle of past and present.

I staggered out of bed, dressed, and went downstairs. A chill seemed to rise from the old kitchen itself. The avocado-colored refrigerator. The dingy black-and-white linoleum. Stieglitz appeared and yowled for food. I opened a can. Tuna florentine with garden greens. One of his favorites.

I raided the box of provisions I'd brought from Santa Monica. I fished out a brown-spotted banana and sat down at the old Formica table. It was littered with hardware: tools and coils of wire and sections of brass pipe. The night before—Franny Fiore in her slicker, the movers, the imagined cough outside—seemed like a dream.

I devoured the banana. There was something brightly colored half-buried in all that hardware. Curious, I moved the stuff around it.

I bounced to my feet with a gasp.

A Cinderella doll. The Disney version. Blonde updo, puffy blue ball gown.

I didn't touch it. Just stared at it. My heart racing. It hadn't been there last night when I was mopping up the rain puddle.

Or had it?

I walked cautiously through the downstairs, checking all the locks and windows, looking under furniture, peeking into closets. I went back to the kitchen. I looked inside the stove, refrigerator. The broken dumbwaiter.

Cars pulled up outside. Doors slammed. Voices, hearty, swearing boisterously. The work crew returning for the day.

A key turned in the mudroom door. Michael Fiore came in, whistling tunelessly. "All moved in, hey?" he said.

He has keys. Could get in anytime.

I pointed to the doll. "Did you put this here, Michael?"

He squinted. "What's that?"

"A Cinderella doll. It wasn't here last night. Did you sneak in and put it there?"

"Hey, whoa, I don't do shit like that. I don't sneak nowhere. Let me see it." He picked the box up. "Are you sure this wasn't there before?"

I hesitated. "No, not entirely."

"Maybe it belongs to one of my guys' kids."

The door opened again. Franny, carrying a red tool kit. Michael held up the box. "Hey, Fran, do you know what this is?"

"Yeah, it's—who do you call it? Cinderella. Like your old ghost, right, Ava?"

"You didn't leave it here, did you?" Michael said.

"Me?" She gave a bewildered look. "Was I supposed to?" She glanced at me. "Was I supposed to bring that for you?"

"She didn't do it," Michael said. "I'll ask my guys." He went back outside, taking the box with him.

"Maybe it's been here all along, Ava," Franny said. "You got so much stuff in this old house, how would you know?"

"Because it's brand new. And we never had brand-name toys. Mom never let us."

"Jamie had Star Wars stuff. I used to play with it when he wasn't around."

That was true, I realized. We'd get stuff like that as birthday presents from our friends. And from Dad sometimes. Just to taunt Mom.

"I was really sorry when your mom died, Ava," Franny said. She deposited the tool kit on the table, on top of the hardware. "Did you know she was going to?"

So she still asked disconcerting questions. "No, I had no idea. None of us did. Not even after she got sick."

"I didn't know my baby would either. It was a real shock."

"I can imagine, Franny," I said softly. "It must have been devastating."

"Yeah, it was bad. His name was Carver, and he was so tiny and sweet. I cried myself stupid for a long time. But me and my boyfriend are gonna try again."

"Great, Franny. I'm glad you are."

Michael came back with the doll. "I asked my crew, but none of them knew what I was talking about. No sign anybody broke in here. But I tell you, there is somebody who gets in, and it beats me how."

"I'm going to call the police," I said.

"You can, but what's the use? They'll see no forced entry. With all the stuff you got here, they'll think you just forgot it was here. Or else they'll think me or one of my guys is lying."

How often had he had run-ins with the law? I was reluctant to cause him more trouble. "Then I want all the locks changed."

"It'll cost you. A couple of grand, at least, for good bolts. You want to pay that just because of some joke?"

"Michael, just do it," I said. "And could you bring me a dog? One that gets along with cats."

"Sure thing," he said. "One guard dog coming up."

I brought the Cinderella doll upstairs. I felt suddenly almost unbearably lonely and confused. That sympathy card. The cough I'd maybe heard last night . . . now this toy. All these things together could not be coincidence and definitely not a joke. But who could I turn to who could help me sort it out? No one, not even Jamie, with this crackle of tension between us threatening to drive us apart.

I gave myself a mental shake. No matter what—new love affairs, inheritance quarrels—Jamie and I would always be close. And Grace, best friend since we were nine: I could count on her forever.

My thoughts turned to Grace's godmother, Margaret, the retired cop I'd met at her party. The one who'd reminded me of a nun. She had told me to get in touch. I fished her card out of my wallet.

CHAPTER TEN

Margaret Zhao showed up shortly after noon. She walked with a cane, laboriously navigating the obstacle course of repairs and workmen, gazing around with frank curiosity. "I remember this place. All this stuff. You should have a yard sale."

"I couldn't," I said. "Most of it was passed down from my mother's family. It belongs here."

"I used to be that way. Then I let go. I sent truckloads off to Saint Vincent de Paul. It felt pretty darned good to lighten up."

She refused anything to drink. I took her to the sunporch, away from the workmen and their racket. She lowered herself heavily onto the wicker fan chair, wheezing a little. "My lung's been acting up. I'm going to have to have some fluid removed."

"Is it from when you got shot?" I asked.

"Yeah."

"Can I ask you how it happened?"

"It was at that women's shelter where your mother served on the board. I happened to be there when a husband broke in with a Remington bolt-action. Shot his wife dead and put two bullets in me before turning it on himself. Stupid of me. I should've been more alert." She glanced out at the ocean. "Some view you've got here. This place must be worth a fortune."

"So everybody tells me," I said.

"I'll bet they do. Okay, let's get down to facts. You say somebody got in while you were asleep last night?"

"Maybe. I found this in the kitchen when I got up this morning." I took the Cinderella doll out of a tote and handed it to her. "It was on the kitchen table under a lot of tools. It might have been there when I arrived last night, but I don't think so."

She furrowed her brow. "Is there a significance to this?"

"When I was growing up, we had a family myth that the house was haunted by a girl who'd been murdered here. It was in the 1920s, in the servants' wing behind the back stairs. There was a fire there years later, and it's still all burned out, so Mom named the ghost Cinderella."

"Anything significant about the murdered girl?"

"We didn't know that much about her. She was a society girl who ran with a fast crowd, and this gangster—a bank robber, I think—fell madly in love with her. He caught her at a party here with a guy from a rival mob and dragged her to the servants' quarters and slit her throat. He was executed at San Quentin for it."

"Very colorful," Margaret said.

"I always felt so sorry for her," I said, "except as a ghost, she didn't seem very sorry for herself. She was very high spirited. And we thought it was fun to be haunted. But then terrible things started happening. My brother had an accident that left his face scarred. My parents fought constantly and then split up. So I began to think, well, maybe the ghost had put a curse on us. And then . . . well, you know, Mom died."

She nodded, pursing her lips. "So you think this doll is from somebody who knew all that?"

"I'm sure it is. There was something else before it." I took out the sympathy card. "This was mailed to me at the house I was renting in Santa Monica before moving up here."

She opened it. "Cinderella again." She glanced at the envelope. "Monterey postmark. So who around here would know about this ghost?"

"Our friends back when we were kids. Some of the people who worked here. But that was a long time ago, so I can't imagine it was any of them." I paused. "My father does, of course."

"Did you ask him?"

"I don't know where he is. We've been estranged for about three years."

"Did he believe in this ghost curse?"

"No, just the opposite. He blew up at even any mention of Cinderella." I sat up a little straighter, remembering something. "There was one time when I was about nine. I woke up at night, and he was in my room. He was drunk and playing at being a ghost. Fluttering his hands and going 'Ooooooh,' in a ghostly way. Then Mom came and yanked him out, and I could hear them whispering angrily in the hall. I pretended the next day I'd been asleep the whole time."

"Huh." Margaret compressed her lips in a line. "First step would be to talk to him. How about people more recently? Who knows about Cinderella?"

"None, really, except Grace, and I'm sure it wasn't her. But I never even told my ex-husband."

"You're divorced?"

"We were only married a little more than a year. I rarely talked about the past. For a long time, I wanted to forget it. I'd lost a lot of memories, and I wanted them to stay lost."

"So what's different now?"

"I don't know." That nunlike quality she had. I felt I could confide anything in her. My words tumbled out, things I'd been bottling up inside. "After Mom's death, I felt a kind of numbness. Like, nothing mattered or would ever be any good, and so why bother to feel anything at all? It's something that's lingered just beneath the surface for me. So now I've decided to come back here and confront the past and maybe bring some of those memories back. Because even if it's painful, it's better than feeling nothing. And maybe if I can figure out what happened to Mom, I can finally get past the pain."

"I understand," Margaret said. She examined the card again. "Let's go back to somebody maybe breaking in. Who's got keys to this place?"

"Me, obviously. Michael Fiore, he's the contractor. He's here now changing the locks." I paused, then added, "My father maybe."

"Any idea how to contact him?"

"No. The last number I had for him is no longer in service."

"And why would he be playing these tricks?"

"He's always claimed this house should have gone to him. He used to call me in a drunken state and make threats. He said he'd burn the place down to the ground before he'd let either Jamie or me ever live here. I finally changed my number and stopped hearing from him."

She fished out a notebook from her bag. "I'll take a crack at finding him. Name? First, middle, last. Date and place of birth."

"Kevin Andrew Holland. Phoenix, November 29, 1962."

"Okay. Anybody else might not want you here? Your brother?"

"No. He'd never do anything so creepy."

"What about that contractor who's got the keys?"

"Michael. He swears he didn't. But he had told me he thought somebody got into the house from time to time. He couldn't figure out how."

"I'll have a word with him. Anyone else?"

Another name came to me. A name I didn't want to share with her just yet.

"No," I said. "But one more thing. Maybe it's nothing." I took the Nembutal vial out of my tote. "I found this yesterday where I'd hidden it just before my brother and I left to go live with our great-aunt.

Somebody had given it to me back then. Told me it would make me feel better. I can't remember who."

"Nembutal, huh." She scrutinized the label. "Beverly Padrillo."

"Is that the last name? I couldn't make it out."

"Yeah. The Padrillos owned one of the biggest canneries in Monterey before that business died out. The name is still on a few buildings around town." She snapped pictures on her phone of all sides of the bottle and gave it back to me. "I'll check if this drugstore is still around." She stood up, using her cane for leverage.

I got up with her. "I don't know what your rates are, but whatever they are, it's fine."

"If it gets more complicated, I'll charge, but it won't be much. I'm not a PI, I consult to the police. But I liked your mother, and the whole thing never sat right with me. That domestic call that got my partner and me up here but came to nothing. And her dying the way she did. And after you called this morning, something occurred to me. There was another poisoning case back then."

"Who?" I said.

"It wasn't my case, so I don't know all the details. The victim survived. I'll see what I can dig up."

The name I hadn't wanted to tell Margaret Zhao was Thomas Rainier.

He was a builder—he'd know how to get into the house no matter how locked or boarded up it was. Michael had caught him trespassing and was sure he was eager to acquire this property. It would be in his interest to scare me away. Then pounce with an offer to buy us out.

But there were other questions he might be able to answer for me, and I wanted to talk to him first. I went upstairs to the spare room I'd picked for my studio across the hall from Mom's. It was stacked with boxes, tripods, rolls of backdrop paper. My desktop computer wasn't set up yet, so I located my laptop in the chaos and googled him.

THOMAS RAINIER ARCHITECTURE AND DEVELOPMENT. An office address in San Jose. He was CEO and chief designer. He employed four other architects and a small squadron of development executives.

I called the main number. Was transferred to a woman with a crisp English accent. He was out of the office for the rest of the day. I left my number.

I did another search: Beverly Padrillo. The name on the Nembutal bottle. One hit, a mortuary-written obituary from twelve years ago. "Beverly Dolores Padrillo, 101, died peacefully on Wednesday of natural causes at her home in Pacific Grove."

She'd have been ninety-six when Mom died. Hardly an age to be running around handing out sedatives and alcohol.

So if she wasn't the one who gave me the Nembutal and Johnnie Walker, who did? And how had they gotten Beverly Padrillo's prescription?

I went shopping for supplies. The Safeway in the complex on Crossroads Boulevard. It was Dad who'd mostly shopped here, coming back with sacks of impulse purchases and cases of alcohol. Mom ordered from specialty stores or sent a housekeeper to the farmers' market with a list.

When I returned to the house, Franny was out front, tossing a squishy yellow ball to a beagle. I jumped down from my Volvo and went to her.

"Meet your new dog," Franny said. "Her name's Betsy. She won't cause you no trouble, and she'll mostly stay outside during the day. And she gets on good with cats."

So this was the vicious dog Michael advised me to get? A frisky, floppy-eared beagle? "You sure she's a watchdog?"

"Outstanding. My brother Terk raised her. He breeds beagles and sometimes labradoodles. He put her out to train as a cadaver dog, but she flunked, and then they tried her out on sniffing drugs, but she flunked that, too, so Terk took her back. Her nose isn't so good, but there's nothing wrong with her ears. She'll let you know if anybody comes near this house." Franny whistled, and Betsy raced up with the ball in her mouth. "Give it a good toss, and she'll love you forever."

I took the slobbery ball from Betsy's mouth and threw my best overhand pitch down the lawn, and she hightailed after it.

"So, do you want her?" Franny said.

Betsy bounded back to me, ball between teeth, eyes drenched with love, tail wagging furiously. My heart was lost. "Yeah," I said. "I'll take her."

That night, with Stieglitz on my bed and Betsy on the floor beside it, I slept untroubled for the first time in months. I woke groggily when the phone rang very early. Started to mute it. Then answered quickly: "Jamie?"

"Yeah, it's me." He sounded distraught. "I'm in my car, I've been driving since two a.m., I'm on the 101 now. I can be in Carmel in a couple of hours."

"What's going on, Jamie? You're scaring me."

"I'm heading to a conference at Berkeley. I'm giving a paper tomorrow. I had a flight but canceled it because I needed time to clear my head." He let out a long breath. "I might have gotten myself into something weird."

"With Sarah?" I said.

"How did you know?"

"You were obviously more involved with her than you were letting on."

"It's even more than that," he said. "We got married six weeks ago. She's my wife."

CHAPTER ELEVEN

SARAH

The second wedding day of my life, and I'm awake at the crack of dawn. Bowing to tradition, James and I decided to spend the night before the wedding apart, so he's at his bachelor's beach house in Laguna, and I'm all alone in bed. It's far too big just for me. A king, with one of those triple-thick mattresses on large springs, so that if you're medium height like me, you've got to hoist yourself butt first onto it using your arms for leverage and then do an equally awkward wriggle to get down. Which is what I do now: wriggle off the bed onto the two-hundred-and-fifty-year-old Oushak rug on the floor.

I slip on my robe. La Perla, silk and lace. *Peignoir*, Gideon had called it when he'd gifted it to me. Then I pad down three hallways to the kitchen. This town house is also ludicrously large for one person. Fourteen rooms plus service areas. In the year after Gideon passed (in the bedroom suite next door to mine), I sometimes imagined I was a Greek maiden trapped in a maze where a Minotaur was lusting for blood.

His will gives me thirty months to live here, all fees and maintenance paid, meaning in just a few more months, it will revert to

Gideon's five middle-aged children—Samantha, Rosie, Chad, Justina, and Austin—from his three previous wives, and who already have his other homes. And the very instant this one does, they will shriek down like Valkyries and shove me and my belongings out onto the street. Belongings that do not include the priceless antique rugs and furniture and paintings by the Impressionists and Picasso.

I don't intend to be here when that happens.

At ten forty-five this morning, I'll be marrying James Blackworth Holland in a civil ceremony at the county clerk's office in Laguna Hills. And then we'll start looking for a new place of our own.

In the kitchen, I fill the electric kettle and switch it on. I select a tea. Ginger, very soothing. There are butterflies in my stomach.

We've kept our affair under wraps. There's no rule at Bradford against instructors dating students, but I've earned every A I've gotten, and I don't want anyone to think otherwise. And James doesn't want to appear unethical.

It's turned out that he's relished keeping it a secret. Despite his interest in fetishists and psycho killers, he's a romantic at heart.

It took only a couple of months before he turned to me in bed (after some very strenuous sex) and asked with appealing tentativeness, "Would you ever consider marrying me?"

And I'd said, "Do you mean it? Of course, absolutely. Definitely!"

My ginger tea looks well steeped now. I blow gently on the surface to cool it and take a sip. It calms the butterflies, but only slightly.

Being such a romantic, James had wanted a white wedding. "I want to see you dressed in white and floating toward me down the aisle. And we'll have a mob of ushers and bridesmaids and a flower girl. Or boy. And dance until dawn with all our friends and relatives."

But I'd already had one of those.

On a private island off the coast of Belize. Gideon had bought it years before from some deposed dictator and built a family compound on it—six peach-colored houses with red tiled roofs. Our wedding cost a quarter-million dollars. My gown was an original Vera Wang, all swishing white silk and tulle. Six hundred guests, business connections, politicians, a gaggle of billionaires. My side of the guests was very sparse—the only family I had left, a second cousin and his wife from Idaho. I was escorted down the rose petal–strewn carpet by a man named Morton Simmonds, who was the CFO of Gideon's corporation.

Not one of Gideon's five middle-aged children deigned to attend.

Gideon had laughed it off during the reception. But afterward, when he and I had retired for the night in the largest of the peach cottages, he'd taken out his rage on me in a variety of painful and humiliating sexual ways.

Behavior I now know originates in the amygdala—the almond-shaped organ in the lizard part of the brain.

I told James some of this. Though of course not all.

And then I'd said, "I've got an idea. Let's not wait until the end of the semester to get married. Let's just run off to City Hall and elope. Like, soon. Next week. We'll keep it a secret until the semester ends and we've moved into a place of our very own, and then we'll announce it to everyone and throw a huge party." I pointed out that I had no real family left to invite. "And besides, I just can't wait to marry you."

Eventually, he came around. A secret elopement. It was even more romantic than a secret affair.

I've downed two cups of tea and eaten a slice of untoasted bread, but I'm still feeling nervous and jumpy. The lock rattles in the back service hall. It's just Paulina, my housekeeper. She's Polish, or at least originally. She'd worked for Gideon through at least two of the three former Mrs. Ellinghams. I always make it a point to be extra generous with household help: I overpay Paulina and give her loads of time off. She loves me for it, or at least pretends to, which is almost as good.

I always want people around me to be fond of me. Some neediness on my part.

"Big day today, Sarah," Paulina says. "I think that Gideon is watching down at you from above, and he is smiling. You were so good to him always, and he is very happy for you now."

"I hope so," I say.

"Do you want me to make you breakfast?"

"No, thanks, Paulina. Just do a quick tidy up of my bedroom. And I've laid out some things in the blue guest room and a bag, if you could pack them for me? You always pack so beautifully."

"Of course, I'm happy to."

I'm giving her the rest of the day off as well as the next three. James and I will be on a five-day honeymoon in Mexico. I'd surprised him with it: a deluxe package including chartered Learjet, five-star resort, all the most luxurious spa treatments.

The surprise hadn't gone down as well as I'd hoped. In fact, he'd been a little angry. "A private jet, darling? For a three-hour flight? What in the world did all this cost?"

I'd forgotten. He'd been brought up not to care about luxury. Easy when you can afford it, not as much when you grew up with less.

I take a long walk on the marina, hoping to settle my stomach. It's shrouded in mist. I think of cruising far out to sea on Gideon's sloop, *Windjammer*, occasionally getting becalmed in a silvery cloud. So quiet. So beautiful. Those were the rare times I'd actually loved sailing.

When I return to the town house, Paulina has already gone. She has set my traveling bag in my bedroom, everything in it exquisitely tucked and folded.

I don't have much to do to get ready. We're keeping it casual. I shower quickly, then blow out my hair and twist it into a French knot. I sit down at my dressing table and apply light and natural makeup. Survey the results.

For one split second, I see my old nose in the makeup mirror.

Poor old nose. Fractured in two places and not brilliantly reset. I think of the sound it made when it was breaking. That crunch of cartilage and small bones.

I recall that feeling of free fall. Of giving in to the almost ecstatic knowledge that I was about to die. It makes me dizzy, and I shut my eyes: and when I look back in the mirror, it's my new nose. A work of art, sculpted by Dr. Arman Coffrey of Beverly Hills.

Thank you, Gideon.

Time is getting short, and I hurry to begin dressing. Another nod to tradition: something old, something new, something borrowed, something blue.

New: the pale-green georgette dress I bought at Saks.

Borrowed: from my life-managing attorney, Lenore Wyatt, a white chiffon scarf. Hard-bitten lawyer though she is, she does turn herself out beautifully.

Old and blue combined: frost-blue La Perla lingerie. Compliments of my dear old former husband.

And one final bit of tradition. I've had a veil made. A short frothing of white tulle on a white satin headband. I fasten it to the crown of my head and pull the tulle to my chin.

Lenore Wyatt is waiting for me in the lobby. Sleek as a seal in a hushed-gray tailored suit. And like a seal, she seems like she's just crawled out of freezing waters. "Don't you look lovely," she says coolly.

I've brought down a baggie of rice. Arborio. Paulina makes an excellent risotto. "Would you mind tossing a little rice after the wedding, Lenore?"

A frosty smile. "I'm afraid they don't permit throwing rice at the Civic Center. It's considered littering."

"Oh, I see." I stuff the baggie in a waste receptacle.

We drive in Lenore's Audi—gray, of course, the engine hushed. The Civic Center is a faux Mediterranean complex, very neat and clean, so absolutely Orange County. Lenore drops me in front while she swings the car around to park.

James is waiting in the courtyard beside a tall, splashing fountain. He's wearing a stunning blue blazer and the Tom Ford glasses I bought him, and he's got my bouquet, a modest spray of pale-pink roses. He turns as I approach, and for one quick moment, his face goes white.

I push the veil up over my forehead. "What's the matter?"

"Nothing. Your veil just startled me."

"Don't you like it?"

"I do, it's charming. Exactly the right bridal touch." He tucks it back down over my eyes.

But he looks like he's seen a ghost.

There are two couples ahead of us, so the two of us and Lenore wait in the clerk's antechamber, making small talk. I'm nervous. I can't shake that feeling that at any moment something is going to happen to prevent the wedding.

Ava. Bursting in, shouting, "Stop! This wedding can't go on!"

No, not Ava.

Didi. That ugly freak.

But now our names are called. We enter the clerk's chamber. A mild-faced, obese woman sweetly manages to not sound bored out of her wits as she performs the ceremony. James and I read each other our simple vows. We slip the rings—plain gold bands, eighteen karats—onto each other's fingers.

James lifts my veil, and we kiss. Lenore applauds discreetly.

It sounds like snow on dead leaves.

And then James and I proceed arm in arm out of the dreary offices and back out into the golden sunshine.

I'm Mrs. James Blackworth Holland.

It's as easy as that.

DIDI

"Did I tell you Christina is getting me a knee replacement?" Mimi, in the passenger seat of the Fiesta, looks like she's on her way to Vegas, not her job as a household drudge.

Only about a thousand times, Didi thinks. She's helping Mimi out today, per their deal. Didi will delay going to college—she was accepted at three out of the four she applied to, despite not being valedictorian—at least for a semester, until Mimi's knee joint is functional again.

"It won't be just cartilage surgery," Mimi goes on. "They're going to put in a new titanium knee joint. I'll be bionic. The Bionic Woman. I'll be indestructible."

Didi, driving, tunes out Mimi's chatter. In her mind, she drifts back to the party on Shoehorn Beach. Her act of incredible willpower. What a joke. The ledge beneath the bluff was invisible in the dark. Only a twelve-foot drop and covered with a blanket of pine needles and dried leaves to cushion a fall.

Minor fractures and bruising. Big deal.

Though now she's glad the ledge was there. It was a sign that her thinking had been wrong. Her wild thought that she should kill just anybody, it didn't matter.

It very definitely mattered.

Mimi interrupts her thoughts. "Merge here, hon, onto that connecting road."

Didi steers onto a worn-out old road that dips below the highway. They're rattling over broken asphalt and loose gravel, probably broken glass. She prays they don't blow out a tire.

This is her second day of helping out Mimi. Saturday was her first. An old lady, Beverly Padrillo, an easy job for Mimi. All Didi had to do was fill these long rectangular pill holders divided into seven compartments, one for each day of the week. Six, seven, sometimes more pills in each. Bev had contracted every disease known to science. Breast cancer. Skin cancer. Intestinal stuff. Two strokes. Arthritis and psoriasis and a zillion other things. But at ninety-six, she just kept ticking.

Mimi sometimes swiped one of the pill bottles. Always one that had expired, like, twenty years ago and needed to be thrown out anyway.

Tomorrow they'd be doing the Rainiers'. Didi's heart sinks, thinking of the blond son. The smart one who'd been at the beach party. Who'd called Mimi a maid.

If he's there tomorrow, Didi thinks, maybe he'll be the one she'll kill.

Mimi suddenly squeals, "That's the driveway!" and it's like this secret road, you can hardly see it through all the trees and bushes. Now the Fiesta is getting scraped by brambles, and they hit a pothole so big it's amazing they didn't break an axle.

"You should bill them for all the damage to your car," Didi says.

Mimi looks at her like she's suggested drowning the Hollands' cat. "Oh, hon, it does the same thing to their cars. People like Christina don't think stuff like that is important."

The house comes into view. This is it? Didi thinks. This haunty-looking old place? The enchanted home of the magical Christina Blackworth Holland? Didi had expected something more like Sleeping Beauty's palace.

She steers around a sort of lot filled with gravel and weird old fountains and statues. "What's this?" she asks.

"It's called the sculpture garden," Mimi says rather proudly. "There used to be a lot of life-size statues, but most of them have fallen over now. The ground is filled with broken bits of them."

"Kinda creepy," Didi remarks.

She pulls into the circular drive in front of the house. "No, hon, park around the side." Didi gives a snort of disgust. The servants' entrance. She drives angrily around and slams the brake near a hedge of twisty old bushes. She gets out of the car and helps Mimi out. "Are Christina's kids going to be here?"

"They went to be with their aunt up in SF. I think she's taken them abroad."

Abroad. Where did Mimi dig up that word? Probably from the very pretentious-sounding Christina.

They enter through a side door into a weird kitchen. Part of it's from the fifties, all worn-out black-and-white linoleum. The tooth colored enamel stove looks even older. A few newer appliances stick out like sore thumbs. There's a guy squatting by the sink, running a flashlight under it, baggy jeans sliding down to show his crack.

"Hello, Michael," Mimi greets him. "Is Christina up?"

He straightens. Kind of a ratty-looking guy. Ripped-off sleeves showing tats on both arms. "Was here just a moment ago." He darts a kind of suspicious look at Didi, then hunches down again and wriggles under the sink.

Didi follows Mimi into a laundry room. Old-time basin, new washer/dryer. They gather up what they need. Four different kinds of cleansers, brands Didi's never heard of. "All-natural," Mimi tells her, meaning they probably suck. The robotic-looking upright Dyson vacuum cleaner should be a lot better.

"So where is the ghost room?" she asks. Mimi's told her all about Cinderella. Being haunted is all part of Christina's mystique.

"You go through the butler's pantry," Mimi says. "It's always locked, but I'll show you the door." They go out of the pantry, hauling pails and cleansers, and head back into the kitchen. "It's through that little corridor." Mimi points to it just past a broom closet, and as she does, an actual ghost comes drifting out. Didi's eyes nearly pop out of her head.

Mimi coos, "Christina! Good morning."

So this is Christina Holland. She's thin and pale and beautiful, with rippling masses of reddish-brown hair threaded here and there with silver. She's got on a light-gray dress with a long flowing skirt, and she's barefoot. Her fingers sparkle with rings. She reminds Didi of a painting on the cover of her paperback of *Tess of the d'Urbervilles*. It has a woman sitting in a tree, with masses of dark red-brown hair and skin so pale it's almost see through.

"Good morning, Miriam," Christina says. "How is your knee today?"

Mimi is suddenly limping twice as much as she was a minute ago. "Oh, Christina, thank you for asking. It's been kind of bad lately."

"Poor you. Hang tight, you've moved up to number thirty-six on the waiting list at the clinic." Her voice is kind of low and whispery so that you have to lean in to hear her.

Mimi gazes at her with drenching gratitude. "Thank you so much, Christina. That's very nice of you."

Christina turns her eyes to Didi. Golden eyes, like a cat's. She's wearing a perfume that has a mossy scent, off-putting but sort of heavenly at the same time. "And you must be Didi. Miriam tells me you're earning money for college. That's wonderful, dear. What are you studying?"

Didi is reluctant to say she hasn't started college yet. "Just English."

"You must love to read. I do, too, especially poetry. Emily Dickinson. Do you know the poem 'Wild Nights!'? It's one that gives me the shivers."

"I do know it!" Didi bursts out. "And I love it too!" She recites, putting feeling into the words,

> "Wild Nights – Wild Nights!
> Were I with thee
> Wild Nights should be
> Our luxury!
>
> Futile – the Winds –
> To a Heart in port . . ."

Mimi makes a sound in her throat like she's inhaled a fly. Didi flushes and lets her voice trail off.

But Christina clasps her hands, jewels flashing all colors on her fingers. "That's lovely, Didi. You have true passion. I believe you must be an old soul." Her thrilling voice, rustling like an autumn breeze. "I think I'm an old soul too. My children aren't, though. They're young souls. They haven't tried on many lives yet."

Didi feels a sort of glow. It's true, she thinks. She's tried on many lives, slipped in and out of them like changing shoes. "I can remember other lives, sometimes," she says, a bit boastfully. "Like, being a completely different person than I am now."

"Yes, me too," Christina says. "Sometimes even animals. I'm pretty sure I was a dolphin once."

Didi isn't so sure about animals. Though if you had to be one, dolphins were certainly of the highest intelligence.

"We need to get to work, hon," Mimi says. "That's what we're here for."

"Whatever you do, Miriam, please don't overtax your poor knee," Christina says.

"I'll make sure she doesn't," Didi says. "That's what *I'm* here for."

"You're a kind person, Didi. I'm very happy to have you here."

And then Didi has the strange impression that Christina kind of shimmers and simply floats away.

"What's that perfume Christina's wearing?" she says to Mimi. "It's an interesting fragrance."

"She never wears perfume because the cosmetic industry is cruel to animals. Maybe she was making paint up in her studio. She makes a lot of her own paints using all these natural things like flowers and dried mud, and the colors are amazing." Mimi's voice sounds proud again, like Christina's talents somehow reflect on her.

Didi suddenly feels hungry to know everything about Christina. "How did she get into the ghost room just now?"

"She's got the key, hon." Mimi unscrews the cap on one of the all-natural cleaners. "Why don't you start with the vacuuming in the ballroom? It's the big room on the other side of the house. Then you can make your way back."

Didi starts dragging the Dyson through the big house. At first, she's puzzled by all the grungy-looking furniture. Where are all the priceless heirlooms Mimi's always talking about? This is just a lot of junk.

But then something comes over her. It's like her eyes have suddenly grown bigger and wider, and she can see that it's not junk, it's all very special stuff, and that this truly is a special place filled with extraordinary and precious things. Windows bordered with stained glass that lets in dancing rainbows. A kind of throne chair made of twisting horns. A painted cabinet with a little theater stage inside of it, and a model of a ship with many, many sails tucked inside an amber glass bottle. Everywhere her eyes land, there's something marvelous to look at.

Maybe she was a Blackworth in one of her previous lives. The thought thrills her. It seems right, somehow. That she belongs here. And now that she's come back, she feels happy.

She can't remember ever having been happy.

Except maybe that one time. Right after Raymond was dead. The blade gone straight into his neck, severing the artery, blood everywhere . . .

But that was a different kind of happy.

This is a kind that comes from being finally in a place she belongs, and knowing that somebody as amazing as Christina—a twin old soul who gets Emily Dickinson—realizes it too. As she passes through the front hall, Didi vows to learn every one of Emily Dickinson's poems by heart and recite them all, one by one, to Christina.

The front door suddenly swings open. A man comes striding in like he owns the place. He's big, with a handsome thin face and bloodshot eyes. "Hey, there," he says. "You're new, aren't you?"

Every fiber in her body goes on alert. "Just temporary," she says. "Helping my mother."

"I'm Kevin Holland." His red eyes sweep her up and down. "I'm temporarily not living here, but I'll be moving back soon."

The dad. Christina's husband, Mimi said Christina threw him out. Why was he here?

Didi just wants to get the shit away from him.

Head down, dragging the cumbersome vacuum cleaner, she continues toward the ballroom, dreading that he'll follow, not relaxing her guard until she's sure he hasn't.

CHAPTER TWELVE

AVA

I suggested meeting Jamie at a Denny's off Highway 1 in Salinas so he wouldn't have to drive much out of his way. It was a place we both knew—Dad always used to stop at it when he drove us up to visit Aunt Willie.

Jamie was already there when I arrived, in a booth bathed in banana-yellow light. I slid in opposite him. He had on stylish glasses. Black, hipster looking. His eyes behind the lenses were ringed with dark circles. Also weirdly hipster. Two mugs of steaming coffee were on the table. "Hey, you," he said.

"Hey, you too."

"I already ordered. A Grand Slam with extra syrup for me. I got you strawberry pancakes with the works."

"Extra whipped cream?"

"Of course." He picked up his mug. His grasp was unsteady.

"You're exhausted," I said.

"I'm okay." He gulped coffee. Set down the mug. Coffee sloshed onto the table. "Shit."

"You're not that okay." I grabbed a wad of napkins and sopped up the spill. "So what the hell is going on?"

"I told you. Sarah and I got married last month. I suppose it was crazy to do it so suddenly, but it felt right. And kind of exciting. We've been keeping it secret until we find a place to live, and then we were going to break it to everybody."

"Why couldn't you tell me? I would've kept the secret."

He shrugged. "I wasn't sure how you'd take it. This whole thing about going back to that damned house. I wasn't sure about your state of mind."

Neither was I. "I'm okay, really. It's your state of mind I'm worried about."

A waitress set down enormous plates. Jamie's Grand Slam pancakes with eggs and bacon and sausage. Mine with chocolate chips and banana and strawberries topped with a tornado of whipped cream. "You think Mom ever knew we ordered like this when Dad brought us here?" I said.

"I'm sure she suspected. She knew we crammed our faces with junk every chance we got." He doused his plate with syrup and dug in.

I tasted the pancakes. The whipped cream was cloying. I had grown up. "So what's the weird thing you said you've gotten into? You meant your marriage?"

"Yeah. I mean, I don't know. Maybe. I want to show you something." He dabbed syrup from his mouth, then picked up a saddlebag from the seat beside him—tooled buffalo leather, from one of our great-grandfathers who'd raised rare white bulls on a ranch up in Mendocino. He drew out a folded piece of white paper. "I found this yesterday inside a book of Sarah's."

I unfolded it and gave a start. "This is me."

"Yeah. One of Mom's sketches."

Me at thirteen, sketched in charcoal. Skinny, all awkward angles. Gripping a badminton racket between my knobby knees while I reknotted my ponytail. "She drew this just before she died," I said. "And Sarah had it?"

"Yeah. Yesterday, I was doing some last-minute revision on a paper for this conference I'm heading to. I was using Sarah's study in her town house. My eyes were hurting. They've been getting a little worse lately. I took a break from the computer and started browsing the books on her shelves. Mostly textbooks from her classes at Bradford but also a few from high school. One was *Advanced Placement English Composition*. A piece of paper was poking from it, so I slid it out. And nearly choked when I saw it."

"Yeah, I'll bet," I said. "Mom never gave away any of her sketches. How did Sarah get it?"

"That's what I wanted to know. I confronted her immediately. She said a girl in high school gave it to her. A Didi somebody. I forget the last name."

"Okay, so where did this Didi get it?"

"She said she didn't know. She's talked about this girl before. She said she was a stalker who followed her around and sneaked things into her backpack. Little gifts. Sarah said she had no idea this sketch was of you or that Mom drew it. She looked stunned when I told her."

"Don't you believe her?"

"I don't know. She told me about her when I first met her. She said Didi had ended up pushing her off a bluff and nearly killing her."

I narrowed my eyes. "Are you joking?"

"It sounds preposterous, I know. It did to me, too, at the time. But now I'm not so sure. Look on the back."

I turned the sketch over. There was a phone number scribbled flamboyantly in pencil. "A Peninsula area code. And the rest of the number looks familiar. Is it somebody we know?"

"I think it used to be Dad's. After he moved out and was living for a while with some woman in Monterey."

I felt a tremor of apprehension. I took out my phone and pulled up "Contacts"—a list that had been transferred through all the phones I'd had over the years. Four numbers for Dad. Whenever he'd gotten a new one, I'd never bothered to delete the old. "Yeah, it was his. Did Sarah know him?"

"She swears she didn't. She says she didn't even know the number was there. She hardly looked at the sketch when this Didi gave it to her. She says she just stuck it in that textbook and forgot about it."

"So it was this girl Didi who knew Dad." *Didi.* The name made something tick in my memory. I couldn't grasp exactly what.

"He did like underage girls. Remember that thing at Forest Hills? The seventeen-year-old on the Italian team? And the way he'd sometimes check out girls I had over."

I remembered. "You think he might have been hitting on her? And gave her this sketch?"

"It's a peculiar thing to give to a girl you're hitting on. But Dad might have thought it was a cool joke. Who knows?" Jamie swirled a last bite of sausage in a pool of syrup and washed it down with coffee. "Anyway, it started an argument between Sarah and me. I told her I didn't believe her about this stalking girl. I accused her of inventing the whole story about being pushed off a bluff. I kept going. Bringing up other things. Like that ring you noticed in my office and said it looked like one of Mom's. I demanded to see it. She said all her jewelry was out being cleaned."

"Okay, that's strange."

"Yeah. And then I started ranting about how much she spends. She'd surprised me with a honeymoon trip to Mexico that cost a fortune. A private jet, can you believe? A suite at a resort that caters to rock stars, with all these absurd spa treatments. Blue agave mud therapy. Jesus." He shook his head. "I'm not even sure how much she actually has. But even if it's a lot, I'm not going to step up my lifestyle with her ex-husband's money."

"Is that why you want to sell our property?" I said. "To have the money to keep up with her?"

He shrugged. "Maybe a little part of it. Anyway, I was in a real temper, so I left and went back to my Laguna place and decided to drive up to Berkeley instead of fly." He took off his glasses, fumbling them a little like he'd done with the coffee mug. "Hold on to that drawing. I've got so many papers with me, I don't want to lose it." He rubbed his eyes. "One thing I want to do—go see Dad and maybe get some answers about this."

"Do you know where he is?"

"Not really. The last time I saw him was, like, five years ago. I had that grant in behavioral genetics at Yale, I came back to visit Willie and went to see him. This place he was renting up in the Santa Cruz hills. It was in the afternoon, and he was already drunk. He tried to hit me up for ten thousand bucks for some investment in a mobile home park in Joshua Tree. I gave him a hundred. He went apeshit, screaming about you and me and saying shit about Mom, and I just left. I still talked to him on and off for a few years, but he'd always get abusive. So I stopped."

"Me too. He got so disgusting that I changed my phone number, remember? It was just after I met Noah. I was still in Boston." I hesitated, then said, "Do you think he beat Mom?"

Jamie's face grew grim. "Yeah, I do. I think it's why she took sedatives. Battered wives often do. And I've thought about what you said. That maybe he had something to do with Mom's death."

I glanced at him.

"I don't know, you could be right. I mean, maybe he didn't intend to kill her. Maybe he just wanted to make her sick so she'd need him to take care of her. A kind of Munchausen by proxy. Remember how he was coming up to the house a lot, trying to get back into her good graces?"

"And maybe having a thing with this girl Didi at the same time." My voice was bitter.

"Wouldn't surprise me." Jamie's voice was bitter too.

"And maybe he tried to make me sick too," I said. "By giving me Nembutal and a bottle of his scotch that night after I found Mom. Or maybe he had somebody else give them to me."

Jamie gave an exasperated shake of his head. "This is insane. Even assuming the possibility he poisoned Mom, he wasn't depraved enough to harm you as well." He glanced at his watch. "I've got to hit the road. It's an important conference, and I need to get some rest before all the schmoozing."

"What about Sarah?" I said. "Will you . . . I mean, are you going to go back to her?"

He hesitated. "I'm the one who overreacted. There's no reason for me not to believe her. It's shaken me up, though. I realize I know so little about her."

"And vice versa."

"Yeah. How could she even imagine the weird background we come from?" He signaled for the check.

"I'll get it," I said. "You go on."

We stood up. He looked really wrung out. "Are you sure you're okay to drive?"

"Yeah, it's only another couple of hours. If my eyes act up, I've got drops. I almost forgot them at Sarah's when I stormed out. She sent her housekeeper to bring them to me." He gave a rueful smile. "She could have let me suffer. But hey, I haven't asked you. Are you really doing okay?"

"Basically, yeah. But there's some things I need to talk to you about. After your conference, okay?"

"Sure." He yawned.

"Oh, and by the way," I added. "Remember Thomas Rainier?"

"Yeah, of course. A strange dude. You used to make moony eyes at him."

My face went hot. "Was it that obvious?"

"To me it was. What about him?"

"I ran into him recently. He's an architect now and a developer. You should see what he's building on the land next to ours. Six gigantic houses."

"I'm not surprised. Somebody was bound to do it."

He left, and I watched through the window as he got into a Range Rover—a fancier car than any he'd ever had before. Keeping up with Sarah. I suddenly wanted to run out and grasp him by the waist and stop him from leaving.

But he was already pulling away.

CHAPTER THIRTEEN

SARAH

He was frighteningly mad. I saw it as soon as I stepped into my study.

He looked out of place in it. It's a very feminine room. Louis XVI writing desk, tulipwood with fancy ormolu. Powder blue striped love seats. The Renoir, two blooming young girls noodling on a piano with a frisky puppy nosing at their feet. I'd had free rein in the decor. Gideon never entered the room. Once he became confined to a wheelchair, he couldn't even make it up to the third floor of this town house: the elevator was too tight a squeeze.

But James wanted a quiet place to work on his paper, and it's the quietest room in the house. He'd been toiling away for over two hours, and I thought he might like some coffee or a snack, so I went up to inquire.

He was at the bookshelves, holding a sheet of paper. His face was drained of blood. A sensation of fear swept through me.

It's that drawing. The girl with the badminton racket. I hadn't thought of it in years. If I had, I would have gotten rid of it. "Where the hell did you get this?" he demanded.

I explained to him it was from Didi Morrison. I told him how I tried to be nice to her but she had no boundaries. She gave me things. It was part of how she stalked me. I told him I had no idea how she got the sketch.

"My mother drew this," he said. "It's my sister, Ava."

My eyes opened wide. I told him I didn't know. I never dreamed it had anything to do with his family.

"Did she give you one of my mother's rings?" he said. "That Victorian one you used to wear?"

"No," I said. I'd bought it in London, I told him, he knew that. I said all my jewelry is out being cleaned, but I'd show it to him when I got it back.

He didn't believe anything I said. That I'd even ever had a near-death experience. Or there was any such girl as Didi. He started on about money, the amount I was spending. Wanted to know exactly how much Gideon left me.

I lost my temper and started shouting back. "If you think such terrible things about me, why don't you just leave?"

I heard Paulina's footsteps retreating from outside the door, and I stopped. How much had she heard?

James began furiously gathering up his laptop and papers. "What are you doing?" I asked.

"You said to leave. That's what I'm doing."

"I didn't mean it, darling. I shouldn't have said it. I'm sorry." I went over and placed a beseeching hand on his arm. "You know I love you very much, James."

He looked at me with his damaged but beautiful eyes. Some of his anger had begun to dissipate. But not all of it. "I'm a little confused right now, Sarah. I need some time to think clearly."

"You've been working too hard. Maybe you shouldn't go to the conference. Call and cancel. Say you're sick."

"No, it's too important. I need to give this paper. I'm going back to my place to finish it and pack. But I think I'll drive there. I'll cancel my plane and start out right after I finish packing."

My throat tightened. "In the middle of the night?"

"I like to drive at night. No traffic, I can get there faster." His voice was still cold. He packed his papers in an old saddlebag. A Blackworth family hand-me-down, he calls it. He put the sketch in it too.

"But you are coming back, aren't you?" I said. "You're not just leaving me?"

He flipped the saddlebag closed.

"I'm begging you not to. I think I might die if you did. I can't imagine living without you anymore. Please say you're not leaving me. When you get back, I'll have answers to all your questions. I'll prove it all."

He gave a sigh. "Look, I can't imagine living without you anymore, either, Sarah. But right now, I need to go."

"Will you at least kiss me first?"

"Of course," he said. He gave me a chill, perfunctory kiss. Then he left the room. I heard the doors of the elevator open and close.

And now I'm alone. I've been pacing in agitation. I can't let him just leave like this. I won't let him.

With a cry, I sweep everything off the desk.

His eye medication. He's forgotten to take it. I scoop the bottle up off the floor.

I have a sudden idea. Something that's sure to make him stay.

I should have thought of it sooner.

CHAPTER FOURTEEN

AVA

Back home, I headed up to Mom's studio. I went to the bank of drawers in back and took the sketchbook out of the bottom drawer. It would have her last drawings—the ones she'd made right before she died—since she'd always hide the books as soon as they'd run out of pages. None of us ever knew where.

I brought the book to the painting table and opened it. A couple sketches of James, a drawing of an old friend of Mom's, and . . . I recoiled. A drawing of Dad. He was naked, toweling off after a shower in one of the guest bathrooms. Mom had inflated his small beer belly into a huge flabby pot sagging over a flaccid penis. A lewd, leering expression on his face.

She'd hated him. Knew he cheated on her.

He'd disgusted her.

She'd had no intention of ever taking him back.

I turned the page. A very sketchy drawing of a woman. Heavyset. Squatting in a grotesque way to pick up some object from the ground outside. The features of her face indistinguishable. Her hair just some lank charcoal lines.

Maybe our last housekeeper? She'd had a bad knee. It would have been painful for her to pick something up. In its way, this sketch was as cruel as the one of Dad.

Mom could be cruel sometimes. The thought struck me like a slap.

I quickly turned the page. The next was not a real drawing. Just wobbly marks. Mom's last attempt to draw before she had become too sick to even hold on to a pencil. *Butterfingers.* What she used to say whenever she dropped something.

Flipping back one page, I noticed two rows of ragged edges from where two pages had been ripped out. I took the badminton sketch of me out of my bag. The ragged top matched one of the missing pages.

What had been on the other one?

The rest of the pages were blank. I focused on the sketch of the squatting woman.

Was she the one who gave the Nembutal to me? A name swam vaguely to my mind. Madeleine. Or Muriel. She had sometimes brought a friend to help her. Or no, a daughter, wasn't it?

Jamie might remember.

My phone sounded. I glanced at it. Thomas Rainier. I felt a little shiver of . . . what?

"I was hoping you'd be in touch," he said. "When do you want to see the site?"

"Soon," I said. "But that's not why I called you. I'd like to ask you some questions." I added, "Personal questions."

"Okay," he said dubiously. "That's intriguing."

"I can come to your office. I'll make an appointment."

"It's a long haul to San Jose. Better idea. I'm usually down at Pebble Beach for the weekend. Drinks, my place, tomorrow night. You remember the address?"

"You mean your parents' house?"

"Same address, but the property belongs to me now. Come at six thirty so you can catch the sunset."

I flashed on the sympathy card. The Cinderella doll. "Will we be alone?" I said.

"Any reason we shouldn't be?"

I hesitated.

"No, we won't be alone. There will be others. Okay?"

I gave an awkward laugh. "Of course. I don't know why I said that. But you'll have to give me the address. I've never been to your place before."

"I suppose not. Why would you have?" He gave the address to me. Said he'd see me then.

"Anya Mei's kicking like crazy." Grace lumbered to a chair at the seaside café where we were meeting for lunch. The baby had been named for maternal grandmothers, one of hers and one of Darsh's. "My back hurts, and I seem to want to pig out twenty-four-seven. Everyone tells me I'm eating for two, but it seems more like six."

"But you look terrific," I told her. "Is everything still on track?"

She lowered her voice. "I've had a little bleeding. My doctor doesn't see anything of immediate concern. We're doing watchful waiting."

"Oh, Grace." I squeezed her hand. "I'm sure it will be fine."

"God, I hope so. And how about you? Doing okay alone in that house?"

"I'm not alone. I've got a cat and a dog. And a ghost who floats around under a white sheet, moaning and trailing bloody footprints."

"Very funny. But really."

"I'm fine. I've been setting up my studio, and I'm dying to start making photos. I wish you could come over." Due to her fragile pregnancy, Grace couldn't visit until the work on the house, with all its paint and chemical fumes, was finished.

"Me, too," she said. "I can't wait to give myself a nice good scare again."

"You won't. It's in the middle of civilization now. Your architect is building homes on the bluff next door."

"Yeah, I heard. They're supposed to be pretty fancy. And I'm sure Thomas is putting a fancy price on them."

"I could find out," I said. "I'm having a drink with him tonight."

She regarded me with a frown. "I saw you talking to him at my party. I don't think you should get involved with him, Ava."

"I'm not," I said. Maybe a touch too insistently. "It's not even a date. I called him to talk about some things from the past. He used to be a friend of Jamie's, you know."

"Oh yeah, I'd forgotten that. Jamie's crowd was so cool and out of my league that I never paid much attention." She let out a belch. "Another new joy. Heartburn. You know about his family, right?"

"Thomas's? Not much. He told me once back then that he hated his mother."

"His parents were both criminals. They were running some kind of Ponzi scheme. His father is now in federal prison and probably will die there. His mother fled to some country with no extradition. Morocco, I think." She leaned closer again. "I've heard rumors that Thomas was the one who turned them in. And then he somehow ended up with the place on 17-Mile Drive. Nobody is sure how."

Turned in his own parents. "If you think he's so shady," I said lightly, "why did you hire him to design your house?"

"It was before I knew any of this. And Darsh doesn't really care. Thomas is a very talented architect, I admit it. Our house is gorgeous. But like I told you, there are some problems he's promised to take care of but somehow hasn't yet."

"He seems to be a really good uncle," I offered.

Grace waggled her head skeptically. "You know what I think? He uses that little boy as a prop. It's very disarming. Even better than a cute dog."

"Are you being serious?"

"Actually, yeah. And I'm not even sure it is his nephew. They look a lot alike, don't you think? And his sister-in-law is pretty cute. Look, sweetie, you haven't been divorced all that long. You're in a vulnerable state. So I'm just saying."

"Noted. But it really is just a drink. Along with other people."

"Okay. I believe you."

"Good," I said. "Now let's get you and Anya Mei something to eat."

There were five entrances to 17-Mile Drive, the looping coastal road, each with a guardhouse; and unless you were a resident, a worker, or a guest of either a resident or a club, you had to pay admission to drive on it. Mom thought that was criminal. "Natural beauty should be free to everyone," she said.

It seemed criminal to me too. The road was gaspingly beautiful. One stunning estate after another, overlooking the ragged and dramatic shore, enhanced now by sunset tints of violet, pink, and azure. I passed the luxuriant greens of the Pebble Beach Golf Course, and I thought of Dad. He'd taken up golf when he couldn't play tennis anymore. Mooched a chance to play at Pebble Beach whenever he could.

A memory flashed: I was twelve. Dropped off by a friend's mother at the clubhouse to meet up with Dad, who would drive me home. I found him talking to a woman, leaning so close his forehead nearly knocked with hers. When I went up to him, he whirled on me with such a savage look that I was sure he was going to slap me. *You shithead*, I remembered thinking. *I dare you to.*

I pushed the memory away as I arrived at Thomas's address. I turned up a well-tended driveway lined by cypress trees to a contemporary home of glass and stone. Like the Greenwalds', it seemed to float above the ground it was situated on, though it was three times larger.

Thomas was standing outside. Arms crossed. Face lit by the intensifying twilight. He looked so intensely alone, I thought, just like he used to seventeen years ago, even in the middle of a boisterous group.

Had my moony faces been obvious to him back then? My face grew hot again.

He stepped forward as I got out of my car.

"Great house," I said. "Did you tear down your family's old one?"

"It was a monstrosity. And besides, I need a showcase to bring prospective clients to and dazzle them." He smiled dryly. "Or not. You can decide for yourself."

We went inside. I had an impression of airy, open rooms and jaw-dropping views. The furnishings were minimal and exquisite. Museum-quality art floated on the walls. I was drawn to a grouping of works by photographers I revered: Nan Goldin, Diane Arbus.

"Okay, I'm dazzled," I said.

"Are you really? I thought you'd find it cold and impersonal. The opposite of Blackworth Mansion."

"It is. And you probably think that's a monstrosity that should be torn down."

"No, I don't. It's a remarkable old house with good bones and lovely quirky elements. A house that's impossible to forget." There was the sound of chatter from a corridor to our right. "Some of my help," he said. "Finishing up for the day."

"Do a lot of people work here?"

"A multitude. It takes a small army to keep this place so empty."

I gave a laugh. He could be funny. I'd forgotten that. "Do I get the grand tour?"

"If you were a prospective client, you would," he said. "But you're not, so we're going to my favorite room. The birdcage, I call it."

This was a stunning solarium at the back of the house—a large high-domed room of glass crossed with thin steel lacings that did resemble a birdcage. A young woman was perched with birdlike delicacy on a couch. Beyond her stretched a view of darkening hills, craggy shore, and the opalescent sheen of the water.

"Hello," she said, getting up. "I'm Clotilde. Thomas's sister-in-law." She was very pretty, with brown skin, straight black hair, thick eyelashes. Her voice had a faint Caribbean lilt.

"Ava." I shook the hand she offered.

"Thomas told me how you rescued my son. It was very sweet of you."

"I didn't really rescue him. I just kept him amused until Thomas caught up with him."

"Ava thinks he's very handsome," Thomas said to Clotilde. "I don't see it myself."

"He's a liar," she told me with a grin. "He thinks Anson is a tiny Greek god. Maybe because there's a resemblance."

"There is," I agreed. "A strong resemblance. Is he here? I'd love to see him."

"He's home with his nanny, which isn't very far away. We live in the guesthouse. That might sound rough, but it's a lot bigger than the house I grew up in. And the plumbing is a lot better."

"Clotilde is from Martinique," Thomas said. "Her home was basic."

"Kindly said, Tommy." She gave him a stunning smile.

A baby-faced man with slicked dark hair came in with a bottle of wine. He opened it with a loud pop.

"Just two, Alberto," Thomas said. "Clotilde isn't staying."

"No?" I said, glancing at her.

"I'm afraid not. I've brought home an enormous amount of work. I'm a CPA, which sounds boring, but I've always liked numbers. I hope to see you again, Ava."

"I do too," I said truthfully. I had liked her instantly.

She kissed Thomas on both cheeks and left through a door that was almost invisible in the intricate birdcage lattice.

Alberto brought over two glasses, each filled to a carefully measured level. Thomas said, "I'll pour out from here, Berto."

Alberto set the bottle on the coffee table, gathered up several items from the bar cart, and disappeared. I had the eerie feeling that, like the house itself, all this had been staged. Clotilde, a charming but sort of chaperoning presence when I arrived, then quickly vanishing. The baby-faced man who'd now also melted from the room. Staged to make me drop my guard.

Against what?

I took a sip of wine. I had guessed it would be as exquisite as the house, and I was right. "I never knew you had a brother," I said to Thomas.

"Big brother Rory." He gave a snort. "The only thing he's ever done right is marry Clotilde and produce a spectacular child. She caught him shooting up next to Anson's crib one night and kicked his junkie ass out."

I shuddered at the image. Then thought of what Grace had insinuated, and I couldn't resist: "Anson does look a lot like you."

"My brother thought so too. He demanded a paternity test to make sure he was his father."

"And was he?"

Thomas's face darkened. "Of course he freaking was. What did you think?"

"Nothing," I said hurriedly. "A stupid question, sorry."

He stared at me angrily a second, then shrugged. "You said your questions would be personal." He lowered himself into a chair. "So go ahead. I'm intrigued."

I sat down on the couch, still feeling unsettled. "Maybe I should explain something first. I'm trying to figure out something about my mother. How she died. I think it's possible . . . well, that she might have been murdered."

He raised his brows. "That's not what I was expecting, but okay. What makes you think so?"

"The diagnosis doesn't fit. Her doctors said a rapidly degenerating nerve disease. But she was getting better. She was back to her normal self. And then all of a sudden, she went into convulsions and died. That doesn't fit any diagnosis at all."

"I remember her getting sick," he said. "She was dropping things a lot. She'd pick it up and say, 'Clumsy,' and then she'd drop it again."

"'Butterfingers,'" I corrected him. "That's what she'd say. She was dropping everything and stumbling and making peculiar faces. It's possible . . . I mean, I really think she was poisoned. Maybe accidentally. But I think deliberately."

He fixed his eyes on me. Sleepy blue eyes with a sharp light behind them. I remembered them too well from the fevered fantasies of my adolescence. "Are you going to ask me if I murdered her?" he said.

"No," I said, startled.

"Good. Because I didn't. And wouldn't like to be accused of it."

I felt even more flustered. Took an uneasy gulp of my wine.

"So what's your question?" he said.

"I'm trying to track down people who were at the house that day. There was a woman who worked for us. A cleaning lady. You told me once she used to work for your family too. Your mother fired her for stealing. Do you remember her name?"

"We had dozens of staff always coming and leaving. Sooner or later, my mother sacked them all. I couldn't tell you most of their names."

"This woman had a bad knee and sometimes limped."

"It doesn't ring a bell. Sorry."

I felt a stab of disappointment. I'd felt sure he'd remember. "Did you ever know somebody named Beverly Padrillo?"

"Did she work for us too?"

"I doubt it. She was in her mid-nineties back then."

"If she came cheap enough, my mother might have taken her on," he said with a bitter smile. "But what about her?"

"Nothing, really," I said. "It probably has nothing to do with this."

In a distant room, a plate smashed on a floor. "Alberto," Thomas said. "He's in training and a bit nervous."

"You're not going to fire him, are you?"

"I'm not my mother. Next question?"

I decided to take a chance. "Did you ever have anybody break into my house?"

His face darkened again. "Any reason you think I did?"

"One of my workers told me somebody had gotten in a few times, even though everything was locked and boarded up tight."

"Michael Fiore, I suppose. He said it was me?"

"No," I said. "Or at least not you personally."

"So one of my henchmen? Who can magically break into securely locked homes?"

I gave a startled laugh. "No. But . . . well, Michael did find you parked there."

"Yeah. I've gone down there a number of times over the years. Sometimes even walked around a little. You're not the only one with a morbid attachment to Blackworth Mansion."

I felt a prick of resentment. "I don't think being attached to my family home is morbid. I can't speak for you."

He slumped lazily back in his chair. "Your house always had a strong pull on me. My parents were crooks. They started shipping me off to boarding schools when I was six, and during vacations they dumped me with servants. My brother, Rory, rolled in and out of every expensive rehab in the country. I couldn't stand any of them. I envied your family. Your house, the way you lived. If I could have just stayed there, I would have in a heartbeat."

And yet he'd always seemed so aloof. As if not wanting to be part of us, or a part of anything, really. "Our family wasn't so perfect," I said. "Even before Mom died."

"I know. Your father was as much of a bastard as mine, just in a different way." He sprang out of his chair. Grabbed the wine bottle and refilled my glass and his own and then slouched back down. "So? Next question."

"Did you send me a condolence card?" I asked.

"No. Should I have? Are you in mourning?"

"No, but somebody did send me one, and it was signed by Cinderella. The name we used to call our ghost back then."

"Yeah, that ghost," he murmured. "No, I didn't send it. Why would I?"

"I don't know. Maybe as a joke. Or . . ." I had to know. "To stop me from living there. Scare me away. So you might be able to buy it."

"Interesting idea. I should have thought of it."

Now he was openly mocking me. I had the urge to sting him. "One more question. Did you turn your parents in to the authorities?"

A frightening expression crossed his face.

"You don't have to answer," I said. "The thing is, what if I'm right about my mother? And what if . . . well, maybe it turned out to be my father? He had a vicious temper. She had kicked him out of the house. If he had anything to do with her death—I'd have to turn him in. And, well . . ." I stopped.

"I did not report my parents," he said. "But if one of them had killed the other, I probably wouldn't have given a shit. I might even have cheered. But if I were you, in your place, and found out your bastard of a father had killed your mother, I wouldn't turn him in. I'd murder him without thinking twice."

Ice ran through my veins.

He set down his glass. Rolled his shoulders as if the oppressiveness of his past had tightened the muscles. Then he stood up again. "Let's go outside. I promised you a sunset, and it's in full glory right now."

"I thought you'd be wanting to get rid of me by now."

"You are through with the cross-examination, aren't you?"

"Yes," I said. "The witness may step down."

He smiled. He rarely had back then, I realized. Or at least not at me. He said, "Then come outside."

He stepped to a small panel, almost invisible in the latticework. Pressed two buttons, and glowing pyramids lit the grounds outside. He opened that almost-invisible door in the fretwork, and we went out into the gardens.

The setting sun had turned everything, hills and ocean and rocks, to fire and blood. We wandered down a serpentine path bordered by reflecting pools to a small promontory where we could see the entire sweep of coastline. The lamps warmed my face and shoulders, but the ocean surging in its wild force made me shiver.

"I suppose I can't dazzle you with this like I do my clients," Thomas said. "You've got the same view from Blackworth Mansion."

"Still, it's so magnificent," I murmured. "I should have come back sooner."

"What kept you?"

"My life went in other ways for a while. Or no, that's wrong. I took myself to other places. I thought I'd never be back. But all along, this is where I've most wanted to be."

He turned to look at me. I couldn't interpret his expression. How did he see me? The geeky girl who used to make moony eyes at him? Or just a nosy woman asking nervy questions. He turned back to the water, framed by the fierce colors of the sunset. I felt a stirring of that desperate longing for him I used to have. It wasn't real, I told myself. All that talk of the past had made me want to recapture something that never really was.

Still, I had the irresistible impulse to touch him. I moved closer to him. I ran my hand down the declivity of his back. A quivering desire shot through me.

He turned to me, smiling again. "What was that?"

"Just getting something out of my system."

"You're a strange girl," he murmured. "You always were."

"How would you know? You never even noticed me back then."

"Yeah, I did. A skinny kid in that awkward stage between cute and . . . something interesting."

Just interesting? "Jamie said the same thing about you," I said. "That you were a strange guy."

"Then I guess you and I match." He placed his hand on my cheek. A gentle caress.

I drew in my breath. Gazed up at those drowsy eyes. They still made my heart turn over.

I lifted my face to him. He smiled softly, then brought his lips to mine. I dissolved into the kiss, tasting salt breeze and wine and something spicy, kissing him hungrily back. I pressed my body closer to his and ran my hands down the length of his long slouchy frame.

"Hey," he whispered. "Are you sure about this?"

"No," I said. "But I don't want to stop." I kissed him again, deeply.

Then he stepped back and took my hand. The sunset was fading: the shoreline was now clothed in pale gray like finespun linen. He led me back into the house, though not through the birdcage, around a path on the side to a guest suite with its own entrance. A ceiling made of glass. A telescope pointing to the evening sky. We kissed wildly, pulling at each other's clothes, tumbling onto a cloud of a mattress.

And then I was drowning in sensations that took me light-years beyond my thirteen-year-old imagination. And I didn't want it to ever stop.

I didn't stay afterward. I went back home. Betsy was insanely glad to see me. Stieglitz fixed his reproachful yellow eyes on me with that uncanny sixth sense of cats.

He knew I'd done something crazy.

And I hadn't gotten any real answers. Just more questions.

DIDI

Didi and Mimi are cleaning for the richy-rich Rainier family today, but Didi's head is still full of the Hollands' house the day before. Christina had floated in and out of Didi's presence, but every time she appeared, she took notice of Didi. More and more, Didi was sure she was right—she and Christina were twin old souls.

Kevin Holland, though. Didi feels some hot sensation flash through her. Hot as in hate, not as in sexy.

He brings back thoughts about Raymond. Everything that happened. All that she desperately tries never to think about.

Kevin Holland is a lot more handsome than Raymond, who had tiny eyes like raisins, a groove carved between them, and big red hands with tufts of wiry hair.

Hands that cupped her butt. Sliding between her legs. Since she was ten, maybe even before.

Mimi pretending not to know, humming in the other room.

Kevin Holland was handsomer, and he had more class. But Didi saw Raymond in the swagger of his grin. His bloodshot eyes. The way his gaze slid up and down her chunky body. Never fixing on her face.

He doesn't live at Blackworth Mansion anymore. Why is he still showing up? But she hopes he won't next time she's there. Didi wants Christina all to herself.

She turns now onto 17-Mile Drive. She's never been on it before. It's only for the superrich. She gives the Rainiers' name at the guardhouse. A phone call. She and Mimi are admitted.

Mimi's pal, Wanda Bautista, is the main housekeeper for the Rainiers. They became pals when Mimi started working here part time. Wanda's got an orange buzz cut and bossy attitude, and she assigns Didi to clean the pool house. "Under no circumstances are you to enter the main residence," Wanda tells her. "Do you understand?"

Like she'd even want to. The Rainier's "main residence" is a kind of cross between an Arabian palace and a big-box Kmart. She pictures herself describing it to Christina. "They're the kind of people who lack all sense of beauty." She says that out loud to herself in a low, whispery tone—she's been practicing Christina's way of talking.

Mimi is ushered into the "main residence." Since none of the Rainiers are home, she and Wanda will spend a lot of the day in the kitchen, gossiping and drinking Fanta (Mimi's favorite) and puffing on Camels. Even though smoking is something else Mimi the so-called Mormon isn't supposed to do.

Didi begins picking up dirty things from various nooks and crannies of the pool house. A bikini top. A jockstrap. Terry cloth robes. Everything reeks of chlorine and sweat and fungus. There's a micro washer/dryer. She stuffs as much as possible into the washer and turns it on. She looks in the shower. *Puke.* It's got about an inch of slime on the walls.

Don't these people care about hygiene?

She scrubs and wipes. Loads and unloads the washer and dryer. The morning crawls. Her shoulders and hands ache.

Finally, lunch!

Being a star house cleaner, Mimi gets to demand the perk of having lunch included. Yesterday, the two of them had the run of Christina's kitchen. It was awesome! All sorts of amazing food. Goat milk and pistachio milk and a dozen different kinds of granola. Blue lettuce. Purple crackers. A canister of grain so golden that Didi wanted to run her fingers through it, like a miser with gold coins.

"It's always so hard to find something to eat here," Mimi had grumbled.

But Didi knew better. This was the kind of food people like Christina ate. People who lived on a higher plane. Didi had sworn to herself, *I'll never eat another OREO again.*

And now finally here comes one of the Rainiers' regular help, carrying a plastic supermarket bag. Didi takes it, her stomach growling with starvation.

It contains one package of Lunchables. Chicken Dunks. She flushes with anger.

Does Wanda think she's nine?

She ought to refuse to eat it. Throw it in Wanda's face at the end of the day. But she's too freaking hungry. She rips open the package.

A few soggy nuggets. A glob of ketchup.

And two non-brand-name OREOs.

She could kill Wanda. She really could.

She's nearly faint with starvation for the rest of the day. She checks the clock continuously. Finally, after about an infinity, there's only ten more minutes to quitting time. Didi folds a last batch of things from the dryer and sets it on top of the rest of the clean clothes and towels stacked in a large basket. She picks up the basket and begins carrying it to the main house—Wanda had told her to leave it outside the back door.

She freezes. One of the blond Rainier sons is coming toward the pool. She shrinks back against the pool house wall. Prays it's not the smart one from the beach who called Mimi a maid.

The blond boy's wearing only cutoff jeans and loafers. His trendy sunglasses glint in the sun. He walks in a kind of shuffling zombie way, like he's half-asleep or high on something.

He takes off his shades and puts them on a table. It's the dumb one, thank God. She doesn't know his name. He's older and shorter than his brother, Thomas. Doesn't have those lazy-looking eyes.

She stands stock still against the wall. Watches as he steps out of his loafers. Wriggles off his cutoffs. Now he's stark naked. He's pale as a mushroom. Patch of blond pubic hair, penis shrunken in the chill air.

He moves to the pool ladder. Starts inching down. Stops and slides a watch off his wrist and sets it on the edge of the pool. Then inches a little deeper into the water.

"Didi, hon! Are you ready to go?" Mimi calls out from a back window of the main house.

The dumb blond son snaps his head toward Didi. "Fuck!" he yells. "What are you looking at? Fuck you!" He hoists himself off the ladder, scrambles back into his cutoffs. "Goddamned frigging servants," he mutters. He grabs his sunglasses and stomps back into the main house.

Didi's face burns. Goddamn *you*, she thinks.

He's left his watch on the edge of the pool. She puts down the basket and goes to it. A chrome Rolex. Flashy. Expensive.

Yesterday, Mimi had swiped a pen from the Hollands' house. Not a fancy one. Just an ordinary click pen running dry of ink.

But the word *servants* is still burning in Didi's ear. She thinks: *If you're going to steal, you should make it something worthwhile.* She considers slipping the Rolex down her pants.

It would be obvious that she was the one who'd taken it.

She sets it back down and picks up the laundry basket and moves to the back door. The dumb son has left it wide open. Like an answered prayer.

She cautiously moves inside the house. It's almost as crammed with stuff as the Hollands', except everything here looks like it's been placed just so, and none of it is old and marvelous. It's all new and shiny. Basically, expensive crap.

She turns into a room that's all mud-brown leather and wall-to-wall oak cabinets and the head of a deer with a full rack of horns on the wall. Mr. Rainier's man cave. She's never seen Mr. Rainier. Only knows him from his laundry. Black briefs and shirts that are yellow in the armpits.

There's a bookcase crammed with stuff, none of it books. She picks up a snow globe with an ornate base. Inside it, a naked man and woman holding each other tight.

She turns the globe upside down, but it doesn't snow.

Then she gets it—you're supposed to turn the base. She does, and the naked couple begins to hump. You can see the man's little pink thing going in and out. *Gross*, she thinks.

But it would be something Mr. Rainier wouldn't make a stink about, even if he realized it was missing. She slips it into the pocket of her sweatpants and pulls her roomy shirt over it.

Then gets out before anybody sees her.

CHAPTER FIFTEEN

AVA

I saw Thomas again the next night. And this time, I could hardly wait until we ended up in the glass-ceilinged guest suite with the telescope pointing to hazy stars. I couldn't get enough of him, his face hardly changed from adolescence, his thick silver-ash hair, his thin body and the sensations it brought out in mine. There was nothing numb in me when we were making love. I was entirely, ecstatically alive.

Afterward, we talked for a long time. He spoke with barely contained enthusiasm about his work. Asked a lot about mine. Offered to come see my photographs. I was evasive. Told him I'd bring finished prints when I had them.

I didn't want him coming to Blackworth Mansion. Not yet. He wasn't after it: I'd almost convinced myself of that. But what if I was wrong? I pictured him there. Pointing out the grotesqueries. The falling-down condition of the house. I'd begin to see it all through his eyes. The chipped and cracked mantels. The sagging banisters and drooping chandeliers. The weed- and gopher-ridden lawns. The Gothic creepiness of the sculpture garden.

And I'd scare myself away.

Once again, I refused to stay the night. And the following day, he returned to San Jose.

I'd finally gotten my studio organized, and now I set to work on my project of photographing my past. First step: preliminary shots throughout the house. I used ambient light, heightening the exposures to create eerie, unsettling images. Bringing out ghosts in the dusty, dimly lit air.

Then I hired Franny Fiore to pose as Mom. Dressed her in clothes I'd found hanging in Mom's closets. Ankle-length fog-colored skirts. Loose linen shirts. They were limp and dusty and chewed by moths, but I easily disguised that.

I made Franny kick off her shoes and brush her unruly strawberry blonde hair down her back, and I had her pose on the staircase, holding Stieglitz and murmuring in his ear. And in the Monster Room, contemplating a dead centipede in her hand. In each shot, a ghost hovered over her shoulder. A glowing image of imminent death.

Single-frame horror flicks. Re-creating my past, but as I now recalled it.

Hoping for something, some clue, to help me resolve Mom's death. But I was still not finding it.

I fitted my Nikon with a gray lens filter. Softened the focus. Trained it on Franny in the ballroom, dancing the way Mom often had to the rhythm of the ocean that echoed from the ballroom's vaulted ceilings.

And through my lens, a shadowy real-life vision of Mom appeared to me. Words whispered in my mind. *Through the past, darkly.*

A memory struck me: a vintage Rolling Stones album Mom used to love. She would scoop up old vinyl albums from the Monster Room—jazz, doo-wop, the Beatles and Stones—and play them on a turntable while she worked. *Through the Past, Darkly* had her favorite song on it: "She's a Rainbow." My favorite was on it too. "Jumpin' Jack Flash."

I took a photo burst of Franny, and another image darted into my mind. *A girl dancing strenuously to "Jumpin' Jack Flash."*

With a start, I lowered my camera.

"Are you okay, Ava?" Franny said.

"Yeah, I'm fine," I said. "But I think we've done enough for today."

I went to my studio and downloaded all the shots onto my computer. My heart beating fast, I examined them—particularly that last photo burst.

That memory of the dancing girl—awkwardly, almost comically, getting into it. Was it real?

Or was I just remembering Mom herself, her horrific dying dance?

Her last sketchbook lay on my desk. I opened it to the drawing of the stocky woman squatting in an awkward, ugly way. But it was a girl dancing that I seemed to remember, not an older woman.

I studied the sketch again. What if this wasn't a middle-aged woman but somebody much younger?

I shivered at a faint stirring of recognition. A heavyset girl who'd worked for us just before Mom died.

The daughter of the housekeeper with the bad knee. Yes. They had come here together for a few months. I tried to summon the girl's face, or even her name. But I couldn't: it was all submerged in that stubborn blackness of the past.

Maybe, by taking more photos, I could pull it out.

Unless there wasn't anything left in that blackness to retrieve. Just empty, dusty spaces.

I shuddered. I shoved the sketchbook into a drawer and slammed it shut.

I was meeting Thomas at his construction site later that day after his crews had gone home for the tour of it he'd promised. I decided to walk;

there was a path through the woods that Jamie and I used to take all the time. As I put on hiking shoes and a rugged sweatshirt, a thought struck me: I'd texted Jamie twice and hadn't heard from him. That feeling I'd had watching him leave—of wanting to force him not to go . . . I brushed off the thought. Shot off another text to him. Then called for Betsy to come with me and set off.

The trail seemed more overgrown now. More densely covered in moss and rotten leaves and fallen cedar limbs. Or maybe I'd just forgotten how difficult it was to follow. I lost the path more than once and had to double back, using the ocean as a guide. Finally the forest thinned, the terrain became rockier. I emerged at the site of a nearly completed house.

Michael was wrong: it wasn't as big as a Home Depot. It wasn't even the size of Blackworth Mansion. Two stories, mostly stone and glass, sitting low on the cliff face.

A vehicle rumbled from an invisible driveway in the trees. An enormous black truck pulled into the site. Thomas jumped down from the cab. Betsy raced to him, wound around his feet, barking, then snuffled at his shoes. He leaned down and pulled her floppy ears. "Who's this?"

"Her name's Betsy. She's my guard dog. Careful, she's vicious."

"I can see that." He grinned. "Where's your car? Did you walk?"

"Yeah. I barely remembered the way, but I made it."

"I tried recently. I got totally turned around, so I gave up and came back. So have you walked around yet?"

"No, I just got here too." I turned toward the house. "It's a lot smaller than I thought it would be."

"The site is zoned for bigger homes, but they would have loomed on it. This is a green design. I went for sustainability and fitting in with the natural landscape. At least that's what I've tried for."

He began walking me in and around the house in progress, pointing out the green features. Solar shingles. A hidden tank to collect rainwater to use in gardening. "The water from showers will be recycled for the washing machine. And we're using the moss we had to take out to construct a green wall on the north facade."

I admired the weathered wood floors.

"Reclaimed from derelict old barns." He talked about power saving and nontoxic materials. I wondered if he'd gone over budget, like with Grace's house. Had to cut any corners. But his enthusiasm was infectious.

"I'm impressed," I admitted.

"So it's not completely evil?"

"Not completely. But I still won't sell you my property to develop."

"I still haven't asked you to," he said.

The light began silvering through the mist rising from the water. "It's too dark to go back through the forest," he said. "Come to dinner at my place. We'll eat early with Clotilde and Anson. Clotilde said she'd love to see you again. And Anson is smitten with you."

"I'd love to, but I need to go home first. I'm covered with cedar needles and sawdust, and I've got Betsy."

"Bring her. I'll have somebody walk her. And nobody's going to be dressed up. But if you want, I'll drive you back to change."

"Okay." I called Betsy, and we followed him to the truck. I paused. There were two additional headlights mounted high on the cab. I flashed on those twin halos hovering in my rearview mirror after my first time back at the house. High headlights diffused by fog.

"What?" he said.

"Did you ever follow me in this truck?"

A tick of silence. "Follow you where?"

I hesitated. There had to be a lot of trucks coming and going from the construction. A lot of them with high-mounted lights. "Never mind, it's nothing. But I think I will walk back first. I know the way now, it won't take me long. I'll come to your place in my own car."

For a moment, something distant came into his face. That don't-give-a-crap look I remembered so well. I felt a tug in my chest, a combination of longing and resentment.

But then he said, "Okay, sure. But don't take too long if you want to see Anson. Clotilde puts him down early." He climbed into his truck, switched on the lights. Just the main headlamps. Betsy barked a joyful farewell to him as he swung back up the driveway.

It was the baby-faced helper, Alberto, who was waiting out front for me this time. He led me down a path to a terrace overlooking the water. Thomas and his sister-in-law, Clotilde, were seated at a table. Anson crawling underneath it, chased on all fours by his nanny, Jeremiah, a youngish man with a gentle smile and soulful eyes.

We drank a pale-yellow wine and ate fried chicken and asparagus with our fingers. "Is it true you live in a haunted house, Ava?" Clotilde asked. "I used to see ghosts as a child, but not one since I came to America."

"I've never seen one either," I said. "Only my mother ever saw our ghost. But I feel the presence of ghosts at my house all the time."

"Then you're lucky," she said softly. I wanted to say, "No. Not lucky at all." But before I could, Anson clambered up into my lap. He twisted around and tugged at my hair. It was a skill he had perfected. Clotilde apologized and signaled it was time to put him to bed.

Thomas and I remained at the table, the heat lamps encasing us in a warm glow. Clotilde had conjured ghosts, and so I found myself talking about Mom, the horrible circumstances of her death. He listened intently. And then about my breakdown afterward. The psych hospital. "I only remember it in flashes," I told him. "Pills every couple of hours. A hospital gown getting tangled up in my legs. Therapy sessions all the time, but all I wanted to do was go to sleep."

"I saw you there once," he said. "Do you remember?"

"No," I said with surprise. "Were you committed there too?"

He gave a sharp laugh. "No, my brother was in the rehab ward, and I'd been forced to come for family therapy. It was a joke. Rory just sat there smirking while my parents ripped each other apart. So I left and went to the other wing. I was stunned to see you there." His voice softened. "You were sitting hunched against a wall in the group room. Your eyes were squeezed shut, and tears were leaking out of them. I came and sat down next to you."

I gazed at him in amazement. "Did you say anything?"

"No. I touched your face and let your tears leak all over my hand. It got drenched. I didn't care. And then a nurse told me I had to leave, visitor hours were over. I said I wouldn't, and a guard came over, so I had no choice."

"I remember a guard making somebody go away. I didn't want them to go. But I couldn't speak, it was like I was hiding at the bottom of a very dark well. If I talked, I'd be found, and that would be dangerous for me." I was silent a moment. "How much do you remember about my mother?"

"A lot," he said. "I had a thing for her for a while."

I stared at him with shock. "For Mom?"

"Yeah. I even kissed her once."

My shock turned to horror.

He grinned. "It was nothing. We were talking, and she was being so sweet and attentive, and it seemed to me that she was the only genuine person I knew in the entire fucked-up world. And she was beautiful. I couldn't help it, I gave her a kiss."

"What happened?" I said warily.

"Nothing. She laughed at me. She called me a lovely boy and said I needed to find a lovely girl my own age. I was mortified. I'd made a total ass of myself."

I continued to stare at him. All the time I was worshipping him from afar, he was lusting after Mom?

"Oh, hey, I've made you upset," he said. "I thought you'd think it was funny, what an ass I made of myself. I shouldn't have told you. Or about the psych ward either."

"No, I'm glad you told me about the hospital. At least I have one good memory of it now. Before, I had none."

A smile played on his lips. "You've got something in your hair."

I reached up. A gooey shmoosh of chocolate chip cookie. "Anson left me a gift."

"He's a generous kid." Thomas handed me a napkin decorated with clowns, and I rubbed off the shmoosh, laughing. Our eyes locked, and I felt something course through me—some emotion that went beyond just physical desire. A feeling that caught me by surprise. I had not expected this. It was nothing I was even ready for.

But there it was, and I clutched the silly napkin, suddenly wanting nothing more except to get closer to him in every possible way.

His phone rang. He glanced at it and said, "Excuse me, I've got to take this." He got up and moved a distance away, and I heard him talking urgently.

I turned my eyes to the darkening water. Thin black clouds were slipping out from behind the hills, smudging the sky like smoke.

He came back. "I've got to go. There's a problem with a home I built. A retaining wall gave way. It could be a drainage problem. The hill behind it is very unstable. If it slides, it could engulf half the house."

"Is it your fault?" I said.

"It's my responsibility. I'll walk you to your car."

I got up. "Don't worry, you've got things to attend to. I can find my own way."

"Okay, good," he said. He turned and hurried into his house.

I stood a moment, confused. He hadn't kissed me. Or even said goodbye.

Grace had warned me not to get involved. She was right. A mistake.

Best that I go back alone to my strange old house. To my animals and my ghosts.

But when I returned to Blackworth Mansion, I wasn't alone. There was a car I didn't recognize in the front drive. A white BMW SUV with rental plates. Lights were on in the house, and smoke rose from one of the chimneys.

Franny Fiore met me at the door. "Why are you still here?" I asked.

"Your sister's come. She showed up a couple of hours ago. I tried to text, but up here, you know, sometimes texts don't go through. I didn't want to leave before you got here. You don't have a sister, do you, Ava?"

"No," I said. "I don't."

Chills of fear ran up my spine. I knew who it was.

CHAPTER SIXTEEN

SARAH

The small, sinewy woman who let me in had taken me to a room with a large fireplace and very efficiently laid a fire. It smokes a little, but I'm grateful for the warmth and move close to it. She left me with a dog, a beagle, to guard me, I guess. But I've got no intention of wandering around. Not yet. And the beagle's very friendly.

I've been waiting for about an hour, and now there are quick footsteps and Ava Holland comes into the room. "Sarah!" In her eyes, there's the terror of a cornered animal. "Has something happened to Jamie?"

"No," I say. "I mean, I don't know. He's missing."

"Missing?" She repeats the word as if the meaning is obscure.

The sinewy woman appears at the door of the room. The beagle sends a bark at her, as if to say it's all under control.

"I haven't heard from him in over three days," I tell Ava. "I've filed a missing person report. And I've called friends of his from the college to ask if he was with them. Nobody's seen him or even talked to him."

Relief mixes with continuing fear on her face. She had already imagined the worst. "When was the last time you heard from him?"

"Right after he gave his paper at a psychology conference on Sunday. He said he wasn't staying for the rest of it. He was going to start driving back the next morning and on the way go see your father."

"He found out where he lives?"

"He wasn't sure. Somewhere up in the hills above Santa Cruz. I wasn't worried for the first day. But then I got very worried when he didn't respond to any of my calls or texts, so yesterday evening I called the police and filed a report. And today I went to the station and talked to an officer. An investigator in the missing persons unit. I gave him a photo and more details about him." My voice is shaky. "Do you mind if I sit down?"

"Of course not."

I sink onto an overstuffed sofa with claw marks on the arms. The furniture is profuse, wildly mismatched, yet it all seems exactly right. "I didn't want you hearing it from a police department," I say. "And, well . . . I was hoping he'd be here. I thought if I just came, he couldn't avoid me."

"We have to do something." Ava takes a few steps in agitation.

"There's not much now we can do. In the morning, I'll get on the police again."

Ava seems about to insist. But then she says, "You look cold. I'll make us some warm drinks. Franny, would you help me?"

She goes out, taking the small woman with her. I hear her telling the woman it's okay, she can go on home, and the woman, Franny, argues a bit, and their voices recede. Ava returns alone ten minutes later, carrying two beer mugs. "Rum and hot water and raw honey. I should have asked you if this is okay."

"Yes, perfect." The drink reminds me of James. Raw bee honey. Dark rum. Grated fresh cinnamon stick. He calls them Blackworth family ingredients.

Ava takes a chair close to me. It's covered in tapestries. "Tell me what the investigator said."

"He said the report had already been sent to all law enforcement and hospitals within two hundred miles. And jails." I give a frightened laugh. "He said the last call made on James's phone was from a gas station in Berkeley, and now his phone tracker isn't registering at all."

"Do they know who he called?"

"Me," I tell her.

"Oh." She takes a deep sip of her drink. Her face is pale as ash.

"The officer was very sympathetic," I continue. "But I thought maybe he wasn't taking it as seriously as he could. Because, well, James and I are basically newlyweds, and I'd been a student in James's class and all that. And I couldn't tell the officer things like who is James's dentist or the personal phone numbers of his friends. I don't know his friends yet." I avert my eyes a moment. "I did get his colleagues' numbers from their instructor pages online. None of them even knew we were married. They were frankly a little suspicious when I called them."

Ava nods in that stunned way again.

"The investigator asked me if James might have stopped to visit a friend. He obviously meant another woman." I warm my face a moment in the steam from my mug. "James told you about the fight we had, didn't he? I had to tell the police about it too."

"He said it was over a drawing you had. He showed it to me. A sketch of me that my mother drew."

"He wouldn't believe me about the girl who gave it to me. He accused me of making her up. He said I didn't even know her last name, and I said, 'Of course I do, it's Morrison. Didi Morrison.' I said I'd get a yearbook from the school and show him, but by that time he wasn't listening." My voice is fading out. I take a breath. "He started accusing me of all sorts of things. Like this ring." I twist off the ring on my right middle finger. "You noticed it when we met in James's office. You said it looked like one of your mother's." I hand it to her.

"It's very similar. But it isn't the same, I can see that now. These pearls are smaller, and the sapphire in hers was rounder in shape."

She gives it back to me, and I slip it onto my finger. My phone sounds. We both snap our attention to it.

"It's nothing," I say, glancing at it. "Spam text."

"Oh." She takes another long swallow of her rum drink.

I pluck a strand of my hair and start to bring it to my mouth but catch myself and let it drop. Trichophagia. I learned about it in James's class. People, usually young girls, compelled to eat their hair. Though I don't actually eat mine, just nibble on a lock from time to time.

"That girl who gave you the sketch of me," Ava says. "Didi? Was that a nickname?"

"No, her mother thought it sounded French. Didi always seemed ashamed of it. She seemed ashamed of her mother too. She was very weird. The other kids ostracized her, so I tried to be nice to her when I transferred into the school. But she immediately wanted to be best friends. Followed me in the halls and messaged me constantly. And she'd sneak presents in my backpack when I wasn't looking." I give a shudder. "I had to pull back from her. When I did, she retaliated."

"Did she really push you off a cliff?"

"Yes. I thought I was going to die. I broke my nose and was bruised all over. And the scary thing is, I still catch sight of her sometimes. Like in a crowd or across a large room. I feel like she's still stalking me."

Ava is silent a moment. Then stands up. "Why are we just sitting here? We've got to do *something*. Start searching for him. Didn't Jamie give you any other details?"

"No. I feel the same way as you, but it's night, and I can't even think where to start."

She takes restless steps. Drains her drink. "Look, I don't want to be rude, but I hardly know anything about you," she says. "Just that you were taking Jamie's class, and your first husband was very rich."

"I'm pretty ordinary," I say. "My maiden name is Sarah Davis; you can't get more ordinary than that. I grew up in a lot of boring places.

Both my parents were military, so we moved around a lot, but nowhere very exciting."

"Jamie said you lived in Monterey."

"Only for half of my senior year. I went to a college in Oregon but dropped out sophomore year. My father had died in a helicopter crash. And after that fall off the cliff, I was never really the same. It was like my whole life got derailed. I moved to San Diego. That's where I met my first husband, Gideon."

"How did you meet him?" she says distractedly.

"I had a job as assistant manager at a yacht club. Gideon kept his sailboat docked there. An eighty-six-foot sloop named *Windjammer*." I look openly at Ava. "Can I be completely honest with you?"

She drops back down into a chair. "I hope you will be."

"I was twenty-five, and he was almost seventy. He was in the first stages of Parkinson's. He'd had three wives before me. And he had certain sexual fetishes. He liked to inflict pain." I see her make a look of disgust, but she quickly hides it. "I'd told him I'd had a near-death experience, and after that, I could stand a lot of pain as long as I knew I wasn't going to die. So we made a deal." I meet her eyes. "You must think that was terrible."

"I can't judge that," she says.

"But I was fond of Gideon. And I had another purpose. My mother had begun to develop Alzheimer's. Sometimes she wouldn't recognize me. She'd scream when I came into her room. I don't know who she thought I was."

A stricken look now crosses Ava's face.

"She needed to be put into a facility, and I wanted it to be a good one. That took real money. So I accepted Gideon's deal."

"Have you told all this to Jamie?"

"Yes, of course. I've always been honest with him. It didn't shock him much. I guess because of his field of study."

"I'll be honest with you too," she says. "I was horrified when Jamie told me he eloped with you. He thinks of himself as always so rational, but he can sometimes act very emotionally."

"Yes," I say. "I know that."

Ava gets up again. "I'm going to start contacting people. His friends from Sausalito and San Francisco. Maybe he did stop to see somebody."

I glance at the fireplace. Such frightening gargoyles. In the dancing firelight, they seem to writhe and twist. I look up at Ava. "Be honest with me again. Do you think James has left me?"

She hesitates just a tiny second. "No," she says. "That wouldn't be like him. He's very faithful to people."

"Thank you, Ava," I breathe. "I can't tell you how much that means to me."

My email alert sounds. My eyes shoot to the screen. "It's from Dr. Florian, the head of Jamie's department."

"Has she heard from him?"

I read it. My shoulders slump. "No. She sounds annoyed that I'm contacting her." I hand Ava the phone so she can read it too.

"Bitch," she mutters.

I pause. "James has been acting a little strange lately. He'll trip or drop something. He says it's his eyes, they've been bothering him a lot. But I'm not sure."

The fear in Ava's eyes quickens. "I noticed that, too, when we had breakfast the other day. He spilled his coffee."

"Your mother died of a nerve disease," I say. "So I wondered . . . do you think it might have been passed down to him? Like, a genetic thing?"

For a moment, she doesn't seem to understand my meaning. Then she says, "No. I think my mother died of something else."

I glance at her. "What?"

"Some kind of poison. But maybe it's not true. I was always the only one who thought it wasn't a disease." She gives a tremulous smile. "I'm glad you're here, Sarah. I don't think I could stand to be alone, going through this."

I stand up. "I feel that way, too, Ava. Maybe that's really why I came."

She moves toward me. And we hug spontaneously.

Just like real sisters.

CHAPTER SEVENTEEN

AVA

It seemed so natural to embrace Sarah. I felt almost overwhelmed with gratitude to her. For her warmth. Her candor.

Her reticent beauty.

After we hugged, she said, "I'm exhausted. Would you mind, Ava . . . I mean, I have a hotel booked, but would it be a terrible inconvenience if I stayed here tonight?"

"Of course not," I said. "I expect you to. I'll make up a bed for you upstairs."

She crossed the room and grabbed the handle of a suitcase I hadn't noticed before. Louis Vuitton. Not an overnight bag—a large traveling-size suitcase. I noticed her understated but expensive clothes. She'd been the wife of a very rich man. Used to luxury. What could she think of this decrepit house? But as we headed upstairs, I was struck by a feeling that she'd come expecting to stay for a long time.

I was wild with fear about Jamie. How could I tell what else I was feeling?

I led her to the south wing. "That was my bedroom, and that one was Jamie's," I said, pointing as we passed. My voice felt on the edge of cracking. I opened the double doors at the end of the hall and turned on the lights. "This was my parents' suite."

"It's lovely," she murmured. "Why didn't you take it for yourself?"

Screaming from behind closed doors. "It didn't feel right. My parents' room, sleeping in their bed. I took the matching suite in the other wing. I've got my own furniture in it."

She moved to the large brass bed. "This must be a family heirloom."

"I don't think of any of our things as heirlooms. We called them hand-me-downs. The mattress is probably musty, but I'll put double sheets on it." *Why are we talking about these nonessential things?* I wanted to scream. For Sarah's sake, I didn't. She, too, was barely keeping control.

I went to the airing cupboard down the hall, glad to have a specific chore. Franny had recently washed all the old linen and hung it to dry outside in the afternoon when the sun was strongest: the sheets now smelled like sunshine and sea. I picked out four large ones and two pillowcases as well as three old wool blankets that were mostly free of moth holes. I returned to the suite.

Sarah was in the adjoining sitting room, staring out the window. "It's so dark out there."

"That window faces the forest. It's beautiful in the daylight."

"So dark," she repeated. We went back into the bedroom, and I put the bundle of sheets and blankets on the dresser.

"Here, let me do the bed," she said. "I could use the activity."

"We'll do it together." The mattress had gone gray now. There were two depressions, one very long, one shorter. Mom had always slept on the right. The sag on Dad's side was deeper. I tried not to look at them.

We shook each sheet and blanket over the mattress, tucking them in. Sarah squared her corners. "A military family," she reminded me, a little sheepishly. She sat down on the edge of the bed and huddled into the oversized mohair sweater she had on. She looked fragile and vulnerable. "I'll keep my phone turned on. Maybe he'll call in the middle of the night. Or maybe just show up here."

"Maybe," I said.

He wouldn't. I was certain of that. He wouldn't come near this house.

I wished her good night. I went back downstairs and tamped down the fire. I got another drink, a stiff shot of tequila. Then took the bottle up to my studio and began doggedly going through old files, dredging up names I hadn't thought of in years, anyone Jamie and I had known in common. I sent dozens of messages to old email addresses. Many no longer existed and were bounced back.

Nobody who answered had seen him. Or heard from him.

He'd vanished into thin air. The thought almost tore me apart.

Stieglitz appeared and crouched on my desk. Betsy, still excited by the presence of a stranger, skidded in and out of the room.

It seemed like days, not hours, since I'd been with Thomas. I began to text him. Remembered his abrupt turning to his house. His mind already elsewhere. I deleted the message.

After some hours, the tequila finally succeeded in making me sleepy. I dragged myself to bed. But I could only fitfully doze.

I was awakened by Betsy barking at the window. Somebody was outside. Jamie. Or police officers with terrible news. Or whoever had coughed that first night I was here.

I got out of bed and went to the window. A figure, moving in the light of an electric lantern. I tensed.

It was Sarah.

She moved slowly, as if searching for something. A hazy moon glowered. I watched her put one hand on her head and lift her face, not to the moon but to the dark sky above the forest. It seemed a gesture of giving up. Of relinquishing hope. I raised the window and called out to her, but my words were swallowed by the surf.

And then she moved out of my sight, into the shadows.

DIDI

Didi loves it when Christina sketches her. She used to like it when Mimi took snapshots of her when she was little. But after all that with Raymond, Mimi never did again.

Didi also loves it when Christina asks for her opinions. Like, of her latest painting: "Your thoughts, Didi?" Didi had scrutinized it, and she'd said, "It's amazing. I mean, everything in it is kind of creepy, but the way you've put it all together and painted it, it's beautiful." Christina had seemed very pleased. Another time she asked Didi to taste a smoothie she'd made, avocado, nut butter, and green matcha powder (gag, but Didi said she could taste the healthiness, and Christina approved of that too).

The warm feeling Christina gave Didi had spilled over to the old lady Beverly Padrillo when she and Mimi went to work for her on Sunday. Didi had volunteered to weed out Bev's bathroom cabinet and get rid of all the expired prescriptions.

Zillions of them. Some from more than ten years ago. Didi dumped them into a trash bag and took the bag out to the bin on the side of Bev's house, but it was overflowing—nobody had bothered to drag it out for the curbside pickup that week. She had stowed the bag instead in the trunk of Mimi's Fiesta. She'd meant to toss it into some dumpster on the way back but forgot.

It's still in the trunk now, as she and Mimi arrive to work at the Rainiers' house on 17-Mile Drive the next Saturday.

It's Didi's fifth time working there. Each time, she's taken something. It's not easy, even though Wanda has promoted her to work in the main residence. First of all, most of the Rainiers' stuff is oversized. Like they were a family of giants or something. Even the knickknacks are gigantic. And Didi's rule is it's got to be things worth something, not junk like Mimi pilfers.

What she's stolen so far:

A crystal shot glass (it got cracked in her purse on the way home).

A miniature Walkman.

A silk scarf with a horse-head design.

The sex snow globe.

It's not like she wants this crap. As soon as she can, she tosses it out in a public receptacle.

Today, Wanda assigns her to scrub the grout in all ten bathrooms. Didi asks for gloves, but no-o-o. Wanda never deigns to listen or even speak to Didi. She snaps instructions for her to Mimi, who has to pass them on, even though Didi can hear perfectly well what Wanda is saying. "Make sure she knows that if she scorches any of Gayle's linen blouses, there will be hell to pay." "She needs to sprinkle the cottons, not use the sprayer." "The copper pots must be scoured and rinsed twice and then hand rubbed."

"She acts like I'm some kind of workhorse," Didi had complained to Mimi. "She never even says my name."

"It's not personal, hon," Mimi said. "Wanda has her ways. They have a lot of staff, so it's hard for her to keep names straight."

"But you're always gabbing with her. Don't you ever talk about me with her?"

Mimi had hummed some lame old Journey song. She always hums when she wants to avoid answering questions. *Is Raymond always going to live with us? Why do you keep letting him hit you?*

It's for Mimi's sake, really, that Didi steals from the Rainiers. A kind of revenge for the way Wanda pushes Mimi around also.

It's now almost lunchtime, and she's only gotten three of the bathrooms done so far. She plods into the family room, which has an attached "commode." Nobody ever seems to use the family room, despite the gigantic Sony TV hogging an entire wall and six-foot-tall stereo speakers. The Rainiers don't seem to spend a lot of quality time with each other.

As she heads to the commode, a statuette on a small table catches her eye. A shepherdess made of china and painted the colors of Necco Wafers. It must be valuable because it's so prominently displayed.

Didi picks it up. Could she hide it inside her waistband? It's roomy enough, but the figurine has got sharp points.

As she's trying to decide, she hears someone coming. She starts to put the shepherdess back, but she's too late. The blond son comes in. The smart one, Thomas, from the beach. She stiffens.

He looks at her, those blue eyes that seem half-closed.

"You don't really want that piece of crap, do you?" he says. "Everything in this house is crap."

"I was only looking at it," Didi says.

"Yeah, sure." He unclasps a very thin silver bracelet from his wrist. It's one of about six he's wearing, some made of leather or twisted string. He holds the bracelet out to her. "This is worth taking," he says.

Her mind races. Is he trying to set her up? The second she reaches for it, he'll start hollering that he's caught a thief?

"Really," he says in a softer voice. "You should have something nice."

Charity for the maid. Her face burns hot as a stove. "I wasn't taking anything. I was simply admiring this ceramic statue." She says it in her new Christina voice, the refined, whispering one she's been practicing.

"Listen," he says. "My mother's on the warpath, she's going to fire your mom today. So you might as well have something before you go." He jams it into her hand. "Cheers," he says and leaves the room.

Didi gazes at the bracelet. It's monogrammed inside. *TLR*. Like all the old Blackworth silverware and plates: they've got fancy *B* monograms. She fits the bracelet around her wrist and snaps the clasp. It's like mercury in a thermometer, silvery and flowing.

It's the most beautiful thing she's ever had.

ᔐ

Only another fifteen minutes now before quitting time. Didi's finished all the grout in the downstairs bathrooms and two of the upstairs and is working on a third. The scouring powder has made her hands itchy and red, but there's that liquid silver bracelet wrapping itself around her wrist and making up for all that.

She hears an angry voice coming from outside. She peeks out the window. On the patio below, Mrs. Gayle Rainier, who's very blonde and bony, is reaming out Wanda. Wanda is cringing like a whipped dog.

Maybe the smart son, Thomas, isn't so smart after all. It's Wanda who's getting fired.

She loves watching Wanda get what she deserves. Didi goes back to her scrubbing with renewed vigor.

At a little after five o'clock, she gathers up the cleaning items and heads downstairs to the laundry room. She hears sobbing. Suddenly, every organ inside Didi feels under attack. She proceeds slowly into the room. Mimi's leaning on the sink, sobbing, on the edge of hysterics. "Wanda fired me. She says I've been stealing. She called me a dirty, sneaking thief. Oh, I never should have, I'm awful, terrible."

"What did she say you stole, Mimi?" Didi asks warily.

Mimi shakes her head. "Once she saw me put something in my purse. She told me she let it slide because she felt sorry for me."

"You're not a thief. If you've ever taken anything, it's because nobody wanted it. Just junk."

"I should never have taken anything. Wanda said I deserve this, and she's right. She's not even paying me for today."

"That's not fair," Didi says vehemently. Mimi's really on the edge of hysteria, so Didi calms her voice. "This was a lousy job anyway. You're way too good for it. And you know what? I think now you're available, Christina will want you on Saturday too."

Mimi looks up forlornly. "Do you think so?"

"I'm positive. Wait here. I'll go get the car and bring it around front."

Didi isn't actually sure what she's going to do. Maybe find Wanda. Confess. Tell her she's the one who's been taking valuable things and get Mimi off the hook.

Screw that.

What she wants is to make Wanda suffer some more. She pictures bashing Wanda's head in with something heavy. Or stabbing her with a knife.

A sharp blade into the side of his neck, that was all it took, so easy, all that blood gushing out . . .

She doesn't want to think about that.

She storms into the kitchen, but Wanda's not there. Didi collects herself. She'd have no justifiable excuse to kill Wanda. She'd get arrested and sentenced to jail or a lunatic ward for the rest of her life, and what would happen to Mimi then?

A gallon bottle of Hawaiian Punch Fruit Juicy Red sits on the counter. Mimi says Wanda drinks it all day long, the way some people drink coffee or booze. It's freshly opened. Didi considers dumping it out just to cause Wanda a little grief, but no, that's not good enough.

Then Didi has an amazing idea. She bolts outside and races to Mimi's Fiesta. Pops the trunk. Takes out the trash bag filled with Bev Padrillo's expired prescriptions. In the car, she crushes pills from a bunch of random vials and dumps them into one of the empties.

She heads back into the Rainiers' kitchen. Her heart is pounding so hard she sees purple spots in her eyes. She pours the powder into Wanda's Hawaiian Punch. Screws the cap on tight. Shakes it up.

Then she goes back outside to pull the Fiesta around and bring poor Mimi home.

CHAPTER EIGHTEEN

AVA

I came downstairs early the following morning and found Sarah in the kitchen, feeding Betsy. "Any news?" I said. She shook her head.

Jamie was still missing. Vanished. A fresh wave of anguish washed over me.

I made coffee by rote in the dented percolator.

"Did I wake you last night?" Sarah said. "I stepped outside for some air but came back in when the dog started to bark."

"I saw you," I said. "I tried calling out to you, but you didn't hear me. Would you like some coffee?"

"No. I'll make myself some tea in a moment." She sat down at the table. "Could I ask you something, Ava?"

"Of course."

"Have you ever considered suicide?"

I looked at her with a fearful start. "Why are you asking that?"

Tears welled in her eyes, enhancing their dark beauty. "Last night, when I thought that if it turns out to be bad news . . . I mean, if James is dead . . ." She raised her eyes to me. "I don't know."

I felt another spasm of dread. I switched the percolator on, then sat down opposite her. "After my mother died, I took some heavy sedatives that someone had given me. But I just wanted to stop the pain I was feeling, not to die. At least, I don't think so. I wanted to live but just not to feel anything for a while."

"You've always had people to live for. If I lost James, I'd have no one left to care about me."

"He's all I have left too," I said.

She looked at me in a shyly tentative sort of way. "Well, maybe . . . I mean, we're sisters by marriage now. Maybe we could care about each other."

I hesitated, just a split second. "I'd like that."

I would, I realized. A sister-in-law. Someone I might grow close to in time. We would share the good news, or the bad.

I couldn't think about the bad right now. I'd go out of my mind.

Sarah stood up. "I need to keep busy. You've got a blender. Would you like a smoothie? I make very creative ones."

"It makes an excruciating noise. Like cats in hell, my father used to say."

"I don't mind." She opened the fridge and began to rummage through the shelves. "James never talks about his father," she said.

"We were scared of him when we were kids. He could get viciously mad in an instant and strike out at us."

"He hit you?"

"Yes. Sometimes."

"Are you still scared of him?" she asked.

"I don't know. I haven't seen him since I was thirteen and haven't talked to him in a few years. But I'm just afraid . . . I mean, what if Jamie did find him? And they had a confrontation? And my father got crazy mad and had some sort of weapon . . . ?" Sarah was looking at me in alarm, and I paused. "It's absurd. I shouldn't be imagining things like this."

I turned as Franny came loping in through the mudroom. "Hey, Ava."

Sarah stepped toward her. "I'm sorry, I didn't introduce myself properly last night. I'm James's wife, Sarah Holland. Ava's sister-in-law."

Franny shot a look at me.

"It's true, Franny," I acknowledged. "Sarah and Jamie got married last month. And we've had some terrible news. Jamie's missing. Nobody's heard from him in four days."

"He's run off?" Franny said.

"Maybe he has," Sarah said in a strained voice. "We don't know." She turned back to the refrigerator shelves. "Just cow's milk? I've been trying to go vegan."

"I don't do the marketing." Franny headed abruptly into the laundry room.

I stared after her, perplexed. "I'm sorry," I said to Sarah. "I'll talk to her. And I'll order anything you want from one of the markets."

"Please don't say anything to her. Or worry about me. I can always make do." She was taking out fresh and wilted fruits and vegetables and now grabbed a bag of raw pistachios. She began chopping the produce and feeding chunks into the blender, wincing at the hellish racket. The pistachios went in and then milk. She poured tall glasses.

I tasted it. "It reminds me of Mom. She used to go on purges, getting rid of toxins in her body. She'd make shakes like this."

"James is not a healthy eater," Sarah murmured. "I don't force him to be, but I worry sometimes." She made a face. "A stupid thing to say right now. And I'm too on edge to drink this." She set her glass down. "I'm going to call the investigator. It's too early, but I'll leave a message."

I had no appetite either. I forced another gulp, then went into the laundry room. Franny had one of Mom's linen shirts on the ironing board and was delicately working the iron. "I rinsed some of these things out in cool water and dish soap and some lavender. They're gonna smell like a garden."

"Why were you so rude to Sarah?" I said.

"I don't trust her. She just showed up here with a suitcase like she owns the place."

"She's married to Jamie and she's my sister-in-law, so she's entitled to be here. And we're both scared to death about him. Can't you understand that?"

"Yeah." She made small dabs at a pleat with the iron. "She sure asked a lot of questions last night. A lot about your mom. Like, did I know her, and was I around when she got sick, and stuff like that."

"Because she's scared about what might have happened to Jamie. If he's coming down with the same thing, it could have caused him to have an accident."

"You think that's true?" she said.

"I hope not."

"Where's she staying?"

"Here, of course. In Mom and Dad's old room."

Franny's face hardened. "You let her?"

"Yeah, I put her there. What's your problem, Franny?"

"No problem," she said.

I felt like firing her on the spot. "I hope there isn't. We all need to get through this together."

She held the shirt up and sniffed it. She said, "I hope Jamie comes back real soon, Ava."

"So do I," I said. "Oh God, so do I."

I spent a long and dreadful morning on the phone in my studio, calling and messaging more people. Grace, who was thunderstruck and offered to contact every graduate of our old academy. Darsh at the hospital, equally stunned. "I'll spread the word in case anyone missed the police report. Or sometimes there's a delay in identification."

"Of a body, you mean." I barely got out the words.

"Well, yes. Or a patient who's unconscious and is without an ID."

I emailed an old girlfriend of Jamie's. She hadn't seen him in a couple of years. I texted Noah. During our brief marriage, he and Jamie had always hit it off well. But he hadn't heard from him since we'd split up.

After a few hours, we began to get contacted by reporters. They'd sniffed out clickbait. Professor whose subject is kinky sex and psychos, now gone missing. Sarah embraced the attention, gave interviews with impassioned pleas to get out search teams, and I passed the calls I got on to her.

I texted Thomas. Asked him to get in touch with any of their old crowd.

He called. "Jesus, of course. I'll do anything I can. But that old crowd, it was always Jamie's, not mine."

"Yeah," I said. "You never seemed completely part of them."

"Hey, are you okay? You sound ready to cry."

"I am. But I can't allow myself to, I've got to keep calling people." I suddenly, desperately, wanted to see Thomas, but he was back up in San Jose and I couldn't leave here now.

We hung up. A huge sob welled up in me and came out in a great burst.

"Knock, knock." Michael Fiore appeared at my door. I struggled back into control. "I heard all the news, Ava. Franny told me. And I just met the wife. Pretty gal. Has a nice way about her."

"Yes," I agreed.

"She says James went looking for your dad up in the Santa Cruz. That covers a lot of area."

"Yeah, it does." My stomach knotted tightly. "The police are ready to send search parties if they have any more specific information."

Michael wiped his hands on his T-shirt—orange, with a leering rat smoking a joint. "I never liked to say anything, Ava, but your dad always was an SOB. I used to see him around a lot after you and James went away, and he didn't change."

"Do you know where he lives?" I said with sudden hope.

"No. I used to run into him at this lounge, Fosca's, up in Monterey. He was a regular there. He'd always be drunk or halfway to it. He talked a lot about how by rights he should've had this place, and how he had big plans to get it back. He was pretty bitter about you and James. He said things no father should ever say about their kids."

"Do you think I could still find him there?"

"Nah, Fosca's shut down maybe a year or two ago. Last time I saw your dad there was sometime before that. I remember he'd picked up some barfly and then later they were both gone. Maybe they left together. After that, I had to quit the booze on account of my liver, so no more bars for me. But I think I've seen him in town once or twice since then."

"Do you know who the woman was he left with?"

"Didn't really notice." He squinched his eyes. "But I've been thinking. Maybe he's the one who's been sneaking in here sometimes. Could be he still has keys."

"I've thought of that too," I said.

"You were smart to change the locks. Tell you what. I'll get some of my gang out driving around the hills. Maybe they can hunt up some sign of your brother. It's a long shot. But keep good thoughts, Ava."

He retreated. I seized on what he'd said about Dad. The woman he'd left the bar with—maybe I could somehow track her down. A barfly. That wasn't Dad's style. But after all these years, who could say what his style was? And if she'd been young, that would've been enough for Dad.

I thought of his phone number on the back of Mom's sketch. The girl who'd given the sketch to Sarah. Didi Morrison.

Sarah's description of her. Overweight. Weird. With a connection somehow to Dad.

My thoughts raced. My memory of the heavyset girl dancing in Mom's studio to "Jumpin' Jack Flash." A girl working here to help out her mom with the cleaning. Not pretty. But young—just out of high school.

She wouldn't have escaped Dad's notice. Another thought came to me: What if she was the girl Dad had given the sketch to?

The same girl as Sarah's stalker? Could that be true?

Even if she was, what did that mean for Jamie's disappearance? I was grasping at straws. But in my panic, a straw was better than nothing.

"Tell me more about that girl, Didi, who stalked you," I said to Sarah.

It was later in the afternoon. We had come down to the beach below the house. I'd been going half-insane from lack of sleep and loss of appetite and sheer terror and needed a respite, and I'd suggested to Sarah that she could use one too. The tide was low. I'd waded a little in the warm tidal pools, other worlds populated with sea stars and meat-eating anemones and barnacles like tiny volcanoes; but then the surf rose, and I climbed up to join Sarah on a lichen-covered crag.

"Why do you want to know about her?" Sarah's face, peeking out from beneath a wide-brimmed sun hat, looked tiny. Almost elfin.

"There was a girl who worked here just before Mom died. She was helping out her mother, who cleaned for us. I was thinking what if it was Didi? And that's how she knew my father."

"Her mother was a cleaning lady. She was ashamed of it."

I glanced at her eagerly. "Then I'm right, it has to be the same girl."

Sarah weighed this. "She hated the rich people her mother worked for. She said they treated her like dirt. That doesn't seem like your family."

"No, Mom treated everybody like they were special. It was just a wild thought. I'm having a lot of wild thoughts right now."

"Me too. I've been imagining all sorts of frightening things." Tucking up her hat brim, she gazed out at the water. "The ocean has always frightened me. It's so enormous and unfeeling. It doesn't care if you live or you die. You can drown in it or sit on a rock and scream at it, and it doesn't care one bit."

"Mom called it her life force. She said if she ever stayed away too long from the ocean, she would simply fade away."

"I used to go sailing a lot with Gideon before he got too sick. Sometimes it was lovely, but if there was any kind of rough weather, I was terrified. But James likes to sail, doesn't he?"

I gave a smile. "We used to race single-mast boats on San Francisco Bay. It was freezing cold. My teeth would literally chatter. Once he capsized us, I think on purpose. We both came down with the flu."

She gave a frightened kind of laugh. "You know this morning, when I asked you about suicide?" she said.

My stomach tightened. "Yeah?"

"It wasn't really about me. I was thinking about James. Because he seemed to be getting the symptoms your mother did. And I thought, What if he knew he was getting the same thing and couldn't stand it? And did something terrible to himself?"

My entire body shivered with dread. "You mean kill himself?"

She gave a despondent shrug. "There's a genetic component to suicide, you know. It runs in families. So if you're right, and your mother did die from poison . . . what if maybe she took it herself?"

"No, it's not possible!" I said fiercely. "My mother did not want to die. Neither does Jamie. It would never, ever be something either one of them would do."

"Oh, Ava, I'm sorry. I shouldn't ever have said that. Forgive me, please. It was stupid."

"No, you were being honest with me. We're both having horrible thoughts. All this waiting." I jumped off the crag. "Let's go back up."

She rose quickly. "Yes. Maybe someone's trying to reach us. Maybe even James."

The probability was dwindling. No one had seen him. No one had heard from him. He'd simply faded away.

I began to walk back up the wooden stairs, Sarah following. I saw a figure appear on the lawn. My heart leaped wildly. Jamie! He had come after all. He waved at me, and I scrambled up the remaining steps and onto the grass.

It wasn't Jamie. It was Thomas. "What are you doing here?" I blurted out.

"I thought you might want me to come."

"What about the hill that was in danger of sliding?"

"We got it shored up in time. My team is putting in stronger foundations."

His eyes were caught by Sarah stepping off the top step of the stairs. He gave a violent start.

He knows her, I thought.

He quickly recovered. "You must be Jamie's wife. I'm Thomas Rainier. Jamie and I were kids together."

"I know, he's mentioned you." Sarah's face, beneath her wide hat, was very pale in the glittering light. "You'll have to excuse me, I can't be very social right now. I've got a thousand things to do."

"Sure," Thomas said.

She continued into the house.

"You looked like you recognized her," I said.

"I did. I knew her first husband, Gideon Ellingham. He hired me to design a small museum for his private collection. I ran into him with her at a benefit. She was gorgeous, young, and didn't speak a word. The next day, Ellingham canceled my contract."

"Did Sarah have something to do with that?"

"I doubt it. Clients like Ellingham change their minds all the time. Money gives them the privilege." He stepped closer to me. "How are you holding up?"

"As best as I can," I said. "Which isn't very well."

"Come back to my place with me. It will be better than staying here. I've got to get back to the office, but everyone there will take care of you. You won't have to worry about meals or anything else."

"I can't leave Sarah alone."

"Bring her with you. And your dog and cat too."

"She wouldn't go. She's got some hope that Jamie might show up here. And maybe I do too."

He looked at me intently. "Hey, I'm sorry I had to leave so abruptly last night. It really was an emergency. There was a family living in that house. I can come back here tonight if you want."

I did. I had a desperate desire to cling to him, as if that would make all this disappear like a terrible dream. Some movement made me glance up at the house, and for one wild moment, I pictured my family gathered there together, a happy, enchanted family that we never were. It made my knees start to buckle. *Jamie, come back. Please, please come back.*

"Hey," Thomas said, taking my shoulders.

Suddenly a darkness seemed to hover around me, crowding out everything, even him. "No," I said. "I can't ask you to come tonight. It wouldn't be fair to Sarah. We need to be alone with each other right now."

That remote look passed briefly over his face. "Okay, sure. No worries. I'll take off."

He turned and began walking away with that attitude I used to find so glamorous at thirteen. Now I saw it for what it was: a shield against rejection. Neglect. All the misery of his youth.

"Thomas!" I ran after him, grabbed his arm. "Don't give up on me. Please."

He gazed at me a long moment. "Okay," he said. Then kept on walking.

CHAPTER NINETEEN

SARAH

I had automatically started to wave.

On the stairs, coming up from the beach, I saw him appear on the lawn. Raising a hand in greeting. Recognizing me. And I'd begun to wave back, but then caught myself. He wasn't motioning to me. It was to Ava.

I'm such a nervous wreck.

I'd gone straight back to my rooms, and five minutes later I heard Franny Fiore out in the hall, busying herself with the linen closet. She's been making it a point to stick as close to me as she can. She suspects me of being up to no good.

I wonder if Ava suspects me of something. Of being at fault somehow for James's disappearance.

She's finally figured out that Didi used to work here. I should have told her from the start, of how ashamed Didi used to be about her mother being a maid. Ava would have started putting things together immediately. But I dreaded making her more upset than she already was. And I so much want her to accept me as a sister.

I think now of Didi toiling away here. A char lady. Mopping. Dusting. Scrubbing on hands and knees. Though nobody scrubs on hands and knees anymore. At least I don't think so.

She'll be coming back here. I know that. She won't be able to keep away.

And when she comes, I'll be ready for her.

Franny's right outside the door again, so I retreat into the sitting room. I sit at the old rolltop desk. It's got initials carved all over it. Generations of bored Blackworth schoolkids. I imagine them from their initials. Louisa Catherine Blackworth: snotty, with ringlets. Nathan Quincy Blackworth III: a fancy-dressed kid bullied by his schoolmates.

This room looks out at the dark cedar forest, and it's become the view I prefer during the day. The sea light in the bedroom is too sharp, too revealing. I like to have some soft shadows on my face.

My heart jumps at every new call and message. But there's been a lull now, and that's the worst of all.

I get up, pace restlessly. Pause before the painting hung above the rolltop. One of Christina Blackworth Holland's. It's unfinished, which gives it a kind of modernist deconstructed look. I can make out the outline of a cat on its haunches, more like the ghost of a cat. A crumpled old pack of Virginia Slims. And a piece of broken sculpture. A section of a carved white face—part of a forehead, some curly locks of hair.

It gives me the shivers.

My text tone sounds, my heart jumps. From Lenore. Wanting to know my immediate plans.

I text her back. Go ahead and cancel the lease on the new house.

She replies: You understand you'll lose first and last month and security?

Yes. It's fine. I hit send. Then text her again. Are the trustees at the town house now?

Two of them. Also an appraiser and Mrs. DiLorenzo and Mr. Austin Ellingham.

Two of Gideon's vulture children, Samantha and Austin. Taking advantage of my absence to mark everything that's to remain in the town house when I leave for good. The vultures are taking no chance that I waltz off with a single fork that's rightfully theirs. Though they are generously allowing me an extra week to remove myself, due to my unfortunate events.

To hell with their pathetic generosity. My movers are arriving there tomorrow. Lenore herself will oversee their packing. Not out of generosity. At her usual rate of $1,500 an hour.

A soft knock at the door. Ava. "Come in," I call.

"Anything?" she asks.

"More of the same. Forest rangers on the alert. Missing posters are up in visitor centers. I've got another TV interview in an hour. Oh, and the college is offering a fifty-thousand-dollar reward. I told them I'd double it."

"I'll add to it too. Are you hungry? Friends just sent us takeout. Greek. Grape leaves, tomato fritters. Baklava. It looks very good."

"I don't think I can eat." I add, "The man who was here before? Thomas? Is he still here?"

"No, he left. He said he met you with your first husband once."

"Possibly," I say. "There were so many people in Gideon's orbit always seeking his attention, but they meant nothing to me."

Ava's phone pings. Like me, she jumps at the sound. She glances at it. Her face goes ashen: she slams the phone to the floor and shrieks, "Fuck you! Goddamn you to hell!"

"What?" I say, with great alarm.

"An e-card. It says it's from Mom. From Christina Blackworth Holland."

CHAPTER TWENTY

AVA

Sarah picked up the phone I'd hurled to the floor. "Maybe you should open the card." She handed it back to me.

I took it, my hand shaking. "I can't."

"I think you should, Ava," Sarah says. "It could tell us something."

Breathing hard, I tapped the link. The e-card cover blinked onto the screen. A wreath of roses on a door. A swell of Vivaldi, the door opened, and a white cat stepped out. The wreath fell and settled around its neck. The cat spoke in a cartoon voice: "To a very special daughter named Ava. Have the best day ever."

Then a signature:

My sweet love, Ava. For all eternity, Mom.

It felt like a punch to my heart.

"May I see?" Sarah said.

I gave her the phone, and she replayed it. "It's so cruel," she whispered. She tapped the email address. "It says you can't send return mail. We can't even find out who sent it. Do you have any idea who it might be?"

"Somebody who knew a lot about us back then. We had a white cat. And Mom sometimes played Vivaldi while she painted. *The Four Seasons*." I was trembling head to toe. "Somebody who knew she called Jamie and me 'sweet love.'"

"Your father would know that," Sarah said.

"Yeah, he would," I said. I told her about the sympathy card signed "Cinderella." And the Cinderella doll on the kitchen table.

"Oh, Ava," Sarah breathed. "That's so scary. If it is your father, then he's a scary guy. Send that e-card to me, and I'll forward it to the investigator."

I did. And also sent it on to Margaret Zhao. She responded quickly. In my office. Come now if you can.

Her consulting office was in a homey-looking professional building in the area known as Outer Monterey. A cubicle-size space containing bare necessities. IKEA desk and chair. Two folding chairs for visitors. File cabinet, large wire rack littered with papers. Pinned to a corkboard was a printout of the missing poster with Jamie's photo on it. Horn-rims. Professorial smile.

"It doesn't look like him," I said to Margaret. "He looks so stiff and formal, and that's not Jamie. If somebody did see him, they might not even recognize him."

"If you've got better pictures, get them out there. Saturate the internet." Margaret pursed her mouth. It was a kind of punctuation. "I heard about your sister-in-law from Grace. You should have brought her."

"She's got an interview with a local news show. She's been handling the media. She's good at it."

"I'd like to meet her sometime." Margaret turned to her computer, tapped the keyboard. I heard the piping Vivaldi of the e-card. "So . . . you've got a hater. Whether it's got anything to do with your brother's disappearance, I can't say. But suspect number one, your father." She flipped open a folder. "I'm still coming up short on his whereabouts. No death certificate, so he's still alive. A California driver's license that will expire end of next year. The address on the license is an apartment in Pacific Grove that's now leased to someone else. No arrest records or recent citations. His credit is good, but a little strange. Just one Visa card, rarely used. I'm thinking he's living with somebody who's footing the bills."

"I wouldn't be surprised. He was good at getting women to support him. For a while, anyway, until he got abusive."

She glanced again at the e-card on the screen. "Any other ideas about who might have sent this? What about your ex? Did he like practical jokes?"

"Noah? No. He wasn't that kind of person."

"Did you get anything in the divorce he might've thought should have gone to him?"

A Tizio lamp. I suppressed a hysterical laugh. "Nothing of any real value, and besides, he makes a fortune. And I don't think I ever told him Mom used to call me 'sweet love.'"

"But your father would know that."

"Yes," I said.

"Your sister-in-law told the police James was going to try to find his place. You have any details not in the report?"

"Not about my father. But Jamie had a fight with Sarah the night before he left for the conference."

"Yes, that was in the report. About money. Typical."

"Partly about money." I took Mom's sketch from my tote and gave it to her. "Also about this. Jamie found it in an old textbook of Sarah's. My mother drew it when I was about thirteen."

Margaret studied it. "She was good. She caught a lot about you here."

"Sarah said a girl from high school named Didi Morrison gave it to her. It was at Monterey Bay Regional. Sarah said she stalked her and gave her presents. And then pushed her off a cliff and nearly killed her."

Margaret lifted her brows.

"Jamie accused her of making it all up. He got furious about that and then about other things. Like about her spending so much."

"Do you think he's left her for good?"

I sighed. "I don't know. I met up with him the next morning, on his way to the conference, and he said he wasn't sure. There's a phone number on the back of the sketch."

Margaret turned it over. "It's local."

"It's an old number of Dad's. His landline after he and Mom separated. It's disconnected now."

"Did your sister-in-law know him?"

"No, Sarah said she didn't even know the number was there. But I've been thinking that Didi Morrison used to work for us just before Mom died. Helping out her mother, who was our housekeeper."

Margaret jotted the name. Snapped a photo of the drawing, front and back. "What was the mother's name?"

"I can't remember exactly. Marion. Or Miriam."

"Okay. Another one to track down." She flipped a few pages in the folder. "There are a couple of things I *have* found out. That Nembutal bottle you've got? The prescription was for a Beverly Padrillo, now deceased."

"Yes," I said. "I looked her up."

"No money to leave anybody. No suspicion of foul play. Also, I dug up the file on the other poisoning case I mentioned to you."

"Yeah?"

"It was more specifically what's called a combined drug intoxication. A housekeeper for a family on 17-Mile Drive ingested a seemingly random combination of prescription drugs. Vicodin, nitroglycerin, and a chemotherapy drug called Cytoxan. She didn't have cancer or heart problems, and she denied taking the drugs. They pumped her stomach, and she was okay."

I was suddenly on edge. "What was the family's name?"

"Rainier. There was a son who was a person of interest, but there was no evidence, and nothing came of it. The family hushed up the whole thing."

"I know the family. There's a son named Rory who was into drugs."

"No, that wasn't the name." She checked the page in the folder. "Thomas."

I felt a deep chill. "Why was he suspected?"

"The usual reasons. Rich kid, sense of privilege. Maybe felt like doing some mischief. Who the heck knows? He's an architect now. He designed Grace's house. Small world."

"Yes," I said. "What was the housekeeper's name? The one who was poisoned?"

She checked the file. "Wanda Bautista. Do you know her?"

"No. But I'd like to talk to her."

"She went back to the Philippines. The Rainiers probably paid her a bundle to go away." Margaret closed the folder.

My text pinged. I glanced with mixed hope and trepidation. One of Jamie's friends looking for an update. I had none to give. I felt a surge of despondency.

"Hey, don't lose hope," Margaret said. "People get lost in those hills, but they also get found. You'd be amazed how many folks are tramping around up there. Hikers, campers. Homeless with cell phones."

I nodded.

"I'll keep working on your dad. I'll find him sooner or later. And you keep the heat on the police and media."

I returned home with a bleakness that matched the blight-stricken pines drooping at the front porch. *He's not dead,* I told myself.

As long as he was just missing, Jamie wasn't dead.

But he wasn't alive either. Like the cat in the physics meme. Schrödinger's cat. Neither alive nor dead until you looked in the box.

I heard Franny talking on her phone in a distant room, echoes of her flat voice muddling with other echoes in the otherwise silent house. I moved heavily toward the stairs. So many echoes. The past colliding with the present.

I froze at the foot of the stairs.

That shadow. I seemed to see it again. That glimpse of ghostly Cinderella, the night I'd found Mom.

Cinderella wasn't done with us yet.

Superstitious crap. Dad's voice, echoing from the past.

I continued up the stairs. My thoughts turned to Thomas. A suspect in a drug poisoning around the same time Mom died.

He had not asked me to sell our property, but I was sure he wanted it. The intimately personal nature of those prank cards—he'd been around our family a lot back then; he'd know what I was most vulnerable to.

What if he was behind it all? Not just the pranks, but Jamie's disappearance as well?

Ridiculous. It couldn't be. I refused to even think about it.

I continued to my studio. I began searching my files for a better picture of Jamie, found one from a couple of years ago that I loved. He wore a T-shirt with a Nirvana logo. His hair was ruffled, his face split in a grin.

I posted it on hiking sites and birder sites and on the websites of a dozen tourist boards, and I made an eye-catching GIF and posted that all over social media. I wrote: "My brother is missing. His name is James Holland. Please help me find him."

And in huge letters, wrote: "$150,000 REWARD."

If nothing else, I thought, that should lure Dad into sight.

DIDI

She's cleaning the claw-foot bathtub in Christina's bathroom, on her knees, scrubbing stains in the porcelain with a powder Christina orders from some old hippy place up in Mendocino. It's all-natural and smells like rotten oranges. It seems to have no effect on the stains, no matter how much elbow grease Didi applies.

She hears Christina wafting into her bedroom. Didi turns on the tap and splashes off the orange powder. Christina appears behind her. She smells like wildflowers and clover on a spring prairie. Not that Didi has been on any prairies ever, but she's just memorized a new Emily Dickinson: "To make a prairie it takes a clover and one bee . . ."

"I don't think these stains are going to come out," she says. "I've been scrubbing them pretty hard."

"Oh, but they shouldn't come out," Christina says. "They're part of this old bathtub now. And a gorgeous part, don't you think so, Didi?"

Didi nods. "Yes, I do. I really do."

"Let's go out and scavenge." Christina's smile, so captivating. "You could do with some fresh air."

Scavenging means searching for unusual objects that Christina can use in her still life paintings. The last time, they'd gone far into the cedar forest, and Didi had scored a triumph. A dead cricket enmeshed in a spider's web. Christina had praised it lavishly. "It's like a tiny mummy embalmed in gossamer thread. Well done, Didi."

Didi jumps up, starts to dry her hands on her shirtsleeves, but thinks better of it and waves them in the air like a symphony conductor. She trots downstairs and follows Christina into the mudroom. It's littered with boots, caps and hats, snorkeling and tennis and rugby stuff, jackets and pails and Easter baskets. Christina puts on a sun hat and selects two large burlap bags, then gives one to Didi.

Didi makes a mental note to get herself a droopy straw hat.

They step outside, and the ocean claims Christina's attention. "Look at that dancing light on the water. And listen to the surf breathing in and breathing out. It's so life affirming. I could never live away from the ocean, Didi. I'd just shrivel up and blow away in the wind."

Didi doesn't know how to swim. The ocean to her is life threatening. But when Christina brings her here to live, she'll overcome that. The ocean will be life affirming for her too.

"Are we going back into the forest?" she asks.

"No, to the sculpture garden. I want to find something anatomical."

It's that weird hexagonal yard filled with gravel and covered with white plaster shards. There's a sweep of small steps over the low wall, but Christina ignores them and steps through a part of the wall that's collapsed. Didi does the same.

She gazes around in awe. Those old dry fountains and all the broken bits on the ground—like some giant kid had a real shit fit and broke a huge set of china. Parts of some of the statues are still attached by rods to their bases, though they're also leaning and crooked. Didi loves one that's just part of a muscular leg and a hand holding a trident. It's Poseidon. She's sure of it.

"Why do you call it a garden?" she asks.

"I don't really know, Didi," Christina says. "We just always did. Imagine, though, when it was brand new. It would be the first thing you saw when you drove down from the road. The fountains would be spouting high, and the sculptures would stand eight feet tall, all white and gleaming."

Weird, Didi thinks. "Why don't you build it back up again?"

"The ruins are beautiful too. Think of the ruins of classical Greek temples and sculptures. We don't want to put those back together again. We cherish them exactly the way they are."

Didi thinks of the Greek word beside her yearbook photo. Τιμωρία. She's dying to tell Christina about it. To tell her what it really means.

She thinks Christina would understand. But she's not totally sure.

Christina has wandered away, and Didi catches up with her. "What are we looking for?"

"Pieces that have recognizable anatomical features." Christina bends down. Picks up a large white fragment. Discards it. "The gravel has shifted a lot over the years, and many of the best pieces are buried underneath."

Didi begins hunting as well. The gravel runs pretty deep, she realizes. Things could be buried a foot down in the rocks and dirt or even a lot deeper. She starts rooting around with the heel of her sneaker. The sun is hot out here where there are no trees.

Her heel strikes something hard. She stoops and digs it out. A part of a head—a segment of forehead, a few tight curls of hair.

"Christina!" she calls. She brings it over to her. "I found this. It's pretty heavy. I think it's actually marble."

Christina examines it. "Yes, it is! Some of the statues *were* made of marble. You have an excellent eye, Didi. And the soul of an artist." She puts the fragment in her burlap bag. But then she's suddenly alert to the sound of a car coming down from the highway.

Kevin Holland's scratched red Mustang convertible appears. The top is up. He's driving. Beside him is a boy with thick light-brown hair. In the back seat, a girl with black braids.

Didi goes rigid.

Kevin toots the horn as he steers around the wall and continues toward the house.

"My kids are back!" Christina thrusts the burlap bag at Didi. "Put this in my studio, would you?" She turns and hurries back through the ruined part of the wall.

Didi remains fixed in place a moment. She's been shuffled off. Like she doesn't count at all.

Like a servant.

She tramps back to the house. There they are, in a tight little family knot out front. Christina with her arms around her two children. James, the boy, all handsome and cocky, despite something strange with one eye. The girl, Ava, who is somehow both ugly and pretty at the same time.

All three are speaking animatedly, and it's only Kevin Holland who gives Didi a glance as she plods around to the service entrance.

In the kitchen, she finds Mimi on her phone. "Hold on a sec," Mimi says into the phone and puts a hand over the mouthpiece. "I'm talking to one of the girls who works for the Rainiers. Wanda is in the hospital. It was touch and go for a while, but she's going to be okay."

"What's wrong with her?" Didi asks.

"They think maybe somebody tried to poison her. It happened the day after we left. The police think it was one of the sons."

"Too bad," Didi says. "But she's going to make it?"

"Yeah, she's out of the woods."

Didi's step is light on the stairs as she heads up to put the burlap bag in Christina's studio. She feels a thrilling new sense of power. She wanted to mess Wanda up, and she seriously did.

And she can do it again, to anyone, anytime.

CHAPTER
TWENTY-ONE
SARAH

I've just finished a radio interview and talked with the police again, barely containing my temper as one cop after another told me for the thousandth time they were doing everything possible.

And Franny Fiore is freaking everywhere. Hammering, sanding. Keeping guard on me. I finally manage to evade her, and the dog, Betsy, as well, slipping out from the sunporch and climbing up into the cedar forest.

It soothes me to be out here. The clean, sharp smell of cedar mingling with decay from the damp floor. The patchwork overhead of white sky and dark trees. Even if I wander off the path into the denser underbrush and shallow ravines, I can't get lost as long as I can hear the sea.

Something catches my eye. A large piece of wood stuck crookedly in the ground. A cross. With an inscription on it, very faded now, but legible. KAHLO BLACKWORTH.

A pet's grave. Probably a cat. There's a small mound with a few stones still scattered on it. And there are other graves. All with the last name of Blackworth.

Christina's family name. Not the dad's last name. Holland. Ava and Jamie's name. And now mine.

I glance up suddenly. Maybe it's being in this spooky little pet cemetery that gives me the sudden feeling that she's here.

Didi.

Haunting me like a dead cat.

I'm mistaken this time. But the next time I'm not, I'll finally make sure she's gone forever.

I return to the house. I'm guessing Ava's in her studio, and she is, at her desk, working on her computer. The black cat crouches among lenses, books, and Magic Markers. It looks at me with glowing yellow eyes, then leaps down and slithers out the door.

"Where have you been?" Ava asks.

"In the woods, walking. I was on the verge of losing it with the police, so I worked off some steam. I found a cat grave out there. At least, I think it was a cat. Kahlo Blackworth."

"One of Mom's cats," Ava says. "She was named after Frida Kahlo."

"Who's that?" I ask.

She looks surprised. "A brilliant Mexican artist." She gives a sad smile. "I remember when we buried Kahlo. Jamie and I were trying not to cry, but we couldn't help ourselves. Mom said that she also wanted to be buried there in the woods, and that made Jamie cry more."

"But she's not, is she?" I say.

Ava gives a startled laugh. "That would be illegal. She's in a very pretty cemetery up in Oakland filled with a lot of our Blackworth ancestors."

I pluck a strand of hair and twist it nervously. "I guess I'm not thinking quite straight."

"Neither am I," Ava says. "I've been sending out photos of Jamie and the reward. I'm getting flooded with replies, people swearing they've seen him in ridiculous places."

I notice a small stack of photos on the desk. "Do you mind if I look at these?"

"They're just work prints, but go ahead."

They're all shots of various rooms in the house. The light is unearthly, and a whitish, unclean-looking haze hovers in the corners. "They're like photos of a haunting," I say. "How did you get this effect?"

For a minute, she looks like she won't answer. Then she murmurs, "Oh, it's a process. I used a slim filter on a twenty-two-millimeter lens and made different exposures. And then played around with the images on Photoshop."

"That glowing in the corners? How did you get that?"

"A halo lamp. Then I layered a long exposure over a shorter one on the computer."

"It gives me the shivers."

Ava raises her too-large, too-wide-spaced eyes to me. "My mother used to say that. It was one of her favorite expressions."

"James says it a lot too," I say. "I must have picked it up from him. I'm sorry. I won't say it anymore."

"You don't have to protect me from memories. That's what I'm trying to get back. All my memories, sad, happy . . ." Another wan smile. "In between."

"Why didn't you take any photos in Cinderella's room?" I ask. "She's the real ghost."

"I haven't been in there since I was thirteen. I guess I'm superstitious about it."

"Do you have the key?"

"It must be somewhere in the bag of keys Michael gave me, but I've never looked."

"Would you mind if I do? I know the story of you and Jamie going there. I'd like to see it. And besides, it's something to do other than just waiting."

She glances at the window. "It's getting dark," she says under her breath. She stands up. "I'll go with you." She takes a rolled-up paper bag out of one of her drawers. It's marked Peninsula Building Supplies.

We head down the back staircase. It's dim and shadowy. Haunty. I give a start as a dark shadow slips past my feet.

That damned black cat.

We go to the kitchen and into the long, narrow butler's pantry, the shelves lined with dusty glasses and decanters, flower vases, serving bowls. That creepy little door at the end. Ava approaches it tentatively. Her breathing is a little quicker.

She grasps the handle. Rattles it. Then she dumps the bag of keys into the rinsing basin and begins trying the smaller keys in the lock. Finally, a click, and she gasps, "This is it."

She pushes the door open a crack. She hesitates.

"Come on." I grasp her hand. We duck through the door and step into a very narrow hallway.

She tries a light switch. "They burned out long ago."

The only illumination is from the butler's pantry behind us. I can vaguely make out two doors across the hallway. There's a hideous damp smell. What I can see of the walls is a kind of coal-like texture. Like being deep in a cave.

Ava is almost rigid. Her breathing is louder. "I still feel like she's in here. I can't help it."

I feel a strange current of air. Colder than the drafts in the rest of the house.

Ava says suddenly, "It's too dark to see anything. Let's get out of here."

She turns sharply and ducks back through the small door. I follow her out through the narrow pantry, and as I pass, something behind me goes crash.

Ava gives a start and whirls. A serving plate has fallen off a shelf and shattered on the floor. Her face goes white.

"I must have brushed by it," I tell her. "Caused it to fall."

We both jump as my phone rings. I look at the screen. Take a sharp breath. "It's the detective in Newport Beach," I say. "The lead investigator."

Spontaneously, we grip each other's hands again. And then I put the phone to my ear.

I whisper, "Hello?"

CHAPTER TWENTY-TWO

AVA

Mom's in a hospital bed, attached to tubes and wires. A machine does her breathing for her. Another one keeps her heart pumping. There's another patient on the other side of the white curtain beside her bed. Mom's eyes open. Amber eyes. Like Jamie's. Like the eyes of a witch. They lock onto mine. Not seeing me. Not knowing me.

Dad hovers behind me. He shouldn't be here. He doesn't belong here. He is going to turn off the machines. I have to stop him before he does.

My eyes shot open. I was in an intensive care unit, but it wasn't Mom's, it was Jamie who was hooked up to the burping, whooshing machines.

And it wasn't Dad standing behind me. It was my sister-in-law, Sarah. She was the one who had the right to pull the plug now. If it came to that. I suppressed an irrational twinge of panic.

"I brought us some fortification." Sarah set down a cardboard caf-eteria tray. Styrofoam cups. Plastic-wrapped pastries. A bear claw, a blueberry muffin. She went close to Jamie and gave his matted hair the gentlest of touches. "Has he woken up?"

"No. They say he won't entirely for a day or more." I moved to the tray. "Do you want the coffee or the tea?"

"I got the tea for myself, but take it if you want."

"No, I'm good with coffee." Small talk. Falsely reassuring. I sipped the coffee, relishing the heat seeping down my throat and the small buzz that followed. I took a few bites of the bear claw, licked sticky sugar off my fingers.

His car had been spotted in the bottom of a ravine by Scouts, two fourteen-year-old girls and a twelve year-old boy. They were volunteer-ing to clear debris from the windy forest road and noticed skid marks. They followed the skidding to the edge of a slope.

Within an hour, a fire department search team had scrabbled down the ravine and found him still in the car, unconscious, but after five days, miraculously alive. The detective who called had told Sarah not to try to get to the accident scene. Jamie was being transported to the ICU at Saint Lawrence Samaritan in Monterey, and we should go directly there.

We shot off. A tense vigil for hours in a waiting room with bland modern furniture. We spoke only intermittently and in monotone. Stopped anyone who seemed in charge. *When can we see him? How bad is he hurt? Why aren't we being told anything?*

Finally, a nurse in scrubs approached us. A concussion. Severe dehy-dration. Ankle broken in three places. Fractured kneecap. Dislocated shoulder and strained ligaments. A horrifying list of excruciating inju-ries, but none life threatening. "We're monitoring him closely for signs of internal bleeding, and he's going to need a lot of rehab, but eventually he should be fine."

He'd be fine. I gave a choke of relief.

"Can we see him now?" Sarah demanded.

"He's in surgery. It could be four or five hours. When he regains consciousness, he'll be in a lot of pain, but we'll try to keep him comfortable."

"Please make sure he doesn't suffer," Sarah said.

"We'll do our best."

We continued waiting, watching the clock hand move slower and slower until it didn't seem to move at all. And then at last, sometime long after midnight, a doctor, an older woman wearing green scrubs and a beautiful smile, told us he was out of surgery, not conscious but resting comfortably. And we were allowed to see him.

The first sight a shock. It seemed truly a miracle he'd survived. His face was swollen black and purple. Surgical dressing on his head and shoulder. One leg elevated and in a thick cast.

Every part of him looked broken.

"It's strange, isn't it?" Sarah murmured now. "James and I have both survived falling from a cliff. It was a shattering point in my life. I wonder if it will be for him."

"He shouldn't have been driving those back mountain roads," I said.

"No, not with his bad eyes. And the strange way he's been acting lately."

A nurse pushing a cart down the ICU halted in front of the room. She told us only one of us could stay any longer.

"I'll be staying," Sarah told her.

"You need to get some rest," I said. "I just took a catnap, so I can stay."

"No." Her face was firm. "I need to be here with him." She turned back to Jamie and bent to him, that gentle touch.

She was his wife, I reminded myself. She came first with him now. It unsettled me, but it was true. "Call me if there's any change," I said.

"Of course I will, Ava. The very second. Depend on it." She gave me a tender look of gratitude. "I'm so glad we've been together."

I felt a burst of warmth toward her. My sister-in-law.

After three days in the ICU, Jamie was moved to a private room. The best in the hospital, light and airy and beautifully appointed, in the most luxurious wing on the top floor. Sarah had seen to that.

She was amazingly adept at dealing with the medical staff and the boggle of hospital procedures. The nurses and orderlies sang her praises, and Jamie's surgeon—a haughty, raven-haired Argentine who traveled with a pack of residents—was impressed by her grasp of medical jargon. She had gifts delivered to sprinkle on all the staff. Gilt-wrapped boxes of handmade chocolates. Scented soaps. Almond croissants and petits fours from a Carmel patisserie.

"I spent a lot of time in hospitals when Gideon was dying of Parkinson's," she explained. "I learned the ropes."

Only later did a thought occur to me. Parkinson's was very debilitating but not in itself fatal. I'd had an uncle who had it—Great-Uncle Jonas—and he lived to ninety-two.

For the rest of the week, Jamie remained on heavy pain meds, drifting in and out of full consciousness. The room filled up with flowers, cards, get-well-soon teddy bears and fruit baskets. He'd always been surrounded by a crowd and still was, even if they weren't there in person. Sarah was a constant presence. If she left the room, it was never for more than five minutes.

He was asleep when I arrived now. I'd brought a shiny bouquet of helium balloons, and Sarah glanced at them with exasperation. "Where are we going to put those?"

I let go of the strings, and the balloons bobbed to the ceiling. "Problem solved."

"We can't have strings dangling into doctors' faces." She seemed on edge. The strain getting to her.

"Okay, then let's keep one and give the rest to the children's ward." I tied a balloon string to the handle of a superfluous cabinet. "I'll take them there when I leave."

"Someone's coming to pick up some of the flowers and baskets to give out. They can take the balloons too."

I saw now that she had divided the gifts into two groups. Give away and keep. I browsed the giveaways, catching up with the names on the cards. One from Thomas: an asymmetrical design of buds and twigs and green leaves set in moss in a wooden slat box. I felt a quick thrill. It reminded me of his buildings: simple, nature based, exquisite. "I think Jamie would like this one," I said. "Let's keep it."

"Fine," Sarah said distractedly. She glanced at Jamie, then said, "Let's go to the lounge for a few minutes. I've been making some plans, and I want to discuss them with you."

We went out to the visitors' lounge off the nurses' station. Luxuriously appointed, like everything on this floor. We took seats in tweedy club chairs.

"I've got some news," she said. "Dr. Marquez told me James will be transferred to the rehab wing in about ten days."

"So soon? He's barely even conscious yet."

"He says the sooner the better. The longer James lingers in bed, the more complications there could be. I've spoken to the director of the rehab facility. She says they'll work him very hard, and he'll need complete rest in between sessions. I won't be allowed to visit him for the first three or four days and only very limited hours after that. I'm not sure you will be at all."

"Not even briefly?" I said.

"Maybe. I'll talk to her about it. But I have to go back to Newport Beach for a few days, so I'll go then. My town house is about to revert to my first husband's kids, and I've got some legal things to do. And the lease on James's house in Laguna is up, so I'll have his stuff put in storage while I'm there."

"That's a lot to do in just a few days."

"My attorney, Lenore Wyatt, has most of it already organized. Almost everything in the town house will remain with the heirs, so it's just my personal things. Most of those I'm having sent beforehand."

"So you've found a new place?"

"That's just it," she said. "We had a house lined up, but it turned out it wasn't suitable."

"Then what are you going to do?"

Her face became animated. "We're going to move in to Blackworth Mansion with you. It's a great idea, don't you think?"

I stared at her in horror. "No," I said. "I don't. Jamie hates the house. He said he never wants to set foot in it again."

"But he doesn't really mean that. I think he actually loves it, the same way you do. He'll realize that once he's back there. And we'll be a family, just like you used to be."

Jamie, back home. For one brief moment, my heart lifted. But then I shook my head violently. "Sarah, think about it. He won't be able to walk very well. The stairs are steep and uneven and badly lit. And the house is cold, sometimes freezing cold, and there's hardly any hot water, and the power is iffy. There aren't even any showers, just old bathtubs with high sides. How could he get in and out of them?"

"I'll hire home help for him. And he'll continue doing physical therapy there. I'll pay for everything, Ava, so don't worry about it."

My eyes widened with dismay. "It's not about the money. It's Jamie I'm worried about. He'd be practically a prisoner there. No, it's a terrible idea, believe me."

"Oh, Ava, I've upset you. I'm sorry. That's the last thing in the world I wanted to do." Sarah rose from her chair. To my astonishment, she sank to her knees in front of me and took both my hands in hers. "I thought you'd be happy about this. Having your brother back home with you."

"I know him very well, Sarah, and in ways I don't think you've discovered yet," I said. "It would be a huge mistake to make him do this."

"But I won't be making him do anything. Believe me, Ava, I would never make James do anything he doesn't want to. I'm going to discuss it with him as soon as he's well enough, and if he hates the idea, of course I won't insist on it." She gave a disarming little laugh. "And besides, I doubt if I could make him do anything he didn't want to. I think I know him that well, at least. He's pretty stubborn."

I withdrew my hands from hers. "He can be," I said. "But he's not his usual self now. I mean, God, Sarah. He's not even always conscious yet."

"But he is more and more. And it will be totally up to him. If he says no, we'll make other arrangements." She stood up. "I'll start looking for other options right away. I'm so sorry I upset you, Ava. I really thought it was a good idea. Please don't be mad at me."

"I'm not," I said. "I'm just trying to make you understand. I think when you talk to him, you'll see that I'm right."

"Yes, you are right, Ava. I'm making too many assumptions. And I will start looking for other places."

Why wasn't I reassured? "Would you do something else for me?" I said. "I'd like to spend a little time alone with my brother. Would you mind?"

"No, of course not! Selfish me, I've been hogging him. You go, and I'll take a stroll around the grounds."

He was still asleep when I got back to the room. I pulled a chair close to his bed. Took out a book from my bag. *Harry Potter and the Prisoner of Azkaban*. His favorite book in middle school. It was still in the bookcase under the eaves of his old bedroom, the cover tattered, the pages creased and stained. I began to read it to him. It was something Mom used to do—read to us even after we had fallen asleep, magical stories from old-fashioned books. "The Tears of Princess Prunella." *The Secret Garden*. So the magic would entwine itself into our dreams, she said.

I'd been reading for ten minutes when I realized his eyes were open. "Hey," I said softly.

"Sarah," he murmured.

I closed the book. "It's me. Ava. Sarah's out taking a walk. She'll be back soon. Do you want me to keep reading *Harry Potter*?"

"I love you," he murmured and then drifted back to sleep.

Who had he said that to? Sarah or me?

To Sarah, of course. His wife.

As it should be.

CHAPTER
TWENTY-THREE

"How much do you even know about this woman?" Grace asked. "I mean, if you think there's something wiggy about her, there probably is."

It was the following night, and I was having dinner with the Greenwalds at their home. Darsh, who prided himself on his cooking, was roasting a wild duck, popping up every ten minutes to turn and baste it. I was drinking the old-fashioned he'd mixed for me. It was delicious and went down easily.

"Maybe it's just me," I said to Grace. "Back in the worst years of my depression, I had delusions. I didn't trust anybody. Sometimes I had the idea that our old ghost, Cinderella, really had put a curse on Jamie and me, and the curse was to set everybody out to hurt us. Crazy stuff."

"Wait, are you saying Sarah's out to get you and Jamie because a ghost curse is making her do it?"

I gave a quick laugh. "No, of course not. I don't know what I mean. And I have no reason to think anything bad of her. She's been very up front with me and told me a lot about her past, even things that aren't very flattering. When I'm with her, I usually feel very warm to her. Like maybe we could become very close."

"And when you're not with her?"

I paused. "It's weird. It's like she seems to slip into the shadows, at least in my mind. Like, I know a lot of things about her, but I still don't know *her*." I shook my head. "I'm doing a lousy job of describing it."

"You mean, she charms you in her presence, but then later you start to realize there's something fishy."

I grinned uneasily. "That's not quite it. It's more like there's something elusive. She's more complicated than she seems."

"Aren't we all?" Grace said. "Just a big old mess of complications and contradictions. But if there's really something bothering you about this woman, Ava, you need to zero in on what exactly it is."

"I can't. It's more of a gut feeling."

She gave a snort. "As a lawyer, I don't consider your gut to be a reliable witness."

"Too bad. It's the only witness I've got."

Darsh came back to us, basting tube still in his hand. "What are you talking about?"

"Ava's mysterious new sister-in-law," Grace said. "Ava, you should get Margaret to run a background check on her. I'll bet she could dig up some real dirt on her."

"I've thought about it," I said. "But don't you think it would be sleazy? I mean, would either of you check up on any of your in-laws?"

"Well, none of my siblings are married, so I don't have any in-laws for Darsh to check up on yet. And his sisters didn't elope with mystery men. They had gigantic weddings that went on for days, and their husbands' families were all present and accounted for down to fifth cousins."

"Not fifth cousins," Darsh said. "Maybe third."

"Okay, third. And besides, none of Darsh's sisters nearly died in a suspicious accident like Jamie."

"There's nothing very suspicious about Jamie's accident. His eyesight sucks, and he was using eye drops that gave him a headache. Sarah's not responsible for that."

"If you ask me, she seems rather remarkable," Darsh said. "I popped into your brother's room this morning after I finished my last surgery, and I spent a little time chatting with her."

"You didn't tell me that," Grace said peevishly.

"Just a few minutes. I was impressed by her grasp of medical concepts."

"Was Jamie awake?" I asked.

"Yes, but he's still on IV analgesics. Hydromorphone, I believe. He was very hazy. I said a few pleasantries to him, and then I left." Darsh reached for a salted radish from a plate of appetizers on the coffee table and crunched it between his teeth.

"Have you been able to talk to him much, Ava?" Grace asked.

"Just a little. When he's awake, it's like Darsh said, he's pretty hazy. We still don't know any real details about what happened." I turned to Darsh. "Would it be possible for you to look at his charts? I want to find out if he's had a tox screen."

"You mean for blood alcohol? Doubt it, because it wouldn't have shown up. Too long a time had elapsed."

"She means other toxins," Grace said. "Like poisons."

"Poisons?" Darsh repeated in a dubious tone.

"Because of her mother. Right, Ava?"

It was what I meant. But why? What would Jamie's accident have to do with Mom's death seventeen years ago?

Dad. It always came back to him. But I wasn't ready to share this with Grace yet. "It's just a wild thought," I said.

"It's damned wild," Darsh said. "But I can give a look at the charts if you want. In fact, you've piqued my curiosity."

"Thanks, Darsh." My text tone sounded. Both Greenwalds looked at me expectantly as I glanced at my phone. I put it down without comment.

Darsh slapped his knees and stood up. "That duck is just about done. Hope you're both hungry."

Grace gave a tiny belch. "Sorry, that's happening more and more. But oh yeah, I'm ready to eat."

❧

The text was a reply to one I'd sent earlier. When I got back in my car after dinner, I sent a short message to Sarah, and then I drove south on Highway 1, but not all the way back to Carmel. I turned off at the Pebble Beach exit. Passed through the guardhouse and continued on 17-Mile Drive nearly to the end. Turned up the well-tended driveway through soldierly rows of cypresses to the large house made of glass and stone.

Thomas was waiting outside for me. He looked ghostly in the mist.

"So, more questions," he said in a wary voice.

"Just one." I approached him hesitantly. The ocean's crash and roar so close.

"It's cold out here," he said. "Come inside."

"No, here," I said. "Your family had a housekeeper who was poisoned around the time Mom died."

His face hardened. "Yes, Wanda. I do remember that. Poisoned with cancer drugs, or something like that. What about it?"

"You were a suspect."

"A person of interest," he said. "The cops desperately wanted to pin it on me. It was absurd. They dropped it after a day." He stepped closer to me. "Are you trying to connect your mother's death to me?"

I hesitated. "I just have to be sure of everything."

"Sure I'm not a murderer." He gave a harsh laugh. "You're obsessed with your mother. You want answers, I get it. Something to believe. But this was just a strange coincidence. Wanda was a tyrant to the rest of the staff. Maids, even butlers, would leave in tears. Any one of them could've played a dirty trick on her."

Obsessed. Maybe I was. Seeing connections to her death everywhere. The prank cards. Jamie's accident. And now Thomas.

"You're shivering like a leaf," he said. "Come on, let's go inside." He came close to me, reached for my hand.

I put my hand in his, felt it close warm around mine. "Jamie's been found, but I feel so suddenly lost," I said. "It's crazy."

"No, it's not crazy. I've felt lost most of my life. Like I told you, we match." He looked at me intently. "You've got to stop thinking all these insane things. I'm not some kind of monster. If you're going to keep thinking I am, this is not going to work."

I was shivering hard, not just from the cold.

"Tell me what you want to do," he said.

I met his eyes. "I want to go to your room. Not the guest bedroom. Your own room."

"Great idea." He put an arm around me and led me into the warm house. We went upstairs to a room that was large, beautifully proportioned, furnished like a monk's cell. And then there was the deliciousness of our naked bodies, making me forget where I stopped and he began, and afterward the comfort of simply lying close together. Not thinking about anything else.

I didn't leave until early the next morning.

CHAPTER
TWENTY-FOUR

SARAH

The head duty nurse lets me stay with James as late as I wish. It's nearly ten o'clock now. I've just received a text from Ava. She's decided to stay the night with her friends the Greenwalds.

I don't believe it. She's with that man Thomas. He frightens me a little, but I don't think he's a real threat to me. It's Ava I worry about.

Why does she feel she has to lie to me? I've done everything humanly possible to earn her affection. What am I doing wrong?

She must be a cold person. Cold and ungiving. She won't trust anybody. But I've got to find some way to make her trust me.

James gives a low groan. He's awake. I hurry over to him.

"Sweetheart." I assist him in sitting up a little. I've requested that lemonade as well as water be always kept by his bedside, and I help him take a few sips of it through a straw. He lies back down, groans again. "Are you in pain, sweetheart?"

"Yeah. It hurts everywhere."

"I'll do something about it." I dart down to the nurses' station and butt into a gossip session. "Excuse me, but my husband's in a great deal of pain. He needs his medication strengthened."

My voice throbs with great distress. One of the nurses—her name is Rosaria, she's fond of me—looks at me sympathetically. "I'll call his doctor. Marquez, isn't it?"

"Yes. Make it quick, please, Rosaria. He's really suffering."

She picks up her phone. "I'm calling him now."

I thank her genuinely from my heart. I return to James's room and soothe him until Rosaria comes in and changes the hydromorphone drip. He relaxes back to sleep. I make a mental note: get something very special for her.

I feel free to leave him now. I drive back to Blackworth Mansion. The house appears dark and gloomy on this moonless night. When I turn the light on in the foyer, it flickers. The electricity is so faulty. It's something Franny Fiore should be attending to instead of spy-dusting outside my bedroom door.

Betsy's overjoyed to see me, and I'm happy to see her too. I take her to the kitchen and reward her with a treat. Even the black cat pokes his nose from the shadows but vanishes the second I turn to him. He still hates me.

I feel spooked, suddenly.

It's the first time I've been alone in the house this late at night. But it's an opportunity I've been waiting for. I just need to steel my mind. Not let it get infected by ghost stories.

I hurry upstairs in the flickering light of that saggy chandelier. So many things need to be attended to. And eventually will be. One thing at a time.

I turn left at the top of the stairs to the north wing and head to Ava's studio. I open the drawer that's got the bag marked Peninsula Building Supplies containing all the house keys. I go through them and find the old iron key to the servants' quarters.

I head back downstairs to the kitchen and turn in to the butler's pantry. I pause, remembering the dish that had shattered right behind me when Ava and I were here.

I had not brushed against it.

I shiver. Ghost stories. The ghost of a murdered girl seeking revenge.

I can understand that. I'm still seeking it myself.

I fit the key in the lock of the spooky little door and step into the narrow corridor. I turn on my phone flashlight and almost gag at the sight of all that gray crud and dust. I continue into the room across the corridor.

Cinderella's room.

That strange icy current twines around me. The nauseating smell of old smoke. I hurriedly shine the flashlight around the room.

I was wrong. What I'm looking for isn't here. There's nothing here at all except two old bed frames and a tiny dresser.

I've got the creeps all over me. I scurry back out and lock the door.

DIDI

Didi nurses the feeling of power she got when Mimi told her about Wanda being in the hospital. She'd turned the tables. Messed up somebody who messed her up first, without anybody finding out.

The Invisible Girl. It's suddenly got new meaning for her. Somebody you don't see coming. And afterward, when you realize you've been screwed, you can't blame it on anybody.

The Invisible Girl is like a ghost. She's there, but you don't notice.

In fact you don't even think she exists.

It was different with Raymond. He had messed her up so much that her life was forever ruined. She had put an end to his. She hadn't cared about being invisible back then.

But the authorities came, and she was taken away from Mimi for months, and then they'd had to move away and start all over again.

But now she's discovered something amazing. How to use being invisible.

How to turn it into power.

"I need the car," she says to Mimi. "I want to go buy something to wear for working."

It's Sunday. Mimi is slumped on the couch staring vacantly at a baseball game, Astros versus Padres, the Astros kicking butt, six to zero. Since she's lost Wanda as her only friend, Mimi's got no one to hang with on Saturday nights and nobody to gossip to all day long Sundays. Also her knee is flaring up. There's been a delay at the free clinic. Christina had said one of the volunteer surgeons was recuperating from a heart attack, so all surgery was backed up.

"Pick me up a couple more pairs of undies," Mimi says. "The polka dots."

"I'm not going to Wal-Mart. I'm going to Tar-jhay." It was the way everyone at school had pronounced Target, like a fancy French bou tique, but in an ironic way. She heads out the door before Mimi starts drilling her on how they've got to watch their money.

She drives to the Target—Tar-jhay—in Sand City. She tries on a baby blue top cropped a couple of inches below her boobs. Jeans that are low rise, but not extra-low. Her stomach bulges in the exposed strip between the top and the jeans, and her belly button winks just above the waistband.

It's a lot like the outfit Sarah Davis had on at Shoehorn Beach. She's heard that Sarah's family moved away to some military base. *It's not fair*, Didi thinks. *We were supposed to be best friends.*

Some dark-red viscosity blinds her eyes a moment. Then it passes. She brings the outfit she's tried on to the register.

Target might not be very expensive but still costs more than Wal-Mart. She's quit spending money on junk food from the Quiki Mart, but the granola and all-natural nonfat yogurt she snacks on now are even more expensive and impossible to shoplift, so this one outfit is all she can afford.

At least she's dropped from size XXL to XL. Still gross compared to the featherlight Christina Blackworth Holland, but it's something.

She wears her new clothes to Christina's the next day—though at the last minute she lost her nerve and covered her bare midriff with an oversized shirt. Christina won't be able to tell she's gone down a size.

If she notices her at all, Didi thinks glumly. She's been there twice now since Ava and James came back. The first time, Christina actually left Blackworth Mansion to drive somewhere with them! Didi was stunned. In her mind, she'd fixed on the idea that Christina couldn't ever leave the grounds of the house, like a princess in a fairy tale under a spell.

The second time, it was only the kids who were gone most of the day. Surfing lessons, riding lessons, some other parent dropped them home, and then they rushed to get ready for another event, a chauffeured car arriving to pick them up. Rich kids were always busy, busy. But that had been a wonderful day, because Didi got Christina again.

"Come up to my studio when you have a minute, Didi," Christina had told her. "I'll show you how I make my pigments."

Didi had quickly found a spare minute and made a beeline to the studio. Music was playing on the turntable. Tingling and mysterious. An old vinyl album, the cover kind of mystical looking, lay beside it. She prefers it when Christina blasts old rock stuff. Sometimes when she does, Didi stops working and boogies out to it.

Christina was busy mashing up a lot of small purple berries with a ceramic mortar and pestle. "So that's going to be paint?" Didi said.

"Eventually, yes. It's the only way I can get the colors I visualize in my mind."

She strained the mashed-up berries through a sieve and added linseed oil to the purple juice, drop by drop, mixing all the while. "This is going to be a legacy shade of purple," she explained. "I love the earthiness of historical pigments. There was a shade in the 1800s called mummy brown. It actually contained the ground-up remains of Egyptian mummies."

Didi had loved that. But she'd said "Ew" because she felt it was expected.

"The color was very popular with the Pre-Raphaelite artists," Christina said. "Are you familiar with them, Didi? Artists like Edward Burne-Jones and Dante Gabriel Rossetti? I have several books I can lend you if you'd like."

Oh my God! Didi had thought Christina looked like the painting on the cover of her *Tess of the d'Urbervilles*, and she'd looked up who the artist was, and it was Dante Gabriel Rossetti!

She and Christina really were connected. Old souls who shared a plethora of passions and thoughts in common. (*Plethora,* a new word for her. From ancient Greek, meaning "full of." You kiss with your lips when you pronounce it.)

She has a big letdown when she and Mimi arrive today.

Christina is busy with window washers. Their faces peer in at every window, upstairs and down. And then a young woman arrives to prepare a fancy lunch with Christina supervising, followed by half a dozen women in casual but expensive clothes, and they have lunch amid the tropical-looking foliage on the sunporch.

They've barely gone when Kevin Holland shows up, bringing back the ugly-pretty Ava from whatever rich-kid activity she's been to. He makes himself right at home. Bossing the window washers from below their scaffolding. Sneaking a shot of scotch, and then another, from a bottle on the bar cart when he thinks no one is looking (Didi was). And following Christina around.

He calls her Daffodil. "You look enchanting today, Daffodil." He leans toward her, and she smiles her dreaming smile.

Didi can hardly believe it. Christina should be spitting in his eye. He's a loser. And a pervert. She already got rid of him once.

Why is she letting him hang around her like this?

Look at him! Didi wants to scream. The trail of slime he leaves behind wherever he goes. She can see it, so why can't Christina?

In the kitchen, Mimi hands Didi a big bowl of garbage. "Take it to the compost, hon." The scraps from the lunch. Veggie parings. Eggshells and coffee grounds. The remains of limp salad greens.

The compost pile is under a tarp on the shady side of the yard. As Didi heads to it, someone calls, "Hello! Hi, wait!"

It's Ava. She's got a fancy camera strung around her neck. "Hi. I'm Ava. What's your name?"

Didi averts her face. "Didi," she mumbles.

"Do you mind if I take your picture?" Ava raises the camera and begins to focus the lens.

"Why?" Didi says.

"I'm learning photography from this gallery that does workshops. And we've been assigned to do, like, candid portraits this week? So is it okay?"

Portrait of a cleaning lady carrying garbage. "I don't want . . . ," Didi starts to say.

But Ava is already snapping away. "Wow, that's great," she says. "Turn this way a little so there's more light on your face."

Didi shades her face with her hand. "I don't want my picture taken."

Ava gets in a few more shots anyway before lowering the camera. "Okay, I won't. Sorry."

Didi suddenly wants a way to sting Ava. "How come your father calls your mother Daffodil?" she says. "It's such a dumb name."

She's gratified to see Ava's face darken. "Because he says she's daffy, which is totally absurd," she says. "It's like a put-down. My mother isn't in the least daffy. She's spiritual and unique."

Ava's not stupid, Didi realizes. She knows her father's a shit. But she's a shit, too, for continuing to take pictures after Didi said to stop. Like she thinks she's entitled to. Didi decides she can't stand her. "I've got to go compost this," she says.

"Oh, okay," Ava says. "See you."

Didi continues to the compost. Christina had showed her the procedure. Mix the garbage with grass cuttings, then bury the mixture ten inches in the muck. She replaces the tarp over it. Pulls off her rubber gloves.

She hears voices from around the other side of the house. Loud, young, male voices, trash-talking each other. The name Rainier hits the air, and she freezes.

She sidles around the corner of the house. It's a boisterous group, James and a bunch of his friends. Among them, and yet somehow looking not quite with them, the smart blond Rainier son, Thomas.

He doesn't belong here, Didi thinks furiously.

She sees Ava sprawled on the grass, her camera by her side. Her huge eyes planted on the Rainier son, like a rabbit transfixed by a cobra.

None of them belong here with Christina in Blackworth Mansion. Not even James and Ava.

They have their father's last name. They're Hollands, not real Blackworths. Young, stupid souls. They think they're entitled, that this all belongs to them, but they're wrong, it doesn't. They've lived no lives before this one. They don't know anything, they're dumb, stupid, and she's invisible to them.

She moves back into the house, almost strangled by the intensity of her emotions. She could kill someone.

And this time, she thinks, why stop at just one?

CHAPTER
TWENTY-FIVE

AVA

Thomas returned to San Jose the following day. I spent the evening with Sarah on the sunporch, watching twilight turn the ocean into opalescence and the sky to fire. I'd brought out a pitcher of frozen daiquiris. "Our family used to gather here on the porch at sunset, drinking these," I told her. "Mom was in charge of making them. Jamie's and mine had no rum, though once he hit thirteen, he began sneaking it into his. Mom knew, I think, but she indulged him shamelessly." I poured the daiquiris into Waterford cut-crystal coupe glasses.

"This one's a little bit chipped," Sarah said.

"They all are. They're over a century old. The original set had more than sixty, but there are only three left. Do you want a different glass?"

"No, don't bother." She tasted her drink. "Mmm. Strawberries and what else . . . ?"

I grinned. "A secret ingredient that only Blackworths are allowed to know."

"I'm a Blackworth now. You can tell me."

No, you're not. It was my automatic thought. But I caught myself: she was Jamie's wife, so in a way she was. "You've got to swear never to reveal it to a soul outside the family."

She held up a hand, mock solemnly. "I swear."

"Elderflower liqueur. I found an old bottle in the dining room bar cart."

"The secret is safe with me."

We sipped and watched the sun die. I was curious about her life with her first husband, Gideon. "He took great pains to teach me how to be rich," she said. "No, *taught's* not the right word. He demanded it. The clothes I wore. The way I looked. He hated it when I talked like a millennial. That's what he'd actually say, 'millennial,' like it was a dirty word. No cursing allowed. And my bad habits. Like playing with my hair. Everything, under his control."

"Did you ever think of leaving him?"

"To be honest?" She glanced at me earnestly. "I couldn't. Something happened to me in that fall off the cliff. My entire life went off the rails. I felt like I'd lost all control. At any minute, Didi could appear behind me and send me falling again. With Gideon's money, I thought I could get back in control, but it was just the opposite. He allowed me none at all." Her face shadowed, and a terrifying expression came into her eyes—something fierce and haunted. So briefly that I wondered if I'd seen it at all. Then she cast her eyes down to the scuffed linoleum floor. "But I would have been penniless and alone if I left him. And I had my mother to think about. I would have had to put her in some hideous county institution. I couldn't do that."

"What was your mom's name?"

She gave a soft smile. "Sharon. Sharon Davis. A very plain name, like mine was." She took a decorous sip of her drink. "I don't want to make it sound like Gideon was a monster. But compared to James . . . well, I guess he was."

It was getting dark. We could no longer see the ocean, just hear its perpetual rhythm. Sarah switched on the standing lamp. "My turn," she said. "I want to know what it was like growing up here."

I drew a reflective breath. "For a while, it felt enchanted. Like we were elves or something. Living in a sort of haunted castle, which we loved. I used to think of us as being perfectly happy until things went suddenly wrong. But part of me always knew there'd been a dark cloud in my childhood."

"Your father."

"Yes," I said simply. Dad. Handsome and charming and vicious. "And Mom," I added. "She was a free spirit but also strange in many ways. She hardly ever left the property. She sometimes didn't get out of bed until almost noon."

"But you and James both worshipped her, didn't you?"

I refilled my glass from the pitcher. The scent of elderflower, dislodging memories. "Yeah. She was beautiful. She had a cloud of auburn hair, and she wore rings that sparkled on almost every one of her fingers, and she loved to go barefoot, so her feet were always dirty. When people met her, they were drawn to her. Everybody, rich people, working people. They wanted to look at her, talk to her. Get close to her. I was a little jealous of that."

"But, Ava, I'm jealous of you," Sarah said. "I think you've always known who you are, even when you can't see it yourself. You're your own person."

"Don't you think you are too?"

"Sometimes I'm not sure. I think by letting Gideon take charge of me, I lost a large part of myself. James never tries to control me."

"No. He'd want you to be yourself." I took another sip of my daiquiri. "Ouch."

"What?"

"This glass is chipped too. It pricked my lip."

"I'll get you a different one." She started to rise.

"Don't bother, you won't find any. And you'll miss the best part of the sunset."

The sky was now ablaze: I held my glass up, and it refracted the jeweled rays. I didn't see a chip; I saw only the radiance.

After the sun disappeared into the sea, we moved to the kitchen. Sarah had stocked it with a rainbow of organic fruits and vegetables, raw grains and beans and nuts, shelled and unshelled—daily deliveries from natural food stores in Carmel. She never bought meat. "Gideon ate steaks that were blood raw. It put me off eating animals forever."

We began making a large salad.

"My mother became a vegan the year before she died," I told her. "Dad sometimes grilled us burgers, always in back of the house, so the sea breeze would carry the smoke up to Mom's studio. Just to taunt her."

Sarah shook a rinsed leaf of frilly lettuce, and the fine spray glittered. "James said when she got sick, she tried to cure herself with natural foods."

"Yeah." I began chopping sprigs of flowering thyme and tarragon, and the oily aromas they released reminded me of Mom's patchoulis. "She'd seen a neurologist but said she could tell just by his touch that he was a fool. She canceled all the tests he'd scheduled and found a holistic healer—a woman with testimonials from movie stars and a Nobel scientist. Mom followed her regimen strictly. She even went to a place in Carmel twice a week for electromagnetic healing therapy. I thought she'd come back looking like the bride of Frankenstein."

Sarah lifted her brows. "Did she?"

"No, she looked like her normal self. Maybe just a little floatier." I smiled. "She began to meditate three times a day. She wouldn't put a thing in her mouth she didn't buy and make for herself, to be sure it wasn't contaminated or tainted with secret sugar or preservatives."

"But she shouldn't have canceled her neurology tests," Sarah said.

"No, she shouldn't have," I agreed. "But the thing is, it was working. Her symptoms had gone away. She stopped stumbling, and drooling when she took a drink, and she didn't make any more screwy faces. She'd even started painting again."

"Maybe something in the paint was making her sick."

"Funny, my father said something like that after she died. That maybe she'd accidentally poisoned herself with something toxic in her pigments. He said there was cyanide in ground-up fruit pits. But I looked it up. She would have had to eat her paints with a spoon to get enough to poison her." I tipped the chopped herbs into a mixing bowl and showed it to Sarah. "Is this enough, do you think?"

"Perfect." She leaned against the sink, facing me, her elbows resting on the edge. "I'm glad you've shared all this with me, Ava. That you feel you can tell me these things."

Had I revealed too much? No, it felt good to talk about it. And she was family now.

I sprinkled the herbs over the lettuce she had washed. "I've been thinking a lot about that last day when I found Mom having horrible convulsions. It's really been weighing on me."

"Okay," Sarah prompted softly.

"When I came home that evening, I went directly to the stairs. And I saw a shadow. It was up on the landing, sort of rushing across the floor, and then it vanished. Then I went upstairs and found Mom, and after that, everything became blurred in my mind. But as soon as I came back here, I remembered that shadow."

"What do you think it was?"

"This is going to sound crazy," I said. "But I think I might have seen Cinderella. I remember thinking so at the time. And I was terrified. I just froze there at the bottom of the stairs." My heart began to beat fast at the memory. "I stood there for far too long before I went up to Mom."

"James says it wasn't your fault, Ava. It wouldn't have made any difference."

"I can't be sure. Not until I'm sure of what happened to her."

Sarah began to assemble our plates. "You might never find out, you know, Ava. What happened to her."

"I think I will. I think whoever sent me those cards might be who killed her. They're trying to scare me off being here, but it won't work. That's their mistake."

"Then it's good that I'm here with you. The more people in the house, the less anyone will try to do anything worse." She brought over the plates. Said casually, "Are you going out later?"

I glanced at her. "No, not tonight."

"It's Thomas, isn't it? The one who was here the other day?"

"Yes," I said.

"I'm glad you're not going out." Sarah set the plates on the Formica table. "I get a little nervous alone here sometimes." She placed two cloth napkins next to the plates. Ironed. Folded, with crisp corners. "Do you want some wine, Ava? I bought you a good Sancerre to go with this."

I hesitated. I'd had three daiquiris. But the evening breeze was settling into the house, chilling me. "Maybe just a glass," I said.

It was more than just the breeze making me shiver, I realized. Though I wasn't sure what else it was.

CHAPTER TWENTY-SIX

My conversation with Sarah left me on edge. I couldn't help dwelling on that fleeing shadow on top of the stairs seventeen years ago.

The next morning, I made a video of the landing from the bottom of the stairs. I downloaded it to my computer. The landing was alive with shadows. It caught the shifting ocean light from windows both upstairs and down, as well as the dim lamps of the chandelier, and all these lights cast forms and shapes that streamed and fluttered across the hall; and watching them on my monitor, both at normal speed and in slow motion, I could imagine any one of them to be a high-spirited ghost.

"Did you know she gets her underwear specially hand-washed?"

Franny Fiore barged into my studio. She wore a boy's muscle shirt that displayed a mythical zoo tattooed on both arms and was carrying a small package. "There's this van that just came to pick it all up, can you believe that?"

"Are you talking about Sarah?" I said.

"Yeah. She says it's all silk and has to be handled special." A snort. "FedEx was here, and this is for you, for a change. There's sure been a lot of things come for *her*." She placed the package on my desk.

"I didn't order anything." I eyed it nervously. Which ghost from my past would it be signed by this time? Cinderella again? Or Mom? Or maybe Aunt Willie?

"Aren't you gonna open it?" Franny said.

"I'm not sure. I don't know who it's from. The label doesn't say."

"You think it might be a bomb?" Her interest shot up.

"No, just maybe something creepy."

"I'll open it." She reached for it.

"No, I will." I slit the taped seal open with a mat knife. Then inhaled a sharp breath. A boxed camera lay nestled in bubble wrapping. A Leica M10-R Digital Rangefinder.

"What?" Franny leaned in nosily. "Oh, it's a camera." Her voice sank with disappointment that it was nothing explosive.

I lifted it from the FedEx box. "It's not just any camera. It's an amazing one."

"So what's creepy about it?"

"Nothing. Except I don't know who sent it." *Thomas*, I thought. No, it was too ostentatious a gift. Not like him.

But then I knew: I looked deeper into the wrapping and found a card. "It's from Sarah," I said.

"That figures," Franny said. "She gave Michael an iPhone, did you know? Brand new, the one that just came out."

"Is she still here?"

"No, just left for the hospital."

Franny left, and I opened the shiny box. Reverently held the Leica in my hands, loving its small, solid heft, the sleekness of the casing. I peered through the viewfinder, marveled at the crystal clarity of the lens. I'd always wanted one. I'd even browsed for this very model not too long ago. But it was over $8,000, so I'd decided no, not yet. The house was soaking up too much of my money.

Jamie was right. Sarah spent extravagantly. Generous to a fault. But it felt uneasily like she was laying the groundwork for something in return. I couldn't accept it. I'd tell her it was too much, she'd have to send it back, when I saw her at the hospital later.

Jamie was alone in his room when I arrived in the afternoon, sitting propped upright, his eyes focused on the wall-mounted TV—a black-and-white movie, Humphrey Bogart, skinny, cynical eyed, rat-a-tat Brooklyn accent. He'd regained full consciousness by now and no longer looked shockingly beat up, but still battered.

"Hey, you," I said. "Which one's that?"

"Some noir. It's got a blonde. I know which one, I can't think of her name." He clicked it off. "Thank God you're here, Ave. Everybody else has deserted me. Sarah's at the rehab, checking it out."

I pulled a chair close. "I'm glad I've got you to myself. We haven't really talked yet about your accident."

"But I told you everything, didn't I?"

"No. All I know is you were going to Dad's place. But then you obviously skidded off the road."

"It was terrifying. I remember the car tumbling, and then I blacked out. And after that, coming in and out of consciousness. I was pinned, I couldn't get out. All I had was a bottle of water and a bag of cashews."

"They probably saved your life."

"Could be." He gave a lopsided smile. "I guess I can't blame this one on old Cinderella. She can't leave the house."

"Who said?"

"Mom did. She said she couldn't go far from the room where she was killed."

"She never told me that." I felt an absurd little twinge of jealousy. "So I guess you never got to Dad's house."

"Yeah, I did," he said. "This was after I'd already been there."

My eyes widened. "You found him?"

"No, the house. I remembered it as high up in the hills, but it wasn't so far up off Highway 1. Old redwood place on a dead end. I rang the bell, and dogs barked, but nobody came."

"So you don't know if it was still his or not."

"It was. I looked in a window. The living room. I saw a tennis racket. An oversized graphite, like he always used. And trophies on a shelf. That black glass one he had."

"The Savannah Open. Yeah, I remember that one!" A tall black obelisk with a gold ball on top. My pulse quickened. Dad was still around here, not very far away. "Why didn't you wait?"

"I did for a while, but my eyes were killing me. And then . . . what? Oh yeah, the dog was at the window, yapping its head off. I went back to my car and put eye drops in, and my eyes cleared up a little. Then I started driving away. And then I saw him."

I leaned closer. "Dad?"

"Yeah. On a tight, winding road. He was jogging. That bobbing way he had of running because of his weak ankle, remember? His hair was the same. And he was wearing that yellow sweatshirt with the arms cut off. With the ice cream cone on it, remember?"

"Yeah, I do." An ice cream cone with a tennis ball instead of a scoop of ice cream. And his bobbing kind of running, the weak ankle that had ruined his tennis career. That and the scandal with the seventeen-year-old. "So what did he say?"

"Nothing. He disappeared."

"Disappeared?"

"There was a bend, and he went around it, and I sped up to catch him, but he'd just disappeared. That's when I went off the road."

"Are you sure it was him?" I asked. "I mean, how could he still look so much the same?"

"He looked older, I guess. But he's probably dyeing his hair. That would be just like Dad."

"Yeah, it would be," I agreed. "So where is the house? I mean, what's the address?"

"Oak Branch something. Lane or Path. You turn up from Moss Landing. But don't go, Ava. You remember how big he is, and those shoulders. Wait till I'm better, and we'll both go." He struggled to prop himself up a little more and winced. He fumbled for the button that controlled his IV. "I wish this damned thing went higher."

"Shouldn't you be off IV meds by now?" I said.

"Yeah, soon. But right now I need them." He pressed the button a few times more, then dropped the device in frustration. "Hey," he said. "Did Sarah tell you we're coming back home?"

"Wait. Home to Blackworth Mansion?"

"Yeah. Surprised?"

A jolt of trepidation ran through me. "When did you decide that?"

"A couple of days ago."

"You can't be serious," I said. "You hate the house, you've said so a million times. You were horror stricken when I called it home."

"But you've been fine, and Sarah really likes it there, so I can see I've been overreacting. It makes a lot of sense for us. We need a place in a hurry, and there it is. It's just until the winter semester, when I start teaching again."

"Maybe you should wait until you're off pain meds to make this decision."

A quick rap on the door, and a nurse—a beanpole of a man—came in to check Jamie's vitals. Blood pressure. Temperature. He jotted notes and then dispensed several pills, which Jamie swallowed with small sips of water.

And then Sarah arrived, carrying a bag marked Veggie Bar. "Ava, hi." She set the bag on a crowded cabinet and greeted the nurse. "Hello, Kenneth. How's my husband coming along?"

"Very well, Sarah. Respiration rate's a little low, but within range."

"Great." She opened the bag. "Would you like something to drink? I've got all-natural fruit soda and iced coffee."

"Not at the moment, Sarah, but thank you." He said a reassuring word to Jamie and left.

She poured soda into a glass, added a straw, and gave it to Jamie. "Watermelon lime, your favorite. Ava? Soda or iced latte? The latte's almond milk, so if you'd rather have a soda, I'll take it instead."

"I could use some coffee." I accepted the cup, took a long sip. It had a faintly bitter aftertaste. Almonds?

Jamie said, "I was just telling Ava we're coming back home to live."

Sarah turned to me brightly. "We talked it over very thoroughly. I had some gorgeous places lined up as alternatives, both up here and in Laguna. It was James's choice."

"Yeah, it was," he said. "It makes so much sense. Sarah says you've fixed it up a lot, Ave, and we'll continue to make improvements. And you've been fine there. You said so yourself."

I set down the half-finished latte. It really did have an unpleasantly bitter aftertaste. "I've got a slight headache. I think I'll go home and take a nap."

"Is there anything I can do for you?" Sarah asked.

"No, I'll be okay. Oh, but Sarah? I got your gift this morning. It's a fantastic camera, thank you. But I can't accept it. It's far too much."

"What camera?" Jamie said.

"A Leica," Sarah told him. "The man I talked to in the camera shop said it was the best. I loved getting it for you, Ava. It seemed so perfect. Please say you'll keep it." She had such an earnest, almost childlike, expression that it seemed like it would be cruel to say no.

"Only if I can give you something in return," I said. "Is there anything in the house you'd particularly like?"

A puzzled look came into her eyes. "But doesn't everything in the house already belong to James and me as well as you?"

No, I wanted to tell her. *Just to Jamie and me. You've got no right to any of it at all.*

"Of course it's yours as well," Jamie said to Sarah, but it felt like he'd read my thoughts.

"I'll think of something," I said.

I went to Jamie and planted a kiss on my palm, and then I put my palm against his temple.

He smiled in a hazy way. "Mom used to do that."

"I remember," I said.

My head really was throbbing, but I didn't go home. I made my way down to the basement cafeteria. The fluorescent glare felt like an assault. Shading my eyes, I bought a can of V8 and sat down at a back table. I pulled the tab and drank the can in a series of gulps, letting the spicy tomato flavor wash out the lingering aftertaste of the almond milk latte. My throat was a little raw: the acidity of the tomatoes burned.

Why did the thought of Jamie coming home disturb me? If he was really okay with it, why not?

And I'd liked having Sarah there. A sister-in-law to confide in. One who cared about me and tried to do things to please me.

Too eager to please. A hidden agenda. But what?

A thought sneaked into my mind: How did she know exactly which camera I'd wanted?

By looking at my browsing history on my computer.

Could that be true? Maybe with the best of intentions. But just the idea of it filled me with horror.

The buzz of conversation in the room matched a buzzing in my head. And the nasty taste still lingered in my mouth.

My email sounded. I fumbled in my bag for my phone. From Darsh Greenwald:

> Checked James's charts. Labs all within normal range. No tox screen. One concern. The dosage of analgesics is on the high side. But that's not my call.

The pain meds were too strong. Jamie obviously wasn't thinking clearly about coming back to the house to live and maybe about everything he'd told me about his accident. Dad, jogging on the road. Still looking the same. And vanishing suddenly.

But some of the details seemed very real. The graphite racket . . . no, Dad had stopped playing tennis years ago. But the trophy from the Savannah Open, that sounded very real.

I had to check it out for myself—the old redwood on a dead-end street called Oak Branch something not too high up from Moss Landing. I pulled up Google Maps. Found the Moss Landing exit off Highway 1. Expanded the area and scrutinized it. With difficulty, my temples throbbing, the buzz in my brain.

There—a squiggle of a road: Oak Branch Trail.

I pictured Dad. Probably drunk, maybe violently so. His vicious tirades. Lashing out.

And suddenly something strange happened. My entire body seemed to clench in on itself. With a groan of pain, I doubled over the table.

It passed. I waited to see if it would happen again. It didn't.

Nerves. The thought of confronting Dad alone.

I'd bring Franny. She was fearless and had to own at least one gun.

No. I didn't want Franny. I wanted Thomas. He probably owned at least one gun as well.

I called and left a message on his voice mail.

"Do you really think it was your father?" He called later in the day. I was home by then. My headache finally diminished. A shot of tequila had vanquished the bitter aftertaste.

"Jamie said he was sure. His hair was the same because he probably dyed it. He had on this yellow sweatshirt that was his favorite for running. And he was running the same way. Kind of bobbing to favor his weak ankle."

"The same sweatshirt after all this time?"

"He used to wear his favorite clothes until they fell apart. There was one jersey he'd had since college."

Thomas gave a skeptical grunt.

"Jamie could be wrong," I conceded. "His eyes had been bothering him. The guy jogging might have been somebody else."

"Or a hallucination."

I hesitated. *The jogger simply vanished.* "There's only one way to know for sure."

"Of course I'll go with you if you can wait till Friday. I'm in Montana right now, checking out a new site. It's spectacular. Thirty miles out of Bozeman, a hundred and forty-two acres with a trout river and high peaks in all directions."

"For a development?" I asked.

"Nope, a ranch. Just one ranch house and several outbuildings. Happy?"

"Happier," I said.

An amused snort. "I get in late Thursday night. I'll pick up the Ram from the construction site early Friday, then swing by for you."

"No," I said. "Come here Thursday night when you get in. Stay with me."

"And what about Sarah?" he said with an edge.

"She won't be here. And it wouldn't matter anyway. I want you to be here."

"Good," he said. "It's about time you had me over."

"Yeah," I agreed. "More than time."

CHAPTER
TWENTY-SEVEN

Jamie was transferred to the rehab wing the following afternoon, Sarah engineering it to be as smooth as possible. She'd be leaving for Newport Beach the next day, Wednesday, and would return around noon on Friday.

I wouldn't be home. I'd be searching for Dad in the hills above Santa Cruz with Thomas.

She returned from the rehab center just as the sky was beginning to blaze. "James has settled in beautifully," she said. "He's got the most adorable roommate, a sixteen-year-old named Aiden. He broke both arms doing something called a tiger claw on an electric skateboard. Jamie told him he used to be a skateboarder, and they bonded instantly."

"That's great. Will I be allowed to visit?"

"I'm not sure. Not for the first week. And I'm leaving tomorrow, so this is my last sunset here until Saturday. Should we go to the sunporch?"

"Sure. I'll make the daiquiris."

"I have a huge favor to ask, Ava." She gave her most fetching smile. "Would you show me how to make them? I bought wild strawberries on my way back. I know the secret ingredient, but I want to learn the entire recipe."

"Yeah, sure. It's not very difficult. I'll show you."

We went to the kitchen. Betsy barked at the back door, and I let her in. "I already fed her, so don't let her con you."

"I'll probably break down," Sarah said. "Slip her a treat when you're not looking."

I demonstrated the daiquiri preparation. "White rum, never dark. And always raw sugar." I carelessly measured both ingredients into the blender. "You don't have to be too exact." I squeezed some limes. "One capful of elderflower liqueur." I added it, then knocked ice cubes out of the aluminum tray in the freezer compartment and added four to the mixture. I turned the blender on to shrieking high.

"We need a new one of those," Sarah shouted, covering her ears.

"Yeah, we do."

"And a new refrigerator with a proper freezer."

"We need a new kitchen." I switched off the machine. "So now you've been officially initiated into the Royal Society of the Blackworth Daiquiri."

"I am honored." She dropped a little curtsy.

I laughed. Poured the daiquiri mixture into a pitcher. "We always serve them in coupe glasses."

"I know that." Sarah took two from the sideboard. I picked up the pitcher, and we went to the sunporch. I began to fill the glasses, then paused. "These are new."

"Yes. Waterford. I sent for a set of twelve, and they came this morning. You won't have to cut your lip on chipped glass anymore, Ava."

I didn't mind, I wanted to protest. *They were Blackworth glasses. They should never be replaced.*

I caught myself. Why would I insist on drinking out of broken glass?

Maybe Jamie had been right: maybe I did expect to find Mom here. If I kept everything frozen in time, she'd come padding into the porch, her bare feet dirty, her hands full of wild grasses.

Was I that crazy? I felt the tickling of blackness at the corners of my mind. "They're beautiful glasses, Sarah," I said quickly. "Thank you." I filled them both, and then we sat and watched the sky light up like olden-days Technicolor.

We didn't make dinner. Sarah said she'd had some food at the hospital and went upstairs to pack. I grabbed some odds and ends from the fridge. After all those days of worry and fear, I still hadn't regained my full appetite.

When I went upstairs to my studio, I thought again of Sarah maybe searching my browser. And of all her extravagant, too-eager-to-please gifts.

I typed a search into my computer. Her name during her first marriage: *Sarah Ellingham*.

Very few hits. Several items mentioning her in connection to charities. She and Gideon had attended a rare-wines auction in Paris, made a winning bid on a 1945 Mouton Rothschild.

Something more interesting. They had donated a multimillion-dollar Henry Moore sculpture to Bradford University. A photo of the two of them posed in front of it. Gideon, balding, sickly looking, leaning on a cane. Sarah, beautiful but looking miserable.

I saved all the items in a file. Then did a new search—for a site that sold digitalized yearbooks. Chose the first one that came up. Entered *Monterey Bay Regional High School 2006* and gave my payment information. Clicked on the link that appeared. It downloaded a plum-colored yearbook with white block lettering. Dolphins leaping: the school mascot.

I fast-forwarded to the senior photos. Midway through the *M*s, second photo down on the left: *Didi Morrison*. I enlarged it.

Freakish. A heavy, broad face, jowls pulled down by an exaggerated frown. Unwashed strands of frizzy dishwater-blonde hair scraggling over her cheeks. Puffy-lidded pale-brown eyes mostly obscured behind the thick lenses of plastic old-lady glasses.

It triggered something in me. A memory. Taking photos with my first real camera, a Canon Rebel. I'd loved, loved that camera. Waylaid everybody in sight for portraits. A girl—older than me—frowning like that. Hiding crooked teeth. Then shading her entire face from the camera.

It had been this girl, Didi Morrison. She *was* the one who'd worked for us. I was sure of it now.

Except she hadn't been that freakish. Overweight, yes. And something sort of beaten about her. But otherwise fairly ordinary.

I continued scrolling forward, searching for other photos of her, doubting I'd find any. She wouldn't have been a joiner—not even chess or chem club. But then I stopped suddenly on page 51.

A girls' lacrosse game in midplay. One girl in the middle foreground, racing down the field with her stick brandished high. Maroon uniform. Long golden brown hair flying into her face. Not Didi.

It was Sarah.

The photo had been taken from a low angle, distorting the perspective, so she looked a little taller. But it was definitely Sarah. And her name in the caption confirmed it: *Sarah Davis, attacker.*

"Ava?" Sarah called from down the hall.

I glanced up with a guilty start. "In my studio," I called back. I clicked off the yearbook.

She appeared, elegant in a sea green silk robe. "I just wanted to say good night. I'll be leaving early in the morning. If you're still sleeping, I won't disturb you."

"I'll be up," I promised. "Sleep well."

I opened the yearbook again. I searched the senior photos for Sarah's. I didn't expect to find it—she had transferred in too late to have one—and I didn't.

I was suddenly very tired. I began to power down my computer but stopped suddenly.

My password was *Cinderella*. Ridiculously easy to guess. I changed it. Then shut off the computer and went to bed.

CHAPTER
TWENTY-EIGHT

SARAH

I don't have to pack much since I'll just be away for a couple of nights. But I'm worried about leaving, even for a short period of time. Not because of James. The rehab facility really is excellent.

Because of Ava. Sometimes it seems we're bonding closely. And then other times she throws a barrier up, one that's high, made of bricks and mortar. Like she's got me pegged as some kind of monster—a female Minotaur lurking in the center of the maze that's Blackworth Mansion.

And now she's seeing Thomas Rainier.

I'm suddenly not so sure what he might tell her.

I think about calling Lenore Wyatt to say I'm canceling my trip. But I can't, I know. I've got no choice but to be there in person to finalize my affairs with Gideon's nightmare kids.

❧

My wake-up music is a strange choice. The theme song from a horror movie, *The Exorcist*. I didn't know that when I chose it. It's not called that—it was simply music that I liked.

It goes off at 6:00 a.m., but I'm already awake. I'm dressed and alert when the driver texts at 7:15 to say he's waiting out in front.

I head outside to find Michael Fiore leaning at the driver's window, probably swapping a few dirty jokes. Maybe they already know each other. Michael seems to know most of the working population on the Monterey Peninsula.

"You're here early, Michael," I say.

"I've gotta leave early today. I've got another job going in Salinas." He ambles over to take my suitcase. The driver pops the trunk.

"I'm glad I caught you. There are some things I'd like you to do here, if possible. James will be coming home in a couple of weeks."

"Coming here?" Michael says.

"Yes. He'll be on crutches, so he'll need a room downstairs. I'm thinking that big corner room on the forest side would be the best."

"You mean the original parlor. It's where their dad, Kevin, had his office. He used to play pro tennis, you know." There's a faded tattoo of a surfing skeleton on his forearm, and he scratches it meditatively. "That room's got no bathroom. Just that half bath down the hall."

"Yes, I know, but I'm wondering if you could expand the half bath to put in a shower. It would have to be done pretty quickly. But the plumbing's already there, so would it be hard?"

He sucks in his lips. "It would require some demolition. We'd have to knock into the dining room. And I'd need my full crew to get it done quick, so it won't be cheap."

"The dining room's enormous, and nobody uses it anymore. I think it couldn't hurt to make it a little smaller." I add with a smile, "I'll be paying for this, not James and Ava, so you can hire however many people you need. And I'll pay a bonus for getting it done quickly."

His eyes acquire an avaricious squint. "Okay, Sarah. No problem. Anything else?"

"Yes, in fact there is. I'd like to get the lawns resodded to make it easier for James outside with crutches. And anywhere there's gravel, add a lot more to replace what's been lost."

"Everywhere? Like the walks around the side and up into the statue garden?"

"Yes," I say. "Everywhere."

"You got it, Sarah," he says.

I get into the car, thinking of my task ahead. Walking through all those lavishly dead rooms in the town house. All the rare French and English antiques. The masterpieces on the walls. Renoirs, Picassos. Monets. None of it belongs to me any longer. I should at least have had the Renoir.

But I will like looking into Gideon's chambers. Saying a last farewell to his deathbed. He's dead and gone, and I have a new husband now who's the very opposite of him. James is young and handsome and romantic, and though he studies fetishes, he's not a sicko like my late first husband.

He's mine and always will be.

DIDI

More and more, Didi is positive she was a Blackworth in a previous life.

She has created a secret file on her Dell Inspiron laptop (a cheapo model that makes a sound like somebody sticking pins into a chipmunk). The file contains the research she's been doing on Blackworths over the past hundred-plus years to find out which one she used to be.

Before World War II, Blackworths dominated the society pages in old San Francisco newspapers, and she's been able to do a lot of the research in the main library in Monterey, reading the papers on microfiche. They covered the family's births and weddings and debutante balls and the many charity galas they gave and attended, and any Blackworths who died got long obituaries.

The more she reads about the family, the more she's sure of several things about her past life:

1. She was a girl. The men in the Blackworth family are handsome but also practical looking, like they were good at business or science, and Didi got good grades in math and science, but not her very best. The Blackworth women, on the other hand, seem artistic and dreamy, like Christina. Sort of existing on a different plane. As Didi obviously does herself.

2. As a Blackworth, she was beautiful. But she also possessed something even better—an inner beauty. Christina had said to her the other day, "Inner beauty is all that counts, Didi. This . . ." She'd fluttered her hand like a pale-feathered bird to indicate her body. "The physical is just a shell. Think of the statuary in our sculpture garden. They were all hollow, you know."

"Hollow?"

"Most of them weren't real sculptures—just plaster casts, shells with nothing inside them. And now look at them. Nothing but broken shards."

But Didi believes that as a Blackworth, she would have had both. Inner and outer beauty. The way Christina obviously does.

3. In her Blackworth former life, she had died young. Not an infant or little girl but in the fading flower of her late youth. Didi's not sure how she knows this. She just does.

And then she finds her! The Blackworth she's positive she used to be!

Her name was Alice Leland Blackworth. Born on New Year's Day 1901. Presented to society on her eighteenth birthday at a dazzling debutante ball at the Fairmont Hotel, escorted by two dashing young officers freshly returned from the fronts of World War I. *The Great War*, the society columns called it. And then the very next day after her debut, Alice had entered a cloistered convent—the Order of Saint Clare—and was no longer allowed to see anyone else, not even her family.

And ten years from that day, she killed herself by swallowing rat poison. She'd been twenty-eight years old.

Finding this out makes Didi's entire body tingle. Rat poison! Like Madame Bovary (one of her favorite novels), who committed suicide with arsenic meant for killing rats.

Because poor Alice was a suicide, she couldn't be buried in consecrated grounds, neither at the convent nor in the Blackworth family plot in Oakland Parks Cemetery. Which was probably the reason she got reincarnated as Didi and has had to suffer some more—to atone for such a grave mortal sin.

Didi studies the photo of Alice as a deb with her two dashing escorts. One of them is exceptionally handsome. His name is Anthony Blackworth Collins, so he must have been related to Alice—maybe a second cousin. He's wearing an eye patch. So romantic. It reminds her of Christina's son, James, that something funny going on with his left eye. And in fact, Anthony looks a little like James, that boyish, fine-boned beauty.

For some reason, this makes something in her chest ache.

She imagines that Alice (who is now reincarnated as herself!) loved Anthony passionately, and he adored her too. *Wild nights! Wild nights!* But their kinship made their love forbidden, which is why she ran off to the convent.

And when her seclusion and prayers failed to quench her passion for her cousin, she ended her life.

The connection between herself and Alice is amazing, Didi thinks. Like with Alice poisoning herself, and Didi had basically poisoned Wanda, the Rainiers' housekeeper. It's like a sign, she thinks.

Poison is part of her destiny.

She can't wait to tell Christina. Not about the poison connection, of course. About everything else.

CHAPTER TWENTY-NINE

AVA

I was glad to find Sarah gone when I got up the next morning. I could work without distraction for the rest of the day.

I was beginning the second and most important phase of my photographs. To re-create Mom's studio exactly as it had been when I found her dying. Or at least as exactly as I could.

I wasn't going to use Franny this time. I'd pose myself. I looked nothing at all like Mom, but I could become her. I could imitate her gestures, her expressions. The way she held her head. Combed her hair. Bit the tip of the paintbrush between her front teeth while she contemplated a painting in progress on her easel.

It frightened me a little. What memories this might dredge up.

What I'd seen that day. What I'd known. Something so horrible I'd had to suppress it.

Or maybe nothing. I had no forgotten memories. Just dreadful trauma, and I'd never get over it, not even with an army of therapists and jug-loads of meds.

But either way, I had to know.

With almost manic excitement, I began making sketches. I taped them to the wall in her studio. Then I took down the filthy gauze curtains and brought them to Franny to wash with the same gentle treatment she'd given to Mom's clothes. I raided the studio's supply closet, trip after trip, for armfuls of palettes and paints—oils and acrylics—and pastel and charcoal crayons, and brushes, some brand new, some stiff with dried paint. Mortars and pestles: one large, one small. Smocks in a rainbow of colors.

Memories, images, flashed and flickered in my mind.

How you were never allowed to take anything away from this room without Mom's permission. Not the cups and dishes that became slick with green mold. Not the candles burned down to tortured writhing shapes or the decomposing mockingbird shedding gray feathers that lifted in mysterious drafts.

I pictured her grinding a cluster of spongy white mushrooms in her mortar and pestle. Shaking an ancient water-warped Bible, dusty pressed flowers sprinkling out of the pages.

Grace thought Mom had been a witch, and she was. Casting spells. Making ghosts appear to her.

I became more frantic in my task as the day progressed. I did a treasure hunt through the cluttered rooms, collecting objects that were suitably bizarre. There was no dearth of them in Blackworth Mansion. I scavenged for more in the woods and on the beach. By the time I got back, Franny had gone home and the last light was fading from the windows.

I grabbed a bottle of tequila from the bar cart (art deco, missing one wheel). I went to the sunporch to watch the sinking sun. It felt suddenly strange to be here alone. The curtains Franny had washed were laid out like shrouds all around me. The ocean was at ebb tide: a low, lugubrious rhythm like a requiem.

Betsy appeared at the outside door, and I let her in. Stieglitz sloped in from some dim part of the house and nestled beside me. I waited to feel that cozy sense of contentment.

But I simply felt alone.

I texted Thomas. He wrote he was heading off to dinner with his clients. Would see me tomorrow night. I sent another text, to Grace. No reply: she was probably already asleep.

I kept drinking tequila. Swallowed another makeshift dinner.

Then I went to the Monster Room. The clicker to the old Sony had disappeared. I turned it on manually and stared at a series of random programs, drinking more tequila shots, until sometime around two o'clock I took myself to bed.

I couldn't sleep. The memories of Mom I'd resurrected were roiling in my brain. They'd brought back all the pain of losing her, still without giving me any answers.

I thought of Nembutal. The bliss of sinking into blackness.

I got out of bed. Went into my bathroom and took the bottle out of the cabinet. I opened it. I stared at the remaining pills inside. Six. No, seven.

My phone sounded from the bedroom.

Jamie. The rehab center. Something had happened. I dropped the bottle and dashed to grab the phone. "Yes, hello?"

Nothing. Just silence.

"Hello?" I said again.

Still no response. But not quite silence. I could hear a faint roar. Not a consistent sound. It surged and retreated, then surged again. The ocean.

The caller was here. Right outside.

The hairs on my arms bristled. "Who is this?"

Nothing. Just the distant, ominous surge and retreat of the tide.

I looked at the caller number streaming at the top of the screen: a familiar number. My heart beat hard. "Dad?" I said.

Still no reply.

"Answer me, you coward," I shouted. "I know you're out there."

A piercing electronic pulse. The line had gone dead.

I stood for a moment, breathing hard. I hit redial. A robotic voice: "The number you are trying to reach has been disconnected . . ."

I darted to the window and pressed my nose against the glass. It was dark, but a faint glimmer from the ocean streaked the horizon.

He was out there.

I backed off from the window. I tried to reason. Betsy was lying on the rug, watching me curiously but without alarm. She would have barked if anybody had been there. And Stieglitz, curled at the foot of the bed, had roused himself briefly but then curled back up in a tight ball.

Just a wrong number. I'd only imagined it was Dad's.

I tapped "Recents." There it was—a Monterey exchange followed by that familiar sequence of numbers. Dad's old landline. The same number written on the back of that sketch Mom had made of me.

He was out there. Playing his tormenting games.

Except that number had been disconnected. I called it again to make sure. Got the same robotic voice telling me it was no longer in service.

Anyone could spoof a number. It was easy. Dad could be calling from any number at all—just taunting me with his old one.

And he could be anywhere in the world, not necessarily outside. The ocean in the background could have been any beach. The Atlantic. Lake Superior. The Indian Ocean.

Still, I should call 911.

A car would show up. They'd see this house, dark, spooky, isolated. Enough to give anyone the jitters.

The caller hadn't made a threat. My dog hadn't barked. My cat had barely budged.

They'd take a cursory look around inside. They'd find all the doors and windows securely locked. Tramp around a little outside.

They'd think: jumpy single woman alone in a creepy old house. I'd have to explain everything. The pranks. The meaning of Cinderella and my mother's strange death and why I'd come back here.

And then they'd think: crazy single woman.

I kept the phone clutched in my hand. If it rang again, I'd call 911.

But there were no more calls. Nothing else to alarm me in the night.

Except sometime right before dawn, the sound of Jazz Age high heels clattering up the back stairs, and it sent goose bumps up my arms.

❧

I got up around eight. Pulled on a not-too-wrinkled shirt and pants from clothes scattered around my bedroom and went downstairs. Fed Betsy and Stieglitz, setting Stieglitz's food on a counter to protect it from Betsy, who'd otherwise scarf it after wolfing down her own. I made coffee in the percolator. It was always too weak or too strong. Thick as mud this morning.

I compulsively rechecked that number in my recents. Still there. Two fifty-three a.m. Still disconnected.

I shoved it all out of my mind. Returned to my work in Mom's studio.

An hour later, I heard Michael's truck pull up in the drive, followed by others. Then sounds of strenuous activity. Doing what? The work here was completed, except for Michael finishing some odds and ends.

I went outside. Three trucks, the beds loaded with sacks of gravel and crushed rock and stacks of lumber and drywall, and Michael's crew were unloading. One of them told me Michael was at the toolshed.

I walked around the north side of the house to the dilapidated wooden shed. When I was six, I imagined some evil creature living in it, a troll maybe, who'd seize me and eat me if I ever went inside. When I was older, the funky smell of fertilizers kept me away.

Michael stepped out with an assortment of implements. Rakes, hoes, long-handled shovels. "Morning, Ava," he said laconically.

"What's going on?" I asked. "Why are all your guys here?"

"We're getting a jump on the work Sarah wants done."

"What work?"

"You don't know?"

"No," I said. "I don't."

"Well, let's see. We're going to restore the front drive, that's what all the crushed rock is for. The gravel is for the driveway and also to fill in that old statue area. I've got a few loads of sod coming to redo the lawns. Sarah wants smoother surfaces to make it easier for your brother to get around when he's on crutches."

"I haven't heard about any of this."

Michael's eyes, the color of sun-bleached denim, fixed on me. "I figured James was okay with it. And well, you know, Ava, Sarah says she's paying for it herself."

With her dead first husband's money. How could Jamie be okay with that? And I certainly wasn't. "I need to talk to her. Don't do anything until I let you know."

"What about that downstairs half bath?"

"What about it?" I asked.

"We're supposed to break into the dining room and make it a full bath with a shower. Your brother is going to be staying in your daddy's old office room while he recuperates. She's paying for that too."

I felt a flash of anger. "There's been a miscommunication. I don't want anything done in this house unless I know about it first. And if there is any more work, Jamie and I will pay for it. Okay?"

"Got it. But you know, if you cancel right now, somebody's gonna have to pay for these supplies. And the cost of lost labor time."

"I understand. Don't worry, it will be covered. Just hold off for now."

"How about that electrical work we're supposed to finish?"

I gave a sound of exasperation. "Yes, of course, finish that. Oh, and Michael? Would you take a look around the grounds and see if there's any sign of someone out here last night? Maybe prowling around."

The bleached eyes locked on me again. "You think there was?"

It occurred to me: *What if it was him?*

"Probably not," I said quickly. "Never mind, I'm sure it was nothing."

"I'll take a look. No problem."

I went back to the house and fired off a text to Sarah. Told her I'd put Michael on hold. That I had to be consulted before anything was ever done. She replied quickly. I am so sorry!! James agreed so I thought it was ok. Didn't mean to overstep. Please forgive me.

Jamie had agreed? To breaking down the wall of our beautiful formal dining room? Making it smaller, ruining its lovely proportions? And to having all that work done on the grounds at Sarah's expense?

He couldn't be thinking straight. The pain meds. Or else he was still badly shaken from the accident.

Or was it Sarah's influence? She was taking him over.

The thought struck me suddenly: just like she was taking over this house.

I felt a tremble of alarm. I texted her: We'll talk when you get back.

I paused for a moment, collecting my thoughts. Then sent another, longer, text, this one to Margaret Zhao. I told her about the spoofed call. About Jamie finding Dad's house. My plan to go there myself. Asked her to call.

She did, shortly afterward. "Don't be stupid. Talk to the police. Tell them he's harassing you. Let them pay him a visit."

"He'd charm his way out. He always could. But he can't with me. And I'm not going alone, I'm bringing a friend." I added, "A male friend."

She gave a grunt. "It doesn't make sense. He's been in the area and kept himself invisible? Was he a loner?"

"Just the opposite. He always needed a crowd to play to. But Jamie could have been wrong. It's what I need to find out."

"So is there something you'd like me to do?"

"Yes, to find somebody else. A woman named Didi Morrison." I explained briefly her connection to Sarah and to my family. "She might still live around here too."

"I can run a trace. Do you have a date of birth?"

"No, but she graduated from Monterey Bay Regional in 2006. Her mother's name began with an *M*. Something like Muriel." I added, "Sarah thinks she might still be stalking her. She says she catches glimpses of her sometimes."

"She's seen her since she's been with you?"

I hesitated. "She hasn't said that, no."

"Huh. Okay, I'll get on it."

"And also, if you can . . ." I paused. "I'd like to find out how much money Sarah has. I mean, how much her first husband left her."

"Always good to know. I do know a little about the first husband, Gideon Ellingham. A secretive guy. The terms of the settling would have been strictly private, but I can reach out to some contacts in Orange County and maybe get an idea."

"Thanks."

"And, Ava? Don't stay in the house tonight. Go to Grace and Darsh, or even a motel. Just to be on the safe side."

"I'll be okay. I've got a friend coming to spend the night."

"Same guy?"

"Yes."

"Hmmph," she said. "But alone or not, you get another call like that one last night or anything funny happens, you get a patrol car there. You got that?"

Another call like that. The idea sent a chill through me. Thomas wasn't coming until late, and whoever was doing these things was getting bolder.

"Don't worry," I told her. "I will."

DIDI

Didi is so excited by her discovery of being the reincarnation of Alice Blackworth that she can't wait to tell Christina about it the next day. But she and Mimi arrive late. Mimi's Fiesta wouldn't start, and they'd had to call AAA and wait for the tow truck to come and charge the battery. The guy charged $59.95 for the service and said Mimi was going to need a new battery, which made Mimi almost burst into tears.

Now at the Blackworth house, Didi soothes Mimi into a kitchen chair and makes her some herbal tea. It has real flowers in it. All of Christina's teas contain real flowers or teeny-tiny leaves, green or brown or golden.

Then Didi races toward the stairs to go up to Christina. She stops. She hears voices on the sunporch. The daughter, Ava. She's home. And she's with her best friend, a Chinese girl named Grace.

Didi keeps her head low. Ava isn't home very much, but when she is, Didi does her best to keep out of sight—out of the way of Ava's big-eyed stares and her pushy picture taking.

She doesn't have to try hard to avoid James. When he's here, he's usually with a posse of at least two or three boys, and sometimes girls as well, and she's invisible to all of them. Though once or twice, James happened to pass her in the hall and he gave his sweet smile, that something strange about his eye, and though he seems to do that with everyone and probably didn't even register her existence, she couldn't help a bounce of pleasure.

She continues upstairs to Christina's studio. The door's open, and she barges in. "Christina!"

But she's not there. She must be down with Ava and the friend. Didi will have to wait to tell Christina her amazing news about her past life as Alice Blackworth.

There's a drawing book on the seat of the swivel chair. Christina has sketched Didi several times, but she's never let her look at what she's drawn, though Didi's dying to. She listens for footsteps. Then she picks up the book and starts turning the pages.

Some drawings of James. Christina's played down his scars, and he looks heartbreakingly gorgeous. Then a sketch of some toothy old lady Didi recognizes as a friend of Christina's.

And then she laughs out loud.

A real porno drawing of Kevin Holland, stark naked and drying his private parts. He looks totally disgusting, especially his junk jiggling below his big, sagging belly. So Christina does know what a pig he is.

She loves Christina. She really does.

She flips the page, and now there's Ava. A badminton racket squeezed in her knees while she's tying up her ponytail. Didi's heart sinks a little. You can see just how much Christina loves her. Ava's teenage goofiness—the way she's got that racket between her knocky knees, how her elbows stick out like chicken wings as she ties up her hair—and in the war between ugly and pretty in Ava's face, Christina has brought out the pretty.

Didi suddenly feels hollow. With a leaden motion, she turns the page.

And feels a blow to her solar plexus.

It's a sketch of her. Bending over to pick up something—maybe a fragment of a statue in the sculpture garden. Her butt looks enormous. Her face is reduced to a few quick, ugly lines.

It's hideous. Even worse than the one of Kevin Holland. Her face flushes red.

She rips it out.

The next page is another drawing of herself. Squatting like she's trying to take a shit with her clothes still on. Looking really fat. Her face is no more recognizable in this one than the first, but just as ugly.

Everything is boiling up inside of her. Hatred. Rage. She hates Christina with a passion. She always has, really; she just didn't realize it.

Someone is coming down the hall. She quickly rips out the second drawing, too, then shuts the sketchbook and moves to put it back on the chair, but before she can, Kevin Holland swaggers into the room.

"Hey, honey." He glances at the torn-out sketches in her hand. "Whatcha got there?"

"Nothing," she says.

He lunges toward her and snatches the drawings.

"I didn't tear them out," Didi says. "They already were."

"Sure they were. Let's take a look." He glances at the first one. "Cute picture of Ava. Why do you want it?"

It takes Didi a second to understand. She must have inadvertently ripped out the sketch of Ava instead of the second one of herself. "I don't want it," she says.

Kevin looks at the second drawing. "Wowie. Christina sure did a number on you." He bares his teeth. "She can be damned mean sometimes, in case you didn't know. They say *I'm* an SOB, but she's the real killer in this family, boy." He chuckles. "If she finds out you've been messing with her sketchbooks, there'll be hell to pay."

"Are you going to snitch on me?" Didi says belligerently.

"Nah." He picks up a charcoal pencil from Christina's table. Scribbles something on the back of the first sketch. Gives both back to her. "That's my number. You better hide these."

She hesitates. She's wearing a new outfit from Target, super low-rise cargo pants and a pink shirt with the tails tied to hide her belly button. She folds the drawings in half, lifts the knot of her shirttails and shoves the sketches down her pants, then repositions the knot.

"I've got to get back to work," she says sullenly. She edges out the door.

He follows her into the hallway. "Hey, did you know I used to be a tennis champion? I broke my ankle a couple of times, and it got too weak for me to compete."

She's noticed he's got a way of favoring one side when he walks. Not a limp, like Mimi. Just a little more swagger on that side.

"Come down to my office when you have a second. I'll show you some of my trophies. I'll tell you what it's like being on the pro circuit. You won't believe some of what goes on."

Didi has seen his trophies. In fact, she's stolen one. A little, shiny bronze globe engraved *Runner-up, Boulder Juniors Open, 1987*, with Kevin Holland's name below that.

"I'm too busy," she says.

"Okay, then give me a call when you're not too busy. You've got my number now."

Without looking at him, she starts toward the stairs, but he grabs her arm. She stiffens. He's big, all right. A lot bigger than Raymond was. Six-one, six-two. And he's got those mile-wide shoulders. Hands the size of catcher's mitts.

His eyes travel to her midriff. The shirttails tied at her navel. "Sexy the way you've got that." He plucks one end of the shirttails, undoing the knot. She tries to yank herself away, but his grip is like iron. He pushes her up against the wall. He tugs on her low-rise waistband. "Let's see if you're a natural blonde."

Rage and fear have turned her blood to molten lava. If only she had something sharp, anything at all, even a pen. She can see the vein pulsing on his neck.

There are light footsteps on the stairs. Kevin drops Didi's arm. "Later, honey." He whirls and strides quickly to greet Christina.

She must have seen what has happened. She already knows what a scumbag her husband is. Didi waits for outrage. For Christina to kick Kevin out of the house again.

But she doesn't. Didi can hardly believe it. She's giving him a dreamy smile. "The girls want to go to the mall," she tells him.

And Kevin says, "No worries, Daffodil. I'll take them."

Christina continues up the stairs and drifts past Didi with a vague smile and goes into her studio, just as if she'd seen nothing at all.

She's not a twin soul after all.

Didi despises Kevin, but she hates Christina even more.

She's not going to tell her about how she's Alice Blackworth's reincarnation. She'll tell Christina nothing from now on.

She has other plans.

CHAPTER THIRTY

AVA

The interruptions to my work on Mom's studio had set me back in schedule—I'd wanted to finish re-creating it by the end of the day, but I still had lots to do. Without the curtains, the sea light glittered through the large windows: I tacked backdrop paper over the glass to dim it. I set up three easels and placed half-finished canvases on each. Then obsessively arranged and rearranged things on the table. Adding objects. Taking others away. There could be no wrong element. Nothing to jar me out of the past.

A tangerine and instant ramen for lunch, and now I was ready to start setting up shots. I carted lights and a tripod from my own studio to Mom's. Positioned the lights, then took some preliminary images, experimenting with various lenses and filters. I studied them.

There was still something lacking from the table.

Mom's rings. There was at least one in every painting and sometimes two or three amid the clutter on her table. The sparkle of the gemstones in contrast to all that grotesqueness—it was what brought her paintings alive. The play of beauty and repulsiveness. One quality animating the other.

Her jewelry was still in the Monterey bank vault where Aunt Willie had interred it seventeen years ago. I glanced at the time. It was too late to go now.

My phone sounded. A text from Margaret.

Sarah is loaded. Per my contact in OC, she owns listed assets of about $45 million. Congrats to James.

I stared at this with unease. She was rich. Definitely not a gold digger. In comparison with her fortune, Jamie's and mine were pitifully small. She could afford to give lavish presents. Leicas. iPhones. Handmade chocolates to hospital workers.

She was in love with Jamie. End of story. Lots of women had been crazy about him before, so why should it be strange?

But I was missing something. I was sure of it. But what?

Franny appeared sometime later with the curtains draped over her arm. "These came out good, Ava. I gave them a touch-up with a cool iron. Want me to hang them?"

"That would be great, Franny. Thanks." I ripped down the backdrop paper. A mist was rising outside. It was later than I'd thought—I'd lost track of time.

Franny nimbly climbed onto the swivel chair and rehung the curtains at the ocean-side window. She dragged the chair to the north window and looped the others back up. Hopped down. Hands on hips, she surveyed the room. "You've sure made this look like when Christina used to be here."

"Do you remember it?" I asked.

"Some. I used to come in here to watch her paint. I liked it when she mashed up stuff. Mud and charcoal and shit like that."

I smiled. "Yeah, I liked it too." I added, "Were you here that last day, when she went to the hospital?"

"No, I had school. But I remember her getting sick before that and walking funny. Michael said she'd started boozing to keep up with your dad, but I never saw her drink anything but a ton of tea."

"What about any of the other people who worked here? Do you remember any of them?"

"Michael. And my uncle Tyrus sometimes, he's the one who taught me electrical."

"How about a cleaning woman with a knee that hurt her?"

"Nope."

"She had a daughter who sometimes came with her. A girl who was sort of overweight and wore glasses."

"Oh, yeah, her."

"You remember her?" I asked eagerly.

"Kind of. She used to hang around Christina a lot. She didn't talk to me much. Or nobody except Christina and sometimes your dad."

"You saw her talk to Dad?"

"Yeah, sometimes." Franny prodded a dead hummingbird on the table—I'd found it on the edge of the forest. Green, with a rust-colored head. "Christina sure liked weird stuff, didn't she? I like it too. One time she had a nose—you know, like off of one of those broken statues? I asked if I could have it, but she said no, Jamie found it, and she wouldn't give it away."

"I remember when he found that," I said. "He was so excited. We all were. It was totally intact." I squinted appraisingly at the table. "That's something I need, some sculpture fragments. I should have thought of it earlier. Could you come help me find some before it gets too dark?"

"I would, Ava, but it's already past five o'clock, and I've gotta get home. Donny's waiting for me. We like to eat early."

"Oh, okay, Franny, go on. I'll see you tomorrow."

"You bet. Oh, wait. Michael said to tell you he checked around like you wanted, and he found some trampling on the grass, but it was probably raccoons. You want me to put some poison out? There's some in the toolshed."

"No! I don't want to poison any animals."

"That's good, because it doesn't work so hot on raccoons. It takes them a long time to die, and sometimes they don't even."

She left. I glanced out the window again. The fog was rising: if I was going to go search for sculpture fragments, I had to do it now, while there was still light left. I crossed the hall to my bedroom, pulled on a sweater, and headed downstairs to the mudroom.

So much of our old stuff, filthy and forlorn, was still drooping from pegs or crammed under the long wooden bench. I heard Betsy yapping a send-off to Franny, and the pickup sputtered, then chugged away.

I unhooked a large, tattered burlap bag. I shimmied a box of Mom's old gardening tools from under the bench, found a trowel, and tossed it into the bag. I slung it over my shoulder.

A flash of memory. Mom heading outside, a burlap bag hanging from her small-boned shoulder. A girl following her, slinging a similar bag. Wearing a droopy-brimmed hat like Mom's.

The girl in the yearbook. Didi Morrison.

That time I'd taken photos of her . . . maybe my little Canon Rebel was still up in my old bedroom.

No. I'd taken it with me to Aunt Willie's. For my fifteenth birthday, she'd bought me a new one, a serious Canon, and the Rebel got donated to one of Willie's many causes.

I opened the door. The mist was coming in fast from the water. I had to hurry if I wanted to find anything. But I hesitated. That eerie, middle-of-the-night phone call.

That sensation that somebody was out there in the night. Watching the house. Waiting for me.

Ridiculous.

Besides, it wasn't even night yet.

I stepped outside.

DIDI

Mimi cries all the way home from the free clinic where she's spent the past five hours getting evaluated. "They're wrong," she laments. "The pain's not just in my head. I absolutely need a knee replacement."

Didi's insanely pissed off about the way it went at the clinic, but she's trying not to show it. "They did x-rays and a lot of testing, Mimi," she says. "Your knee joint's not that bad, that's what the doctor said."

"He thinks I'm lying about how bad I'm in pain." She starts sniffling again. Digs an already snotty Kleenex from her pocket and blows her nose. "If Christina would've been there, they wouldn't have turned me down. They couldn't have gotten rid of her like they did with me. She would've insisted they do the replacement."

Didi silently agrees with her. That smirking creep of an orthopedic surgeon. So freaking pleased with himself, donating a little of his precious time to charity cases. He'd sized up Mimi immediately. A whiner. A middle-aged lady with some aches and pains. She ought to just grin and bear it.

He wouldn't have been so quick to reject her if Christina had been there, working her wiles on him.

She *said* she was going to be there. On Friday, Christina had met them outside the house when they arrived, she was so excited to tell them the news. "The most wonderful thing, Miriam!" she'd said to Mimi. "A patient at the clinic had to cancel a presurgical appointment, and you're being slotted in. Isn't that exciting? I'll go with you, of course, and make sure everything goes well."

Mimi was so excited that she hopped up and down, momentarily overcoming her excruciating pain.

But Christina had been a no-show today. Didi and Mimi had been made to wait over two hours until, hallelujah, Mimi was taken into the exam room. Didi had to hunker down in the waiting room for another two hours plus. Lunchtime came and went. Not even a vending machine in the clinic.

Finally, she was summoned into the inner sanctum, where Mimi was sitting on an exam table, finished with all the tests and waiting to consult with Dr. Hotshit Orthopedist. They cooled their heels (literally—it was ice cold in the exam room) for another half an hour until he breezed in.

"I've got very good news for you, Miriam." He pulled up an x-ray on a computer screen. "I've gone over your x-rays, and I am not seeing any significant deterioration of the knee cartilage or bone."

"You're not?" Mimi said in a tiny voice.

"No, so you can rest easy on that. However, I am seeing significant scarring from previous fractures in three places on the left femur." He made a circling motion with his hand at the area on the screen, then lifted an inquiring eyebrow at Mimi.

"She was hit with a socket wrench pretty hard," Didi blurted out. "My stepfather used to get carried away."

Mimi shot her a furious look. She's not supposed to share this information.

The doctor lifted both brows. "Was it reported?"

"Sure," Didi said. "It was all reported. And he's gone now, anyway."

The doctor kind of cleared his throat and turned back to the image on screen. "What I'm seeing is that some arthritis has set in to the old breaks. When the arthritis flares up, it's likely you think the pain is coming from the knee. That's not uncommon. We call it referred pain. It feels like it's coming from one place in the body but actually originates in another."

Didi got it instantly. He was turning Mimi down for a new knee or even an injection of any kind. Mimi tried to argue, but the doctor was done. He recommended exercise and over-the-counter pain relievers—Motrin because it was an anti-inflammatory, or else Tylenol. He wrote a prescription for six sessions of physical therapy. And then he was out of the room like a bullet.

Didi wanted to murder him. She really did.

But the one she blames the most is Christina.

She *said* she was going to come. She freaking promised.

She lied.

At home now, Didi settles Mimi on the ratty brown couch, two pillows under her leg, and gets her an ice pack. Then she goes to her room. She hates Christina like nobody ever before, not even Raymond.

Raymond was just an animal; you can't really hate an animal, you've just got to put them down.

But Christina's not an animal. She just freaking doesn't care.

Didi goes to her closet, and from the back, she pulls out her treasure chest. It's like Mimi's bag of pilfered souvenirs from her clients, except it's not a bag, it's a box from a pair of Vans. It contains bottles of expired pills—the ones Didi cleared out from the old lady Bev's medicine cabinet. The pills she'd used to mess up Wanda at the Rainiers' house.

She spills them out onto the bed. Counts them. Thirty-two bottles in all.

On her computer, she opens a new file. She begins looking up the various meds one by one and writing each one down in the file. What it's prescribed for. What the side effects are.

There's one that gets her pretty excited. Nembutal. It's a sedative. Sometimes called the suicide drug. Very lethal if taken with alcohol. Almost never prescribed anymore, except for pet euthanasia.

She types an asterisk in front of it.

She marks another of the drugs with an asterisk. Bufanenil, 100 mg.

Side effects: loss of coordination, confusion, agitation, and hallucinations.

It comes with a warning label: *Do not chew, divide, or crush the tablet.*

She finishes making the list. Picks out the two prescription bottles she had starred. The Nembutal she secretes in a pocket of her purse. She shakes out a bunch of the Bufanenil and crushes them on her desk with the jar of rancid skin cream Mimi had given her as a graduation present. The one Mimi had fished out of Mrs. Rainier's trash basket.

Didi sweeps the crushed pills into an envelope from a card Gram had sent her for her seventh birthday. It's adorned with a pink unicorn, and it says, "To a Magical Granddaughter!"

She doesn't open the card. She doesn't want to see Gram's writing right now.

She returns all the rest of the pill bottles back to the cardboard box. There's one other treasure inside it, and on an impulse, she takes it out.

It's the silver bracelet Thomas Rainier gave her—the one that seems to flow like mercury around her wrist. She's been afraid to wear it.

Mimi's got an eye like an eagle when it comes to anything expensive. She'd want to know how Didi got it.

But Mimi won't be going to Christina's house tomorrow. She'll be still resting. So Didi will be free to wear the bracelet. To feel the cool, pliant metal slip-sliding against her skin.

Enabling her in what she's going to do.

CHAPTER
THIRTY-ONE

AVA

The mist was fast weaving into a silvery-gray gauze as I began walking up the gravel drive, but sun gleamed through the darkening cedars. I still felt a little jumpy. But this was home, Blackworth Mansion. Jamie and I had wandered every inch of these grounds, even in the fog, even in pouring rain, playing among the rocks and tidal pools on the shore and chasing each other deep into the forest, and as long as there was daylight left, I had nothing to be afraid of.

But the light that flickered through the trees gave me the sensation that somebody was lurking in the woods. Keeping pace with me, darting from tree to tree.

I gave a start as Betsy came scampering up.

She raced on ahead, then came back and zigzagged past me, chasing a squirrel or some waving fern.

Nobody is lurking in the trees. I repeated it to myself.

Nobody would be prowling around in daylight.

The sun had a rusty twilight tint, and a breeze had come up off the forest, the undertone of rot heightened by the damp fog. And the fog amplified sounds: every snap of a pine branch sounded like a rifle shot. My heart started to beat a little faster.

I could now faintly make out the sculpture garden through the mist—the eerie, listing shapes of those statues that were still partially attached to the iron rods. The fountains, dry for many decades, black and also tilting. I quickened my steps.

Some reddish shape flickered through dark branches on my right. I whipped my head.

No one. Nothing. Of course not.

Betsy barked from ahead. She was inside the sculpture garden. I quickened my pace to the surrounding low wall and circled to the section that had been pushed down by flooding water over the years. It was even more crumbled now. The torrential rains this past winter—Michael said they'd swept gravel and debris all the way up to the house.

I stepped through the rubble into the enclosed gravel yard. Betsy was at the other end, barking—at a dead gopher, a skulking rat, or for no reason at all, like she sometimes did.

I gazed over the field of gravel and broken plaster fragments. Images from the past darted through my mind.

Jamie at nine. Holding up a partial piece of a face. *Hey, Ave! I got a nose.*

Mom, turning a rippled fragment in her hand: *Look, sweet loves! This one's made of real marble.*

I walked farther through the yard. The top layer of gravel had been washed away, and what was left formed drifts and hillocks. In the red-lit fog, it seemed Martian, the white shards the ruins of an alien civilization.

The most intact fragments were always buried deeper in the gravel. The mist was thickening by the moment. I needed to work fast. I began searching for a particularly shallow area where the erosion was heaviest.

An opaque scarf of fog momentarily blindfolded me, and I paused until it shredded into tatters. The air was damp and chill. The breeze had shifted away from the forest. It came off the water now, carrying the dismal moan of a low, receding tide.

Betsy began barking again. Agitated yips.

I moved through the ruined fountains toward her, caught sight of her digging furiously at the base of one of the partially upright statues. It was one I remembered well. Just a jagged section of face attached to a leaning rod, the features eroded to a smooth and impassive mask.

Mom had called it an allegory of time. She said it was like how time sanded everything away, love and passion and hate, until it was all just this smooth and uncaring mask. It had scared me silly when I was little.

Not Jamie. It was his favorite. He called it Ernie.

The rains had sluiced gravel, plaster shards, and plant debris high against Ernie's base, leaving a shallow depression in front of it. Betsy was digging furiously into the depression, barking and whining.

"Okay. Let's see what you've got." I pulled her back by her collar. I crouched and looked into the hole she'd made.

Nothing.

I set the bag down, took out the trowel, and began to dig deeper into the hole—eight, then nine inches deep. The trowel blade nicked something. I peered down again.

A faint gleam of white. A sculpture fragment—possibly one that was fairly intact. I scraped carefully around it with the trowel—old plaster was fragile, and even old marble broke easily. And then I set the trowel down and used my hands to gently clear more dirt and gravel away.

I drew an excited breath: part of a plaster finger. It seemed to be in excellent condition. Maybe even marble. I continued to very gently excavate it. It was even better than just part of a finger—an entire one. With joints that were meticulously defined.

Far more defined than on any other sculpture, I realized.

This was not marble. Or plaster.

I felt my blood turn very cold.

I sank back on my heels. I heard the ocean hiss. The wind muttering through swaying cedar branches. Betsy, barking again. She wouldn't stop.

Then the sound of a car engine. Headlights floating through the dense white mist, dissolving back into it.

I collected myself. Knelt again and looked back into the deep hole. Another dim gleam poking through the side. And now I seemed to be lapsing into an almost trancelike state as I began to clear around it. I used my hands again, scraping away gravel and debris. It was something larger than a finger, much larger, but it was getting so hard to see: the twilight was dimming to gray through the streaming mist.

I kept scraping around that dim gleam, and a rounded white shape emerged, and then the ridge of a brow, and then beneath the ridge, a gaping black void where there had once been an eye.

A black void staring up at me from out of a skull.

The sound of a car again, sweeping by in the opposite direction, heading back up to the highway. I only vaguely registered it. I felt pinned in place by the fog and the ocean and the suddenly threatening forest. Immersed in horror.

I knew whose skull this was. Whose bones were buried here.

Betsy, failed cadaver dog, wouldn't stop barking.

I raised myself to my feet. For a moment, I didn't know which way to go. I stretched out my arms as if trying to grope at something in the fog. And then I began stumbling my way back to the crumbled-down section of the wall, and I made my way over it and onto the driveway. The house, lights in the windows faintly glowing through silvery gray, seemed impossibly far away. I pushed myself on, one step after another, but my feet felt unattached to my brain, which was whirling with hideous images.

And then I froze: a figure was coming toward me. It appeared to be gliding without touching the ground, and my heart pounded so hard I felt it would tear itself apart.

Amid the chaos in my mind, a thought rose up: *Cinderella*.

But then the figure took more tangible shape. It was striding firmly on the ground. It was not a ghost, nor was it a hallucination.

It was my sister-in-law, Sarah.

And I felt in my wild, turbulent state an even greater dread.

CHAPTER THIRTY-TWO

SARAH

I had planned to stay at the Ritz-Carlton until the following morning. I had a full day of services booked: my hair cut and layered with fresh tints, a pulse-light facial, some subtle fillers. Not luxuries. Necessities.

But then I received Ava's texts about canceling the work I had asked Michael Fiore to do. I'd made a mistake. I could wait on these treatments, get them done in Palo Alto or some other town in Silicon Valley. I had my travel people find me a flight for this afternoon—another small private plane that could land at an airfield inland. Fortunate, because Monterey Airport was socked in by fog. Flying commercial, I'd still be delayed in Orange County.

A car and driver were waiting at the private airfield, and we began a slow journey down the foggy coast road to Carmel. But now finally we're on the access road. The driver misses the hidden, unpaved driveway to the house. I suppress a snap of annoyance as I direct him back. As we head down, we are ensconced in an even thicker cloud. The driver mutters as a branch claws the roof.

The house looks dark. Mysterious. Those tall, witchy gables on both wings. The pines in front, dying for years and yet refusing to die. There are a few lights burning in windows, but they seem neither cheery nor welcoming.

The driver swivels to face me. He's an older Black man with pouchy eyes and superb posture. "Are you sure this is it?" he asks.

"Yes, this is my house," I say. "Thank you."

He gets out and opens my door for me and takes my bag out of the trunk. A large tip has already been written into the bill, but I give him an extra fifty. He looks concerned to be leaving me at what is evidently the lair of a mad scientist, but I turn and head briskly up to the front door. It's unlocked, and I step inside.

I call out to Ava so she won't be startled by my sudden appearance. No answer. I run upstairs and call down her hallway, but she's not up there either. I deposit my bag in my own suite.

The window in my sitting room is partially open, and a slightly rotten smelling breeze from the forest is blowing in. Did I leave it open?

Was I getting so careless?

As I go to shut it, I hear the dog, Betsy, barking from outside. Ava must be taking a walk with her. Strange, in this fog, but Ava is strange to me in ways I can hardly count.

I go back downstairs and head outside. Betsy comes bounding up to me in a delirium of excitement. The dog is hyperactive. Any little thing makes her go bonkers with excitement. But she's particularly frenetic right now: she races off again up the drive.

I go after her curiously. I can't see very far ahead, so I walk slowly. I *am* getting careless: I should have brought one of those hurricane lanterns. I'm about to turn back when suddenly I see her—Ava—standing stock still, as if horrified by the very sight of me.

And suddenly I'm seized with horror too. I have the instinct to turn and run.

She recovers herself and strides toward me, yelling my name, and I step forward to meet her. She looks wild. Almost out of her senses. I grab her by the arms. "What's happened?" I say.

She shakes her head wildly. "I need to call the police."

"Why? What is it?"

"I need to call them. Now."

"Ava," I say. "Tell me. Is it something you've done?"

"No, nothing. I mean, I found something." She's panting; hyperventilating.

"Found what?"

"My father. He's there."

"Where?" I look quickly at the blackening forest around us, right, then left. "Where is he?"

"In the sculpture garden. He's buried underneath the gravel. It's him."

"You're not making any sense." She's frightening me terribly, but I try not to show it to her. I wonder if she's maybe on the verge of another breakdown. "Please, Ava, try to calm down. It's okay, I'm here."

She draws some deep, slower breaths and regains some control. "Okay, I'm okay."

"Tell me what's happened."

She glances over her shoulder, then back at me. "I was in the sculpture garden, I was searching for fragments. You know, pieces of sculpture, I was looking for a good one, something still intact. And then Betsy started digging, and I went to see, and I dug deeper into the hole she'd made, and I found something. A bone. A finger bone. And near it, there's a skull."

"An animal," I say.

She shakes her head frantically. "It's him. It's my father."

"What?" I say incredulously.

"They're his bones. He's buried back there."

"I'm going to go take a look, okay? You've had a shock, but it's probably not what you think."

"No," she insists. "Don't go back there. You don't want to see, it's too horrible." She shivers hard. "I've got to call the police and tell them. I left my phone in the house."

"Okay," I say in a soothing voice. "Let's go back to the house. You can call the police, but you need to calm down a little."

"I am calming down," she says fiercely.

"Okay, great. Let's go back."

I start walking with her toward the house. She says suddenly, "Why are you here?"

"I was done with my legal affairs. I was planning to stay another night, but then I got your texts and decided to come back right away. I was afraid you were mad at me."

She looks at me as if I'm the one not making sense now. She murmurs, "All this time I've been thinking he's been out here. Stalking me. Those awful cards. And then a phone call. I had the horrible sense he was here, somewhere close by. Somewhere right outside the house." She gives a harsh laugh. "I was right. He's been here all along."

"You see, you've scared yourself," I say gently. "We'll find out what it all is. It will all become clear."

We climb the steps to the porch, and I open the door and we head inside, the dog scooting in with us.

"My phone is upstairs," Ava says.

"Use mine." I hand it to her. "But before you call 911, wait. Don't tell them you think it's your father. Don't say anything except that you found what looks like human remains on your property."

"Why?"

"Things can get so easily misunderstood. My first husband taught me that. Anything else you say, you should have a lawyer present. I can call my attorney, and she can get somebody for you quickly."

"No, I'll call my friend—Grace Zhao. She's a lawyer."

"Does she do criminal defense?"

Ava stares at me. The word *criminal* has thrown her.

"You don't want a civil case lawyer for this," I say. "You'll be talking to the police."

"Grace deals with police all the time."

"Okay, good. I'll give you privacy." I turn and head down the hallway, stopping at the thermostat. I'm chilled to the bone, and I imagine that Ava, in her shock, is even colder. I revolve the dial up to high, for all the good it will do. This ancient heating system is next to useless.

I continue into the kitchen and light with matches all the burners on the old ceramic stove. Ava comes in several minutes later. "The police are on the way. They'll be here soon. And Grace is coming too."

The black cat, Stieglitz, rubs her leg. It disturbs me how he seems to just materialize from some otherworldly realm. She scoops him up, hugs him tightly, then puts him back down. She seems to be in a dream state, not totally conscious of what she's doing. She goes into the butler's pantry.

For a moment, I think she's going into the servants' quarters. That horrific place.

But I hear her open a cabinet and take out a bottle. She brings it into the kitchen. It's Johnnie Walker scotch. I feel a momentary shudder.

She pours a stiff amount into a water glass. She gulps it and grimaces.

She doesn't really like scotch.

"I've got to call Jamie," she says suddenly. "Before he hears about it from somebody else."

"We can't now," I say. "He'll be exhausted and sore from physical therapy. And we don't even know what this is yet."

"He'll know I'm right. It's Dad."

"Ava, listen. It can't be. Jamie saw him, remember? Jogging on the road up in the Santa Cruz hills."

"He was mistaken, it was somebody else. Or maybe . . ." She pauses.

"Maybe what?"

"He said the jogger just disappeared. So maybe his eyes clouded over. Or . . . those eye drops he used. Do you know what they are?"

"No. They're by prescription, that's all I know." I can tell what she's really thinking. He was hallucinating. There was never a jogger there at all.

"If anyone calls him, it has to be me, Ava," I say firmly. "But we need to wait until we know more."

She stares at me like I'm a total stranger, not somebody who belongs here, who has any connection to James or to her. Then she takes another gulp of the scotch she hates. It almost seems like a penance. "As soon as we know more," she says.

Within an hour, Blackworth Mansion is swarming with activity. Police and coroner's office vehicles and an ambulance—just in case, I guess, there's a spark of life left in those old bones. The county sheriff's deputies have buff-colored uniforms with six-pointed stars. Plainclothes detectives are the ones in charge. Several TV vans show up, oblivious to trespassing. It's too foggy for helicopters, but they'll come as soon as it isn't.

Grace Zhao-Greenwald had arrived quickly, despite her far-along pregnancy. She appears to be on familiar terms with the investigators and a lot of the coroner's crew. I gather that they've confirmed the bones are human.

Ava had spoken to the detectives before Grace arrived, but Grace was in time to stop her from saying too much, and now we're all closeted in the library, the one with the gargoyle carvings. Ava and Grace and me. Grace has informed the police there'll be no more questioning for the night.

"But why shouldn't I tell them it's my father?" Ava says. She's switched to tequila, her favorite, I've noticed, for serious drinking.

"Because we don't know that it is," Grace says patiently. "It could be a total stranger. This property was deserted for a long time, so it would have been an attractive place for somebody to dump a body. We don't know how long the remains have been there. Or if there's even been a crime. Let's let forensics determine all that."

"Is that what we're supposed to call him now?" Ava says. "Remains?"

Grace gives her a tolerant smile like you'd give a child asking why the sky is blue. "I think it's best, sweetie. It will take a few weeks for the coroner's unit to release its preliminary findings. They're always backed up."

"How can it not be a crime?" Ava insists. "It's obvious somebody killed him."

"Sweetie, we don't even know yet if it's a him. And it could have been an accident. A slip and fall."

"But somebody buried the body."

"Maybe not. The gravel might have gotten swept over it by rains and wind over the years."

Ava considers this a moment. "Michael Fiore would have seen it at some point. He was the caretaker all those years."

"It's at a place hidden from the road, so if you're driving, you wouldn't see it. How often did Michael actually go into that area?"

Ava shrugs. "He had to sometimes."

"The police will question him, so let's not make any assumptions."

"I think Grace is right, Ava," I say softly. "We shouldn't jump to conclusions about anything."

She darts a glance at me, as if she'd forgotten I'm there.

Grace is summoned by a detective: apple cheeked, mustachioed. The name on his badge is Bissello. Ava refills her glass. She's brought the bottle.

My text tone sounds. It's from Lenore. I scan it hastily. She's got a top criminal defense lawyer in LA ready to assist James if necessary. And me as well if need be.

Ava snuggles deeper into the couch, a long pale-gray throw pulled around her, her glass in hand. She plucks at the hem of the throw in a distracted manner. "My Aunt Willie wove this," she murmurs. "She used eleven different shades of silver and gray thread. Silk thread for the warp and cashmere for the weft." She's rambling to distract herself.

"It's very beautiful," I tell her.

She tugs it tighter around her. Drains her glass. "I know it's my father out there. I'm sure of it. And I'm sure he was murdered, and it must be by the same person who killed Mom."

"But you were sure he was the one who killed your mom, Ava," I say carefully.

"Yes, I was. But this has changed everything. There's something else I've been thinking of. It may be crazy. But that girl who used to stalk you in high school?"

"Didi Morrison?"

"Yes. She was the girl who worked for us back then. I got a copy of your high school yearbook, and I saw her photo."

I give her a look of surprise. "I never even looked at it after graduation. I didn't have a photo in it."

"Except in the lacrosse photo," Ava says.

"Oh, lacrosse. I forgot about that." I pluck a strand of my hair and twist it. "So you saw Didi Morrison. A real oddball, wasn't she?"

"She is in the photo. But you can tell she's made herself look very freaky. I remember now from when she worked here that she wasn't all that freaky looking. She was standoffish and didn't seem to like anybody, except for Mom. She used to follow Mom around. Like the way you said she followed you around at school."

"That's pretty interesting," I say.

"Yeah. And Franny told me she remembered her talking with Dad. My father had a thing for very young women. So now I've been thinking. I mean, what if she had something to do with Mom's death? Like, maybe Dad hit on her. His phone number's on the back of that sketch she gave you. And maybe they had some kind of relationship. And Mom found out and turned on her." Words are tumbling out of her now in a manic way. "She was crazy enough to try to kill you when you rejected her, right? So maybe with Mom too. Maybe she poisoned Mom. And then maybe decided she wanted to kill all of us. She tried to kill me by giving me Nembutal and scotch. She must have come back for Dad years later."

"No, Ava," I say.

"Why not? It all fits. And now she might be trying to get at me again, and who knows, maybe Jamie as well. She could have been the one who sent me those cards. And I got a phone call last night, it said it was from Dad's old number, but it wasn't, it was a spoofed call. Like she's taunting me, letting me know she's coming after me, and who knows what she's going to do?"

"Ava, stop!" I say emphatically.

She looks at me, startled.

I go over and sit beside her on the couch and take her hands in mine. "Please, just listen to me. It can't be Didi. She's dead."

She stares at me.

"Didi Morrison died in Canada several years after high school," I tell her. "She and her mother moved to Vancouver Island sometime after graduation. It's where her mother was from. Didi was killed by a drunk driver a few years later."

"How do you know?" Ava says.

"I had Gideon do a search for her because I couldn't stop being scared of her after what happened. I had the idea, the same as you do, that she was coming after me again. I couldn't get it out of my head. He hired an investigator to track her down and found out she died."

"But you said you've seen her since then. You told me you catch glimpses of her from time to time."

"Oh, Ava," I say softly. "I was speaking figuratively. I meant that I see her in my mind's eye. She haunts me, just like you're haunted by what happened with your mother. I had no idea you were taking me literally."

Ava shakes her head, and locks of her thick dark hair fall into her eyes. "I don't believe you. You're just trying to keep me calm. You don't have to, I'm calm enough."

"Gideon showed me the death certificate. And if it turns out you're right and it is your father out there and he was murdered, I think there are more likely suspects. Michael Fiore, for instance."

She pauses. "I've considered Michael," she admits. "But why would he?"

"Maybe it was an accident. After an argument. Maybe he caught your father on the property with no business being here, and things got out of hand. Or something about money. Michael seems to be very fond of money."

She glances briefly away. She likes Michael. She doesn't want to think anything bad about him.

"And there's something else you should know," I say. "When I talked to him about doing that work on the grounds, he was the one who suggested adding more gravel to the sculpture garden."

"He had no reason for poisoning Mom."

I say gingerly, "You have to consider something else, Ava. The possibility that nobody did. That your mother wasn't murdered, she really did have a disease. It's what James thinks. And maybe after this you should stop being so obsessed with the past."

"Jamie changed his mind," she says. "He told me I could be right about Mom."

"Really? I'm . . . well, surprised. He always seemed so sure."

There are voices out in the front hall. Grace Zhao. She's come back inside and is talking with one of the investigators. She continues talking as their footsteps head toward us. She appears at the door, but not with an investigator.

She's with Thomas Rainier.

Our eyes meet, and prickling sensations course through my entire body. I quickly look away.

But not before Ava has noticed.

CHAPTER THIRTY-THREE

AVA

My heart gave a leap at the sight of Thomas. I had texted him what happened, and I'd told him he should stay away, the police probably wouldn't let him on the property. I hadn't heard back from him and assumed he wasn't coming. But he had, and I smiled up at him gratefully.

But he wasn't looking at me. His eyes were fixed on Sarah.

I watched a silent dialogue pass between them.

He'd lied. They both had. The thought burned through my mind. They'd known each other far better than they'd let on. They'd been closely involved.

And maybe they still were.

Sarah was the first to withdraw her eyes, ducking her head in that reticent way of hers, and Thomas came over to me. "Hey, are you okay?"

"I suppose so." I shrugged. "How did you get past the police?"

"I just did. Nobody stopped me."

Sarah rose rather abruptly. "If it's okay, I think I'll go upstairs and lie down. Unless, Ava, you still need me for anything?"

"No," I said.

Grace grasped Sarah's hand warmly. "Thank you, Sarah, for being so supportive of Ava."

"I hope I have been a little." She smiled gently at me. "Good night, Ava, I'll see you in the morning." She nodded at Thomas and left the room.

Grace said, "I'm going to take off now too. This is going to go on all night. Ave, could you walk me to my car? I need a word with you."

"Of course." I got up. "I'll be right back," I said to Thomas.

I followed Grace out to the front hall. "I'm glad you have Sarah with you," she said. "I like her. She's warm and capable, and she seems genuinely concerned for you." In the light of the chandelier, she looked exhausted.

"You should have sent somebody else," I said. "You need to be taking care of yourself."

"I am, sweetie. I just want to mention a few more things. At some time in the next few days, you'll be asked to come to the precinct. I'll come with you, of course. You'll give a more detailed statement. We'll decide beforehand if it's okay for you to talk about your father. If you do, they'll want a DNA sample to help with the ID. You don't have to agree to it without a warrant."

"Why wouldn't it be okay?"

"I'll need to know a few things first. Like, when exactly was the last time you saw him? And where were you in the time period following that?"

"Wait," I said. "Am I going to be a suspect?"

"If it is your father and there's any evidence that there was a crime involved, they're not going to rule out any family members, at least not immediately."

"I can tell you the last time I saw him. It was right after Mom's burial. We were all here, in this house. Dad was drinking scotch. The ice in his glass clinked because his hands were trembling." I took a breath. "He had pulled the plug on Mom. I heard him say that to Aunt Willie. He said she'd been brain dead for a week."

"Oh, Ava," Grace murmured.

"The last time I talked to him was about three years ago, when I was still in Boston. I wouldn't lend him any money, and he got abusive. After that, I never took any of his calls again. I even changed my number."

"Okay. We'll get into more details tomorrow. I'll be asking Jamie the same questions when he's up to it. But don't worry much. After all this time, it will be almost impossible to find any real evidence. The site's been compromised by rain and wind. It will probably end up as just another cold case in a file."

That sounded so bleak. She opened the door. Through the fog, flashing smears of red and white lights, with spectral figures moving around them.

"Am I allowed to leave?" I asked. "I mean, leave the property tonight?"

"With Thomas?" She regarded me warily. "I wasn't totally surprised to run into him here."

"I figured you wouldn't be."

"There's no reason you can't leave. You're not charged with anything. All I can say, Ave, is I wish you wouldn't."

"I might not," I said. "I don't know."

We hugged, something that had become increasingly difficult with the size of her pregnancy. I returned to the Monster Room. Thomas was crouched at the fireplace, examining one of the gargoyles—a shrieking three-horned imp with long pointed ears. "I remember this dude. Your mother said he was straight from Hieronymus Bosch."

"Yes. A painting called *Hell*."

"I might have guessed." He straightened up and came toward me. I drew back. "Hey, sorry I didn't text you back. I was on a small plane flying through a line of thunderstorms. It was intense. We got in late, and I didn't check messages until I was in my car."

"That's not it," I said. "What's your real relationship with Sarah?"

His eyes became guarded.

"I saw the way you looked at each other. I know there's something more than what you told me."

"Do you really want to talk about this now? After what you've just been through?"

"Yes. I want to talk about it."

"Okay. The truth? It's not much different than what I told you."

"I think it is."

"It's not. I did meet her with her husband at a charity event. But I didn't just run into them. Ellingham had invited me. I was seated at his table next to Sarah. I drank too much and began flirting with her. Heavy flirting. I was practically falling into her lap."

"Did she respond?"

"Yeah, she did. I think she enjoyed the attentions of a man a lot younger than her husband. Ellingham couldn't help noticing. He would have had to be blind not to. He canceled my commission to design his museum the next day." He shrugged. "I thought about suing, but he had dozens of lawyers who could stall it forever. My lawyer said don't bother."

Stieglitz seemed to have suddenly appeared at his feet. Stieglitz never came out for strangers. I had a memory: Thomas at fifteen, picking up Mom's white cat, O'Keeffe. Nuzzling her head. An affinity with cats.

"What happened after that?" I said. My voice felt strange. Depleted. "Between you and Sarah?"

"Nothing. The next time I saw her was here, when she came up from the beach. But I've always wondered if it had cost her. I'd heard some things about Ellingham. That he liked rough sex, among other things. Just now, I was trying to convey to her I was sorry."

He wasn't telling me everything. But I felt suddenly overwhelmed. I sank into a chair. Everything was strange and dark. If I could just see what I already knew—pull it out of the shadows of my mind—I'd have what I was looking for.

"What are you thinking?" Thomas asked. "Tell me."

"I don't want to talk anymore."

"You should. You've got to be in shock. Please, talk to me."

I met his eyes. I suddenly didn't care what secrets he had. What he had or hadn't done. I just wanted him. "Take me out of here. Someplace high and not closed in, where I can see forever. Now, before I go out of my mind."

"Okay, I can do that." He took my arms, lifted me to my feet. "You'll need something warm." He grabbed the wrap Aunt Willie had woven on her attic loom and draped it around me.

We went out, and I told one of the plainclothes cops I was leaving for a while. Thomas led me to his truck—the hulking black one with the high-mounted headlights. We drove up the eroded gravel driveway, encircling the sculpture garden. Yellow crime-scene tape strung around the wall. The glare of huge lights, the hum of a generator. Dogs, milling people in uniforms.

I averted my eyes.

We continued to the highway. I didn't ask where we were going. He drove up snaking streets and steep narrow lanes in the Carmel Highlands, ascending above the fog line to a high promontory. He parked. Reached for an old flannel jacket behind his seat. We got out and walked among ancient cedars, all twisted bare trunks and flattened canopies. Thomas spread the jacket on the ground, and we huddled down beside each other.

The wind was sharp. Below was a thick white quilt of cloud. The horror of the evening lay buried below it. But above us, stars pulsed faintly through a transparent mist.

I let myself be thirteen again. The simple proximity of his body to mine setting every nerve on fire.

DIDI

September 2006

Didi's stomach is fluttering when she arrives at the Hollands' house. She's got the birthday-card envelope containing the crushed-up prescription pills in her shoulder bag, and it's not like anybody's going to be searching it, but still, she's a little nervous.

Ava and James's school, Sanderson Day Academy, started back up today, so they're already gone from the house, and after school, they'll have a full schedule of activities. There are people working inside, but there always are. Spackling and painting. Ripping out wires. Replacing moldings. Fixing that old-time enamel stove that Christina is so in love with. But Didi's perfected the art of blending into the background. Keeps her head low and scrunches her body into whatever task she's doing, and they rarely give her a glance.

For a change, Christina is already up, and she's in the kitchen, arranging flowers in a cut glass vase. "Good morning, Didi," she murmurs. "Where's your mother?"

"Her knee is too sore after the clinic yesterday. They made her move it around a lot."

"They told me the good news. She doesn't need a knee replacement. She must be so relieved!"

"Why didn't you come?" Didi can't keep a surly tone out of her voice.

"I couldn't, dear. Jamie and Ava were going crazy getting ready to go back to school. I had to help them sort out their clothes and organize other things."

Resentment rises inside Didi like a burning balloon.

A kettle on the stove starts to scream bloody murder, and Christina, hands full of white snapdragons, says, "Shut that off, would you, Didi? And could you take down some tea for me?"

Didi switches off the flame. She opens a cupboard. The paint is peeling inside. "What kind?"

"There's a hibiscus flower imported from Nigeria that came in yesterday. It's supposed to be rich in antioxidants. They prevent cancer, did you know that, Didi?"

Didi locates the bright flower-decorated box. Natural Hibiscus Blossom Antioxidant Tea. Christina carefully situates the last of the snapdragons in the vase, then opens the tea box and scoops four heaping tablespoons into a speckled blue teapot. There's one of her sketchbooks on the counter. She tucks it under her arm and then picks up the vase and heads into the butler's pantry.

Bringing flowers to a ghost. A few weeks ago, Didi would have been in raptures over such a poetic gesture. Now she just finds it pretentious.

But it's the opportunity she's been hoping for, though she'll have to be quick.

She takes out the birthday-card envelope. She grabs a large pinch of the crushed pills and sprinkles it into the teapot.

The mudroom door slams open. Didi hurriedly replaces the lid. She stuffs the envelope back into her purse.

The little girl, Franny, who's the handyman's daughter, comes trooping in. "What are you doing?" she asks.

"Making Christina's tea. Why aren't you in school?"

"It doesn't start for me until next week." Franny wrinkles her nose. "That doesn't smell like tea."

Didi's nerves go on alert. "It's a special kind. Made from tropical flowers."

"Like what?"

"Hibiscus." Didi shows her the box with the crimson blossom. "See, it looks like this."

"Can I have some?"

"No, it's not for kids."

The door in the butler's pantry opens and closes again, and the key turns. Christina reappears, now carrying a tarnished silver vase of dead blooms. "Oh, hello, Franny," she says. "No school for you today?"

Franny shakes her freckled head. "You want me to dump those in the compost for you?"

"No, love. I'm going to paint them just like this."

Franny points to Didi. "That lady is making tea with flowers."

"I know, isn't that lovely? Didi, would you bring me up a cup when it's ready? A good strong one. Let it steep about ten minutes."

Do this, Didi. Do that, Didi. Wait on me hand and foot like a good servant.

"Sure, Christina," she says.

Christina continues out to the hallway, carrying the dead bouquet, Franny trailing after her, peppering her with dumb questions. A poem Didi read just yesterday wafts into her head:

"Love, strong as Death, is dead . . . Among the dying flowers."

It's by a Victorian poetess named Christina Rossetti who Didi's been reading like crazy. Her poems are mostly about death. Didi loves it that her name was also Christina. And even better, she was the sister of the artist Dante Rossetti, who painted the red-haired woman on Didi's copy of *Tess of the d'Urbervilles*—the painting that had reminded her of Christina Blackworth Holland.

It's all so intertwined and connected that it's got to be a sign.

The tea has steeped long enough. She lifts the lid and sniffs tentatively. It smells like a sweetish flower, nothing more. She dabs a finger and tastes. A little cloying, but nothing suspicious.

She fills one of Christina's hand-painted mugs and carries it carefully upstairs. She doesn't spill a drop.

CHAPTER THIRTY-FOUR

SARAH

I've been pacing since I've come upstairs, walking back and forth between the bedroom and sitting room, trying to imagine what's going to happen next. Ava's terrified by what she's found, and I'm scared by it too.

I lied to Ava. Didi Morrison is not dead.

I do sometimes see her. She's become fatter and homelier over the years—it's pathetic how she's let herself go. I might not even have recognized her now, except her face is etched forever in my mind. She does nothing more except let me know she's tormenting me. Pathetic freak.

Gideon was supposed to get rid of her for good. It was our deal. "Make her disappear," I'd said to him that first night he took me out on his boat. That enormous, phallic schooner, *Windjammer*. "I'll do anything you want. Just make sure she's gone forever." We were in his stateroom below, and I was down on my knees, tears wriggling down my face. "Please," I begged him. "I don't care how you do it. Just get rid of her."

And he had made her disappear. I thought it was forever.

I was wrong. It could be just a matter of time before Ava and even James start getting glimpses of her and spoil everything for me. I can't let that happen. I'll make certain that she's gone for good. That, too, is just a matter of time.

I look out the forest-side window, where everything is usually black, but now the property is lit up like Christmastime. There are people in uniforms with devices like metal detectors roaming here and there, and dogs—real cadaver-sniffing dogs, not wannabes like Betsy—are sniffing and barking. There's a lot of digging going on. They must think if there's one buried skeleton, there's got to be a dozen more.

But I'm not being fair to Betsy. She's the one who sniffed out the bones.

But Ava was the one who found them, and it's pushing her to the brink of crazy. She's getting out of control.

My thoughts turn to Thomas Rainier. The way he slouched into the Monster Room with Grace Zhao-Greenwald and fixed his eyes on me. Like broadcasting our connection out loud. Ava caught it immediately.

Stupid of me to have left them together; I should have stayed with them, all night if necessary.

I pull out my phone. And I write a carefully composed email to Thomas.

Not threatening, not pleading. Simply detailing certain facts and certain consequences if he starts telling Ava about things he shouldn't. I mention a few things I have in my possession. I drop the name of my attorney, Lenore Wyatt.

He doesn't reply for a long time. And then finally he does. Just two words: Got it.

CHAPTER THIRTY-FIVE

AVA

Forensic activity on the property continued for another four days. The investigating unit and its dogs roamed the property all day and into the evening. Betsy had to be shut up in the house, and she ran up and down like a crazed creature. Stieglitz took up permanent residence under my bed.

I couldn't work. My phone sounded nonstop. Franny nailed a handwritten sign to a pine trunk at the highway: **PRIVATE PROPERTY NO TRESPASSING!!!** with a drawing of crossed revolvers, but news vans and rubberneckers came anyway, only taking off when Michael stalked by them with a shotgun under his arm. Helicopters whapped overhead, and the footage they shot of Blackworth Mansion made it look perpetually enwreathed in an ominous mist.

"The House of Horrors" became a media catchphrase.

A message from Margaret Zhao: Stunned by the news. Still want me to do trace on Morrison?

There was no point. Didi Morrison was dead. Unless, I thought, Sarah's husband had lied to her. Fabricated a death certificate. To keep Sarah in control.

I wrote: Yes, tho she might be dead. Car crash Vancouver Island some yrs after high school. Would like to see death cert.

The coroner's office released its preliminary report. Male, roughly fifty years old. Date of death, two and a half to three years ago. No immediate sign of a criminal act. Cause of death, undetermined.

The following day, I gave a statement to a pair of detectives at the precinct with Grace seated beside me. Described the sequence of events leading to my digging the bones up. Told them it might be my father—he'd dropped out of sight two or three years ago. I refrained from mentioning anything about how I knew with some sixth sense that it was him. I agreed to a cheek swab.

That night, I stayed with Thomas in his gorgeous, near-empty house. The very opposite of Blackworth Mansion. I drowned myself in a long bout of lovemaking and afterward sobbed furiously in his arms. And then I felt a little better.

I began obsessively taking photos of Mom's studio. I shot in black and white and in color and used halo lights in some shots and ambient lighting in others. I made dozens of images and studied them closely.

The sparkle of her jewels was still missing. I added a couple of my own rings to the table. Better. But still not right. Only Mom's rings had the right perfection of glitter and light to them.

Unless everything was absolutely right, every detail exact, I would never unlock my memories. Ever. Just the thought of that drove me crazy.

Crazy. The word floated into my mind.

What if I really was going crazy again?

I was feeling increasingly strange. My throat was tight. My stomach sometimes did that clenching thing again.

My thoughts jumped and skittered wildly like grasshoppers in tall weeds.

I had to get a grip.

I'm rushing into the house. There's something urgent I have to do. The hallway at the top of the stairs is encased in shadows. A large shadow goes bobbing across it, swift and ghostly: it makes a creaky sound that terrifies me.

And now I'm in Mom's studio, and she's in the corner between the two windows, that mockery of a dance. Grinning at me, her head a skull, her eyes two black voids. There's somebody or something right next to me. Pinching my arm. I hear myself scream.

"Ava?" Sarah called.

I sat up with a bolt. I was in bed, and Stieglitz was next to me, round eyes open wide. I was sweating. My pulse racing.

I looked at my arm. He had nipped it, but just lightly: a feline wake-up call.

"Ava? Can I come in?" Sarah cautiously opened the door. Stieglitz leaped off the bed and scurried under it. "Bad dream?"

"A nightmare. I'll be okay in a second."

She picked up a tray from the floor beside her and backed into the room with it. "It's almost noon. You didn't come down, so I thought I'd better bring some coffee up to you." She set the tray on my bed table. A small pitcher of coffee. Another of steamed milk. A wide-rimmed china cup. A spoon. A saucer of raw sugar lumps. "I sent this up on the dumbwaiter. It's now working like a charm."

"It creaks, doesn't it? It got into my dream."

"Oh, Ava, you're sweating. It must have been a terrible nightmare."

"It was."

"I'm sorry. Would you like a café au lait? Coconut milk. I found a French press in one of the cupboards."

"It was Dad's. He made three cups of strong coffee every morning and laced it with Black Label. Yes, I'd love some."

She poured the coffee and steamed milk in identical streams. "I learned the trick of this while I was with Gideon. He demanded that I learn it, actually. It had to be precisely right." She handed the foamy cup to me.

I sipped. "It's really good."

"Not too sweet?"

"No, perfect. Thank you."

She perched on the edge of my bed. She was wearing no makeup, and it made her look not older, exactly, not any less lovely, but different somehow. "I've been having nightmares too. For a long time. Actually the same one every night, over and over."

"Me too. The same one. Just the details change."

"Tell me about yours."

I let out a sigh. "It's a version of when I found my mother that last day. Doing this jerking kind of dance and making convulsive faces. Sometimes in the dreams, she points at me like she's accusing me. Other times she reaches her hand up, like pleading for my help. Just now, her head melted into a skull." I gave a grim smile. "It doesn't take Freud to interpret that one."

"You're processing your most recent trauma. That's a function of dreams."

"I suppose so," I said. "Tell me about yours."

"Oh God. I'm back on that cliff in high school. I'm standing on the edge, looking out at the moonlight on the ocean. It's so peaceful and beautiful. And then suddenly I'm in free fall, and at first it's a kind of . . . I don't know, ecstasy. I just let myself go, and it's, well, sublime. But then suddenly it turns to terror. Like sheer terror, and I'm desperately flailing and trying to stop falling. But I can't. I keep falling and falling, and I know for sure I'm going to die." She gave her shoulders a shake. "I felt it was so unfair. And all I could think about it was that I wanted to get even."

"With Didi?"

"It's terrible to think about it, but yes. I wanted to get even with that freaky bitch." There was a venom in her voice I'd never heard before. "When I wake up from these dreams, I'm sticky with sweat and my heart's going a mile a minute. It's PTSD. Posttraumatic stress disorder. You and I are living out our old traumas over and over."

"You're probably right." I swallowed the rest of the coffee, and Sarah refilled the cup, those perfect twin streams, one dark and rich, the other white and frothy. "Do you know what I'm most terrified of?" I said to her.

"What?"

"Of falling back into the state I was in after Mom died. I had delusions. I thought everybody was a threat. There was danger everywhere. I needed to protect myself by huddling up in a deep, dark space. The thing is, I'm afraid that if I do ever slip back into that place, this time I'll never get out. I'll be locked in it forever."

"Oh my God, Ava." Her dark-brown eyes gravely met mine. "We'll get through this together. I promise you."

I felt that rush of warmth toward her that I sometimes did. I took another fortifying sip of coffee.

"I've got a surprise for you," she said. "James is coming home at the end of the week."

I lowered the cup. "He can't. He's got another week of therapy to go."

"I know, and I tried to argue with him, but he insisted. He hates being there. They cut him off too quickly from his pain meds, and he's been in agony. He'll feel better once he's here."

"Will he be up in the suite with you?"

"Not at first. He'll need a hospital bed. I'm going to do up his old bedroom for him."

"How will he get up and down the stairs?"

"With help, he'll be able to. And downstairs, he'll have a wheel-chair, so he'll be self-sufficient." She stood up. "I've got a lot to do today. I've ordered the medical bed for his room, and it will be delivered very soon. Two of Michael's men are going to start painting and refinishing the floor. And I need to go to the rehab center and deal with a mountain of paperwork."

Her phone sounded. Music. It was familiar. "What's that music?" I said.

She made a face. "My alarm clock. Some movie theme song I just happened to like. I must have accidentally reset the time." She turned it off, then reached for the tray. "Do you want me to leave you the coffee?"

"No, thanks," I said. "I've had enough."

I had a kind of coming-down-with-a-flu feeling, weak and sweaty. I thought of Jamie leaving rehab early. Being back in his old bedroom.

It felt so wrong that maybe it was making me sick.

I shouldn't have told Sarah about my fears of slipping back into that dark place. I'd never told anyone about it. Not even Aunt Willie, who I'd loved so much. Or even Jamie.

I dragged myself up. Took a long bath, as hot as I could get it. As I was dressing, I heard heavy footsteps clumping up the front stairs. Men's voices. Bringing up something heavy—the medical bed for Jamie's bedroom.

This is wrong.

I felt a slight wave of dizziness. I really was coming down with something. I lay on my bed again. The music from Sarah's alarm revolved in my mind. Where did I know it from?

It came to me: one of those old vinyl albums Mom used to play while she was painting. "Tubular Bells." That particular song was used in *The Exorcist*.

I was so sleepy. My eyes closed. I dropped back into unconsciousness.

DIDI

October 2006

Christina has been sick for over a month now, and she won't see a doctor. "She says she's just absent minded," Mimi tells Didi. "She's not paying attention, so that's why she's clumsy and dropping things."

Didi grins to herself. Sure it is. Tripping over her toes and smashing antique crystal glasses because she's got her mind on something else.

But then later that day, Christina's aunt comes steaming down from Marin County. Wilhelmina Blackworth, an eccentric-looking old lady with a mane of reddish-gray hair. Didi overhears her talking with Christina in the studio. (Didi has become an expert at listening from behind closed doors. Not pressing her ear to keyholes or anything as creepy as that, just hovering outside and keeping her ears open.) Wilhelmina has a deep and raspy voice, and she's throwing a fit, bullying Christina into going to some fancy-sounding neurologist up in SF. Christina's voice—low pitched, murmury—is harder to make out, but she stands her ground, or at least at first. But then she capitulates.

The next day, they're both gone. Wilhelmina had spirited her off the night before.

A week later, Mimi relays Christina's diagnosis to Didi in a portentous semiwhisper. "Creutzfeldt-Jakob disease. That's what the neurologist thinks. It's the worst possible thing to get, it's like a death sentence."

Didi represses a snort. The fancy neurologist is a moron.

Though to give him a little credit, there's no way to detect the small doses of the drug Didi has regularly been feeding Christina. Still, she decides to knock it off. She can't risk this doctor raising suspicions.

Christina does not accept the death sentence part. She's confident she can heal herself. A brown-skinned woman who's an expert, supposedly, in self-healing comes to the house, and Christina now spends the majority of her time doing what she prescribes. There are smelly herbs and oozy mudpacks, and Christina is constantly sniffing aromatherapy oils. An elderly blind man with Chinese features shows up every afternoon and sticks tiny needles into the soles of her feet. Most of all, Christina is forbidden to put anything in her mouth unless she can verify it's 100 percent organic and all natural, so she prepares everything she eats and drinks herself.

Didi couldn't have put anything more in her tea or anything else, even if she'd wanted to.

And Christina gets better. Everybody except Didi hails this as a miracle.

"She says she's never going back to a regular doctor," Mimi tells her. "She says they've all been brainwashed by the AMA."

Judging by the fancy neurologist who'd said Creutzfeldt-Jakob, Didi thinks maybe Christina's right.

She feels empowered. A word she's heard used a lot these days, and it fits. Being invisible has empowered her. The way a ghost can supposedly wreak so much fear and havoc, even though nobody can see it.

She feels empowered enough to wear Thomas Rainier's silver bracelet. When Mimi says "That's new. How much did it cost?" Didi is ready.

"I got it dirt cheap on this internet auction site," she said. "It's called eBay."

Mimi accepts that. When it comes to the net, she's sort of clueless.

❧

"Didi?" Christina calls from the kitchen. "Are you here?"

Didi and Mimi are taking a break in the formal dining room, munching slightly stale powdered sugar crullers from a bag left by a plumber. Didi has sworn off junk food, but any kind of doughnut she can't resist.

"Go on, hon," Mimi says.

With a sullen motion, she wipes sweet powder off her chin. Goes into the kitchen.

Christina's at the Formica table, strumming her fingers through a box of dried berries like she's playing a harp. "Look at these," she says. "Did you ever see such a ravishing shade of lavender? But they're hard as rocks."

"Are you going to start making pigments again?" Didi asks.

"Yes, I think I'm well enough. Could you go to the toolshed and fetch me a mallet? I can't go in there, you know. There are pesticides."

So it's okay if she, Didi, goes in there and breathes poisonous fumes and gets brain cancer and dies, but not Christina. Didi feels like telling her to drop dead. But she's made a decision—she's going to quit soon. The Thanksgiving break is coming up, meaning Ava and James will be around more, and Didi has decided to quit right before that and get ready to matriculate at Santa Cruz in January.

She stomps out the mudroom door, her thoughts snarling. A poem resonates in her head. Edna St. Vincent Millay, "The Ballad of the Harp-Weaver."

There sat my mother
With the harp against her shoulder . . .
And her hands in the harp-strings
Frozen dead.

Maybe she hadn't gone far enough, poisoning Christina's tea. Maybe she should have seriously messed her up. Like she did to Wanda, the Rainiers' housekeeper. Put her in the hospital.

As usual, there are people working on the grounds, buzzing and bumbling with lawn mowers and other garden implements. Keeping her head down, Didi trudges around the north side of the house to the rotting toolshed near the compost heap. She creaks open the door.

A powerful stench makes her gag. Pesticides. Also rust and dirt and manure and the ammonia smell of animal pee. Crinkling her nose, she steps inside. She begins scrounging around in the heaps of rusty old tools, keeping an eye out for black widows. There are hammers. Drills. Wrenches.

A heavy socket wrench.

And now that old movie, the one she can't stop replaying in her mind, starts up again. It's always in black and white, except for the blood, that's in color. *Mimi, howling like a wild animal caught in a claw trap. Raymond whirling with the socket wrench. Didi, just turned twelve, a wildness of her own, flying at Raymond . . .*

She presses her hands on both sides of her head to turn off the movie, and it stops. She's back in the here and now.

She continues searching the tools until she finds a small mallet coated in dried straw. She grabs it and turns to leave.

Her eyes fix on a rack crammed with old boxes and bags. Some are marked with pictures of diseased flowers and leaves, others with ants or mice or rats. Some are ripped open, and the spilled contents pool in damp lumps on the floor.

Some of the packages have little skulls and crossbones on them, meaning the contents are potentially lethal. The oldest of them probably contain poisons that have been banned for years because they were so deadly.

Rat poison was the way Alice Blackworth, the debutante turned nun, had chosen to die. Alice, now reincarnated as Didi herself. Didi feels a shiver.

It's a sign.

CHAPTER THIRTY-SIX

SARAH

It takes both medical attendants to help James hobble upstairs on his metallic blue crutches. I wait at the foot for them to clear the landing before I follow.

With every step, James gives a moan that rips at my heart. The attendants pause every fourth step to let him rest, and when they do, he looks around in confusion. Like he's come to some strange and unknown place and can't figure out how he's gotten here.

"How's he gonna get up and down?" Franny Fiore has planted herself behind me and watches, hands on her boy-slim hips. "He can't hardly walk, even with those guys holding him up."

"He'll have physical therapy twice a day, and the therapist and I will help him with the stairs. You can help, too, Franny, when you're here. During the day, he'll stay down here in his wheelchair."

"Yeah, but he's, like, really hurting. It's like they're torturing him."

You've got no idea what torture is: it's on the tip of my tongue to say that. But I don't, of course. "The therapists want him to push himself. The more he does, the faster he heals."

"You ought to get skilled nursing help. I got a cousin, Shasta, who's licensed. Want me to see if she's available?"

"I'll keep it in mind, thanks, Franny, but I've already lined up someone for home visits. And I've had some experience in nursing, so I think we're good."

The attendants semi-hoist James onto the landing. He gives a loud groan.

"Shit," Franny says. "Where's Ava?"

I'm so tired of her rudeness to me. "She didn't know he'd be discharged so early, so she went out," I say crisply. James had been released earlier in the day than I'd expected. They'd actually been a little hostile at the rehab facility because he was leaving before their recommendation, and they'd rushed through the discharge.

Ava is probably with Thomas. They seem to have become very thick. But after the email I sent him, I think I can trust him. He's not stupid.

I now head upstairs and follow as James and his attendants make their slow progress to his room. It's just a few steps down the hall from my suite. I've transformed it. There's a medical bed; it's ugly, I couldn't help that, but I've fitted it with Frette linens and matching blankets in calming shades of dark azure and ivory. The freshly painted walls glow in a pale sea blue. I've collected several of the better antiques from various rooms in the house—a tall walnut bureau, a smaller burled-maple chest of drawers (both of which I sanded until my elbows ached, then waxed twice), an ebony Chinese cabinet for a bed table. I've placed on the cabinet a silver water pitcher (polished to bring out the elaborate *B* monogram) along with two new crystal tumblers. I've set his laptop and the TV remote on the rolling overbed table.

I had debated whether to hang anything on the walls. I'd decided no. I'd hate to inadvertently pick out something that might bring up bad memories.

The window looks out onto the forest instead of the sea. Ava's old bedroom has a sea view, but I thought he'd prefer his own. And anyway, she'd have gotten her hackles up if I had attempted to redo it.

The attendants settle James into the bed. One of them elevates his ankle cast on a large foam block, then adjusts the complicated sling that has replaced the plaster cast on his shoulder. His facial swelling has gone down, and the worst of the cuts and bruises have healed, so his face has recovered much of its handsomeness. He'll have a few new scars to add to the old ones, but that won't do him any harm.

I go downstairs with the attendants. They show me how to fold and unfold the state-of-the-art electric wheelchair and demonstrate its features. They leave, and I return to James. "Feeling a little better now?"

"Yeah. These sheets feel great."

"Oh, good. How do you like what I've done with your room?"

His eyes dart around it. "Where are the rocket ships?"

"The old wallpaper? It was so stained and moldy that I had to get it scraped off and repainted. This color is called Borrowed Light."

"I picked that wallpaper out myself when I was eight. Mom let us choose our own. Ava's was horses. She was wild about them when she was a kid."

"It's still there in her old room. When you're up to it, you can go see for yourself how dirty and shabby it is."

The sound of chimes echoes faintly from downstairs.

"What's that?" James says with a start.

"The old grandfather clock in the front hall. I had a specialist come and fix it. He said it was an original Craftsman from about 1910."

It begins to strike the hour: three . . . four . . . five. So faint it's like something heard in a dream.

A shade of panic crosses James's face. "I'm not so sure this was such a good idea, Sarah."

"The clock? I'll stop winding it if you don't like the chimes."

"No, my coming here. I'm not so sure I should be here." He struggles to sit up more and winces with pain. "Damn. Did you get ibuprofen?"

"Extrastrength. It's right here."

I open the Chinese cabinet and take out a bottle of Motrin IB. I shake out four pills and give them to him with a glass of water. "The rehab said you can take this dosage twice a day. Three, if it's really necessary."

He swallows them quickly.

I open the valise he brought back from rehab and start putting his things away, making light conversation. After about five minutes, he lets out a sigh. I turn to him.

"I feel better already," he says.

"Thank heavens." I go over and brush his lips oh so gently with mine.

"I love you," he murmurs.

"Me too," I say. "Very much. Promise you'll let me know if there's anything at all you need."

I've texted Ava that we're home. She returns forty minutes later, charging up the stairs and bursting into the room. She has more energy than she has had for a while. "Hey, you!" she says to her brother.

James smiles dreamily. "Hey, you," he replies.

"I got takeout from a Chinese place in Monterey. Spiky sea cucumber and preserved eggs and things. You're going to love it."

"I don't have a huge appetite."

"Maybe just a few bites. You look thin."

"So do you," he says.

"Yeah, I've lost a little weight recently. Hey, remember those ivory chopsticks we used to have? They had little elephants carved on them."

"Yeah. From Great-Uncle Whoosis, who shot elephants."

"Oh my God, yes!" Ava says.

I speak up. "They're probably still here. I'll see if I can find them for you."

"They're not," James says. "Mom said we couldn't use them anymore."

"Yeah," Ava says, "she said the elephants died horribly just for their tusks and it was criminal to even own the chopsticks. So then we had a burial for them, remember, Jamie? Next to Watson's grave in the woods."

"Yeah, and remember, Mom found a Buddhist prayer, and we all chanted."

Ava dissolves into laughter.

"Who's Watson?" I ask.

"This parrot Mom inherited from her grandfather. He was supposed to live to a hundred. He only made it to eighty-eight."

"He used to recite limericks. Dirty ones."

"There was a young girl from Nantucket . . ."

I feel like an outsider. With my face pressed up against the window. "I've got an idea," I say.

James and Ava turn their faces to me. They don't look anything alike, except in some strange way they do, that identical Blackworth expression, a mixture of quizzical, dreamy, and just the slightest bit superior. "I'm going to make some daiquiris," I say. "The authentic Blackworth kind. Ava gave me the secret recipe, James."

He smiles vaguely. "Extra rum in mine."

"You can't have any alcohol," Ava says. "Not while you're still on meds."

"Just ibuprofen. One drink won't kill me."

"A splash of rum for you, darling," I say. "I'll send them up in the dumbwaiter. I got Franny Fiore to fix it."

"Remember how we used to squeeze into it and hide from Mom?" James says to his sister.

They are instantly back in their insular world, and I'm just as instantly excluded.

I head down to the kitchen. I start throwing fruit into the shrieking old blender. I'm ordering a new one today.

I hate being treated as an outsider. I always have.

And I refuse to be in my very own house.

CHAPTER
THIRTY-SEVEN

AVA

Sarah is dangerous.

The thought had been sneaking into my mind since Jamie had come back. Or more of a feeling, dim and watery: something hovering just below the surface of my thoughts.

I was feeling that way about other things too. The absence of traffic lights in the village of Carmel, part of its charm, but it was dangerous, you could have a head-on collision. And so was the village's quaint lack of addresses, you had to go by directions—Camino Real NW Corner 11th, meaning the eleventh house on Camino Real, so you could get dangerously lost in the fog or after dark. The art gallery on Casanova where Mom had sometimes exhibited her paintings, the young man with too-white teeth who ran it now, his smile wide and white, "If you ever want to sell more of her work . . . ," but I didn't. Who had told him I would? He was dangerous.

The kind of paranoia I'd had with my breakdown. That kept me at the bottom of that dark well. It was creeping back.

Starting my car was unsafe. The construction sounds that still carried from the neighboring bluff when the wind was right—they gave me a sense of dread.

Thomas's construction. He was very dangerous, but I couldn't stay away from him. He was an addiction. Like heroin. Or meth. I'd kick it sometime. I'd have to. But not now.

These crazy thoughts. I couldn't get them out of my mind.

"Am I doing something wrong, Ava?" Sarah asked.

I glanced at her with a start. We were in the pretty sitting room of her suite. It was twilight; we were drinking daiquiris, and Jamie was with us too. The sunporch was too bright, he said; the rays hurt his eyes. Sarah had made the drinks and sent them up in the dumbwaiter.

That squeaking sound it made. It unsettled me.

"You've hardly touched your daiquiri," Sarah said. "I thought I'd followed the recipe same as always. Did I screw something up?"

I picked up my glass. I no longer wanted it, but I made myself take a polite swallow. "It's perfect," I said. "I'm just feeling out of sorts. Maybe it's the forest. It sometimes sends a rotten smell into this side of the house."

"I'll close the window," she said.

"No, don't," Jamie said. "I've missed that smell. I had the ocean in Laguna, but not the cedars, and I missed it. You never minded it before, Ava."

His voice was strained, agitated. Every day, one of three revolving physical therapists came to the house and worked with him, and the sessions left him irritable and aching, until he took painkillers—drugstore meds, Motrin, Tylenol. Nothing very strong, but enough to make him sometimes vague and sleepy and other times snappish.

Sarah gave a charming laugh. "I've stopped noticing the rotten odor, to tell you the truth. I just notice the cedar smell, and it reminds me of hope chests and old closets, which I love." She refilled Jamie's glass from one of two pitchers. One was extremely light on the rum for him. The other contained our traditional amount.

She replaced the pitcher on Mom's beat-up old rolltop desk. Except it wasn't Mom's any longer. The thought tumbled into my mind. It was Sarah's. The entire bedroom suite belonged to her now. She'd changed the arrangement of the furniture. Added new touches. Linen lampshades. Silk throw pillows. This morning, a brand-new mattress had arrived, made by a Danish company I'd never heard of. It had probably cost a fortune. The old gray one with the two body-shaped depressions was hauled away.

She'd lived in luxury. She was worth tens of millions. Why did she want to live here, in the gloom of a drafty old house where every stick of furniture was burdened with an eccentric family's history?

Why wouldn't she want some shiny, huge new mansion of her own?

She's dangerous.

I took another swallow of my drink. It really wasn't right—Sarah had screwed up the recipe somehow. Or used bad strawberries. Maybe they'd picked up some mold. I put the glass down.

I looked at Jamie. He was slumped a little against the back of his chair, and his eyes seemed to be drifting shut. Sarah had done everything possible for his recovery. He was improving in strength. He could walk farther and longer with his crutches.

But he wasn't getting better.

My stomach clenched. Could that be true?

Or was it just another of these wildly confused notions that were skittering through my head? Danger and threats everywhere.

I got up. "I think I'll go work for a while. There's some editing I want to get done."

Sarah shot me a look of concern. I didn't want her concern.

I wanted her to go away.

I went to my bathroom. My face felt burning hot. I splashed it with icy water. I heard a quick jitterbug of steps behind me. The hairs on the back of my neck prickled.

I raised my dripping face to the mirror.

There was nothing behind me.

I was still imagining Cinderella after all these years.

Thomas called later and invited me to a dinner party at his house the following night. Impromptu, for his Montana clients and a few others.

"I can't," I said. "I'm not feeling very well."

"I've noticed. You're stressed out. This will be good for you."

"I'm really not up to socializing."

"I'm never up to it. This is work. I need you there. I've got to have at least one other person as strange as me."

I forced a laugh. I reluctantly agreed to attend.

The dinner was in the birdcage—that spectacular domed room with latticed glass. The clients were a lively couple who'd made a killing with robopets: dogs, rabbits, potbellied pigs that purred and squealed and apparently even fetched things for you. There was also one of

Thomas's associate architects, a man with silver hair and a patrician jut to his jaw, and his elegant Syrian-born wife, an engineer with a degree from MIT.

Clotilde was a guest—she brought Anson out to be cooed over, and then she joined us solo.

The conversation was vivacious. The Thai-inspired food, prepared by Thomas's cook, exquisite.

But I still had little appetite. My mouth tasted bitter. My head was jangling and tight, and I'd had that sensation again—the one I'd had the first time I came to Thomas's house—that this was all staged, including the people assembled.

Just theater. Designed to trick and seduce.

It was theater, I reminded myself. A showcase. Thomas had never pretended it was anything else.

I really wasn't fit for socializing, but I made the effort. Smiled. Laughed when appropriate. Tried to hold up my end of the conversation. But it was a relief when it was over and the guests departed.

Thomas poured us snifters of Courvoisier, and we took them out to the gardens. The warmth of the heat lamps seeped through me, but I was already feverish and hot. I moved out of their range, into the moist compress of ocean air. Thomas came up beside me. "Don't get cold."

"I won't. It feels good."

He regarded me with a frown. "You really aren't feeling well, are you? You barely touched your food."

"Was I a terrible guest?"

"No, you were a fine guest. Just sometimes it was like you were somewhere else." He gave a smile. "Like on a different planet."

"I warned you." I paused, then added, "I'm worried about Jamie. We've always been so close. But suddenly we're not."

"Things have changed. He's got a wife now."

"I know, but it's more than that. *He's* totally changed. It's like he's not really Jamie anymore."

"Who does he seem like?"

"I mean, he's different. I can feel it in a thousand ways." I took a sip of the Courvoisier. It burned like jalapeño in my tight throat. "He gets irritated with me for the least little thing. He still insists it wasn't Dad buried in the sculpture garden. He says it can't be when he saw him jogging up in the hills. He accuses me of not trusting him or anybody anymore." I paused. "And then at other times he seems to be sort of fading away. As if he's turning into a ghost of himself."

Thomas gave me one of his sleepy, skeptical looks. "You need a break from that house. I'm going back up to Bozeman at the end of the week. I'll be finished with what I have to do in a couple of days. Why don't you fly up and meet me there? We'll go riding in the mountains." Another smile. "When's the last time you've been on a horse?"

"No," I said. "I mean I can't meet you there. I'm afraid of leaving Jamie. Of leaving him with Sarah. I'm not sure why."

Thomas was silent for a second. "Maybe you should be," he said.

I felt a tremor of apprehension. "Why?"

He hesitated.

"Tell me. Why should I be?"

"Nothing," he said. "I don't know any reason."

I turned to face him directly. "Did you have an affair with her?"

"No," he said quickly. "Absolutely not."

"I don't believe you. I think you did."

His eyes darkened.

The young helper, Alberto, stuck his head outside the birdcage door. "Thomas, a moment? We've got a problem."

"One second," he said sharply. He glanced back at me.

"I saw that look between the two of you," I said. "It was about more than what you told me. A lot more."

"We need to talk about this. I'll be right back." He went inside.

I stared out at the water. That ghostly phosphorescence on the breaking waves. A thought took form:

Thomas and Sarah.

They were in it together. They had conspired right from the start. Of course. Why hadn't I realized that before?

They'd been having an affair. Maybe still were. Thomas wanted Blackworth Mansion and all its land to develop. And Sarah was helping him get it.

The two of them all along. Seducing Jamie and me. Manipulating us through what they knew of our past traumas.

No. It was too wild a thought. Depending on too many probabilities. If only I could think straight. This low-level flu or whatever that wouldn't go away . . . putting my entire body out of sorts. Muddling up my brain.

I had to leave before he got back. Just until I could think straight.

I walked quickly back inside, into the birdcage. My purse was missing. Someone had confiscated it. To keep me here. My car keys were in it. My phone.

My heart began to pound.

No, there it was on the dining table, where I'd left it. I grabbed it and then hurried through the house, dreading I'd run into somebody on the way.

My Volvo was the only one remaining in the drive. With a shaking hand, I opened the door. Got in and gripped the steering wheel.

It was greasy. I felt like I could hardly keep my hands on it. A dusty kind of grease.

It had been on the wheel when I'd left home, I realized. I must have left the window open a crack the night before. My hands would slip. I'd drive off a cliff into the pounding ocean below.

Thomas burst out of the house. He yelled my name.

I gripped the wheel tight and drove away.

I was still missing so many things about him, about Sarah. And Sarah's stalker, Didi.

The puzzles just got more convoluted. I had to figure everything out.

DIDI

"Is this the right size?" Didi holds out the mallet she's brought from the toolshed to Christina.

Christina looks up from her half-finished canvas, her brush poised at the tip of her mouth. "Yes, perfect." As she takes it, her eyes fix on the silver bracelet on Didi's wrist. "Where did you get that?" she says.

"On eBay," Didi tells her. "It was really cheap. Did you ever go on eBay, Christina? You can get some amazing deals."

She regards Didi with a penetrating look. "Didi . . . do you ever take things that don't belong to you?"

A tingle of fear creeps up Didi's spine. Then her mouth sets in defiance. "No, never. Why are you asking me that? I wouldn't ever."

"Are you sure?" Christina's voice is gentle. "I know you and your mother worked for Gayle Rainier and that she had to let the two of you go. Did you ever take anything from the Rainiers, Didi?"

"No! She accused my mother of stealing, which is so disgusting. Mimi sometimes takes things out of the garbage, but that's not stealing."

"But what about you, Didi?" Christina says.

"I'd never," Didi repeats stubbornly. "This bracelet cost sixteen dollars and ninety-nine cents on eBay, and it's just a cheap thing, and I don't even like it." She squeezes her hand out of the bracelet and drops it on Christina's painting table. "Here, you can have it."

"It's okay, Didi. Thomas Rainier owns a lot of bracelets and can buy himself more if he wants. Losing one won't hurt him."

"I don't know what you're talking about. I resent being accused of things. How would you like it if I accused you of stealing?"

"You can talk to me, Didi," Christina says. The light through the curtained windows bathes her in a kind of holy way. "I know what happened to you and your mother. Your mother told me all about it."

Didi goes stiff with rage. If she could kill Christina right this second, she would. "My mom talks crap sometimes. You can't listen to what she says."

"I'd already heard it from people in social services. I felt so badly for both of you and wanted to do something. That's why I hired your mother, and I asked Gayle Rainier and Beverly Padrillo to take her on part time as well."

Bullshit, bullshit. Mimi's a star cleaning woman. She can pick and choose her clients, and she selects only the best.

"I'm not going to fire you," Christina continues, "but please don't take anything else. My family jewelry can't be replaced. Do you understand what I'm saying?"

Didi searches for words but can't find any through her rage.

"And, Didi? You need to keep away from my husband."

"I don't come on to him, if that's what you think," she says with fury.

"No, dear. I mean, you need to avoid him as much as you can. He can get very ugly, especially when he's drinking. He's hurt me a few times. He broke three of my ribs once."

"I don't believe you. He's here all the time, and you let him suck up to you."

Christina sighs. "If I don't, he retaliates. And he tries to turn my kids against me. He can't, of course, but it's traumatic for children to be forced to choose between parents. Ava is high strung. She breaks easily. And Jamie is very impressionable. When they're old enough to be independent, I'll file for divorce."

Bull bull. Shit shit. Ava is conceited. She had no right to take those pictures of Didi. And Jamie's always got so many friends, he could deal with anything.

Christina's just too stoned out to stand up to Kevin. She drifts around in her druggy haze, letting him throw his weight around. Didi doesn't believe he broke her ribs. Christina is all bullshit.

But Christina's eyes are lifted to her now, and they are clear and alert and not druggy at all. She offers the bracelet to Didi. It looks all silver and slippery, like a baitfish. "Take it back, Didi. It's okay, I won't say anything."

"I don't want it, I told you. You can throw it in the garbage." Didi turns and stomps out the door.

She hates Christina, she really does. All her phony-shit caring and understanding, it's such crap. And she hates Mimi for blabbing to Christina about what happened to them.

Why is Mimi always sucking up to her? Why can't she see through her pretentiousness the way Didi can?

Mimi's a lousy house cleaner.

The thought suddenly hits Didi like something gripping her throat.

At the Rainiers', she spent most of her time gossiping with Wanda. And her job with the old lady Beverly Padrillo is super easy, a junior high kid could do it.

And Christina's got an army of people to do the real cleaning: window washers and floor polishers and laundry people and a company that beats and shampoos all the rugs and curtains.

Mimi's a charity case. She's too loopy and crippled and lazy to do much of anything. She and Didi are both charity cases.

There's a noise in Didi's ears like the banging of drums. She presses her hands over them and continues downstairs.

She finds herself in the ballroom, the huge living room with high coffered ceilings. The one that has the echo. She slides down against a wall and sits with her hands over her ears.

The movie starts up again in her mind.

She's twelve, beginning to develop, breasts, hips, pretty face. Just come home from school. Raymond, her stepdad, fixing the leaking radiator, tools scattered around. Baggy jeans sagging, a plumber's crack. "Your mom drew overtime," he says. "Get over here, I need your help." She doesn't want to, she drags her feet. He yanks her closer. "When I say come, you move your ass." He looks at her a moment with a grin. Then shoves her to her knees. Drops his jeans to below his erection. Fat, red, angry looking. Pushes her mouth against it. Everything in her brain goes red.

But then Mimi is there. She's shrieking. Coming at him, yanking his thin hair, scratching at his face. He grabs a socket wrench and swings.

The crack of a leg bone, and Mimi drops, howling in agony.

And Didi is on Raymond, scratching, biting, but he overpowers her and slams her face into the iron bars of the radiator. The crackle of smaller bones.

He throws her on the floor and flips her over and straddles her and wraps his hands around her throat.

Didi feels her larynx being crushed, the pain bright yellow. She can't even gasp. She knows she's going to die, his grip tightening, crushing . . .

She gropes at the scattered tools around her, a screwdriver, long sharp blade, she thrusts blindly at his throat, it's easy, like a knife into pudding. His grip relaxes. She gulps a painful breath and pushes the blade in deeper. He's a deadweight on her now, blood from his throat, slippery, rust-smelling, mingling with her own blood that's seeping from her smashed-up face . . .

Something ghostly brushes against Didi now, scattering away the memory. Her eyes go wide. But it's just Christina's white cat, named after Georgia O'Keeffe. A streak of green paint on her ruff. She rubs against Didi again, and now her fur feels good.

It had felt good to kill Raymond. Making sure he'd never hurt Mimi again. Or do disgusting things to her, make her touch him. It had felt so good knowing none of that would ever, ever happen again.

She wants that feeling back now.

But she's got to be ultra-careful.

She can't risk getting caught.

CHAPTER THIRTY-EIGHT

AVA

I felt increasingly sick over the next few days. I could hardly struggle out of bed. I slept a lot but felt worse when I woke up. Sarah was solicitous. What did I need? Coffee? A little juice or toast? Something from the pharmacy to settle my stomach?

Her face suddenly didn't look human to me. It was too perfect. The face of a plaster sculpture.

I locked my door to keep her out. I kept the curtains drawn and cuddled Stieglitz until he yowled in protest.

Jamie came to the door, but I wouldn't let him in either. I was clearly ill. Dizzy and headachy. Many things felt strange to my touch. He was convalescing. He shouldn't be exposed.

I let Franny in with fresh sheets, as well as fresh bottles of Pellegrino. It was the only thing I wanted. "You're not coming down with what Christina got, are you, Ava?"

"No," I said. "It's just a bug."

"A virus? Two of my uncles died of COVID, and Michael almost did."

"I didn't know that. I'm sorry. But I don't think I've got anything that serious."

"I don't feel so great myself," she said. "I might knock off early. Sarah's got this team coming to do deep cleaning. Did you know that?"

"No," I said. I felt so weak. "Leave early if you want. Take care of yourself." I burrowed into the fresh sheets and fell back asleep.

I was a little better the next morning, refreshed by crisp sheets. I glanced at my phone for the first time in several days. Grace's assistant had just texted, asking me to meet Grace at her office later.

I felt a tremor of dread. I knew what it was about. I wrote back that I would.

Thomas had texted and called a dozen times. He'd give up eventually. Like Dad had stopped calling.

No, Dad had stopped because he was dead.

My mind was still in confusion. I wasn't entirely better.

I went downstairs. Thumping music issued from Dad's old office. Jamie having a physical therapy session in the room Sarah had chosen for them.

I thought of different music. "Tubular Bells." Mom used to play it. And it was on Sarah's phone.

I prayed Sarah wouldn't be in the kitchen. She wasn't.

I had to eat. There was a porridge Mom used to make. Muesli, yogurt, banana. She made it for herself: Dad had a liquid breakfast, black coffee with a pick-me-up of scotch; Jamie and I only wanted Count Chocula.

I reconstructed the recipe as best I could. Ate as much as I could. It wasn't much. My mouth was so bitter tasting.

୨ᡛ

I arrived at Grace's law offices at four. She came out to reception to meet me. "Today's my last day working from here," she said, leading me to her office. "My ob-gyn wants me to do bed rest until the birth. Just to be on the safe side."

"Grace!" I said with alarm. "You should go home right now."

"It's really just out of an abundance of caution. I'll still be working from bed, so don't think I'm deserting you."

"Please don't worry about me. The baby's the most important thing."

"She is. But I worry about you anyway."

We went into her office and shut the door. A thicket of bottles covered most of her desk: OJ, FIJI Water, Perrier. "I hydrate all day long and all night too. And then dehydrate in the john all day and night." She let out a laugh. "The joys of late pregnancy. What would you like, sweetie?"

"Maybe a small glass of Perrier."

She poured me a full one and a glass of orange juice for herself. Motioned me into a chair.

"There's been an ID, hasn't there?" I said.

"Yes. The lab report came in this morning."

"And it's my father, right?"

"Yes, it is. The DNA was conclusive. Without your cheek swab, it could have taken months to identify him. I wanted to tell you in person, and I wanted to see you anyway. I'm so sorry, Ava."

I thought with horror of being back in the sculpture garden. Digging in the dirt and gravel. That gleam of white veiled by streaming fog. A shudder ran through me.

"I don't know if I feel sorry," I said. "Or sad or anything."

"I know you didn't have a great relationship with him. But maybe as time passes you'll have some better memories of him."

"No. It's like the more I remember of him, the worse it is. He terrorized us. Jamie and I knew it but pretended we didn't. We liked to think Mom just floated above him, like she seemed to float above everything else." I stared at the fizzing water in my glass. "We wanted to believe she could never be touched. But something did touch her, and it was terrible. Something even worse than the way Dad treated her."

Grace regarded me with deep concern. "You look flushed, Ava. Drink that water."

I gripped the glass without drinking. "I thought my father had poisoned Mom. When I came back to the house, I thought I could prove it. And then I thought maybe he was after me and maybe Jamie too. But now . . ." I stopped. "I'm not sure what I think now. It's like I'm suspicious of everybody."

"Ava," Grace said gently. "Your hand is shaking. When did you last get a checkup?"

I clenched the glass tighter. "It's cold in here. I'm not used to air-conditioning."

"Please. You live in one of the most freezing-cold houses ever. I've got a terrific GP, I'll refer you. Or Darsh can recommend someone. And Ava . . . ," she added delicately, "Maybe you could also use a shrink. To talk things out with."

A wire seemed to tighten around my head. "I've got a psychiatrist in LA I check in with periodically. He adjusts the meds I take."

"Okay," she said. "But maybe somebody local to see more frequently. Keep it in mind."

"I will." I took the slightest sip of water, more like a wetting of my tongue. "So what's going to happen now? With the police, I mean."

"They'll have more questions for you and Jamie. But the statements you both gave were pretty comprehensive, so unless you've got anything else to add, nothing should change. There's a chance they

might try again for a warrant to search the house, but it was unoc-
cupied and completely boarded up all those years, so they won't have
any real grounds."

"And that will be that?"

"It will remain an open case. But without new evidence, it should
be the end as far as you and Jamie are concerned."

৯৪২

I left her soon afterward and headed back to my car. The steering wheel
still had that dusty-grease texture. My fluish feeling was returning. But
I had one more errand to do—retrieve Mom's rings from the bank they
were stored in. It wasn't far away—near the Old Town Historic District,
a fifteen-minute drive.

It was a small family-owned institution. Murals from the 1940s
fading on the lobby walls. Ornate brass cashier screens. An elderly man
in banker's gray brought me into the vault and showed me my two
safe-deposit boxes. As I turned each key of my own, he used a dupli-
cate key to unlock it in tandem. He apologized that I'd only have seven
minutes: the bank closed at five thirty. He withdrew.

I slid the drawers open. A large jewelry box lay in each. One, black
mahogany and gold, a relic of the Gilded Age. The other Edwardian,
walnut inlaid with mother-of-pearl. I remembered them so well, on the
mirrored vanity table in Mom's bedroom.

I carried them to the ledge. Opened the mahogany box. Three
black-velvet-lined tiers filled with a glittering jumble of rings, necklaces,
bracelets. I pictured Mom: gliding downstairs, rings on her fingers. *I
had the sweetest dream about you last night, Ava . . .*

A sharp pain crackled through my body.

I looked again at the tangle of jewelry. It dazzled my eyes: I couldn't
focus. I was searching for something, but what?

Rings to add gemstone sparkle to the painting table.

I flashed to my meeting Sarah for the first time in Jamie's office. My thought while driving back to Santa Monica: Her ring wasn't just similar to Mom's. It was the exact same one.

A small ring. Sapphire and pearls in a Victorian setting.

I combed quickly through the pieces. Mom's wasn't here.

I opened the walnut box and rifled through it. Not in that one either.

The vault felt suddenly oppressive. Rows of brass-and-wood safe-deposit boxes lined the walls like tiny crypts. The bank employee returned to tell me my time was up. I picked up both boxes and took them out to the parking lot, cradling them protectively against my body.

My hands were still shaking as I opened the car door. I fumbled the mahogany box, and it flew open on the asphalt. I tossed the other one onto the passenger seat, then bent down to gather the scattered pieces. Red flashes in my eyes: my head felt like it would explode.

And then suddenly I was sitting on the ground.

I did need to see a doctor. Tomorrow, I'd get the name of Grace's GP and make an appointment.

I gathered up the jewelry and flung it back into the box. A few pieces had rolled under the car. I groped for them. Two rings and a silver bracelet. The bracelet was simple. Modern looking.

It didn't belong with the rest. Mom never wore anything but old family jewelry. Even her wedding ring had been worn by two Blackworth brides before her.

I slipped the bracelet onto my wrist. It hung loosely.

Thomas. The bracelets he always wore stacked on his wrist.

I shook it off and examined it again. Initials engraved on the inside. *TLR.*

Thomas Laurence Rainier.

I felt a tremor of horror. He must have given it to Mom.

He'd had a crush on her. He had kissed her.

She'd laughed at him, and he'd been mortified. So much that he'd killed her.

No, not possible. I didn't want it to be possible.

I threw myself into the car. Slid the gears into reverse and swung out in a too-wide arc, skidding onto the grass barrier. I straightened out and pressed the accelerator and sped out of the lot. I was shaking and short of breath.

Count backward from a hundred, Ava. Dr. Patti, my old shrink: *Count slowly. Let your breath follow.*

I forced myself to count. *One hundred, ninety-nine, ninety-eight . . .*

My breathing returned to normal, but I still felt jittery and strange. The steering wheel with that dusty grease coating it. So slippery, and the coast road was so dangerous. Steep drops to the ocean on one side. Towering sheer cliffs on the other.

I batted down another rising panic.

I turned onto the access road paralleling the highway. Paved, not the rough and jolting dirt road of my childhood. Hammers slammed. Whining saws and Spanish talk radio.

Thomas's construction.

I steered sharply onto our unpaved driveway. Dry brush scratching at the windows like something trying to claw its way in.

The yellow police tape sagging on the low wall of the sculpture garden. Dad's makeshift grave. Worms devouring him. Leaving nothing but bones.

Mom had been cremated. Worms couldn't get to her.

Thoughts tangling like worms in my mind.

Blackworth Mansion loomed before me. That shadowy old house. There were ghosts in it, but I was no longer afraid of them. I was more terrified of the living.

I came to a jerking stop in front, and the jewelry boxes tumbled off the seat to the floor. I left them there and got out. My legs were unsteady. I stumbled on the porch steps.

Mom. Stumbling over her own bare feet. Dropping everything she picked up.

Poison.

The word fought through all the jumpy tangle of thoughts in my brain.

I was being poisoned.

DIDI

The more Didi learns about poisons, the more fascinated she becomes.

So many different types, each one acting in different, interesting ways. Some you need to breathe in, and some you absorb through your skin. Arsenic will make your breath smell like garlic, and if you expose phosphine to water, it stinks like rotten fish. If you ingest a superlarge amount of vitamin D_3, you vomit your guts out and start to twitch, and then your kidneys shut themselves down.

Didi particularly loves the mushrooms. Deadly ones that are birthday-party beautiful, all yellow polka dots or candy-red stripes, and others that are mousy and hide shyly under trees. Some could be found not too far away. The death cap, for instance, which is greenish with white gills and sprouts beneath oak trees. Or the beautiful creamy white one called the destroying angel. The names are like poems, she thinks.

But they mostly grow in the forests north of San Francisco, and even there they aren't very easy to find.

Doesn't matter. She has poisons right at hand. The rat poisons in the toolshed—the old ones with skulls and bones marked on them.

She's made her choice. One that contains strychnine. It comes on quickly. Ten minutes, twenty tops. It's got a slightly bitter taste, but it's not too obvious.

And most important of all, it's almost impossible to detect afterward.

Yesterday, which was Wednesday, she'd made another trip to the toolshed. That was the riskiest part. She could never be entirely sure who might pop up or who was already watching. Michael Fiore, that freaky handyman, he might be up on the roof spying down on her. Or his kid, Franny, suddenly trailing behind, asking nosy questions: *Where are you going? What are you doing that for?* It was a school day, but Franny seemed to sit out a lot of school days.

But Didi was pretty sure she hadn't been seen yesterday. Plus she'd gone first to the compost heap and dumped food scraps in case anybody even saw her heading to the area.

Today, Thursday, will be her last day working for the Hollands. She's going to tell Mimi she's quitting tomorrow. No one will be in the house all day today, except herself and Christina. Ava has riding after school, and Jamie, cross-county. Kevin almost always picks them up afterward, so he won't be around until late.

Mimi is home in bed, out like a light, due to the Nembutal Didi had crushed in her coffee.

She's told nobody she's going to quit yet. She needs everything to be as normal as always today.

Christina doesn't get up until very late, shimmering downstairs in a long, shushing, dove-colored skirt. Her white cat is draped over her shoulder like an ermine boa. Didi, dusting the stained glass in the entrance hall, doesn't even hear her until she speaks: "Good morning, Didi," that thrilling, whispery voice.

Didi turns. "Morning." It was past noon, but so what? "I looked up online what made the spots on these windows, Christina. It's limestone from where rainwater has leaked in. They say use distilled water and only soft cotton cloths."

"Wonderful, Didi. I'll tell that to my window washers." She sets the cat down, and she pads away. "You do like this house, don't you?" she says.

"It's interesting," Didi mumbles.

"I love it so much. I know my children will want to leave when they're grown and go live someplace livelier. But I never will. You might be one of the few people who can understand that."

In spite of herself, Didi feels a lift of pride. "I do understand."

Christina adds, "Besides, what would happen to Cinderella if I left?"

"You don't think she's real, do you?" Didi asks.

"Oh, I know she is. I've seen her, didn't you know that? She appeared to me in my studio."

Is she making fun of me? Didi wonders.

"Why don't we go out on a scavenge later?" Christina continues. "Wander in the woods and see what treasures we can collect."

"Okay," Didi says. "Whenever you're ready."

They wander beneath the dappled canopy of the cedars, collecting unusual things: misshapen cones, a lichen-covered strip of bark. Didi finds a bright-blue mountain jay feather, and Christina rhapsodizes over the color.

"Oh, and look, Didi!" Christina sinks to her knees before a dying tree.

Like a druid, Didi thinks. Like a tree worshipper.

She's found two frilly yellowish mushrooms growing from the rotted-out roots. "Cauliflower mushrooms. Very rare. They look like little brains, don't you think?"

"Are they poisonous?" Didi asks.

"No, just the opposite. They're a great delicacy. When they grow larger, I'll collect them and make the most delicious soup. I think you'll like it."

Like I'll still be here, Didi thinks.

At four o'clock, she goes up to Christina's studio. "I'm done, so I'm taking off now, Christina. Unless there's anything else?"

Christina is at her easel, absorbed in sketching a still life arrangement. She's using a gray pastel crayon and has a black one clamped between her lips. She had used black charcoal in those disgusting sketches of Didi. She murmurs a response.

"Goodbye," Didi says.

She goes downstairs and out the front door, shutting it loudly behind her. She heads to her car, parked beside the garage, and starts to drive, not up the dirt lane to the highway but instead on the rough ground behind the garage that leads to the toolshed. She parks the Fiesta in a hidden grove behind it.

She fishes beneath her seat and grabs what she's hidden there—the envelope from the birthday card Gram had sent her so long ago. It no longer contains the crushed-up pills she'd put in it before. She gets out of the car.

She doesn't go into the shed. She'd already gotten what she needs from there yesterday, and it's in the envelope. Skulking in shadows, she heads around the back, past the juniper hedge where Jamie had scarred his handsome face the year before. She feels a pang, thinking about that.

She comes to the mudroom door, unlocks it quietly, and creeps into the kitchen. She stands there a moment, listening.

A chinaware teapot sits on the round Formica table, filled with cold tea that Christina had brewed earlier. Didi lifts the lid. It's got an earthy odor. Like walking in the forest.

She sets the lid back on the teapot, then turns and walks into the butler's pantry.

She glances at the small locked door that leads to the servants' quarters. In the olden days, that's where the help like her and Mimi would have lived.

Servants.

No! She wasn't a servant in her previous life. She was a Blackworth. The beautiful Alice Blackworth, who swallowed arsenic rather than living separated from her beloved cousin.

Didi has the soul of Alice Blackworth. But she does not intend to poison herself.

She opens one of the upper cabinets in the narrow pantry. It's crammed with liquor bottles. Vodka, tequila. A lot of scotch, all Johnnie Walker. Many bottles of rum, also all the same brand—El Dorado, clear as water, not like any kind of rum Didi's ever seen. A lot of weird liqueurs. They have beautiful colors: amethyst, pale gold, glowy green.

She already knows the bottle she wants, one that's about three-quarters empty. When she replaces it in the cabinet, she won't be putting it back right in front but two rows behind. She doesn't want it drunk right away, but in a few weeks or so from now, when she's been long gone.

She places the bottle on the narrow counter and twists open the top.

A thudding sound makes her freeze.

She glances quickly at the creepy little door. *Cinderella.* Christina had said the ghost materialized to her, and it suddenly seems like there's something cold here, some icy breath-like draft that makes her shiver all over.

She's got to hurry. Before long, Kevin will be back with Jamie and Ava. She wants to be off the property well before then.

She tips the edge of the birthday-card envelope on the lip of the bottle. This part is tricky. She has to take care not to get any of its contents on her fingers.

She's nervous. Her hands shaky. Why? She's done this before, at the Rainiers'—the smooshed-up pills she put in their housekeeper Wanda's bottle of Hawaiian Punch.

But that was just to mess Wanda up. This time it's different.

It's real poison. It's to kill.

Something moving at her feet startles her. Her hand jerks, knocking the bottle over completely. "Shit!" she mutters.

Christina's white cat, scuttling out from some shadow, scoots into the kitchen. Cats never like her. She doesn't know why.

She sets the bottle upright. She grabs a polishing cloth, dampens it in the miniature sink, and dabs up the spill. Then she positions the envelope again at the lip of the bottle.

A shadow ripples over her hand.

She feels a cold tremor of dread.

CHAPTER
THIRTY-NINE

AVA

I made it up the porch steps to the front door, the thought still twisting in my mind. I was being poisoned.

Was it true? Or was it some fatal neurological defect? A genetic thing, it ran in our family. Jamie and I had inherited the gene. Both of us condemned, like Mom, to an early death.

I lurched into the dim foyer and continued toward the staircase. It had once seemed so grand to me, and now all I saw were cracks and sags and ingrained dust and rot. My eyes traveled up to the second floor.

Again, that memory. The dark, shadowy shape rushing across the landing. Keeping me frozen in place. Too scared to go upstairs.

Too late to help Mom.

Cinderella. I'd seized on the idea that I had seen her because I didn't want to admit what I'd really seen. Not a ghost. Or just a play of shadow.

A person.

Mom had been poisoned, and I'd seen the shadow of the person who had poisoned her. Running away from her studio to the back stairs.

No. There had been nobody there when I came home that day. I'd been alone, Jamie said. I had called 911. Still had the phone in my hand.

Except I could remember hearing footsteps. People running upstairs to help me. The memory was too vivid to be a delusion.

My head ached too much to think about it. And there was a creaking coming from somewhere. It reverberated from the passageway that led to the sunporch. The sound of the glider. Someone rocking it slowly, the way you'd rock a cradle.

Dad. Rocking in that chair. Ice clinking in his glass.

She ate her paints.

It couldn't be Dad. He was dead. His bones long buried in the sculpture garden. Brittle as plaster.

I went cautiously toward it. It was Jamie. Sitting on the swing, eyes closed, using one of his crutches to rock himself. Betsy was there. She trotted up to me, tail wagging vigorously.

"Jamie," I said softly. His eyelids drifted open. "I thought you didn't like this room."

"I don't. It's too bright." He blinked. "Where are my glasses?"

"I don't know. Where's Sarah?"

"She had an appointment. I don't know what's keeping her so long."

I crouched beside him. "Stop swinging a moment. I've got something to tell you."

He pressed the cane against the floor, and the glider stopped.

"I just went to see Grace. She said the lab made a positive ID. It was definitely Dad buried out there."

"It can't be. They screwed up."

"No. It was a match with my DNA sample."

He shook his head. "I saw him, Ave. He looked right at me. Do you think I wouldn't recognize him? That look on his face, it was just the same. And the way he ran with that fucked-up ankle. I'm not wrong. It was him."

"I think you were wrong, Jamie. I think maybe you just imagined it."

"Hallucinating? Come on, Ava."

"Your eyes were acting up. Maybe you couldn't focus."

"I put in drops before I left his house. My eyes were perfectly clear."

I slogged through the confusion in my mind. The eye drops. There was something he'd told me at Denny's when we'd met for breakfast. "You said you forgot to take them when you walked out on Sarah?"

"Yeah, but her housekeeper brought them to me. I did have them. I wasn't hallucinating it, if that's what you're implying."

"No," I said. "What I mean is . . ." What did I mean?

Poison. In his eye drops.

He began rocking again. That creaking sound. "I need another dose of ibuprofen."

He sounded fuzzy. Drugged out. Not like himself.

"How much are you taking?" I asked him.

"Enough," he said vaguely.

"Are you sure it's just ibuprofen that you're on?"

He didn't answer. He turned his head toward the ocean. "The tide's coming in. It sounds like it's going to be a heavy swell."

The surf was starting to hit the rocks with thunderous force. My head throbbed painfully. I put my hands on the rocking glider and stopped it. "Listen to me. I think you're taking something stronger than just ibuprofen."

"I know that," he said.

I looked at him, confused. "You do?"

"You can't imagine the kind of pain I've been in. I need something stronger until I'm over the hump."

"Does Sarah get it for you?"

He hesitated. "No, a friend of mine. A psychiatrist in Laguna."

He was a rotten liar. He always had been.

"Where's Franny?" he said.

"It's late, she's gone home. Listen, Jamie. I think I'm being drugged. Listen to me, okay? I've been feeling anxious and having a hard time concentrating. And I'm getting cramping pains and headaches. I think I'm being poisoned."

"What are you talking about, Ava?"

"It's Sarah. I think she's been giving me something. In the daiquiris she makes for me. And the coffee. And maybe other things."

"Jesus, Ava. Are you crazy?"

"I don't think so. I think it's some poison building up inside me."

He gazed at me with faraway eyes. "You need to talk to somebody, Ave. A good therapist. I'll get you a name. They'll adjust your meds."

I couldn't get through to him. The ocean outside, that relentless crash and retreat, seemed to mock my even trying.

A text sounded, and I gave a violent start.

From Margaret: Emailed 2 docs. Come to my office tomorrow, 10 a.m. Will have more info.

"I'm going upstairs a moment," I said to Jamie. "I'll come back."

"Could you get me a drink? Not a fruit daiquiri. A real drink. Vodka, rocks."

"Yeah, I will. In a minute."

I headed to the stairs. A wave of vertigo washed over me as I reached the top. I sat down on the step. I did need a doctor: I should get to urgent care; but I couldn't drive like this.

I texted Franny. Asked her to come and take me. It didn't send right away.

Then I opened the first of Margaret's emails. Clicked on the attachment.

A document. The words blurred. I waited for my vertigo to recede enough to focus, and then I scanned it. A police report from twenty-two years ago. A town called Everly, Idaho. A chilling crime. A physical assault, a sexual assault of a minor, and a homicide.

A name leaped out at me. Miriam Morrison, forty-three.

Miriam. The memory flashed: our housekeeper with the bad knee. That was her name.

She had been assaulted by her second husband with a socket wrench five years before working for us. Femur broken in three places.

The husband, Raymond Hoxie, forty-four. He had also sexually and physically assaulted Miriam's twelve-year-old daughter (name redacted) from a previous marriage. Was pronounced DOA by police when they arrived. Jugular vein pierced with a long-blade screwdriver.

The minor daughter allegedly the perpetrator.

Didi Morrison.

So she'd killed her stepfather after he had brutalized both her and her mother.

The thought came to me: *Five years later, she'd been capable of killing again. She had tried to kill Sarah.*

I began to stand up, but my head was still swimming. I sank back onto the step. I opened Margaret's second email.

> Did not find a COD for a Didi Morrison or similar
> name in British Columbia within time specs. But
> did find this.

Another attachment. A death certificate from 2014. Sarah Jennifer Davis.

I stared at it. It made no sense.

I continued reading through blurring eyes:

Age: 26.

Place of Death: Victoria, British Columbia.

Cause of Death: traumatic injuries sustained in vehicular collision.

A young woman named Sarah Davis had died in a car crash on Vancouver Island. Not Didi Morrison.

But it did make sense. A part of me had already put it together.

Mom's music on Sarah's phone. Mom's favorite sayings—*It gives me the shivers*—on her lips. Other things. An occasional inflection in her voice. An expression on her face.

I got up and went to my studio. My computer wouldn't start up. I felt a panic, then remembered: I'd changed the password. *Butterfingers.* I entered it.

The keyboard had the same gritty-greasy feeling as my steering wheel. My hands were clammy. Everything was starting to feel that way.

I pulled up the yearbook from Monterey Bay High. I advanced to the senior photo of Didi Morrison. Dragged it to the desktop screen.

Then I opened the file I'd compiled of items about Sarah and her first husband. Selected Sarah from the photo of the two of them with their donated Henry Moore sculpture and dragged her image next to Didi's. I enlarged both.

Didi. Heavy and defeated-looking. Pale eyes almost invisible behind thick lenses.

Sarah, elegantly dressed, beautiful. Looking miserable.

What was I seeing?

Both of them frowning. Didi's exaggerated. Sarah's a natural look of misery. But something similar about both frowns.

My eyes began to blur. I squeezed them shut a moment, then focused again. I looked at the quote beside Didi's name in her senior photo. One word in Greek lettering.

I highlighted it and clicked on Translate.

It meant *revenge*.

A terrible chill ran through me.

Sarah, telling me about her recurring dream. In free fall. Wanting revenge.

But it was Didi Morrison who'd chosen it as her yearbook quote.

I had to be sure. I needed a better picture of Didi. One where she hadn't made herself into a freak. The drawing in Mom's sketchbook was too primitive.

But Mom had always been sketching. She must have drawn Didi Morrison other times before she got too sick to hold a pencil steady.

Where did she hide her other sketchbooks?

I suddenly knew. Maybe I'd always known. A place where she was sure they'd stay totally private because she was the only one who ever went there.

The servants' quarters.

I stood up, trembling. I went across the hall to my bedroom. Stieglitz was curled on his cat bed. I roused him, turned over the bed, and removed the iron key I'd taped to the underside. Hiding it from Sarah.

I scooped Stieglitz up. A shield against ghosts. I carried him downstairs. Stopped at the bottom, listened for voices.

Nothing. Sarah wasn't back yet.

I continued to the kitchen and then into the butler's pantry. Clutched the squirming Stieglitz with one hand as I fitted the key in the lock of the small door and turned it.

So dark inside. The lights burned out long ago. I'd left my phone on my desk. There was an electric lantern on one of the pantry shelves. I grabbed it, set it on the counter. Switched it on. It glowed. Who'd put in new batteries?

Sarah. Her first night here, wandering outside in the middle of the night.

I picked up the lantern and pushed the door open with my shoulder. Stieglitz growled loudly. He'd never growled at me before.

I set him down, and he shot off, back into the kitchen. I continued to the room across the narrow hallway.

My heart began to pound hard as, for the first time in seventeen years, I stepped into Cinderella's room.

My gorge rose. Fetid odors: mold, charcoal, filthy dust. I steadied myself a moment with a hand on the doorframe, then moved farther into the room.

Oozing slime on the walls. The twists of petrified dust suspended from the ceiling. Those stark iron bed frames. Skeletons of beds, Jamie had called them.

Fragmentary images flickered through my mind.

Jamie, shifting his legs nervously.

My eyes shooting open: "Something touched my hair."

Jamie, leaping up in terror. "She kissed me on the lips."

My pulse was now beating in a weird, jumpy pattern. I couldn't remain in here very long. I swept the lantern around the room. That tiny dresser veiled in cobwebs: there were shards of glass covered in dust on the charred floor in front of it. A broken vase. Mom's last tribute of flowers to Cinderella.

I wanted to run. Forced myself to sweep the light again, more slowly this time.

There was no place she could have hidden the sketchbooks. The dresser was too small, and there was no closet. Wait. There! An outline near the bottom of the wall opposite the beds.

A low built-in cupboard nearly obscured by dust and ashy slime. The knob was gone, but the door was warped. I crouched down. A wave of dizziness. I waited until it passed, then pried the door open. Shone the lantern light inside.

Nothing. Just a dense, sticky fabric of cobwebs.

But this was Blackworth Mansion. Hidden chambers behind other chambers.

I took off my cardigan and wrapped it around my hand, making a sort of mitt. Then reached into the cabinet, the sweater-mitt collecting a thick, webby membrane and sending spiders scurrying to the edges. My stomach flip-flopped, and I yanked out my hand.

I unwrapped the sweater and, steeling myself, thrust my bare hand back inside, gagging. I tapped a spot on the back wall. And then another.

A panel slid open. I jerked my hand out. I lifted the lantern again.

Inside the hidden chamber, slumping stacks of sketchbooks. Just as I'd known there would be.

I grabbed a few from the front stack. Crumbling. Moldy. I felt suddenly too weak to stand; I sat on the charred filth beside the lantern. I opened the top book.

Faces of my adolescence appeared.

A much younger Michael Fiore, slamming a nail with a hammer. Franny, a little kid, mouth agape.

Me with Grace. Our arms thrown around each other's waists.

Thomas. I drew a breath. At fifteen, slouched on a bench in back of our house. Looking both aloof and yearning at the same time. I lingered on it a moment. Then turned the page.

And then I paused. My body was trembling, and so was my mind.

I was looking at a drawing of my sister-in-law, Sarah.

CHAPTER FORTY

SARAH

The bitch.

The bloodless freaking bitch.

She was in Santa Cruz, her text said. She needed me to meet her at her hotel.

I didn't ask why. If Lenore Wyatt requested a meeting, it had to be something important. I had messaged her recently about Didi, my intentions of getting rid of her for good. A rather long message. I thought it was what we'd be discussing. How she could facilitate it.

It was at the Hilton off Route 17, luxurious and impersonal, so typically Lenore—but not in her suite or in the restaurant. In a meeting room on the first floor. She was waiting when I arrived, spotless white shantung jacket, bloodred lipstick, seated all alone at a conference table for twelve. She had a look on her face I'd never seen before. Concern. Lenore never looked concerned.

My pulse jumped. The police. They'd begun asking about me.

I calmed myself. If that was what it was, she'd see to it that I was protected.

But it wasn't about the police. The fucking bitch.

Brisk as death, she came to the point. She was withdrawing as my attorney. She said I had caused representation to be rendered unreasonably difficult.

"What does that even mean, Lenore?" I said.

"It means that your requests have become extreme and your behavior increasingly erratic. I find it impossible to represent you anymore."

She couldn't force me to take medication, she said, nor would she wish to. But my behavior without such medication had led to a breakdown in our attorney-client relationship.

She handed me a bound set of printed pages. "This document details cause. I'll give you some time to read and digest it." She stood up and left the room.

I didn't read it. I didn't even look at it. I tore the pages out of the binding and ripped them up. I scattered the pieces on the table.

Who does she fucking think I am? I'm Gideon Ellingham's wife. Has she forgotten that?

Though I'm not. What made me even think that? I'm Mrs. James Blackworth Holland now.

She returned fifteen minutes later. Didn't blink an eye at the torn-up pages. She informed me I'd be receiving a registered letter confirming her withdrawal. It would allow time for me to employ other counsel. Her voice softened in a way I'd never heard before. "I know you think I'm very heartless, Sarah. I've had to seem so, dealing with you and your particular situation. I've had to keep a distance because I knew that this moment would arrive at some point. You'd go past the point of reason. I'm truly sorry it's had to end this way. That's all I can really permit myself to say." She extended a hand. "Goodbye, Sarah. I do wish you the best of luck."

I wouldn't touch that hand. I got up and walked out.

I must have been speeding, I've gotten back in record time. I'm nervous as hell. What am I going to do without Lenore Wyatt behind me, putting everything right? Whatever I needed, she provided. A private plane. A tech wizard. Somebody to make anonymous calls or break into an old house. Never a problem. And now she thinks she can drop me, just like that?

I fantasize about killing her.

But I couldn't, even if I tried. You can't kill something that's already dead.

I screech up in my car to the front of the house, gravel and rocks scrunching beneath the tires. I can't go in yet. Not in the state I'm in.

I've lost all control. I need to get it back.

I walk toward the woods, where it's dark and cool. I'm wearing ladylike medium heels. I dressed up for that bitch. I've always wanted to look my best to impress Lenore. The heels make walking in the forest a little tricky, but I can handle it. I'm familiar with the path by now.

Here's that pet cemetery. The police dug up all the old graves. How surprised they must have been. Two dead cats, a parrot, and some chopsticks with elephant carvings on them. It's hilarious when you think about it.

I have the sudden feeling that Didi is very close by. I turn in a full circle, looking for her.

Gideon was supposed to get rid of her for good, but he didn't. That was his final way of torturing me. He let Didi Morrison go on living.

The light is getting dim. I have to go back, but I'm suddenly not sure which way to go. It all looks the same. The ocean, I can hear it rumbling like a warning to me. *Keep away.*

But if I follow its rumble, keep it to my right, I'll be going south, in the right direction. It's hard, the sound keeps shifting with the wind.

And these goddamn heels. I stumble over a fallen branch and slip and fall on a bed of rotting cedar needles.

Or was I pushed? I get to my feet and look wildly around again. How does she slip away from me so fast?

I'm covered in needles and dead leaves. I try to brush myself off, but they're tenacious, clinging to the georgette dress I put on to meet with Lenore.

Pale-green georgette. It's my wedding dress. And now it's ruined.

I'll get even with her. With all of them.

I continue weaving through black trees as I follow the ocean. I'm breathing hard. And now finally I emerge in the clearing next to that horror of a sculpture garden.

I don't want to look at it, but I can't help myself. Those broken statues leaning on iron rods. Staring at me. Judging me.

They've got no right to judge. Lenore had no right.

Gideon constantly judged me. He thought I'd always do anything he wanted. But he wasn't totally right about that. When the time allowed, I did something on my own. He was weakened by Parkinson's and was going to die anyway.

He just went sooner than he expected.

As I enter the house, James calls out. "Sarah? Is that you?"

He meets me in the hall, his progress on crutches excruciatingly slow.

"I'm sorry, darling, I got held up," I say. "I had to fire Lenore Wyatt. I discovered she's been skimming money from me. She didn't take it very well. She caused a scene."

"You've got leaves on you."

"I know. I slipped in a pile of them leaving her hotel. I'm not hurt, but my dress is ruined. It's my wedding dress, remember?"

"Yeah, of course I do," he says.

"You shouldn't be walking by yourself. I can't have you falling."

"I wanted to go back upstairs," he says. "I'm starting to really hurt."

I support one of his arms and help him to the staircase, and then I take one of his crutches so he can grasp the banister. We slowly climb the stairs, and I give him back the other crutch, and we head back to his bedroom.

"It's time for me to move into the suite with you," he says. "I don't need a hospital room anymore."

"I'd love that, darling, but let's just see how you do for a couple more days." I help him into bed and smooth the luxurious covers over him. I open the Chinese cabinet and take out the bottle of Motrin.

"What exactly have you been giving me?" he says.

I look at him with puzzled eyes. "You know what it is. Motrin Extra Strength." I show him the bottle.

"Come on, Sarah. I know it's some sort of opioid. What is it? Demerol?"

"No, of course not. It's just brand-name ibuprofen."

"I know what the bottle says. I feel far too good after taking it. And why am I still in so much pain?"

"You were badly injured, darling, and it takes a lot of time. You know that."

"No. These therapists you hired are pushing me too hard. They're doing me more harm than good. I'm firing them. And where's my computer? I want to look up the pills in that bottle."

I set the Motrin bottle on the cabinet. "If you don't trust me, you can have Ava get something from the pharmacy. I'll get her to go right now. That way you can be sure it's just ibuprofen."

He hesitates.

"Oh, James," I say softly. "Is that what you really want?"

"I don't know." He lifts his eyes to me. Such a beautiful amber gold, except the part that's kind of milky. "No. Maybe not quite yet."

"Are you sure, darling?"

"Yeah, I'm sure. It hurts so damned much." He grabs the bottle and attempts to open it, but it's got a childproof cap, and he's essentially still one armed. "Shit!"

I take it from him and shake out four pills. He starts to take them, then stops and puts two on the cabinet. Swallows the remaining two with the glass of filtered water beside his bed. "Are you drugging Ava too?" he asks.

I stare at him in astonishment. "I don't understand. Does she think that? Because that's insane." I sigh. "I'm worried about her. I think everything that's happened has been too much for her."

"Maybe," he says.

Ten minutes later, he drifts off to sleep. I leave his room, turning off the light behind me.

I feel like I'm still in the darkening forest. I can't see the right path. Everything's blocking my way.

I'm losing control.

I have to find Ava. Before she has time to say anything else to him. Turning him against me.

They all keep turning against me.

I head down the opposite wing. Ava's not in her studio, but her desk lamp is on. She's been in here recently. I go over to the computer. The screen is black. She has a password on it, but she probably didn't shut it down yet. She makes that mistake a lot.

I use a pen to tap the keyboard. I don't want to get anything on my fingers.

The black screen is replaced by two photos side by side. One is of me.

The other is a photo of that other one.

I start breathing very hard. I've got to get back in control.

I send both photos crumbling into the trash file.

Then I turn and leave the room and go across the hall to Christina's studio. I gasp. In the dimming light, it looks exactly the same, like Christina is going to come in here any minute.

Gasping, sighing, grunting . . . these are all forms of breathing.

The part of the brain that lets you control your breath connects directly to the amygdala—the organ in the lizard brain that triggers fear. And also flight or fight.

I've always chosen to fight.

CHAPTER FORTY-ONE

AVA

It wasn't actually a sketch of Sarah I was looking at. It was Didi Morrison.

Heavyset. Round faced. A frizz of blondish hair. No glasses. Something battered looking about her flattish nose and the set of her jaw. A hint of very crooked teeth beneath her half smile.

But Mom had seen how beautiful the shape of her eyes was, despite the puffy lids. She'd chiseled off some of Didi's extra weight and brought out the quality of her cheekbones.

She had sketched an idealized portrait of Didi, and it revealed the woman I knew as Sarah.

An iron band tightened around my head. I felt both vertigo and cramping in my stomach. I was getting worse. I had to get to a doctor immediately.

Straining, I reached out to grab the post of one of the bed frames and, still clutching the sketchbook, struggled to my feet.

There was somebody in the kitchen. I feebly called out, "Jamie?"

A figure appeared in the doorway. Backlit from the light of the kitchen, dark, like a negative. Like that shadow on the top of the stairs. A dimmer shadow fluttered on the floor in front of it.

"What are you doing in here?" Sarah asked.

A whip of pain snapped in my stomach. I gave a groan.

"What's that you're holding?" she said.

"Nothing. Let's get out of this room. It's not healthy in here."

"It's horrible." She approached me. "Let me see what you've got."

I pressed the sketchbook against my chest. "Just some drawings my mother made. They're private, I can't show them to anybody."

"Your mother is dead, Ava," she said. "She's nothing but ashes now. Any lawyer can tell you she's got no more right to privacy." Her eyes darted to the open cupboard. "So that's where they were. I didn't see that cabinet before." She stepped closer, and now I could see she had something in her hand.

"What's that?" I asked.

"This?" She looked at it. "It's a tool. I'm not sure what you call it."

"An awl." Scratched-up wooden handle, very rusty, but the point was still sharp. I had found it in the mudroom and had put it on Mom's table.

Sarah took another step toward me. She yanked the book out of my hands. She looked at the drawing it was turned to. "Ugly freak."

"No, she's not," I said.

She threw the book violently into a corner of the room. I flinched. Watched her warily. She stood half in shadow, half illuminated by the lantern. Both Didi and Sarah now. I tried to focus: let her know I understood. That it was okay. She didn't have to be afraid.

My throat was starting to feel like acid. I forced myself to talk. "You changed yourself," I said. "You lost weight. You changed your nose and jaw and got your teeth fixed. Your eyes are darker. Contacts." I paused. My throat and lungs all burned. "You made yourself into somebody else. The pretty girl in high school. Sarah Davis."

"You've lost your mind, Ava," she said. "You don't even know what you're talking about."

I was on the verge of collapsing. I clung to the bedpost. My thoughts tangled, jumping. I searched my mind for that dark place, the one that always hovered at the edges—not to give in to it, but to use it now as a focus. To steady my thinking.

The glass shards. I could almost reach them. If I could keep her distracted . . .

"I don't blame you," I said. "I know what your stepfather did. And what you did to him."

A breeze shivered through the rotting window frame with a kind of wheezing sigh, and her eyes darted to it.

I took a step closer to the shards. "Gideon made it happen for you. He paid for you to become Sarah. To change your looks. Your whole identity. Did he have the real Sarah Davis killed?"

She looked back at me. "You're crazy." But with something uncertain in her face now.

"He made you into her. And in return, you did whatever he wanted."

"You've got no idea of what he wanted," she said shrilly.

That iron headband tightened. "You were abused by your stepfather. You found another man who abused you. That often happens."

"I know the studies, Ava. You don't have to tell me."

"But Jamie's different, isn't he? You love him. You always did, even way back then."

That confused look on her face again. "He walked out on me. I won't let that happen."

A thunderous crash of surf: the window frame wheezed, and the shadows on the ceiling twisted and danced. Her gaze shot upward. I attempted another step toward the shattered glass. She looked back at me, and I froze.

"You loved your mother too," I said. "You wanted to give her the best of care. Her name was Miriam, right? Mom liked her very much."

"Bullshit!" she shrieked. "She didn't show up at the clinic. If she did, that doctor would have given Mimi a new knee."

I didn't know what she was talking about. I glanced at her hand grasping the awl. A ring on her middle finger. Pearls and a sapphire. Victorian setting.

"You stole my mother's ring when you were Didi," I said. "I recognized it when we first met. You had a new one made to fool me. The one you're wearing now."

She looked at me, in deep confusion now.

"Where is Mom's? Do you still have it?"

"No," she whispered. "That poor saleslady at Saks. She looked so tired."

What was she talking about? But I was close enough to the shards now to pick one up. I faked a groan and doubled over.

Sarah lunged again and pricked my neck with the awl. I shrank up against the wall. A wave of pain and nausea spun through me.

"Your nose is bleeding, Ava," she said.

I dabbed at it. Bright blood. "You're poisoning me. You're trying to kill me."

"Maybe," she said. "I haven't decided yet."

I felt a deep spasm of alarm. "You don't have to. Everything will be okay. Let me get to a doctor."

"Why won't you accept me, Ava?" she said. "We should be sisters. I'm a Blackworth, too, you know. I was one long before you. I was Alice Blackworth, and I belong here more than you do."

My throat was so raw. My voice a rasp. "I don't understand."

"You can't understand. You're just a new soul, and you don't know anything yet. You're not even a real Blackworth. You're a Holland, that's your last name, like your father."

She was making no sense. Or maybe I just couldn't process it; my head ached so much, and my mind was jumping. "You killed my father."

She smiled. "He deserved it. He was a pig."

"Did he touch you?"

A small shrug.

"But why did you kill my mother?" I said. "What did she do to you?"

"I didn't," she said.

"You did. You poisoned her, like you're doing with me. You made her sick, and she died."

She stepped very close, brandishing the awl.

"I never would have killed Christina," she said. "We were both old souls."

"I saw you. Your shadow when you ran from her studio. Running to the back stairs."

"No," she said insistently. "I loved Christina. I would never, ever hurt her."

"Sarah Davis wouldn't. But you're not Sarah, you're Didi Morrison. You tried to kill the real Sarah. You pushed her off a cliff."

"No, that's not it . . ." Her voice trailed off. She looked around the room in deep confusion. "I was in free fall. I wanted to die. But I didn't."

I looked at her, not understanding at first. But then I did. Words came from my burning throat. "You didn't push the real Sarah Davis, did you? You stepped off that bluff yourself. You tried to commit suicide but survived. But you wanted revenge."

"No," she says again, but tentatively.

"You're Didi Morrison," I whispered. "You want revenge for all your own misery. That's why you inflict pain on everybody else. You killed Mom."

Her face suddenly twisted in hatred. "You're so stupid, Ava. You think you're so smart and superior, but you're not, you can't even know what's true and what's not. I would never have killed Christina."

She was lying. I'd seen her, her shadow, running away.

But then a memory flew up, out of that darkest recess of my mind. Even through my fear and the pain and nausea racking me, I saw it clearly. That shadow, bulky but agile and moving in a bobbing sort of way, and the terrible creaking sound it made.

She wasn't lying.

"I believe you, Sarah," I whispered. "It wasn't you. You didn't kill my mother."

CHAPTER FORTY-TWO

SARAH

She doesn't really believe me. She'll say anything to save herself now, even though it's too late. Her eyes were always too big, but right now they're like full moons; they glow with a strange light, the reflection of the lantern.

There's that whistling sound at the window again. Something trying to get in. Or maybe get out. This room gives me the horrors.

Ava's watching me carefully with those huge, glowing eyes. Waiting for me to make a mistake.

"It was my father, wasn't it?" Her voice is like a croak. "It was his shadow I saw. A bobbing kind of run. And he made the floor creak. He was the only one big enough to do that."

She's just telling me what she knows I want to hear.

"I knew that when I was thirteen. I didn't want to believe it. That my father killed my mother. It nearly made me go insane. I told myself I'd seen Cinderella."

I don't want Ava to talk about Cinderella. It spooks me too much. The window won't stop whistling, and there are strange kinds of shadows on these horrible walls and ceiling.

Ava gives a groan of pain. For real this time. She sinks to the floor. Looks up at me in a pleading way. Her breathing is getting laborious. "Tell me what happened to my mother."

I sit down, too, but I keep the sharp tool clutched in my hand. My pale-green wedding dress is ruined. It's stained with rotten leaves and cedar needles and now charcoal and dirt.

"Please tell me," Ava says. "I need to know."

I don't think that's true. But it doesn't matter.

She doesn't have long to live.

I give a sigh. "I had an envelope with rat poison from the toolshed. I told Christina I was leaving for the day. But I came back."

A shudder runs through her body.

"I went to the butler's pantry. I started putting the poison into a bottle of scotch. Johnnie Walker."

"Dad's." I can hardly hear her voice, it's so weak. "He was the only one who drank it. You tried to kill Dad."

"He hurt Christina. He broke her ribs. I bet you didn't even know that."

"No," Ava says in that croak.

"He wasn't ever going to stop." My voice is so much higher. It's losing its refinement. "He was going to kill her sometime. I had to stop him. But he came back early. He wasn't supposed to." I can see it all again. Like a movie in my head. "He looked into the envelope, and he got a grin on his face. He said, 'Are you trying to poison me?' He grabbed my arm, he twisted it, I felt it start to break."

Ava makes a strange sound.

"I told him what the poison was, and he laughed. He said, 'You stupid, ugly freak. You just made it easy for me.' And then a pain exploded in my cheek, and I blacked out."

"He knocked you out."

"Yes. And when I came to, I was locked in his office. My face hurt. I knew what he was going to do, and I had to stop him. I got one of the windows up. It was hard, but I did it and got outside. It was dark, and there were flashing lights in front. And voices. I knew she was dead."

"Not yet. She was in a coma. Dad pulled the plug later." Ava clutches herself in a spasm of pain. "Why didn't you tell anyone?"

"He had the envelope, and it had my name on it. He'd put the blame on me. I was afraid he would anyway. I went around the back to get to my car. To leave before anybody saw me. I heard this terrible noise. Like somebody being tortured."

She lifts her feverish eyes to me.

"It was you, Ava," I say. "On a rock facing the ocean. It was too black to see the water, but the sound of the waves was very loud." The waves sound very strong now. Like giants smashing their fists against the shore.

"You gave me Nembutal," Ava says.

I smile at her. "I had it with me. I gave some to Mimi that morning."

"And a bottle of scotch. You wanted to kill me too."

"No. You already had it with you. I didn't know it was scotch. You were so young, and it was black all around."

Something mingles with the pain in Ava's face. "I remember," she whispers. "I took it from the kitchen. I wanted to feel nothing." Her voice sinks away.

She's getting sicker.

She says, "You came back for my father. You found him in a bar in Monterey."

I smile again.

"You were Sarah by then. Not Didi anymore. But you still wanted your revenge."

I breathe out a giggle. "He was bragging about the mansion he had rights to. He wanted to show me. I drove him. I stopped at the statues.

I said, 'Let's have a drink first.' I had a bottle of Johnnie Walker. The Blue Label. The most expensive kind."

"You poisoned it," she says.

"Strychnine." It's a word I like saying. It's from ancient Greek. "The same poison he killed Christina with. His whole body arched, and he made faces. Then it was over. I was just going to leave him there, but I got scared."

"Why?"

"People saw us together at the bar. And maybe getting into my car. And then another car came down from the highway. A truck. I took a rock and hit my face and arm until they bled. And I ran to meet it."

"Michael."

"No, not his truck. A big black one with extra lights. You know it."

Ava shudders again, very hard. She looks like she's on the brink of passing out. She can barely talk. "Did you give me strychnine?"

"No. Ant poison with sodium cyanide. Only a little at a time, but yesterday and today a lot more."

Her eyes glow. "My steering wheel."

"Yes. With a gel to make it stick. And your keyboard. And some in your pillowcase."

She lets out a sort of sob. "What are you giving Jamie?"

"Just OxyContin. Left over from Gideon." I sigh again. "He belongs to me. He always has. I won't let him leave me again."

"And his eye drops. You put something in them."

I have to strain to hear her. She's so weak. It will just be a matter of hours. There'll be convulsions. Her lungs will stop working.

"I switched bottles with one of Gideon's. For glaucoma. I peeled off the labels and put Gideon's on James's. I switched the caps. I didn't want to hurt him. I thought he'd use them before leaving. They'd make his eyes blur, and he'd have to stay."

Ava's breathing is strange. "Please, Sarah, let me get help."

"No," I say. "I'm not going to do that."

"They'll know it's you if I die. You won't get away with it."

I look at her with pity. "Of course I will. I always get away with it. Everybody will think you've had another breakdown. They'll think you committed suicide."

Her eyes are huge with fear. She knows that's true.

CHAPTER
FORTY-THREE

AVA

The room is sinking into twilight. I try hard to concentrate, but my thoughts keep dissolving into pain and that overwhelming desire to sleep.

I'm being poisoned by cyanide. Fruit pits have cyanide, Dad once said that; if you grind them up, apricot pits, cherry pits, they've got small amounts of cyanide. But it's not Dad who is poisoning me, it's Sarah.

A wave crashes and booms. The room shivers, and a breeze slaps the window. Air hisses between the dirt-coated window and sill.

I need to get to a hospital.

Another wave slams the rocks. The house vibrates. Dust spools up from old crevices and is illuminated in the glow of the lantern. It holds me in rapture. It's so very beautiful.

"What did you say?" Sarah says.

Did I speak out loud? "It's so golden and beautiful. Can't you see it?"

Her eyes shift nervously to the lantern. "What do you mean?"

I sense a tinge of fear in her voice. It gives me hope, and I experience a little surge of adrenaline. I can play off her fear. I grasp the bedpost and pull myself to my feet. "It's Cinderella. She's here. This is her room."

Sarah gets up, keeping the sharp point of the awl trained on my throat. "You're the one who believes in ghosts, Ava. Not me."

"Cinderella is real. Mom saw her, and now I see her too."

Her eyes fix on the lantern. "I don't."

"She hates anyone coming in here. You know what happens when they do."

She lunges again, and the awl nicks my arm. I give a cry of pain.

"You're very sick, Ava," she says. "You're seeing things. It's because you're dying."

"It is true. Cinderella's here. She's right behind you now." Thin streams of cold air drift in from the rotting window frame. I draw some strength from it, and I find a stronger voice. "She's standing behind you, blowing on your hair. Can't you feel her breath? It's so cold."

She gasps. She reaches a hand to the back of her hair.

"She's put her curse on you. You know what's going to happen to you."

"No, I don't believe you!"

I am very sick. On the edge of delirium. But for one fleeting instant, I do seem to see her, Cinderella, just like Mom described her: small and dark and lovely. With such sad eyes. "She's right behind you, Sarah," I whisper hoarsely. "She's touching you with her cold breath."

"Where?" She whirls.

I gather every last ounce of my strength and step behind her, then push her against the iron bed frame, catching her off guard, and with a sharp cry, she crashes backward into the metal rungs. I stumble to the door and make it out of the room and back into the butler's pantry. I shut the door and turn the key in the lock. I clutch the counter for support.

The doorknob rattles. "Ava! Open the door."

"No," I say. "I'll never let you hurt my family again."

"I am your family," she pleads. "Let me out."

"You're not, you're Didi Morrison. You destroyed us. If it hadn't been for you, Mom would still be alive."

"No. I loved Christina, it wasn't my fault. I told you, and you believed me. I'm your real sister, why can't you accept that, Ava? I belong here."

I feel a revulsion that goes deeper than my racking pain. "You'll never belong here, Didi." I try to say that, but the words are now too hard to get out.

She gives an unearthly shriek. "Let me out! Ava, there's horror in here. I can feel her. I feel her breath on me. Let me out!" I flinch as I hear her slam the awl against the lock. "Don't leave me in this terrible place. Let me out!" Again and again, she slams the awl on the door and the lock face. The doorframe is rotted, it's just a matter of time before it splinters, and the old screws on the lock's metal plate will give way.

I stagger through the kitchen, dizzy, trying hard not to vomit as I make my way to the back stairs. The screaming from the servants' quarters becomes another echo among the many reverberating through the house.

Clinging to the banister, I pull myself to the top of the stairs and continue to Jamie's room.

"Jamie," I say in a hoarse whisper. "Wake up." I shake him, rousing him from his opioid dreams. "We've got to get help. Now!"

CHAPTER
FORTY-FOUR
DIDI/SARAH

I shriek and strike the door again and again with the sharp awl.

The horror is all around me, it oozes on the walls and twists down from the ceiling, and there are ghosts dancing and weaving, their cold breath wraps around me.

The lantern light flutters dimly, the battery is dying. It gives a final flicker and goes out. It's all black now; there's just the faintest glow from the window in the room behind me. The moon rising.

"Let me out of here!" My voice sounds so high to my ears. "Let me out of this terrible place!"

I scream it again and again, gripping that tool, the awl, with both hands. I furiously stab the lock and plate. I strike and stab, again and again. A crack of wood. Something has given way. I heave my body against the door, and it gapes open. And then I fling myself out of that terrible blackness, and I'm in the butler's pantry.

Christina. I've got to find her.

I run into the kitchen. She should be there. Arranging flowers to bring to the ghost. She'll bring a sketchbook, too, and she'll leave it in that room along with the flowers.

She's an old soul, just like me. She knows I belong here, that I'm a real Blackworth. Those others are just stupid young souls, they don't know anything yet.

"Christina!" I yell out. "Where are you?"

I start walking through these gloomy hallways, letting this tool that's in my hand drop to the floor. It clangs and brings up murmurs and echoes from behind every door and dark corner. So many voices. Mimi. Her knee is killing her. Poor Mimi, she deserves better. I hear that bitch Lenore, her voice is cold as ice. An old man's voice, his name is Gideon, he wants me down on my hands and knees. A man whose name is Raymond: *When I say come, you move your ass.*

And another man, he's big, with bloodshot eyes: *You stupid, ugly freak.*

Those men with the voices. They're all gone now. All of them dead.

I have to tell that to Christina. She'll be proud of me. She'll understand it's what I had to do.

She must be upstairs in her painting studio. Making her pigments. I pause at the foot of those grand stairs.

There are other voices up there. James and Ava. It doesn't matter. They won't even see me. I'm just a servant.

Didi, dear, let's go out and scavenge.

Christina! She's not upstairs. I keep walking, looking for her, until I come to that glassed-in porch. But where are all the tropical-looking plants? Who took them away?

"Christina!" I shout again.

She must be outside, in the forest, scavenging for things to paint. I step out of the door, into the moonlight.

There's such sharp, clear air, and I feel it cleanse away the horror of that room. Those ghosts and deathly cinders. I walk quickly across the backyard as it slopes up toward the trees. It's thick with overgrown weeds and pockmarked stone benches. I stumble a little. Stupid shoes. Christina is always barefoot. I take off my shoes and carry them and keep walking in my bare feet.

I've come to the forest now. The moon casts my shadow very long on the ground. The old trees, their branches crisscrossed, are etched in black against the dark sky. Pebbles and twigs are painful under my feet, but I don't care. I can take a lot of pain.

A huge shadow glides off a high tree limb. Black and silent.

An owl, Christina's favorite bird. It's a sign. It's showing me the way.

The path is getting very narrow, and it's climbing steeply, getting close to the edge of the bluff. I hear a siren sound in the distance.

Police cars. Ambulances. Like the ones that came that day after what I did to Raymond. The screwdriver going in so easily, and then his blood mixing with mine.

I'm walking now along the very edge of the cliff. I stop and look out at the ocean. The moonlight creates a shimmering staircase on the rolling water, and the surf crashes on the rocks below. It frightens me. The ocean always has.

Didi. Christina calls my name again.

My heart beats very fast.

And now I see her. Standing just ahead, where the bluff juts out farther into the shore. She's smiling. She's so beautiful. Her long skirt rustles. Her red-gold hair is like a loose cloak around her face and shoulders.

I hear her murmuring voice even over the thrash of surf. "Didi, sweet love," she murmurs. "I've been here waiting for you."

My heart rises to my throat. Christina understands. She's the only one who does.

I put down the shoes I'm still holding. I open my arms wide.

I go to her.

And now suddenly there's nothing beneath my feet. No painful hard stones. No jagged cliff. Nothing but free fall. No sound at all, not the deadly surf below, not even the rushing wind. It's silent all around, and I'm falling, and it fills me with such bliss.

I'm not afraid anymore. I feel nothing but boundless joy.

CHAPTER
FORTY-FIVE

AVA

After I shook him, Jamie woke up quickly. He'd taken a lesser dosage of Oxy—two pills, not four—and the sight of me was enough to shock him into a lucid state. "Ava, Jesus. You're really sick."

"I've been poisoned." My voice barely a croak. "Cyanide. Call 911."

The operator sent an ambulance, then transferred Jamie to poison control. He relayed their instructions. "Get out of your clothes, Ava, and get into a bath. EMS will bring an antidote kit."

I rallied enough to climb into a bathtub and soap myself. I put on Jamie's robe. I told him as much as I could manage about what had happened. My lungs were aching, my throat raw.

We heard Sarah downstairs, calling out for Mom. We tensed. Waited for her to come up. She didn't.

Minutes later, EMS came screaming up with a patrol car not far behind. We made our way downstairs. Both police and paramedics were wearing masks and double gloves.

I told them I'd been exposed to ant poison with cyanide while clearing out an old shed. The paramedics got me into the ambulance and inserted an IV. "You come, too, sir," one of them said to Jamie. "You need to be checked out. So does anyone else who lives here."

One of the cops said they'd seen a woman going up the ledge of the bluff into the forest.

"My wife, Sarah," Jamie said, leaning heavily on his crutches. "She's been showing signs of an escalating dissociative disorder. She wouldn't agree to a voluntary commitment. I've been recuperating from a bad accident, so I couldn't tend to her." He begged them to go search for her. "With all the sirens and commotion, I'm afraid she might have had a psychotic break. I'm worried what she might do."

He said he wouldn't leave until he was sure she was safe.

The paramedics whisked me to Saint Lawrence Samaritan, where Darsh Greenwald was an attending surgeon. Even in my delirium, I was glad he wasn't on rounds. I didn't want Grace to worry when she could be going into labor at any minute.

The next day, Jamie told me what happened afterward.

Franny had shown up. She'd gotten my text and had been trying to reach me. She'd agreed to stay with Jamie as long as he needed. And for once didn't ask any questions.

The cops had called for backup, which arrived with dogs. They spread out in the dark forest.

It wasn't until dawn that they saw the body mangled on the rocks below the very highest point of the bluff.

"I feel like I've snapped out of a dream," Jamie said.

It was two weeks later. We were in the sunporch, though not drinking daiquiris. We were having tea. I'd been lucky—I'd been treated for cyanide poisoning in time to have no lasting liver or heart damage. But I didn't want to push my luck and had cut way down on drinking.

Jamie was on a maintenance dose of OxyContin. Tomorrow, he'd be checking into an ultra-discreet detox ranch in the Carmel Valley.

"When I look back now," he continued, "I see a thousand things that should have stopped me from marrying a woman I hardly knew. It was like I'd been in an altered state. A kind of temporary insanity."

"She was fixated on you, and that's hard to resist," I said. "Especially when it's someone so charming and beautiful. And maybe you sensed there was something very broken about her. You wanted to be her white knight and come to her rescue."

He thought a moment. "Do you think she was fixated on me?"

"Yeah, I do. Going back to when she was Didi and working here. It was all part of her delusion. Of being a Blackworth and belonging here."

"So you're a psychologist now?" he said teasingly.

"Maybe," I said.

His face turned somber. "Mom stuffed our heads with ghost stories and fairy tales. I became a scientist to reject all that. But what if I'd sensed something deviant about Sarah, and that's what attracted me? Like an irresistible case study."

"I don't believe that," I said. "I think you're a true romantic. Just like Mom. Like our great-great-whatever-grandpa who built this house. And like me too. It runs in the Blackworth blood."

He gave a skeptical snort but didn't contradict me.

I sipped my now-lukewarm tea. Flowering herbs. All-natural and organic.

It reminded me of Mom.

Also of Sarah.

The search team found her shoes at the edge of the cliff, which apparently pointed to suicide. "The ones who jump off cliffs and bridges often do that," a detective told me. "But not usually if they go out a window. Go figure."

Jamie repeated to investigators that she'd had a worsening mental disorder. "She had become obsessed with the idea our house was haunted by an evil ghost." He'd said that if she did have a psychotic break, she might have committed suicide, but it could have been accidental—there was just no way to tell.

Sarah's attorney—a powerhouse lawyer in Orange County named Lenore Wyatt—told police she'd met with Sarah on the day she died to inform her she was quitting as her attorney. Sarah's requests had become too erratic and unreasonable for her to continue. Basically meaning she thought Sarah had gone crazy.

The coroner listed cause of death as "traumatic injuries sustained from a high fall." No evidence of a crime, though there'd be an official inquest later.

Franny took down the door to the servants' quarters, removing all evidence of what had happened in there. A cousin of Michael's came in a hazmat suit and scrubbed down my car and studio and bedroom.

There'd been another flurry of media attention, but a bigger scandal broke at the same time—a teenage TikTok star, a tech billionaire, explicit videos—so we were minor news.

No one suspected that Sarah had once been Didi Morrison, a girl who, at twelve, had murdered her stepfather. There was no reason to. The new identity Gideon's money had forged for her was simply too good.

Outside, Betsy was barking, and a squirrel scolded. I set down my drained teacup. "Do you think you'll ever forgive her?" I asked Jamie.

"I don't know," he said. "I can't really blame her. I blame myself more. She had survived terrible trauma physically but not emotionally. She tried to reject that damaged persona. When she met me again, it might have stirred up her old Didi obsessions. With Mom. And becoming a Blackworth. And taking revenge on anybody who stood in her way."

"I suppose she was the one who sent me those cards," I said. "And made that spoofed call from Dad's number."

"I'm sure. To unnerve you. She needed you off balance to keep you under control." He gave a bitter smile. "I should have realized. I had my head in the clouds."

I was silent a moment. Mom was dead because of her. Maybe I'd forgive her sometime. But not yet. And maybe never.

We had told nobody what had happened to Mom. No one needed to know. Her murderer was dead.

And we'd told no one that Sarah had murdered Dad.

These were Blackworth secrets.

We had closure, dreadful as it was. It would have to be enough.

But there was one more thing I did need to know.

I had called Thomas from the hospital the day after I was admitted. He'd caught the first flight back from Bozeman and came directly to the hospital. I was released two days later, and he brought me back to his house in Pebble Beach, where I was pampered by his entire household. He fetched Stieglitz from Blackworth Mansion to be with me, Stieglitz yowling with outrage at being torn away from his beloved shadows.

And now we were having a picnic with Clotilde and Anson at Shoehorn Beach, a small cove near Monterey sheltered by a semicircle of mottled green bluffs. Jamie had taught me to bodysurf there. One of the bluffs was known as Lover's Leap. I'd always wondered why. It looked no different from any of the others.

It was under Lover's Leap that we laid out the cloth and the picnic baskets. Anson's nanny, Jeremiah, struggled to get him into his swim diaper and shirt, but Anson refused to give up his regular T-shirt—one I'd given him. It had huge dinosaur jaws and the word *Chomp*.

Thomas built him a sandcastle with four turrets and a moat and a driftwood drawbridge, but a half hour later, a high wave flooded the moat, and another took a bite from the castle keep, and then Anson gleefully knocked it all down. He'd lost a lot of his shyness around me. Whenever Jeremiah scolded him—always ever so gently—he ran to me for pretend protection, burying his head in my lap or against my shoulder, and I'd feel a burst of love with a twinge of some aching pain.

We gorged on sandwiches—Serrano ham, Gouda, arugula—and homemade chicken nuggets and saucer-size cookies. Then Anson curled up asleep on the picnic cloth next to his mom. I sat with Thomas on a log of driftwood bleached white as milk.

We were silent for some moments. It had been a perfect afternoon. I was tempted to just remain sitting in contented silence. But I couldn't.

I said, "There's one more question I need to ask you."

"Just one?" he said.

"It's a difficult one."

"Your specialty, isn't it?"

I made a chagrined face. "I can't believe some of the things I asked you. That first time at your house. I'm surprised you didn't tell me to go to hell."

"I considered it. But the thing is, I didn't want you to go anywhere."

"You didn't?"

"No. You had stuck in my mind all those years. I'd always had a sense that we were sort of alike. It's pretty rare for me to feel that way about anybody."

"You did about Mom."

"I thought I did, but she set me straight. I was just a fifteen-year-old with the hots for a gorgeous older woman. But with you, it was something very different. You took my breath away."

I flushed with pleasure. But I turned my face and looked out at the luminous blue water.

He took a swig from a sweating bottle of pinot gris. "So what's your difficult question?"

I said, "You came to Blackworth Mansion the night my father was killed, didn't you?"

He was silent. I felt a terrible tightening in my chest.

"You knew all along that he was buried there," I went on. "And that Sarah had killed him. You were there. You had the same truck you have now."

"It was brand new at the time," he said.

So it was true. I turned to look at him. His eyes were hidden behind dark glasses. I couldn't read them.

"Were you meeting her there?" I asked.

"No. I told you, I used to go to your house from time to time. It was the only place I'd ever felt happy as a kid. I was stunned to find her there."

"So you did know her."

"I recognized her. Gideon Ellingham's wife. That benefit I'd made a fool of myself at."

"Did you help her kill my father?" I said.

"No," he said emphatically. "Absolutely not. He was already dead." He took another swallow of wine. "I was coming down the driveway, and a woman came running up, screaming for help. It startled the hell out of me. Even more when I recognized her. She had bruises on her face. She told me she'd been assaulted and the man had tried to rape her. He'd had a stroke and was dead. There was a car parked by the sculpture garden. I went to look."

A shiver ran down my arms. "Did you know it was my father?"

"Yeah, right off. And he was definitely dead. His body was twisted, and his face was bright red and distorted. He had vomited, and he reeked of scotch. His belt was unbuckled. I supposed it could have been a stroke." His face hardened. "The truth is, I didn't care. I was actually glad he was dead."

"Why?"

"I'd always hated him. I knew he slapped you and Jamie around. Jamie had told me things. I was pretty sure he beat your mother. He was a shit. He belonged in my family, not yours." He gave a short, mirthless laugh.

"Were you the one who said to bury him?" I asked.

"No, of course not," he said. "It was her idea. She said her husband was a monster, and if any of this got out, he'd do things to her that would be worse than death. I knew enough about Gideon Ellingham to believe that was true. I told her I wouldn't say anything, she could just leave the body and there'd be no way of connecting it to her. But she said people had seen them together. She seemed genuinely terrified. She begged me to help bury him and swore she'd have the body moved later." He paused. "I only discovered she never did when you found him."

I reached for the wine. I didn't drink. Just held the bottle by the neck. "Then what happened?"

"God. It was ghoulish. There was a greenish kind of moon, and the ocean was slamming the rocks like I'd never heard before. I had tools in the truck. I started digging. Then I looked over and saw her. She was removing his clothes and watch and things in this matter-of-fact way. It freaked the fucking hell out of me. I realized I'd made a terrible decision." He lifted his face up toward the top of Lover's Leap. Then looked back at me. "It was a horror. But in some way, it also felt right. A kind of justice. For you and Jamie. And for Christina. How he treated you all."

There was a sudden loud squawking: seagulls fighting over a rind of cheese. I watched them peck and flap and scream.

I said, "You knew I was afraid that Dad was after me. Why didn't you tell me this?"

"I wasn't sure how you'd react. I wanted you to know me well enough first so you'd believe me about what happened. I was going to tell you the night I came back from Montana. But you were in shock. And then I got a text from Sarah. She made threats. She said she had photos she'd taken. I didn't really believe that. But she did have powerful connections." He shrugged ruefully. "I guess I thought it didn't matter, since you knew now you didn't have to fear him anymore."

The breeze slapped wet salt across my face. It stung. "These past weeks, I'd started to think I was having another breakdown," I said. "That maybe I was having delusions. About Dad. And then about Sarah and then practically everything. If you had told me this, I would have realized I wasn't. That it was Sarah who was crazy, not me."

"I don't think you were ever crazy," he said. "Not even when you were in the psych ward. I think you feel things very deeply. Sometimes too deeply." He touched my cheek. "I do too. We both have our ways of covering it up."

I stared at the bracelets on his wrist. I'd kissed them many times, as if they were a natural part of him. I still had a desire to.

I set the bottle on the sand, digging it in deep, and I stood up. "I'm going to take a walk down the beach."

He looked up at me. He didn't reply. He knew I wanted to go alone.

I began walking underneath the cliffs, succulents trailing down their steep faces like slick hair, strands of broken rock strung at their crumbly napes. The sand was firm and damp and cool beneath my bare feet.

I could keep on walking and not go back. I could climb one of the sets of stairs up to the parking area. I had my own life. My own work. I could call for a ride back home.

But where was home? Was it Blackworth Mansion?

I kept walking on sand so firmly packed I scarcely left footprints.

Thomas had kept a secret from me that nearly cost me my life. It was far from his intent, but it's what had happened. He didn't know Sarah was insane, but he had known she was ruthless. He hadn't warned Jamie or me. It would be impossible not to blame him, wouldn't it?

But I wasn't so blameless in other ways.

Seventeen years ago, I'd frozen at the base of a staircase, too scared by a shadow to move. And then I'd chosen to believe that what I'd seen was a ghost rather than my father.

I'd locked my sister-in-law in a room, and I had filled her with horrors, maybe pushing her into suicide.

And I would remain silent about both my parents' murders forever. As would Jamie.

I saw myself suddenly at fourteen. In the office of a therapist. Dr. Patti, with her basket of beanbags. A box of no-brand tissues on a blue table. A happy print of leaping goats on the wall. A purple octopus soft in my hand.

Let it go, Ava. Throw it hard against the wall.

I picked up a stone and threw it with all my strength against the cliff. It dislodged a stream of rocks that tumbled into the rubble below.

A peal of laughter rang faintly from a distance behind. Anson had woken up from his nap.

I turned and looked back. I saw Thomas standing between the bluff and the shore, shading his eyes to watch me.

For one stupefying moment, I thought, *I'm never going to see him again.* I'd keep walking and call a Lyft from the highway.

But then Anson, no longer so wobbly legged, came running to his uncle and wrapped his arms around his legs, and Thomas scooped him up and swung him high above the damp sand. A renegade wave frothed high, submerging his sun-browned ankles, and Anson was shrieking with delight, his arms stretched out like he was flying with the wind.

I thought: Thomas seemed like home. Going back to him would be like going home. There would be no more secrets.

And I thought that maybe if what I used to think when I was a child was true and I had inherited a little bit of witchy clairvoyance from Mom, it might not always be about terrible things.

Maybe it could also predict something good.

I felt a little lift of happiness. And I began walking to the man who was swinging a happy, shrieking little boy.

ACKNOWLEDGMENTS

My grateful thanks to the following:

Nancy Yost, superagent, and the terrific team at NYLiterary

Charlotte Herscher, editor extraordinaire

Liz Pearsons, for excellent guidance and support, and the amazing crew at Thomas & Mercer

Katie Milnes, brilliant source of toddler info and much more

Travis Kirby, ingenious source for all things '90s and right now

Sara Jane Boyers, for generous insight into photography

Susan Wald, perspicacious early reader

Peter Dorsett Graves, luminous observer of both inner and outer worlds

ABOUT THE AUTHOR

Lindsay Marcott is the author of *Mrs. Rochester's Ghost* and *The Producer's Daughter*, as well as six previous novels written as Lindsay Maracotta. Her books have been translated into eleven languages and adapted for cable. She also wrote for the Emmy-nominated HBO series *The Hitchhiker* and coproduced a number of films, including Hallmark's *The Hollywood Mom's Mystery* and the feature *Breaking at the Edge*. She lives on the coast of California.